RAVE REVIEWS FOR DAWN MacTAVISH!

THE PRIVATEER

"Dawn MacTavish transports readers back in time with this enchanting tale. *The Privateer* is full of characters you'll either love or love to hate but I can guarantee you won't be bored as you immerse yourself in this regency storyline. Beautifully written Ms. MacTavish! This is regency storytelling at its best!"

—Romance Junkies

"I readily recommend *The Privateer*. It's an exciting book with a fresh plot and likable, lifelike characters."

—Romance Reviews Today

"Adventure on the high seas, family drama, rescue from a fate worse than death, passionate love; what more can a romance reader ask for? Dawn MacTavish draws us right in and paints her absorbing story with authentic historical detail in *The Privateer*....Through her intriguing book, Ms. MacTavish allows the reader to escape to another time and place, so mesmerizing is the tale. Snuggle down with a "cuppa" tea and your copy of *The Privateer* by Dawn MacTavish and enjoy!"

—Single Titles

THE MARSH HAWK

"*The Marsh Hawk* is historical fiction at its very best. A breathtaking, sweeping adventure. No one does period romance with such style and panache. *The Marsh Hawk* stole my heart!"

—Deborah MacGillivray, Author of *Riding the Thunder*

"If you're looking for something fresh and lively...Dawn MacTavish's tale of a London beauty of the ton who isn't afraid to impersonate a masked highwayman, including robbery and possible murder, and the real, sapphire-eyed highwayman who pursues her, will keep you up reading all night. The love scenes are luscious. *The Marsh Hawk* is a winner."

—Katherine Deauxville, National Bestselling Author of *Out of the Blue*

"*The Marsh Hawk* will enchant the reader from page one. This sweeping Regency will capture the reader's imagination and make you fall in love with the genre all over again."

—Kristi Ahlers, The Best Reviews

"A master of vividly accomplished tales, the author ups the ante yet again with *The Marsh Hawk*. From the first suspenseful page, I was captivated!"

—Kenda Montgomery, official reviewer for The Mystic Castle

"Brilliant!...A breathtaking historical romance. *The Marsh Hawk* will run the gamut of your emotions—from laughter to tears....You won't want the story to end."

—Leanne Burroughs, Award–Winning Author of *Highland Wishes*

FEELING IS BELIEVING

"You heard the gendarmes when they removed my helm and saw my face."

"But...you are beautiful!"

"Lass, you *are* blind," he said.

"Oh, no," she contradicted. "My hands are my eyes, my lord, and they see quite well. I bathed your face a good many times while you slept. Your jaw is firm and squarely set, and your chin wears a fine, deep cleft. Your lips are strong, and your cheeks are like that of a marble statue I once touched in a great cathedral. Your nose is arrow-straight. It is the proud nose of a Celt, from what I have heard told—bent ever so slightly below the bridge. Your brow is broad, and flat, the eyes deeply set beneath the ledge of it. They are marvelous eyes. They are the most marvelous of all."

"Oh, child, you dream."

"No," she insisted. Grasping his hand, she raised it to his face. "Here...see for yourself." He tried to pull away, for he detested the feel of it, but she held his hand securely. "Trace the bones, my lord," she instructed. "Feel deeply...feel what lies beneath the scars. Pay them no mind. They only mar the skin on the one side, and go no deeper. The other side was not touched by the flames. The bones themselves have not been harmed. Their structure is sound. Feel both sides now...see? You are...beautiful! I can see you just as God made you."

Other *Leisure* books by Dawn MacTavish:

THE PRIVATEER
THE MARSH HAWK

Writing as Dawn Thompson:

THE BRIDE OF TIME
THE RAVENING
THE BROTHERHOOD
BLOOD MOON
THE FALCON'S BRIDE
THE WATERLORD
THE RAVENCLIFF BRIDE

Prisoner of the Flames

DAWN MacTAVISH

LEISURE BOOKS NEW YORK CITY

A LEISURE BOOK®

November 2008

Published by

Dorchester Publishing Co., Inc.
200 Madison Avenue
New York, NY 10016

ISBN 10: 0-8439-5982-7
ISBN 13: 978-0-8439-5982-6

Visit us on the web at www.dorchesterpub.com.

To:

My sister, Diane Mae Thompson—
thank you, for giving me Green Darkness.

The Ladies of Goth Rom, who gave me
the foot in the door.

Candace Gold, Leanne Burroughs, Jacquie
Rogers, Victoria Bromley, Rowena Cherry
and Monika Wolmarans.

DeborahAnne MacGillivray—never enough thanks
for all you do.

And Miss Fuzz.

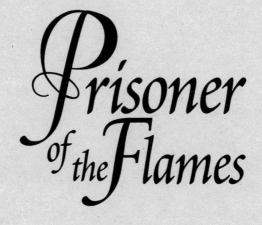

Prisoner of the Flames

Prologue

Hume Castle, Scotland
April 1533

The nursemaid lowered the Laird of Berwickshire's heir into his cradle in the nursery. He was just a sennight old, born of the lady Gwen to her husband Robert Mack. They had come to celebrate the Easter feast with Laird and Lady Hume, Lady Gwen's half sister, who was herself enceinte.

The bairn, having just come from his mother's breast, made no protest, and sleep soon closed his eyes. The night was cold and the young nurse tucked a throw made of pelts about her charge. Howling winds assailed the turret walls and tortured the candle flames, which threw long fingers of fractured light across the child's face. Cascades of molten beeswax, sculpted by the drafts, flowed along the candle shafts until they overflowed the drip pans and anchored the tapers to their stand behind the cradle. Now and then some wax spattered upon the herb-strewn floor and hardened there. The nursemaid took no particular notice. She paced impatiently before the hearth, evicting a large bullmastiff reclining on the stone. The animal lumbered off complaining, finding safer sleeping quarters along the curve of the turret room wall.

The nurse raised her arms above her head and stretched like a cat, sliding her open palms along her body as she lowered them again. She moaned as they slid over her breasts, the hardening nipples protruding through her homespun shift, and let them linger there, fondling, until a rush of aching warmth started deep inside her.

Would he never come? She began to pace again, watched by the dog that gave a warning growl each time her path crossed too close to its tail. Its ears pricked up as a faint knock came at the nursery door—one rap, then a pause, then two quick raps—and the nurse hurried through and into the arms of the young bondservant she had been expecting. He whisked her quickly away to a vacant chamber on the far side of the corridor, and gathered her into a frenzied embrace that soon saw them naked in the lightning-touched darkness, their anxious bodies entwined on a pallet of straw in the corner. Her duty forgotten, the young nurse spread her legs and let her lover fill her, exchanging moan for moan in their illicit coupling.

In the nursery, the baby stirred. The loud voice of the storm bled into his sleep, and a clap of thunder overhead startled him awake. His crying brought the dog. Frightened by the noise and rampant lightning flashes spearing through the arrow slits, the animal began to whine and bark and prance about the cradle, pawing the side with its great clumsy feet, which only made the child's cries more acute.

All at once, a great clap of thunder rumbled overhead, reverberating through the sparsely furnished chamber. The mastiff spun wildly at the sound, displacing the tall candle stand with its rump, and the candles fell upon the cradle, igniting the child's loose-fitting cap, fur rug, and long Holland gown. The infant's cries echoed along the corridor, arousing his mother, asleep in the arms of her husband in their chamber next door, and she reeled into the room screaming at the top of her lungs. Barefoot and tugging on his leggings, the duke was close behind, but before he could stop her, Lady Gwen had plunged her hands into the blazing cradle, snatched up the child, and smothered the flames against her breast.

The fire spread quickly. Fanned by the drafts from the window, the flames traversed the floor and ran up the timber supports to the exposed beams above. Drenched in pitch, they were soon aflame, and fire rained down all around.

New shouts, riding the plumes of acrid smoke that belched through the wide-flung door, soon mixed with those of the Macks. Laird and Lady Hume had arrived, and the young nurse leapt from the arms of her lover and groped her way into the hall. Her long hair loose of its headdress, and her trembling breasts barely covered by the gaping shift she'd donned without a girdle, the girl screamed at the sight of the chamber engulfed in flames.

Mother and child shrieked hysterically, gulping smoke-filled air fetid with the stench of burnt flesh and hair: both the child's and the dog's. Laird Mack dragged them through the billowing curtain of smoke that the drafts had pulled into the corridor and past a string of castle guards and serfs rushing in with buckets of water and sand.

"Bring the healers at once!" Lady Hume shrilled at one of the guards over the conjoined rackets of pandemonium and storm. She seized the inconsolable nurse, and thrust her toward her husband. "Hold her!" she charged. "She dies for her pleasure this night."

Dawn rose on the gutted turret nursery still trailing smoke through a gaping hole in its roof, but the young nursemaid did not see it. She had been put to death for her negligence—her lover as well. Such would have been the dog's fate if it hadn't died in the fire, for its part in the tragedy was clear. It was found beneath the heavy iron candle stand it had knocked over.

Heavily dosed with poppy and herbs, Lady Gwen Mack tossed in the elevated bed in her chamber, her scorched hands and forearms slathered with an unction made of marigold and comfrey and bound loosely in linen gauze. Drugged though she was, her moist eyes flashed toward her approaching husband and Baldric, the head healer.

"Our son . . . ?" she pleaded, addressing Laird Mack. But it was the healer who answered.

"Calm yourself. He lives, my lady," was the reply, and the man lifted her head to administer more of his drugs. "And he will recover. You have my oath. He is of strong warrior stock."

"Haddock stock," she said, her words riding a sigh of relief. She was speaking of her own ancestral line, the Haddocks: fearsome champions of the border wars. Though her lineage had always been a sore spot and a jealous bone of contention where her husband was concerned, since the Macks had not the legendary reputation of the Haddocks, she could not curb her boasting. Even now. "I want to see him," she said, her voice slurred. The drugs were working. "Bring him to me."

"Not . . . yet," Baldric said. His response was a little too loud and quick to avoid her exchanging glances with the duke, whose eyes also held a silent question. This exchange prompted a slow wag of the healer's head in a disparaging, silent "no." "He wants rest, and so must you, my lady."

"But I must nurse him," she groaned. She hadn't missed the two men's guarded exchange. What was Baldric keeping from her? Many a healer had lost his life for nothing more than bringing bad tidings to nobility, and he'd doubtless seen the freshly severed heads of the nurse and her swain impaled on pikes along the stronghold wall, a grim warning to the rest of the servants. Was the news of her son so dreadful that he dared not speak it for fear of his own head? If not so, why was he so slow to reassure her?

"A wet nurse will suckle him for now," the healer replied to her mumblings. "You cannot hold him as you are, and the poppy has surely tainted your milk in any case. Take ease, my lady. All that can be done is being done."

"Has God been . . . merciful?" she pleaded. "Tell me the truth—the pair of you. Would it have been best if—"

"God evidently thinks not, my lady," the healer interrupted. "Else He would have surely taken the boy. It is nothing short of a miracle that he lives."

"It is worse than I feared!" she groaned.

"My lady," the healer said, hesitating. "What the young laird has need of in this life, we must pray that the Almighty has left him. You must give thanks that the heir lives to carry on the line . . . and leave the rest in the hands of God."

One

Mount St. Michael, off the coast of Cornwall
Early autumn 1562

$\mathcal{D}$arkness was falling over St. Michael's Mount as the third Laird of Berwickshire disembarked the ferry. It was a lighter vessel than that which had carried him most of the distance from the Scottish borderlands, and his belly rumbled from nausea as well as hunger, for the Channel was beset by storms, and it had been a rough crossing. Travel by sea, however, had been a wiser choice than hacking his way over land through God alone knew how many border wars and internal skirmishes then in progress. While the young laird was a seasoned warrior, his sojourn this time was a peaceful one of a highly personal nature, the gravity of which left no room for distractions.

He was grateful that the light was fading as he prowled the wharf, threading his way through dockworkers, hawkers, and patrons making last-minute purchases from vendors anxious to close up shop for the night. His late father, a formidable battle strategist, had always held that all cats were gray in the dusk of evening. Hoping that to be true, he began his climb, leaving behind the mingled dockside smells of fish, tar, rotting meat, and overripe produce, all seasoned with the salty tang of the sea.

A silver helmet concealed half of his face like a macabre masquerade mask, dividing it in half from forehead to chin, and calling attention to the very thing it had been fashioned to disguise. Despite a strategically placed opening on the hidden side for air intake and a clever retractable visor for anonymity, the weight and the suffocating heat it generated in warm climates made it a gross inconvenience, aesthetic considerations notwithstanding. But the Scot endured it all with stubborn resolution to placate his pride.

He scaled the Mount easily, with light, agile steps, thankful for the rigorous conditioning among the legions that had left his long legs well muscled, but it was fully dark by the time he reached the summit. Passing the nunnery by, he knocked at the abbey portal. Presently, a hinged aperture in the heavy door came open, and a stern-faced, hawk-nosed cleric squinted up at him through the narrow opening. A breath of dank warmth that smelled of stale incense, spoiling food, and stagnant air puffed through the window, and the young Scot shrank from it.

"Who comes?" the dark-robed individual barked impatiently. It was well past vespers, and Robert knew the monks would have long since retired.

"I am Robert Mack, Laird of Berwickshire, come from the borderlands seeking audience with my uncle, Aengus Haddock, a monk of this abbey."

"The hour is late, my lord," the cleric intoned loftily.

"That I cannot help," Robert said. "I have traveled a great distance—many days upon the water. If you would but tell my uncle I have arrived, I am certain he would bid you admit me."

The cleric breathed a nasal sigh while shutting the little window with a crack, and it was some time before he returned and threw the bolt, allowing Robert to enter.

"Follow me, my lord," he said, shuffling along a winding, dimly lit corridor—so narrow they could not have negotiated it side by side—that emptied into a refectory. "Brother Aengus will receive you directly," he told him, "and food is being prepared. He held his hand out, motioning toward the Scot's helmet. Robert didn't respond, but his eyes narrowed behind the lowered visor as the cleric worked his outstretched fingers. "Come, come, there is no need to helm yourself for battle here, my lord," the cleric snapped.

"My helm is worn to spare you, not myself, good monk," Robert said, staring down at the little man through the clever shuttered eye slot in the helm that left his vision unobstructed, while hiding his eyes from view. After a moment, he took a bold step toward the monk, removed the helmet, and thrust it under his arm. "The 'battle' that won me my scars was waged and lost in my cradle, good brother," he said succinctly.

The cleric backed away, his wide eyes on the young Scot's face. Robert did not need a looking glass to see the sight the holy man saw. It was etched in his memory since the day he'd ambled to the stream that threaded its way through his domain, and stretched himself out over the bank to take a long, cool drink. He was nearly ten, and, though he'd felt it, he hadn't seen his face before. His mother had removed all the polished metal mirrors in Paxton Keep for fear of it. He would never forget what met his steel-blue eyes that day, staring back at him from the still, silvery water. While the right side of his face was untouched and handsome, much of the left side looked as though it had melted. The burnished auburn hair that he wore rather long, waving across his broad brow and curling about his earlobes hid some of the disfigurement. The scar tissue, however, that narrowed his left eye, and pleated the corner of his mouth beneath, having stretched to its limit as he grew, was a shocking sight.

"F-forgive me, my lord," the cleric stammered, genuflecting helplessly. "I . . . I had no idea! Please," he urged, gesturing toward the helmet, "avail yourself."

Robert shook his head. "I cannot eat in it," he said. "You did say food was coming?"

"Y-yes, yes, my lord . . . at once, of course, my lord . . . at once!" the cleric babbled, scurrying off.

Robert gave the closest thing to a devilish grin as the scars around his lips would allow. He sank down on a bench beside the nearest table, slapping the helmet down on top of it, meanwhile stealing a sidelong glance at his distorted reflection in the polished silver, as he often did, hoping against hope that it would show him a kinder image. Like always, however, his visage was the same, dissolving his triumphant smile forthwith.

Presently, the cleric returned with a trencher of *colcannon*—a hearty pottage of cabbage, turnips, and carrots—a loaf of freshly baked monk's bread, for which the abbey was famous, a generous slab of cheese, and one of sweet cream butter. Another quick trip to the larder yielded a copper bowl heaped with apples, pears, and plums from the abbey orchards, and a flagon of nut-sweet spiced wine.

The moment the young Scot was alone he began to wolf down the food ravenously. Eating was awkward, and—he'd learned early on—repulsive to view, which was why he never ate in company. He hadn't finished when his uncle entered, robed in the traditional black Benedictine habit, a knotted scourge girding him. Robert vaulted from the bench and let the monk embrace him, but when he took his seat again, though his belly churned with longing for the delicious meal before him, he would not lift a morsel to his lips.

"Eat, Robert," said his uncle, "lest we vex Brother George, whom I've wrenched from his bed to prepare it. I have seen you eat before, son." After a moment, Robert returned to his meal, and his uncle smiled sadly. "All is well in the borderlands," he prompted. ". . . and with my sister, your good mother?"

"She fares well enough, Uncle Aengus."

"Ahhh," the monk breathed, clearly relieved. "What, then? Have you come to make your poor uncle a happy man, at last?"

Robert scowled. "No, sir, I have not come to join the order," he said unequivocally. "I am not cut of the stuff to make a monk, Uncle Aengus." That argument had surfaced many times before, and he was on the defensive, steeled against it.

"Your mother presses for it."

"My mother would shut me away for safekeeping. It matters not where. She longs to spare me from the world—a doting mother's foolishness. Ha! What worse could happen to me, eh? I would go mad shut up in a monastery. If the fellow who admitted me is any example, your brethren here are a sour and shortsighted lot. I mean no disrespect, but I'd sooner die in battle than entomb myself in a Benedictine abbey and risk becoming like such an insipid, bleached-white shell of a man."

"There are far worse things, son, than being shut up in a Benedictine abbey," his uncle murmured, frowning.

"Not for me." He hadn't set out to be argumentative. He had forgotten how they used to lock horns, like two Highland stags. His uncle had a gentle thrust that made the wounding crueler, and he had yet to prevail, much less win out against it.

"Why have you come, then?" Aengus prompted.

Robert hesitated, choosing his words with care. "You served in France before coming here, did you not?" he queried.

Aengus nodded.

"I mean to go there, and I will need a sponsor. I am hoping you can recommend me to someone of esteem—or possibly even the man I seek himself. I hear there is unrest there now, and foreigners are frowned upon—some sort of religious dispute."

"Who is it that you seek?" said Aengus, his frown deepening.

"His name is Michel de Nostredame, called Nostradamus, a healer of great renown. Do you know him, Uncle?"

The old man's faded blue eyes widened. "I know of him, Robert, but we are not personally acquainted. What is it that you seek in this man?"

"I have heard that he has worked miracles with his healing arts. I want to see if he might work a miracle for me."

"Ahhh, Robert," said the old man, "your good mother has consulted every healer in the land over you. You know it is quite . . . hopeless. Why do you torment yourself?"

"But not *this* man," the young Scot interrupted.

"You are nearly thirty summers. Can you not resign yourself?"

"Uncle, I am a man with the face of a beast—not even! I have the same needs . . . the same urges as other men. I long for a wife and family, but none save whores will have me, and even the most hardened lightskirts shrink from the sight. I want no more congress with strumpets."

"Years ago, when it was feared that your father was dying of his battle wounds and I was summoned to his bedside, he begged me vow that I would be your friend and your protector, that I would look after you in his stead if he should die. You were little more than a bairn on that occasion. Now you come here bringing tales of whores, and hopeless quests. I, too, have grown shortsighted. Much of this is my fault. God forgive me for failing you, Robert."

"You have not failed me unless you refuse my request," he replied. "I will go, with or without your help, Uncle Aengus. I am resigned."

"You embark upon a fool's errand."

"If there is even the slightest chance—"

"You are just like your father—mulish and reckless! Those were the noble traits that finally killed him, you know. He knew not reason, nor caution when drunk with battle madness. And what of the border wars? Have you left your mother all alone to defend the keep—armed her with sword and mace and ax, and instructed her in the fine art of warring? Is your memory so lax that you've forgotten what occurred when your good aunt, Lady Hume, tried to defend Hume Castle against the English? You were eleven that year and at your father's Paxton Keep, praise God, or you would have been there when your mother's noble half sister held out until the invaders commenced to hang her little son, your cousin—close to your own age, mind—in front of her very eyes, before she yielded. The border wars still rage, young son, and will for some time to come. How could you leave your mother prey to such dangers whilst whoring after vanity?"

Robert scowled. He wasn't sure he ought to address that question. To do so would mean breaking a trust and betraying a confidence, and he wasn't sure it was his place to discuss his mother's personal affairs.

"Well?" the old man urged him. "Explain yourself, Nephew!"

"The duchy is well defended," he hedged. "It shan't come to Mother riding into battle mailed and armed to defend the keep."

"By whom?" his uncle insisted.

"You know him . . . Hamish Greenlaw," Robert grumbled, defeated, and knowing it. "You knew him when he was Father's captain of the guard. He swore fealty, and Laird Hume knighted him for valor and awarded him lands before he died. He commands my garrison now."

"And why, pray, does he command your garrison if he has gained title and lands?"

"He is my mother's consort," Robert said angrily. It wasn't any use. He had never been able to hide anything from Aengus Xavier Haddock.

"I have been away from home too long," the monk replied. "My sister has become a whore, and my nephew is off on some mad quest that will surely bring him low, with naught but some ruttish lummox who commands the army to instruct him. How could she take a lover with your father only in the ground two summers?"

"That is neither my affair, nor yours, Uncle. I tell it only to put your mind at ease in that, come time of invasion, Hamish Greenlaw will defend my mother and the keep with his life. She loves him, and he her. I trust him."

"Love!" Aengus ground out. "Carnal lust, you mean. The love of God is the only true love. All else is false. He will use her, and steal your birthright."

"With all due respect, Uncle, I beg you take that up with her, not me. Many others offered for her properly, the stiff-necked sort I'm sure you would approve of, who did not know which end of the sword to grasp, much less thrust. Was I to leave the domain in the hands of one of those so they could 'lose' my birthright for me? Forgive me, but you cannot rule Berwickshire from St. Michael's Mount. And none that I have ever known, including Father, could rule Mother. She is no maiden, and she has made her choice. Now, enough of Mother! Her fate is sealed, and my mission is plain. I need to get an heir. I should like to do that with a willing wife, which is hardly likely as I am. Will you help me?"

The old monk fell silent for so long a time that Robert cleared his throat to prompt him.

"There is one man with whom I am acquainted who might sponsor you at my recommendation," Aengus said at last. "His name is Michel Eyguem, seigneur de Montaigne. He is, I think, only months your senior, but do not scoff at that. He gained a seat in the Parliament of Bordeaux when he was only twenty-four summers. He is a brilliant essayist, and a magistrate of some renown—a very esteemed and respected man, and he should be in Paris now at his château, unless he has gone off early to winter at his country estate in Bordeaux. I do not think that likely yet."

"Is he acquainted with the healer?"

"All of Paris is acquainted with your healer. He is both revered and feared, and in most cases both. I will draft you a letter of introduction, but I do not want to raise your hopes, son; it isn't likely that either man will be able to help you, and you put yourself at great risk going."

"Hope is all I have, Uncle," said Robert, "and this is my last. I am willing to vow that if this healer Nostradamus cannot help me, I will concede defeat, accept my lot, and trouble no one further about it."

"Then you had best have another tankard of wine, and pour one for me as well. Since you will not see reason, there are many things you should know before you set foot on French soil these days."

Robert obliged him, and waited somewhat less than patiently while the old man took a deep swallow of the fragrant spiced wine and leaned close, crouching over the table before he went on, speaking hardly above a whisper.

"Your sojourn to that country is ill-timed," he said. "To begin with, what is going on in France these days is no mere religious dispute, it is bloody civil war between the Catholic Royalists, and the French Protestants—the Huguenots."

"They are Calvinists?"

"Yes, they follow the teachings of John Calvin, and they are many in number, much to the chagrin of the Crown, though that is the Queen Mother's fault. Straddling that fence has cost her much, and will cost her more before 'tis done. But I shan't go into the whys and wherefores. I shall leave all that for seigneur de Montaigne."

"Where does he stand in this civil war?" Robert wondered.

"He is exempt," said his uncle. "He is a Jew, of Spanish-Portuguese extraction. At least that is his heritage. What his religious or political position is in these troubled times, who can say. He is, however, a very wise intellectual, one of the great thinkers of our time, and he remains neutral. Although he is a favorite of the queen, he relishes a certain amount of anonymity. You would do well to respect that."

"The king is but a child, I'm told."

"He is a lad of twelve, but make no mistake. Catherine de' Medici, his mother, rules France, and will until she dies, no matter who sits on the throne. Even now, the factions sue for the king's favor. He might make a good ruler if he lives to manhood. Those who manipulate him tug him in many directions, and some whom he trusts should not be trusted. It is difficult for even an adult to brook and discern wisely, and the young king is swayed by his mother's views, which fluctuate between the Catholics and the Protestants daily. She changes sides the way she changes partners at her precious court fetes, and if the boy is not soon counseled rightly, his rule will fail, and France will suffer greatly."

"I doubt I shall have contact with any of these," Robert said. "I want only an audience with Nostradamus. I don't intend to get caught up in civil strife in a land not my own."

"Nonetheless, it's best that you are aware of these things. You will be far less likely to become embroiled in civil strife if you are armed with the means to avoid it. Bear with me, Robert. If you must go, go prepared for what awaits you, and my conscience will be clear in the matter."

"Yes, Uncle," Robert said humbly. There were times, like now, when the old man seemed more warrior than monk. It had to be the lusty Haddock blood. How it had turned out a holy man was a mystery.

"You would do well to heed Montaigne in all things," Aengus went on. "While I can only warn you, he, being in the midst of it, will be able to counsel you far better than I. Things are changing hour by hour there now. What was true a sennight ago could be very different by the time you reach Paris. You know how long it takes for word to travel."

"Who leads these Huguenots?"

"First, Louis I de Condé, in France and abroad, but it is Admiral Gaspard de Coligny and Henry of Navarre who lead the troops. Coligny vies to hold sway over the boy king, but Coligny's archrival, who rules the Catholics, currently has the king's ear, and he is by all accounts the greater danger. He is far more ruthless."

"And, who is this . . . archrival?" Robert asked, avoiding his uncle's scowl. He should have known the answer to that question without asking. Hadn't Mary of Guise married

James V of Scotland, producing Mary Stuart? He muttered a low-voiced curse at his own stupidity.

"The Guises rule the Catholics," Aengus mouthed, his words no more than a whisper. He leaned closer still. "Young son, if you heed nothing else I've said to you, heed this: do not cross swords with Charles de Guise, Cardinal of Lorraine. I run a great risk speaking against him even here—especially *here*. The very air we breathe has ears, and that man's arm can reach beyond French borders. Avoid him at all costs, and if you do find yourself in his company keep your wits about you, and commit to *nothing*—not even an opinion on the weather. Do not let his youthful good looks fool you. The stairs he climbed gaining his place in the hierarchy were the bodies of the dead whose blood anoints him, and the bent backs of lowly monks such as myself, whom he has broken to his will.

"You have had dealings with this man," said Robert.

"Dealings? Oh, yes, young son, I have had 'dealings' with Charles de Guise. I spent a good many years serving the Church in France, and I watched ambition spoil him, like the beetles spoil the plums out in our orchards, leaving the tender fruit to rot on the trees. I made the mistake of going against him whilst I was serving there under his jurisdiction. We were at loggerheads on canonical issues, and social reforms, as well, the very ones that have led to the unrest there now. He thinks he punished me in my assignment here—my banishment, as it were. Actually, I engineered it to get out from under his yoke." He chuckled. "Don't think to use me as a reference with that one, laddie. To this day I marvel at my prowess gaining freedom. My age, and his vainglorious complacency won it for me. If he had any inkling that I wanted out, I would still be there, I assure you."

"If a prince of the Church is corrupt, who, then, can be trusted?"

"Save Montaigne, no one that I can recommend," Aengus

said flatly. "He is no stranger to adversity himself. Most important, he is beyond reproach, and has thus far accumulated no important enemies, which is a miracle in itself. No, I'm afraid he is the only man in France right now that I can personally vouch for. Now! Do you still think you are equal to the task you have assigned yourself? Is seeking out this . . . ill-reputed heathen . . . this soothsayer worth your life? For you will lose it, helmed for what they will perceive as battle in that land now. All factions are certain to hold you suspect."

"I have come this far, Uncle. I cannot turn back now."

"So be it!" Aengus said almost in anger, giving a crisp nod. "I have done all I can to dissuade you. If, after all I've said, you are still determined, the consequences are upon your head, not mine. Now then, it is late, and I am weary. Let me hear your confession, and then sleep, while I draft your letter. On the morrow you receive the sacrament before you depart on your mad journey."

"Thank you, Uncle Aengus."

His uncle hesitated, and after a moment said, "There are some who say that your Nostradamus is in league with the devil, you know, Robert. He has uncanny sight, and is at best a mysterious fellow."

"And, what say you, Uncle?"

"I say that the devil is in this somehow, and I fear that I am about to send you whoring after him."

Two

*R*obert woke before the cock crowed, received the sacrament, and ate a hearty breakfast before most of the monks arose. Those who worked in the kitchen provided him with barley bannocks, oatmeal porridge, which reminded him of the thick *crowdie* he ate at home, ale, and boiled eels—much more than the monks ate, which was usually only dinner at midday. Only in summer were bread and ale occasionally permitted at the breakfast hour if the monks were to labor in the heat, and sometimes a light supper was allowed. Fish and vegetables were the mainstay of their fare. Benedictines ate no meat. It was forbidden to all save the gravely sick.

Aengus fasted, though he sat with Robert while the younger man ate ravenously. Then after enduring one last vain attempt on his uncle's part to dissuade him, Robert bid his uncle farewell, and left St. Michael's Mount, his leather traveling pouch bulging with barley bannocks, a generous wedge of goat cheese, and a skin of the abbey's own mead, flavored with honey and herbs, but not cut with water as the monks usually drank it.

It was barely first light when he took the ferry back to the mainland, where he booked passage on a merchant vessel bound for France. But traveling in autumn by way of the English Channel was treacherous and unpredictable, and the ship tossed for many days, blown off course at the mercy of wild maelstroms, howling winds, and torrents of horizontal rain before finding calmer waters in the *Baie de la Seine*, where the river met the channel, and the ship sailed southeast, along the Seine itself, to Paris.

Dawn was breaking over the city when he disembarked the vessel. The citizens of Paris were just beginning to mill about by the docks and in the square, and the vendors were setting up shop along the various routes that led into the city proper. It was a busier place than any of the markets he had experienced in the lowlands, and he soon found that he attracted far more attention than he had at home, where his affliction was well-known. In an effort to remain as inconspicuous as possible, he had opted not to go abroad in Scottish dress, and chose instead to travel in a padded, fitted doublet made of brown fustian, with darker brown sleeves, and hose of pease-porridge tawny, laced knee-high boots of soft leather with sturdy soles, and a short cloak with a stand-up collar to protect him from the weather. He kept his razor-sharp *sgian dubh*, the infamous black knife of the Scots, tucked out of sight inside his boot, carried a short English sword at his side, and had exchanged his ornamental sporran for a codpiece. His strategy had seemed sound, but he may as well have worn his comfortable tartan and strapped his Claymore on his back, for he hadn't taken two strides upon French soil before he realized his tall, helmeted presence among the more slightly statured French was doomed to be at best a curiosity, and more than likely a great danger. Voices speaking in hushed whispers echoed all around him in a blood-chilling murmur of sound that did not bode well, and though his belly craved food, and his weary eyes drooped wanting sleep, he decided that it would be best to put all else aside and seek out seigneur de Montaigne.

He slipped the letter of introduction his uncle had given him from his pouch and examined the address. He was approaching a footbridge that spanned the river and descended to the edge of a road that wound eastward toward a modest collection of city dwellings, and westward away from the city. According to Aengus's directions, Montaigne's chalet lay to the west, so he tucked the letter back inside his pouch and started across the bridge, when a disturbance on the other side caught his attention.

For a moment, he hesitated. The last thing he needed then was to make himself conspicuous by becoming involved in the affairs of the locals, but a young girl was being accosted at the foot of the bridge. Two rowdy drunkards, evidently still abroad after a night of revelry, were passing her back and forth between them like a ball, and her cries echoed over the water, amplified by the morning mist.

At first he took it to be a confrontation between two men and a girl of ill repute, but closer scrutiny revealed quite something else. The girl was a flower vendor, and the men had tipped over her cart. The damp cobblestone street was splotched with color where they had trampled most of her wares underfoot as they tossed her back and forth, groping her body familiarly. Glancing behind, he noticed two gendarmes at the foot of the bridge behind him, who saw the scuffle also, but they made no move to interfere, and without further hesitation, Robert vaulted over the bridge and put himself between the two bullies.

The drunkards looked bewildered, and the laird took advantage of their confusion. Shoving the girl out of the way, he launched a powerful right fist that sent one of the men over the upturned flower cart, where he landed sprawled on his back against the curb with the wind knocked out of him. Robert then took a quick step toward the other, who was very drunk, and had run at first, but who now started to reel back in his direction. Whether he meant to collect his friend or fight was unclear. Meanwhile, the man he'd hit scrambled to his feet, put himself between the two men, and turned his comrade around. The pair staggered off, and Robert turned his attention to the girl.

Whimpering, she knelt foraging for the coins that the men had spilled from her pocket in the tussle, and Robert squatted down and lent his hand to the search.

"Are you aright, lass?" he inquired. How lovely she was, with the sun gleaming in her long honey-colored hair, and exertion rouging her cheeks, her throat, and the creamy skin showing above the neck of her cinched-in blouse. She was a feast for his eyes, and he drank her beauty in greedily.

"My coins," she despaired. "I had so few."

"We shall find them, lass. See? Here are two more, and there is another by the cart behind you."

She groped the cobblestones at her back without finding it.

"No, no—by the cart, lass . . . there, see? A half-pence."

"I cannot see, monsieur, I am blind," she sobbed.

Robert had wondered why she hadn't seemed to notice his helmet. For a moment he stared at her. Then his posture sagged, and he ground out a bitter laugh as he picked up the coins in question.

"There is no harm in being blind, monsieur," she said defensively.

"No, there is not, lass, forgive me," he said.

"Were you with them, then?"

"Hardly," said Robert, righting her cart. "In my country, men do not abuse young lasses—blind or otherwise."

"You speak the language well enough for a foreigner," she observed. "Where do you come from, then?"

"I am Robert Mack, of Paxton, Scotland, Laird of Berwickshire. I was tutored in French as a child, but not nearly well enough in manners. I beg you forgive my want of conduct. I have come in search of Michel Eyguem, seigneur de Montaigne, of this city. I have a letter of introduction from my uncle, a monk at the abbey on St. Michael's Mount."

"Ahhh," she breathed. There was great relief in the sound.

"What are you called, lass?"

"My name is Violette Cherier, and I am in your debt, my lord. Those men . . . they were quite rowdy, and would, I fear, have had their way with me if you had not intervened."

"I think they were a mite too drunk for that," he said. "If you were sighted, you would have seen it."

"You have saved my coins. What of my flowers? Have they ruined them?"

"Some still remain," he said, frowning toward the scant few that hadn't been trampled. Stooping, he retrieved what was left of the blooms and placed them back into the cart somewhat clumsily. "You will have to sell them quickly," he informed her. "All the water has been spilt . . . unless you tell me where to fetch more?"

"I will fetch more water, my lord. I have detained you long enough. I know seigneur de Montaigne. He is known and loved in the vendors' quarter, as he is everywhere in Paris. His chalet lies on the western fringes of the city. If you had but turned to your right when you stepped off the bridge, and not become involved with me, you would have nearly reached it by now."

Robert was following her directions with his eyes, when all at once the two gendarmes who had been watching him since he left the docks, took hold of him from behind. Resisting, he cried out in protest as they shackled him in irons, groped the doublet beneath his cloak for his coin purse, and relieved him of the sword and dinner knife sheathed at his side. One of them opened the purse and probed its contents, stirring the coins. Juggling it in his hand, he assessed its weight, discarded the letter of introduction Aengus had given him, which floated to the ground, then tightened the thong cord again, and thrust it beneath his own belt.

When the other grabbed hold of his helmet, Robert fought back with a well-aimed foot that found the man's genitals beneath his codpiece, doubling him over. Loosing a string of blasphemous oaths, the other reached around to remove the device himself, while the first man recovered himself.

"Please!" Violette cried. "This man is a foreign noble, come seeking seigneur de Montaigne. He has done nothing wrong. He has papers. He . . . he saved me from rowdies who laid hands upon me and upturned my cart!"

"Keep silent, wench!" barked the gendarme who still had the power of speech. "He's done something now. He's attacked an officer of the French police, papers or no, and he goes to the Bastille, your foreign noble."

"She speaks truth." Robert thundered. "Do not remove the helm. *Do not*, I say!"

But the injured gendarme was on his feet at last, and between them they yanked it off his head.

"*Mon Dieu!*" cried the first, reeling away from the sight. "*Plague!*"

The other let Robert go, meanwhile wiping his hands on his tunic, and Violette rushed forward, kicking air until she found the man's shins, at which point she gave them a healthy drubbing with the toe of her shoe.

"Jean-Claude Geneaux, you lout! I know your voice," she accused, "and you also, Henri Flammonde. Where were you when those drunkards were accosting me? I will report you! This man has done nothing."

The one called Henri, still soothing his genitals, pulled her off Jean-Claude, shoving her aside roughly, and she fell to the cobblestone street beside her flower cart.

"Garboneaux can deal with this," said Jean-Claude, slapping the helm back in place on Robert's head. "Bring him, and be quick!"

"No!" Violette shrilled.

"Keep still, unless you want to join him," Henri warned her.

"I have no plague, you fools," Robert insisted. "I have been burned, and the scars redden when confined for long periods. The helm spares such as you the sight and me embarrassment for it. If you will but loose these accursed irons, I will show you my credentials."

But they paid him no mind, nor did they heed the girl's cries as they hauled him quickly away.

Violette heaved a weary sigh as the sound of their voices grew distant. She had the gendarmes' terror of plague, and their panic to be shot of it to thank that she hadn't been hauled off with him. She was certain she had bruised Jean-Claude's shins severely. Scrabbling up to a kneeling position, she began to grope the cobblestones for her straw hat, which had been lost in the struggle; only her lawn cap remained, tied neatly in place under her chin, with her long hair hanging down in back. Not finding the hat nearby, she extended her search, spreading her arms in wider circles, and her hand brushed a crumpled piece of parchment on the cobblestones that had come to rest against the wheel of her cart. Fingering it carefully, she felt the sealing wax, and her heart leapt—the laird's credentials? Could it be?

She jumped to her feet, her first thought being that she go at once to the jail with it. She had taken only two steps in that direction—for she knew most of the city by heart—when she hesitated. The gendarmes were as much a danger to her now as the drunken pair she had encountered earlier. They had arrested many a vendor for far less than she had just done. Who was to say that they wouldn't tear the laird's papers up, and throw her into prison herself? Did she dare chance it after telling them she knew who they were? The blindness that had always been her shield in the past would not help her now.

No. She spun around, slipped the parchment into the

pocket concealed beneath her apron, and set out in a different direction.

The two gendarmes dragged Robert before Captain Phileppe Garboneaux of the Paris police, jailor at the small, dank castle prison. It reminded him of the makeshift prison keeps at home. Due to the dubious nature of the situation—the officers were convinced they were dealing with plague and feared a panic—they took the laird below to a cubicle deep in the bowels of the foul-smelling prison to be examined by the jailor well out of the other guards' view.

Flares in sconces along the passageways they passed through perfumed the lower regions with the putrid odor of rancid oil. It hung heavy on air fouled with mildew, and, when they reached the cell, it stank with the lingering stench of the body odor, excrement, stale urine, and vomit left there by its last inhabitant.

Robert had ceased his struggling. Still shackled, he lay in a urine-soaked pile of dung-matted straw where they had flung him. Wise enough to realize that he could not escape, he decided to reason with these men who had curtailed his mission before it had even begun.

Jean-Claude and Henri backed quickly away, but the jailor stood his ground scrutinizing, him arms akimbo, a formidable-looking baton in one of the fists he had braced on his hips.

"What's he done, then?" he growled toward the officers behind.

"I have done naught but come to the aid of a poor blind child who had been set upon by drunkards in the square," Robert put in before either of the gendarmes could answer. "They had overturned her cart and spilled—"

"Hold your tongue!" the jailor snarled, smacking his baton hard to the side of Robert's helmet, cutting him short. "Nobody's asked you!"

Robert groaned. The impact of the blow was doubled, amplified by the clang of the truncheon reverberating inside the helmet, and blood began to run from his ear.

The jailor reached for the helmet.

"Don't touch him, Captain, it's *plague*, I tell you!" Jean-Claude spoke up. "Don't go too near. He kicked Henri here hard enough to deaden his balls."

"Trying to defend myself," Robert groaned. "They had no business laying hands on me. I had done nothing, and I have no plague. Is this how you treat all foreigners who sojourn in your land—gendarmes ambushing them from behind, whilst they are doing their job for them? *They* should have gone to the girl's aid. They saw it all—they followed me from the docks. They would have let those cup-shotten roaring boys take her down."

Another blow all but rendered him senseless, then the jailer lifted the helmet and thrust a torch close to his face. Robert shrank from the fetid stench of the oil, from the sudden light in that dark place, and from the heat of the flames as Garboneaux conducted his examination.

"Umm," the jailor grunted, grimacing as he took a step back. "Addle-wits! This is no plague here so far as I can tell. These scars are old." He slapped the helmet back in place, then tethered Robert's ankle to a leg iron chained to the floor, and swaggered out to join the others waiting in the passageway. "Nasty sight," he opined. "Leave him awhile. We'll show this insolent Scot how we treat foreigners who assault gendarmes in Paris, eh?"

The heavy door slammed shut on Robert, taking the light with it, and he slid the helmet off and laid his head back in the moldy fouled straw. Blood from his ear ran down his neck, and his head ached, the reverberation of the blows still rumbling around in his brain. His head was reeling, and his last thoughts before vertigo finally rendered him unconscious were of the little blind flower vendor, Violette Cherier, as he had last seen her lying prostrate on the street where the gendarmes had flung her. He recalled the long honey-colored hair spread like a fan over the cobblestones, spilling from beneath her white cap, and her sightless eyes, so thickly wreathed with lashes, staring into nothingness. Praying that she would not face a similar fate for attempting to champion him, he succumbed to the pain and the dark hopelessness that overwhelmed him.

Three

*M*ichel, *seigneur de Montaigne had already left for a court* audience at the Louvre when Violette reached the château. She had started out bravely on her own, but soon realized that, though she had traveled the route many times before, she had never attempted it on her own; there had always been another vendor with her, and that had been some time ago. She soon realized that she had taken on too much in her blindness, and had it not been for a dairy cart passing her by on the way to fetch more butter to market, and the dairyman agreeing to deposit her at Montaigne's château on his way past, she might never have reached it. That, however, was the reason she arrived too late to deliver Robert's credentials to the magistrate before he left for his court appointment.

A bondservant answered her knock. Hearing her tale, he brought the steward, who informed her of Montaigne's absence and promptly closed the door in her face. She wasn't surprised. The situation in Paris was critical then, and Montaigne was a public figure. The servants would have been instructed to admit no one, least of all a toil-worn, blind flower vendor, much the worse for wear due to her ordeal with the drunkards and misuse at the hands of the gendarmes.

She sat down on the step, smoothed out her hair and skirt, and straightened her cap. She couldn't go back on her own, even if she wanted to, which she didn't. Montaigne would return eventually . . . unless he stayed on at court. Her heart leapt at that possibility, and she crossed herself and said a quick prayer against it. But blindness had heightened her other senses, and as the day wore on, she began to fear that prayer was in vain. When dark clouds began rolling in after the sun reached its zenith, she could not see them, but the constant gray she did see grew steadily darker, the way it always did at night, and the sun no longer warmed her face. The wind changed direction sharply and grew stronger blowing in off the Seine. She filled her lungs and licked her lips, tasting salt. The bird music changed, too. The sweet voices of lapwing, sparrow, and mourning dove were suddenly drowned out by the harsh, rasping cries of gull, tern, cormorant, and plover seeking shelter inland from the approaching storm. This far inland in autumn, it would be a ripper.

Reading the weather thus was vital to her livelihood. Setting up shop in the square with a storm brewing would be a costly mistake—especially now, when so few good days were left before winter. She thought of her cart by the bridge, praying that one of the other vendors had collected it for her. But that couldn't be helped. She was where she had to be, doing what she must do. What was right to do . . . unless she should have followed her first instinct and gone straight to the jail.

She shuddered. It had grown suddenly colder, and the gusts stronger still. Twice now, she had taken her apron back from the wind, and all her labor making herself presentable earlier had gone for naught at the mercy of the gusts. She was tired and cold and her belly churned wanting food. Did she dare knock at the door again? No. What would be the use? They wouldn't admit her, but there might be an overhang, an arbor, or some attachment that she might seek shelter beneath, for the rain was imminent, and, judging from the sound of the waterfowl clucking about her, this was to be no mere brief shower.

Groping her way along the steps to the façade of the house, she felt for such a shelter, but found none. She couldn't see the roof above, of course, but the rain had begun, and flattening herself against the building did not spare her a drenching, suggesting that the residence was sheerfaced. And she felt her way along the rough brick wall until she found the door, recessed enough to spare her somewhat. There she stayed until the gray world she lived in grew deeper still as night fell, and she was just about to knock at the door again and beg that someone lead her to the stable, where at least she might wait out of the weather, when a voice close beside her made her lurch violently. She had not heard him approach above the racket of the wind and rain.

It was Montaigne.

"Violette?" he breathed. "So it is! What are you doing here? You are drenched to the skin, child."

"I have a letter that I believe is addressed to you, seigneur," she cried. "Your steward would not admit me, and I . . . could not leave it you see, because they have taken him to . . . prison, and you would have no way to know it!" Sobbing in relief, she leaned against the strong arm he had wrapped around her as he ushered her inside out of the weather.

"What's this?" he said. "Taken whom to prison, Violette?"

"The Scottish laird," she wailed.

"Child, you are soaked to the skin," he observed. "And I've no idea what you are talking about. Come sit by the chimney and warm yourself. I shall have my steward bring ale and a blanket to warm you, then you will tell me calmly what all this is about, eh?"

The closest lit chimney, a portable fireback and grate, was located in a small parlor room Montaigne used as a study behind the Great Hall, and he left her there seated beside it in a Glastonbury chair to seek his steward, who returned with him, bringing ale and a blanket, which the magistrate wrapped around her shoulders. After setting a tankard into her hands, he dismissed the steward and took a seat in a similar chair on the other side of the chimney.

"Now then," he said, "what is all this business about a laird, and a letter for me? Tell me slowly, from the beginning if you please."

"A Scottish laird helped me today," she began. "Two drunkards were using me cruelly by the bridge. They had overturned my cart, and were tossing me back and forth like a poppet, and he put them off. He said he had come in search of you . . . that he had a letter of introduction from his uncle . . . a monk, I think." She drew it, damp and crumpled, from her pocket and handed it to him. Leaning close to the chimney, he broke the seal and read Aengus Haddock's words.

"*Mon Dieu!*" he breathed. "You say they've taken him to jail? What was his crime?"

"He did no crime," she shrilled, "but for saving me."

"Calm yourself, child. He must have done *something*. Think."

"From what I heard of their speech, I believe they followed him from the harbor. There was something . . . wrong with him. He wore a helmet, and when they laid hold of him and removed it, they screamed—'*plague*'! But he said not, and they took him anyway. I think he injured one of the gendarmes. I . . . I'm sure he did, seigneur."

Montaigne sighed. "You know all the local gendarmes, don't you, child? Who were they? Did you recognize their voices?"

"I did. They were Jean-Claude Geneaux and Henri Flammonde."

"I know them. This does not surprise me."

"They took his money pouch, his sword, I think, I heard it clinking, and traveling bag, and hauled him off to the Bastille. I tried to help him, seigneur. I kicked Jean-Claude hard in the shins. I told them I would report them, and they threw me down."

"You should not have done that, Violette," he scolded.

"Now they will likely seek a reprisal. But that cannot be helped now. Go on, child, what more?"

"I found the letter in the street, and came here to you. I wasn't even sure it was the credentials he spoke of, but the seal suggested it might be. At first I thought to go to the Bastille with it . . . but they were so . . . unreasonable with him that I feared they might just discard it—"

"And likely lock you up as well," the magistrate interrupted, "especially since you recognized them; a wise decision. You've done well, Violette—very well. Is there more?"

"No, seigneur," she murmured, "except . . ."

"Except what, child?"

"I feel . . . responsible. It never would have happened if he hadn't tried to help me."

"And, where were they, Jean-Claude and Henri, whilst he was doing their job for them, eh?"

"Watching."

"Nevermind, child. There is no fault in you. Drink up. My steward is preparing a basket of food. You must be starving. It is nothing fancy, I'm afraid. Since I was not in residence, and dining at court, no formal fare was prepared, but there is some trencher bread left over from the servants' meal that they have not yet given over to the poor, some cheese, and some pears. As soon as it's brought, and my carriage is readied, I will see you safely to your quarter. Then I will deal with this muddle you've brought me."

"You have a *carriage?*" she marveled. She had never heard of anyone except the royals possessing one, and certainly never dreamed she would ride in one.

"A very small one of sorts," he replied, "nothing anywhere near so grand as the king's, I fear. I do not use it here in Paris, only for my trips to and from Bordeaux. It will keep you drier than the cart, and I would not sit you on a horse blind—storm or no."

"Thank you, seigneur," she said. "You have always been

kind—even buying my flowers when I know that you have no one to give them to. God bless you!"

"So, you've found me out, have you?" he chided. He laughed outright. "Well, it may interest you to know that I shall be shopping for a wife once all this unrest is settled, and then you will be seeing me more often at your flower cart."

"Can you free him?" she urged. She couldn't imagine it, and not even his laughter, or the prospect of riding in a carriage could coerce her to smile.

"Not sitting here," he said. "The hour grows late, and this needs my immediate attention. That makeshift dungeon is no place for the guilty, much less the innocent."

Robert had no idea if it was night or day, or how long he'd been held there when Garboneaux unlocked the heavy cell door and thrust the flare lighting Montaigne's way as he entered.

"*Mon Dieu!*" the magistrate murmured, raising a handkerchief to his nose. "Get him out of that!"

"How was I to know?" the jailer grumbled. "He had no letter on him when they brought him in. They feared plague. Just look at that, seigneur! And he attacked one of them—kicked him in his privates. He's still all swoll up."

"Probably from the pox," snapped Montaigne. "That's not all that's going to be 'swoll up' before I've done. You have to answer for this, Garboneaux—all three of you. Well? Why are you still standing there? Remove those irons!" He ventured nearer. "What's this?" he demanded. "Why is he bleeding? Has he been treated? Speak up!"

"N-no, seigneur," the jailer stammered, unlocking the shackles. "I . . . I mean, yes, that is . . . I—"

"Nevermind, I can see that he has not. Get his belongings—his traveling bag—his sword, and be quick!" Shoving the jailer aside, he snatched up Robert's helmet, and helped him to his feet. "Can you stand, my lord?" he queried.

"Y-yes," Robert murmured. "Seigneur de Montaigne?"

"Yes, my lord," he replied. "I will explain, but first let me get you out of here. Come."

Robert donned the helmet, and let the magistrate lead him up through the narrow passageways and out into the rain to the waiting carriage, which he eyed skeptically, never having ridden in one. It had to be a dream—but for his aching body, bruised from the beatings he'd suffered in custody, he would have sworn to it.

"The first thing we must do," Montaigne said, "is get you home and summon a physician."

"No," Robert returned. "I will mend without that. There is only one physician whom I need to see in France."

"Ahhh yes, so your uncle said in his communiqué. Once you are rested and refreshed, we will get to that."

"How did it ever come into your hands? I'd given up hope of being found."

"You have Violette, a little blind flower vendor of your acquaintance, to thank for your good fortune."

"The girl by the bridge?" he breathed, incredulous. "I feared they would arrest her as well. She foolishly tried to defend me. Quite the little tigress."

"She found the letter in the street and brought it to my château. I had been summoned to court early, and I had already left for the Louvre when she arrived with it. I returned quite late, otherwise I would have been here sooner."

"All this happened *today*?" Robert queried, scarcely able to believe he'd only been incarcerated for a few short hours. It seemed like a lifetime.

"Poor fellow, we haven't exactly made you welcome in France, have we?" Montaigne observed. "I beg you forgive my countrymen their want of conduct. All Frenchmen are not oafish want-wits."

"She waited for you, then?"

"Yes, fortunately for you. I never would have known you had been arrested otherwise. Without her, the letter would have meant nothing. I found her on my doorstep in the pouring rain when I returned. She had been waiting there since the morning. My servants admit no one these days. One cannot be too careful. This country is at war with itself, I am ashamed to say."

"Where is she now? I would thank her, seigneur."

"There will be plenty of time for that on the morrow. I returned her to the vendors' quarter well rewarded. I will be happy to direct you. But first we must become acquainted, and you must be fed."

Robert would not argue with that. He was beyond famished, and while a wooden tub was being prepared with soothing bay, and fennel in what was to be his sleeping quarters, Montaigne had the steward prepare a meal consisting of a boiled salad, olive pie, and sauced capon that were slated for the following day's meal, served on fresh trencher bread.

A comely serving maid, whom the magistrate introduced as Francine, brought the food to Montaigne's study for privacy; she set it on a thick wooden table along with jugs of sack and ale, and left them. The fare smelled wonderful, and Robert salivated in anticipation, but he was reluctant to remove the helm.

"I have already seen your misfortune, my lord, and I am no worse for the experience," Montaigne said. "We are quite alone here now, and shall remain so. Please remove the bonnet and have your food before it grows cold."

Hesitantly, Robert set the helm aside and drew his eating knife from its scabbard, grateful that the magistrate had retrieved it, and his sword as well from the jailer. He would have had his *sgian dubh* in any case, since none at the jail had found it concealed inside his tall, laced boot. He had not been so successful where the coin pouch was concerned; neither gendarme would admit taking it, and Garboneaux was innocent of that crime since it was disposed of well before he ever set eyes upon Robert, its contents divided between Jean-Claude and Henri. But the young Scot was not so foolish as to travel abroad with all his funds in one purse. The bulk of his coinage was concealed in his codpiece.

"Why a heavy helm of silver?" Montaigne queried, nursing his tankard of ale. "It must be beyond bearing in the summer months, even though it covers only half your face. And the weight! I should think a simple traveling mask would suffice, no?"

"Wars are being waged on all fronts these days, and many sojourners travel about helmed; it is fast becoming the fashion of the times," Robert responded. "Believe me, I attract far less notice in that headgear than I would in a cloth traveling mask, and, of course, at home my helm is known and respected. I have never been to France before, and I assumed that my . . . solution would work as well here as at home. But, I don't believe it was the helm that attracted those guards as much as the fact that I am recognizably a foreigner. We Scots are somewhat . . . less delicately built than you French. They would have suspected me if my face were unblemished and I'd arrived bareheaded."

"You may have a point, my lord. There are none here that compare to you that I can call to mind, and you certainly would have caused a stir bareheaded."

Robert rolled his eyes and moaned. "This fare is outstanding," he complimented. "You steward is to be commended, seigneur."

The magistrate smiled. "You should join me at *Montaigne*, my home in Bordeaux," he said. "Gaspard, my steward there, outshines Alain, but do not dare let Alain know that I said it.

He is very jealous of his talents, and one must never tamper with the temperament of those who prepare one's food. Those, my friend, are words to live by."

The meal was quickly eaten, and as soon as the last morsel had been swallowed, Robert reached for his helm.

"There is no need of that here," Montaigne said, arresting him with a quick hand on his arm. "We are quite alone. We need to talk. Why not be comfortable to do it, eh?"

"Forgive me, seigneur," Robert responded, drawing his hand back without the helm. "An old habit."

"Your uncle asks that I sponsor you here during your stay in France."

"Yes," Robert said, "but do not feel as though you must entertain me. I seek your sponsorship in order to arrange an interview with Michel de Nostredame, the great healer. My uncle tells me that you are acquainted."

"Because of . . . ?" the magistrate queried, gesturing toward the obvious.

"Yes," said Robert, nodding

"I will send word to him first thing on the morrow," said Montaigne, frowning, "but . . . I do not want to raise your hopes."

"You do not think he will meet with me, then?"

"He is a . . . peculiar fellow, I will admit, and who can say if he will or he won't, but that is not what I meant. I doubt that even he can help you. How did it occur, your tragedy?"

"In my cradle, when I was a sennight old. There was a fire."

"There were no healers in Scotland to help you?"

"No, I have found no healers equal to the task, but I have heard that Doctor Nostradamus has healing powers no others possess."

"And if he cannot . . . ?"

"Then I will be satisfied that I have left no stone unturned . . . and go home. It is not vanity, as Uncle Aengus supposes—not really. No decent lass will look at me. Even the strumpets in the local stews back away in disgust. I want a wife and family—not only for Berwickshire . . . for myself; if that be vanity, than I am vain."

"No, my lord, that is not vanity. It is no more than any man should expect as his God-given right in this life. You are exhausted. Let me show you to your sleeping quarters. We need to talk, it's true, but we can do that on the morrow when you are rested, no? Come, your bath awaits."

Robert's sleeping chamber was small, though well appointed, boasting a boarded bed fitted with two mattresses stuffed with carded wood, and down pillows instead of the bolsters he was more accustomed to. There was a close-stool and chamber pot, a small table with a beeswax candle, basin and water crock upon it, and a box chair. The wooden tub was set beside a portable chimney, and he quickly shed his clothes and sank into the warm, fragrant water, ducking his head beneath to wash away the dry, crusted blood that had hardened on his neck, running from his injured ear. He lingered there until the water grew cold around him before he climbed out, dried himself with the linen towels laid there, and donned his shirt, which also served him for sleeping.

He poked the mattress. It had been some time since he'd slept on anything so fine. The bed in his cell at St. Michael's Mount was no more than a pallet of straw. Throwing back the sheet and coverlet, he climbed beneath, and set his helm on the box chair beside the bed. He always kept it within reaching distance.

He was about to extinguish the candle when a knock on the door stopped his hand as he reached toward it. "Come in," he said, supposing it to be Montaigne. Instead, it was the dark-haired maid, Francine, who entered, and he quickly put the helm on while her back was toward him as she closed the door. "What do you here, lass?"

"The master thought you might like a little . . . company," she said, strolling nearer the bed.

Robert stared as the undulating wench unlaced the girdle she wore over her shift and set it aside. Sauntering nearer, she slid the shift down, baring her pendulous breasts. They swayed, their tawny nipples erect, as she threw back the bedclothes, hiked up her shirts, and straddled him. She smelled sour, of sweat, spiced malt ale, and residual kitchen grease, and he grimaced beneath the helmet.

"Do Scotsmen always sleep decked out for battle, then?" she chided, laying hands on the helmet to remove it.

"No!" he said, grabbing her wrists to prevent her. Lowering her hands, he let them go. "This will not do," he said. "I thank your master for his hospitality, but I wish no company tonight."

"I will be chastised if I do not pleasure you," she crooned, groping beneath the hem of his shirt until her skilled hand closed around the shaft of his member. "You would not want to see me flogged, then, would you, my lord?"

"Seigneur de Montaigne does not seem the type of man to whip a woman," he opined, grabbing her wrist again, for exhaustion always heightened his libido, and she had aroused him.

She only laughed, guiding his hands to her breasts, and crushed his fingers against the tall, protruding nipples as she attempted to capture his member with her body by lowering herself upon it. Now that his hands were occupied trying to forefend that, she lifted his helm, and he quickly turned the burned side of his face aside as she gasped and shrank back from him.

"You were warned," he gritted, lifting her off him, "and I told you I wanted no company."

"Liar! That there says otherwise," she shrilled, gesturing toward the erection he quickly covered. "What? You thought you'd get better in such an important master's house? Who but somebody paid to, do you think would let you cock a leg looking like . . . like *that?*"

"*Get out!*"

"What? After you've got me ready?"

"You ready easily, I think," he said with a humorless laugh, "and will find relief elsewhere quick enough." It was no less than she deserved. Montaigne meant well, but this was beyond bearing, and he retrieved his helm and put it back in place. He would have welcomed the release, but not in such a one as she. Never again in such a one as she! If he had to bend to Aengus's will and enter the monastery, he would have no more truck with strumpets. "Get out," he said again. "I shall tell no tales to your master. If he should pay you again to keep me 'company,' take the tribute as you will, but do not come to me again. *Get out* I say!"

"You'll have no luck for humiliating me," she warned him, snatching up her girdle from the floor and tugging her shift back over her breasts. "It can rot and fall off for wanting before I come near it again!"

Crashing through the door, she disappeared, and Robert vaulted from the bed and dropped the wooden bar, locking the door behind her. After extinguishing the candle flame in his open palm with such a heavy hand that it squashed the beeswax taper flat, he crawled between the sheets, exhausted. Only then would he remove the helm and trust himself to spiral into a deep, dreamless sleep.

Four

*R*obert *did not mention Francine's nocturnal visit to Montaigne* in the morning. He broke his fast with barley bread and ale and then set out for the vendors' quarter in search of Violette. The magistrate lent him a fine bay gelding from his stables for the occasion and for his continued use during his stay in France.

He had no trouble finding the area Montaigne had mapped out. It wasn't far from the foot of the bridge where he'd last seen her, though she was not there today. The heavy rains had ceased, but the day was still sodden, spitting rain, and blustery, and the air had turned colder. He reached the home of Jacques and Justine Delon, where he was told Violette kept lodgings. It was easily recognizable with its unique Lincoln green door. But the door was slammed shut in his face after the woman insisted that Violette was not there, that she had not been in a day and a night, and that she had no idea where she'd gone. Her cart, however, was there. Robert's sharp eyes glimpsed it lying empty behind the mews.

He knocked on every other door in the quarter with the same result—no one had seen Violette since the incident. He rode back to Montaigne's château acutely disappointed. He wanted to thank her, yes, but more than that, he wanted to see her again. The sight and scent of her was still with him. Those beautiful eyes, like a frightened doe's in color and expression tugged at his memory, as did the long fall of satiny light brown hair cascading down her back from under the tight-fitting white linen cap, tied under her dainty chin.

He took a deep breath, recalling her scent. The clean, rain-washed air seemed infused with it—mum, nasturtium, and the provocative, clovelike gillyflower. Even the memory of it blotted out the real smells of food rotting in the alleys, of musky, lathered horseflesh, and sooty smoke belching from poorly drawing chimneys and braziers.

He arrived at the château just in time for the noon hour dinner, and joined Montaigne in the study, where a veritable feast was laid out including boiled beef, pickled herring, and mutton, as well as more of the savory olive pie. Boiled salad and trencher bread were also offered, along with jugs of ale, sack, and also perry, made of succulent pears, for which Montaigne professed a partiality. Robert ate heartily while they waited for the magistrate's messenger to return with Nostradamus's reply to the missive he'd sent that morning.

After they ate, Montaigne suggested a stroll through the gardens for their private talk, out of earshot of anyone who might eavesdrop.

"Your uncle made you aware of the situation here in France, no?" the magistrate queried, as they progressed through the various plantings.

"He told me something of the conflict, yes, and warned me to beware of the Guises. I think he felt that I best wait and consult you for the details, since the situation is so rapidly changing here now."

"Indeed. Your uncle has had dealings with Charles de Guise, and knows firsthand the danger in that camp. I can only reinforce whatever he has told you. Have no truck there if you can avoid it."

"I am hoping to have concluded my business here and be away before I've had the pleasure of his acquaintance, seigneur."

"The Guises rule here now, no matter who sits on the throne," the magistrate warned. "Their power fell away briefly after Francis II died, when Catherine de' Medici, as regent, dominated the government. But just last year, the duke, Francois de Guise, the cardinal's brother, formed a triumvirate of sorts with Montmorency and Marshal Saint-Andre, putting them again at the head of the Catholic party in a formidable bloc—more powerful than they had ever been. This is where we stand now, and their opposition to the Calvinists has us on the brink of civil war here."

"These Huguenots . . . what is their stand? Why can they not coexist peacefully?"

"They are no different from the Protestants you have encountered in Scotland, my lord. Their beliefs are intolerable to the Catholics, in that they would make all men—and *women*, privy to the Scriptures, not just priests and the hierarchy, as it is now. Both factions vie for supremacy, and neither will yield. The Guises have mustered a daunting army, with men like General Louis de Brach, a ruthless, self-serving social climber, who like the cardinal himself, has risen in the ranks over the bodies of those who dared oppose him—Huguenot and Catholic alike! He is the cardinal's constant companion here of late, fighting for sway over the boy king with Condé and Coligny, the Protestant opposition. That is the real conflict, and they must also sway the Queen Mother, and Catherine de' Medici is a force to be reckoned with. She walks the thin edge of a sword between them right now, swinging like a pendulum, and as she goes, so goes the king."

"Where do you stand in this conflict?" Robert asked.

"On a similar edge of a similar sword," Montaigne responded. "My office allows it. Were I to take sides now, it would ring my own death knell. I am wise enough not to declare myself—even to you, and being a Jew, I am not pressed. I do have a personal opinion that I will share, though, for your ears only."

"And that is . . . ?"

"That God . . . the God we *all* worship, who has given us

free will, has not denied us free expression in our humble attempt to worship Him. It is man, who has done that, and man must answer for it how God wills."

"Well said."

"Only to you."

"I understand, and I am flattered, seigneur, and honored to be privy to your innermost thoughts. I shan't ever betray them."

"I am counting upon it."

"You can. A Scot's word is his bond."

"I have consulted your healer on the subject of war. He is not encouraging."

"Is he really able to see into the future?"

Montaigne ground out a humorless laugh. "Ask the Queen Mother," he said. "His prediction of her husband King Henri's death is legendary. He has written books, which, I might add, she carries with her, and he doubtless will write more. Some of his predictions, I will admit, are without precedent, but who can say, eh, considering that all he has prophesied of the here and now has come to pass. Catherine idolizes him, and after forecasting Henri's death so exactly, his word is sacrosanct. She is a very superstitious sort. She has consulted the astrologer Ruggiero for years. There are dark rumors there as well, just as there are concerning Nostradamus, who has, I fear, been suspected of consorting with the Devil himself."

"I know you do not believe he can help me," Robert said, dismally.

"I know, my lord, that you must hear that diagnosis from Nostradamus himself before you will yield to reason. Nothing I can say will dissuade you from seeing him, and so I shall not even try."

As if on cue, a servant hurried along the garden walkway bearing a sealed missive. But he was not alone. Two others came apace behind, one robed, the other uniformed.

"*Mon Dieu!*" Montaigne crammed the letter into the pocket of his gown. "So much for concluding your business and being away before making the cardinal's acquaintance," he whispered. "Take care! The other with him is Louis de Brach, the general I spoke of. Leave this to me."

"Are we interrupting something?" the cardinal asked, hooded eyes raking Robert from head to toe. "Don't let us keep you from your missive there, Montaigne. The way your man all but trampled us to deliver it, it must be rather . . . important."

"Another summons from the Queen Mother, your grace," Montaigne responded silkily. "Heaven knows I am no architect, but she will consult me over every detail—monumental decisions, such as should there be a gallery in the renovated wing, where must the privies be, and how the new gardens should be laid. My poor gelding will be swaybacked soon for traveling back and forth, I fear. I will be much relieved when the Louvre restorations are complete."

"Ummm," the cardinal grunted. "And this is . . . ?" he inquired, inclining his head toward Robert.

"My houseguest," said Montaigne flatly. "Forgive me . . . Robert, Laird of Berwickshire, may I present Charles, Cardinal de Guise, and General Louis de Brach."

Robert nodded his helmeted head and studied the two most feared men in Paris with not a little interest. The cardinal's robed presence was indeed formidable, but it was the captain who interested him more. This was a warrior, someone with whom he could identify, if not agree. What he read there was plain—the man had loyalties to no one save himself, and eyes like a ferret's, sharp and black, that missed nothing.

"With which army are you aligned, my lord?" the captain queried. "I do not recognize your . . . uniform."

"Neither army, sir," said Robert steadily and succinctly.

"Your rudeness is insulting, then," the general responded.

"Who has taught you manners? Remove the helm, so that we may see with whom we speak."

"You have been told you with whom you speak," Robert replied. "I wear the helm not out of rudeness, but rather compassion—what lies beneath is hideous to view."

A spark of recognition flared in the cardinal's eyes. A hissing sound accompanied the look, and he held up his hand toward the general, cutting his next words short.

"Of course," he said, "Robert of Paxton, nephew of Aengus Haddock. I know him well, your uncle. A childhood injury as I recall . . . your deformity?"

"A fire, your grace," Robert replied, close eyes on the general, who still viewed him with suspicion.

"What brings you here to Paris—more to the point, to Montaigne's château, eh?"

"I am his sponsor whilst he visits Paris, your grace," Montaigne interjected.

"*You?* Why you?" the cardinal demanded.

"Are you not a Catholic, then?" the general put in, speaking to Robert.

"Now, now, Louis, let us not be hasty here. Let him speak," the cardinal soothed.

"Won't you step into the parlor for a refreshment?" Montaigne offered.

"We shan't be staying," the cardinal said, his voice like ice. "We heard of your . . . guest, and we have come to see whom you have taken into your home in these troubled times. Mere curiosity, Montaigne. You entertain so seldom."

"What is your alliance?" the general persisted, strolling nearer the Scot. "Declare it!"

"I am a Catholic," said Robert. "It is well known, I think, without my telling it to you upon demand."

A quick look from Montaigne told him this was not the tack to follow. A sidelong glance in Louis de Brach's direction reaffirmed it. The general's posture had clenched, and the hands at his sides were flexing in and out of white-knuckled fists.

"Then, how is it that your uncle has chosen Montaigne here, a Jew, to sponsor you and not myself, my lord? I should imagine I would have been the most logical choice."

"Most probably because he did not want to burden you with keeping me whilst you have such press upon you here now," Robert said, thinking on his feet. "You would, I am sure, have gone to great lengths to accommodate and entertain me, which would have taken you away from the dire situation at hand here. He simply did not want to impose; neither do I. My stay shall be brief, and I wish no fuss made over me."

"Why *are* you here, then?" the general insisted. "What mission brings a Scot from the borderlands in time of war with English invaders into the midst of another stew in France, pray?"

"A personal one," said Robert.

"*Personal?*" the general erupted. "Explain."

"I have come to see a healer over my . . . condition."

No one spoke. Would they accept it? One look at the cardinal's hard, cold stare, and the general's overt skepticism told him it wasn't likely.

"Who is this healer?" the cardinal queried.

"There is only one healer who can help me, I think," Robert replied, "Michel de Nostredame."

The cardinal made an indistinguishable sound in disgust that closely resembled the hiss of a cobra, and waved the notion off with a hand gesture.

"You lie!" the general roared. "Remove the helm! Let us see what you would have the charlatan Nostradamus heal."

Robert glanced toward the magistrate, who nodded, and, without hesitation, he slipped off the helm.

But for a brief tremor in his cold eyes, the cardinal made no response. The general, on the other hand, had much to say.

"I was right!" he triumphed. "You lie, indeed! What? Do you take us for fools, here? *No one* could repair *that*—not even God, who has evidently marked you so. Now then, I shall ask you once again, 'my lord,' why have you come here? Why are you not tartan-clad? Are you ashamed of your country, or are you come to some clandestine purpose that you fear might bring shame upon it? Speak up! With which side are you aligned? Come, come, these are not difficult questions. You are either on one side, or the other. Declare yourself!"

"I have told you, I am not politically aligned here," Robert said, donning the helm again. "I want no truck with your civil warring. I wear plain dress for anonymity."

"He lies!" the general said, addressing the cardinal. "He smells of heresy. I can sniff out a heretic downwind a league away, and this man is one—Montaigne as well if he has sponsored him. Catholic, eh? We are not so backward here that we do not know the Protestant John Knox was ordained as minister in the 'Church' of Scotland three years past, and just two years ago, the Latin Mass was outlawed there."

"That does not mean there are no Catholics left in my homeland," Robert served. He turned to the cardinal. "And Queen Mary—a very Catholic relative of yours, your grace, as all here know—returned to Scotland a year ago this past August."

"Take care where you sling your arrows, Louis de Brach," the magistrate warned. "You have no right to come here uninvited and accuse this man, who has just professed his Catholic faith, much less me, of heresy without proof. Alienating me will not help your cause. It would do you well to remember that I have the Queen Mother's ear, whilst all others in Paris scrap over it like dogs over a marrow bone."

Again the cardinal's upheld hand stayed the captain. "I have been slighted," he announced. "Let us first deal with that. Your uncle has made a serious and costly error offending me . . . again. It shan't go without reprisal, unless amends are made. You have just joined the Catholic cause against the Huguenots, I think," he declared smugly, a triumphant sparkle in his narrowed eyes. "Since you have blundered upon the Church in trouble, you have no recourse that I can see, but to defend it. What say you, Louis, will that satisfy?"

"There is a planned . . . event to take place soon," the general mused, stroking his pointed chin. "A raid. Two days hence, we march upon the Huguenot village north of the city. If he would prove himself, let him join the fray."

"I do not need to prove anything!" Robert said hotly. "I've stated my business here. You cannot force me to fight your battles. I am a foreign noble."

"Oh, no one is forcing you to, my lord," the cardinal responded. "You are simply proving your loyalty to the Church . . . and to your uncle don't forget, as well as your sponsor here. Oh, yes, you'll lend those broad Scottish shoulders willingly enough to our cause I'm thinking."

A chuckle erupted from the general's throat at that, and Robert knew he was caught. Run through by his own sword. His deformity, the very thing he'd called upon to exempt him, had damned him instead. They did not believe him. Oddly, for all the danger he found himself in then, what bothered him most was that they didn't think Nostradamus could heal him either.

How right his uncle was about this man, who claimed to be a prince of the Church. Not only would he be putting Aengus in jeopardy if he refused to fight, but Montaigne as well, who waited pensively, close, unreadable eyes upon him, anticipating his reply.

"Very well," he said, through clenched teeth, glad that

they couldn't clearly see the jaw muscles ticking beneath his helm, or the hard, lipless line his mouth had become. "I will join your battle, but not your war. As you have pointed out, I have wars at home to attend to, and I am sure that neither of you would be willing to come and lend me a hand with that."

"Louis?" the cardinal intoned, soliciting the general's approval. "Will that suit?"

"For now," the general begrudged. "We shall see how well he fights for our cause in the field first."

"When is this battle to be?" Robert queried.

"Patience, Laird Mack. I will come for you when 'tis time," the general assured him, "and for your sponsor's sake, not to mention your uncle's, you had best be here when I do."

"I have given my word," Robert reminded him, "and a Scotsman's word is his bond. We shall soon see how the French measure up by comparison."

"Montaigne," the cardinal said, with a nod. "We take our leave . . . for now." Then to the general, he said, "Come, Louis, we shouldn't want to overstay our welcome."

Both men turned then, and made their way back along the garden path without a backward glance.

"I am sorry, my lord," said Montaigne, "that was regrettable, but unavoidable, I'm afraid."

"It is I who am sorry, for involving you in my conceited cause. I will not see you chastised for my vanity, nor Uncle Aengus, either."

"You do not want to fight this battle," the magistrate said, answering his own question.

"I do not want to fight *any* battle in this land, seigneur, least of all a raid upon unsuspecting civilians. It is uncivilized."

"The times are uncivilized, and I think, considering that we are both ingredients in the same stew here, we might dispense with formalities. I am Michel, and you are Robert, *consenti?*"

"Agreed," said Robert. "Will the one raid satisfy them, do you think, or have I signed on for the duration of this senseless bloodlust of Christian against Christian?"

"Only time will tell."

"Then I must conclude my business with Doctor Nostradamus now—before this raid. Perhaps if they see that I am in earnest . . . that I really have come to seek his counsel—"

"Ah!" the magistrate interrupted. Reaching into the pocket of his gown, he produced the sheepskin the servant had handed him earlier, untied the ribbon wrapped around it, unrolled it, and read, his sharp eyes flitting over the lines of a script that looked both regal and primitive to Robert. "Your audience is granted this midnight," he said, perusing further, "—at the ruins. It is encrypted, thus, I read between the lines. Could he have known the cardinal and Louis de Brach would come on the heels of it? He must have. I told you he had uncanny sight."

"That is from Doctor Nostradamus? I thought the Queen Mother—"

"No, no, I only said that to dupe them. They would not dare tamper with a royal missive—at lease, I hoped not."

"You were very convincing," Robert said, through a guttural chuckle.

"A latent talent for performing in the mystery plays, I fear. I have always wondered what the life of a bard would be like. I do believe I've just had a taste."

"I am to be watched, I take it."

"I would count upon it, which is evidently why he has chosen the ruins over his rooms in the city for your meeting."

"He has more faith in my ability to elude pursuers than I have," Robert responded.

"It will take the general time to mobilize his spies. It would be best that you set out at once—now—in daylight, when you can see if you are being followed. The ruins stand on a knoll in the valley to the south that borders a copse dense enough for you to conceal your mount. Come, while I have my steward prepare a food pouch and a skin of mead for you to sup upon while you await your interview. I will draw you a map."

"And if I am followed despite all your precautions?"

The magistrate smiled. "If Doctor Nostradamus has gone through this much trouble to bring you, my friend, you may rest assured that you will reach him safely."

Five

$\mathscr{R}$obert reached the ruins at dusk and tethered his bay gelding in the forest close by. Taking stock of the structure and the land around it, he surmised that it had once been a keep used for defense. Its elevated vantage gave a panoramic view of the surrounding land. Now only the attached smoke-house and parts of the walls were still standing, and what remained seemed to be held together by the climbing wood-bine that nearly covered it.

The inside was strewn with rubble, where the keep had collapsed in upon itself, and once he'd satisfied himself that he hadn't been followed, he decided to wait and eat the food Montaigne had provided. Out of the view of any who might venture near, he relaxed, removed his helm, and opened the provisions sack.

There was a skin of spiced wine, a small loaf of cheat made with bran, a slab of butter wrapped in a grape leaf, and a generous wedge of nut-sweet hard cheese unlike any he had tasted at home. It was delicious, and he ate ravenously, washing it all down with the wine. Afterward, he stretched out alongside the highest wall and watched the moon rise full and round and brilliant. After a time, his eyelids grew heavy and finally closed, the darkness behind them diluted by the brightness of the moon, until something blotted it out. Seasoned warrior that he was, he sensed a presence and vaulted to his feet, drawing his sword and donning the hel-met he'd set aside in one motion.

He stood in the presence of a short, vigorous man, whom he calculated to be in his late fifties or early sixties, darkly gowned, wearing a four-pointed cap. The brilliant moonlight revealed rosy-apple cheeks, a high, square forehead, straight, determined features, and extremely keen eyes. He could not make out their color, but they shone like polished silver.

"Doctor Nostradamus?" he breathed.

"Take ease, my lord," the healer soothed. "Sheath your sword and remove the helm. I have already seen what lies beneath."

Robert raised the helmet and set it on a shelf of rubble, while the healer came forward and took hold of his chin, tilting it this way and that in the moonlight.

"Can you . . . help me?" Robert urged, studying the healer's pursed lips and narrow-eyed scrutiny.

"Does it pain you?" Nostradamus queried.

"No. There is occasional tightness, but no pain."

"I can give you an ointment that will soften the skin and relieve the tightness, young Scot, but the scars will remain. Those burns go deep, and were acquired early in your life. You are fortunate that only one side of your face was affected; the other is quite handsome."

"I was but a bairn in my cradle, a sennight old, when it happened," Robert said, desolate.

"Ummm," the healer grunted. "Growth has distorted the scarring. There is no treatment. But one day, such will be remedied as a matter of course, though not in your lifetime I fear. When were you born—the month, and day?"

"I was born the thirtieth day of March, in the year of 1533."

"The fire-sign of the ram. The flames have marked you. Warring is your . . . occupation?"

"Yes . . ."

"You have chosen well."

"You were my last hope," Robert despaired, "and in coming I have put many in danger—my Uncle Aengus, who is a monk at the abbey of St. Michael's Mount, seigneur de Montaigne, and an innocent little blind flower vendor, who has become caught up in my trouble; all for naught."

"I am not your last hope, but we will come back to that. Tell me about the flower vendor? How has she come to harm?"

"Her name is Violette Cherier, and I do not know for certain that she has," Robert admitted. "She seems to have vanished."

"Hmmm," the healer mused, "let me hear how little Violette has become embroiled in your . . . adventure."

"You know her, then?"

"All Paris knows Violette, young ram. Her flower cart has been a fixture in the square for years, and her beauty and vivacity have won her many friends. What has she to do with you?"

Robert sank down on the ledge beside his helm, and recounted his capture and release from the Bastille, and the strange reception he received in the vendors' quarter when he went there to thank her. When he had finished, the healer did not speak directly.

"Do you know what's become of her?" Robert asked.

"The vendors protect one another," he replied. "She is probably in hiding. Jean-Claude and Henri would be looking for her, seeking satisfaction for their chastisement. Rumor has it that they have been dealt with severely, and Garboneaux has been demoted in rank. You are under Montaigne's protection. She has no such champion, and she is blind. You can be assured that her vendor friends have spirited her away to some safe haven. They will keep her whereabouts secret so that no one can lead the gendarmes to her. It is wise thinking. Do not trouble yourself about her. If she had met with foul play, we would certainly have heard of it. One thing you must know about Paris, young ram—the very air you breathe has ears, and word travels quickly."

"I feel responsible for her," Robert confessed. "She tried to help me, and I have cost her her livelihood, and endangered her life. She heard them holler 'plague,' when they removed my helm—she heard their panic, and yet she did not fear it. She even attacked the gendarme called Jean-Claude, followed his voice and kicked him soundly in his shins. That man was restraining me, and she was close enough to touch. What if I did have plague?"

"We should all be so 'blind' as our Violette," the healer observed.

"Sir?"

"For all her blindness, she sees far better than you ever will, young ram, because she sees with her spirit."

"Riddles? Montaigne warned me to expect them."

" 'Tis no riddle. *Pay attention!*" he thundered. "Step out of yourself, and hear words that one day may well save your life, *or hers* if you will but heed them."

"I do not understand your convoluted speech. Can you not speak it plain?"

"Violette cannot see with her eyes, and so she sees with her spirit—her instincts. It is common knowledge that when one of our senses fails, other senses are heightened to compensate. In Violette's case it is her sense of perception that has been heightened."

Robert's ragged sigh, and brows knit in a puzzled frown replied to that. He was no student of philosophy. It had no hilt to grab, and no sword point to thrust.

"You still don't understand?" Nostradamus said, vexed. "*You* are the blind one. She knew without seeing you that you did not have plague. Her instincts told her. She did not need the physical proof her eyes might have provided to know it was safe to champion you—to come near to you. She saw this with her spirit. *You* must learn to see with your spirit, young ram. There will be times when it will be vital that you do so, and you are so preoccupied with how others view *you*, you cannot see *them*. I would advise you cultivate the art—and quickly. If you take nothing else away from this interview, take that advice to heart. As gospel."

"It is a warning, this?" Robert asked.

"Riddle—warning—prophesy—call it by what name you will, but know it as plain fact. You are out of your element here. This is not Scotland, where war means hand-to-hand combat on an open field, and there is at least some semblance of honor in it. War here means something else entirely—something more political than physical, though blood lust is an integral part of it. It is waged primarily in the shadows—clandestine—deceptive. There are no real 'sides,' only ambitions, and a man can lose his head without even knowing why. You are ill-equipped to wage this kind of war, my blind young ram."

"But I learn quickly. I have met your Charles de Guise, Cardinal of Lorraine, and his henchman, General Louis de Brach."

"What do think you of these men?"

"Guise is unfit to wear the robes of a cardinal, and Louis de Brach thinks he rules him, but that unholy prince of the Church will cut him down like wheat in the field the minute he is of no more use to him. This is why he keeps him close, so that he may use him up before he strikes like the viper he is."

"You are learning. Tell me, how do you view the Huguenots?"

"I pity them! Blind faith in God empowers them, but faith need not be so blind as to annihilate God's faithful. They are too gullible. They should be warned, and I cannot do it, else I put Montaigne and my uncle in grave danger. The Huguenots are unprepared for what will come, and many will die needlessly."

"Who is speaking in riddles now?"

"There will be slaughter done, and I am to be part of it. I

have no choice. You must know, or we would not be meeting here in these ruins at the midnight hour, but openly in your rooms, and your reply would not have been encrypted."

"Never grieve for what cannot be changed," the healer said.

"Montaigne tells me that the boy king is seduced by both factions now, and that the Guises head the Church in France and vie for the Queen Mother's support. How does young Charles IX feel about such atrocities in the name of God?"

"His sympathies, like the country, are divided. He is very fond of Admiral Coligny, and intimidated by the Guises, particularly the cardinal, who has intimidated half of France—the literate half."

"He will not sit long upon the throne, I think."

"He will sit long enough to make the massacre you fear look like one of his mama's mystery ballets, young ram," the healer ground out through a bone-chilling chuckle. "But we will both be gone from here by then—you to your destiny and me to my rest. It is no secret. I told her long ago that she would see three of her sons become king, but that the royal Valois line would vanish with the last, without descendants. Though, while he lives, your 'boy king,' he will shed more blood than you could in two lifetimes of soldiering."

Robert did not probe that augur. The way the healer spoke held his tongue. It really didn't matter. He would have no dealings with the boy king, or any of these that Nostradamus spoke of. He would fulfill his obligation in the looming battle, and be away. There was no more reason to remain in France, though he did hope to see Violette before he returned to Scotland.

"Will I see her again?" he said, as though speaking to himself. "I would like to find her—to thank her. She was kind to me. Not many have shown me . . . kindness in this life."

"You will find her when you do not seek her," Nostradamus returned.

More augur; it was maddening. Why couldn't the man speak plainly if he knew? But he must know, else he would not have said it. The esteemed Michel de Nostredame was not one to waste words. Or was he simply trying to salve his disappointment with hope—any shred of hope?

"And what of you, Doctor, are we to meet again?"

"Somewhat . . . abruptly, young ram, when you least expect it."

"Doctor Nostradamus," Robert said haltingly, "before you said that you were not my last hope. What did you mean by that? If, as you say, there is no way to make me whole . . . ?"

"That marvel puzzles you, does it? I speak not of the aesthetic, but of what lies beneath. Hear my words—you, born of the fire sign, beware, for it has marked you. All your life, the flames will stalk you, Robert of Paxton. Listen well and remember, for I speak this augur only once: The flames attend you. They will spring to life about you at each turning point your life takes 'til 'tis done, for the winds of change fan them like a bellows. Tempt them not, but heed them well—they will guard you, and they will guide you to the woman your heart desires, but they also herald Hell itself. You must learn to divine them, young Scot. You must school yourself to divine them quickly, and well or you will see all you hold dear lost to the flames."

"They say you are a sorcerer that you can foresee the future thus . . . that you know of things yet to come."

"There is no sorcery in predicting the future, young ram, since the past so often repeats itself. What is the future, after all, but the bastard child of time—the illegitimate, ill begotten blunders of man? Why I have been chosen to see it, I cannot say, unless it be to warn mankind that he must change it, for it is truly terrible—beyond imagining."

"I still do not see—"

"See with your spirit," Nostradamus intoned. "What have I just been telling you? Do not plow what can be under the soil of what cannot. You are a prisoner of the flames that have disfigured you 'til you—like the Phoenix—rise above them. Chew on that food 'til next we meet. Look past the obvious. See with your spirit, Robert of Paxton. . . ."

Six

To Robert's surprise, Montaigne was waiting up for him when he returned to the château. It was very late, but the magistrate had wine brought to the parlor study, and sat in his favorite Glastonbury chair beside the chimney while Robert highlighted his interview with Doctor Nostradamus.

"I'm sorry, Robert," Montaigne said, genuinely. "I know you do not think it, but I had hoped."

"It was folly, my coming. I think I always knew it. I shan't pretend that I am not disappointed. And worse yet, I must take part in this raid I want no truck with. Has there been any more word about when it is to be?"

"No, but there is something else," Montaigne said. "After you left, I did receive a summons from the Queen Mother, which is just as well, of course, because it legitimized my lie. I am to have an audience with Catherine de' Medici on the morrow, and you must come with me."

"But, why?"

"Because you are not safe here alone," Montaigne told him. "If they should come for you, I will not know of it, and I cannot protect you if I do not know what has happened to you."

"I don't see how you can protect me in any case," Robert said dismally.

"I must try. We must be inseparable now, you and I. Between your battle prowess, and my wits, we might just be able to get you out of France all of apiece."

"It isn't my hide I'm worried about." Robert said. "It is yours, and Uncle Aengus's."

"Then indulge me."

"I can hardly march into the Louvre helmed. At the very best, I would be viewed as insolent. And if I dared to venture in without it, there would surely be a hue and cry over plague."

"There is a maze, and gardens, with stone benches in the walled courtyard at the Louvre. You may wait for me there. It is quite beautiful this time of year, and private. You will not be disturbed. I will advise the Queen Mother of your presence, and your need for privacy. No one would dare to take you from the court without her permission, and the king would not do such a thing without consulting her. It is what must be, Robert. I will not leave you here alone. God only knows what plans are hatching."

"How much will you tell her, surely nothing of the raid?"

"No, no," Montaigne assured him, "only that which pertains to your . . . personal misfortune, and your mission here to consult with Nostradamus. I will plead your cause to spare yourself embarrassment, and the court your helmed presence."

"As you wish," Robert conceded, "but I believe you are being overcautious."

"Better that, than sorry after. Now then, you must to bed. We rise early. Though, I could have Francine visit your quarters . . . if you have need of . . . company beforehand?"

"No. Do not disturb her. I have more need of sleep than company. Thank you, Michel, you are most generous, but I think it best that I abstain from carnal pursuits for the remainder of my stay here. I must have my wits about me and my strength unsapped if I am to do battle—on the field and off—and wenches muddle both."

"As you wish, but if you should change your mind . . ."

"I will be sure to make it known. But for now, you must let

me prepare for battle as I always do . . . in solitude, and prayer."

The day dawned fair, and they broke their fast with ale, fresh baked bread, and boiled eels, for it was a fish day. They ate heartily, since they had no idea if they would be returning in time for dinner. This was more for Robert's sake than the magistrate's. Montaigne would certainly be provided food at court if his stay was to be a lengthy one. Since anonymity would deprive Robert of similar fare, he convinced the Scot to take along two ripe black Worcester pears, should he grow hungry waiting in the garden. Then, setting out on horseback, they rode leisurely to the Louvre.

They hadn't gone far when Montaigne informed him that they were being followed. The spy wore no uniform. He wore plain dress in colors that blended well with the color of his mount, making him nearly invisible. They were both expecting surveillance, and made a game of making his task difficult. When they reached the Louvre, they did so with a flourish. Let the nodcock carry tales to Louis de Brach, or the cardinal—whomever he pleased. All they would learn was that Montaigne was where the cardinal already knew he would be, answering his summons from Catherine de' Medici, which he himself had seen delivered.

The maze fascinated Robert. Paxton Keep had none, and he set out at once to walk it leisurely, his feet crunching the graveled path. It was rather high as mazes went, sculpted out of juniper, as was the even taller hedge wall that enclosed the entire garden. Every so often, there was a stone bench, and he didn't have to wonder at the wisdom of that. By noon, he had become quite lost, and took advantage of one to rest and get his bearings. It wasn't long before he started out again, but he hadn't gone far when a boy rounding a corner ran headlong into him.

"Whoa there, poppet!" he cried, staring down toward the fine blue eyes of a prepubescent boy, whose quick intake of breath was no surprise; they had collided heavily, and both were winded.

"Are you a knight?" the boy said, as Robert steadied him and let him go.

"No," Robert said, noting the boy's deflated posture at his answer, "just an admirer of these wonderful gardens here."

"Oh," the boy said dejectedly. "I thought perhaps there was to be a joust. We haven't had one in some time you know, not since King Henri died in one. I would so enjoy some excitement. All this restoration fuss is boring, and it shall go on, and on. Grown-ups are never satisfied. I will be old and gray, and still the Louvre will be under construction."

Robert laughed, taking the boy's measure. There was nothing unusual about him, just a child in plain dress, with grass-stained hose and windblown hair, and yet he was extraordinarily engaging.

"Do you often run the maze?" he queried, as they began to travel it again. He had changed directions following the boy's course in hopes of finding his way out.

"Not often enough," the boy said, scowling. "I'm not supposed to run. I have this cough, you see, and running makes it worse. They always know when I've been at it. I wheeze, you know. Then I catch it. Doctor Nostradamus says my lungs will collapse if I don't take care, and then I shouldn't be able to breathe. I worry about that sometimes . . . what it would be like not to be able to breathe. I've once even held my breath until I saw stars. It was not very pleasant."

"You know Doctor Nostradamus, then?"

"Oh, yes, he treats all the children here at court, and the adults, too."

"You like him, I take it?"

The boy shrugged. "He frightens me," he whispered. "Some of what he has foretold has come true, you know. He predicted King Henri's *death*! He won't predict my future, though—to me, that is. But I see something in his eyes at times . . . something disapproving. I do not think he likes me much."

"Children are often frightened of adults," Robert opined. "I was when I was a boy. More often than not, when they gave me disapproving looks it was for my own good."

"The words of a true adult," the boy chided with a gusty sigh. "Are you sure that you are not a knight? You look like one."

"I am sure."

"Have you never jousted, then—not even once?"

"Not even once."

"Ummm, a pity. I would really like to learn more of the sport from someone with firsthand experience."

They had come to a stone bench, and the boy was still panting hard.

"What say we sit a spell?" Robert suggested. It was a shady spot, though the sun was warm beaming down, and once they were seated, he took the pears from his pouch. "Will you join me?" he said, offering one.

The boy licked his lips in anticipation of the juicy pear and swallowed audibly.

"Go ahead, take one," Robert coaxed.

"You shall have to taste it first," the boy lamented.

"Why?" Robert said. "They are quite fine, black Worcester, very ripe and delicious."

"I am the king," the boy said flatly. "All of my food must be tasted, you see."

Robert vaulted to his feet and bowed awkwardly, almost dropping the pears. "*Your Majesty!*" he breathed. "Why did you not say so? I had no idea!"

"Sit, sit, I did not want you to," the boy said, still eyeing the pears.

"Are you supposed to be out here unattended?" Robert

queried. Watching the boy's eyes devouring the fruit, he withdrew his eating knife, and sliced a piece from the larger of the two. Now what to do? He didn't want to remove the helmet before the king, and he turned his back, loosened the lower edge enough to eat the slice of pear, and then turned back, offering what remained. This time the boy took it, having observed the ritual with not a little interest, though he said nothing then. The pear had his full and fierce attention, and he sank his teeth deeply into it, making loving little moans as he made short work of it, ignoring the rivulets of sweet, sticky juice running down his chin.

"You didn't answer my question, Your Majesty," Robert urged. "Should you not be attended on your . . . outings?"

"I suppose," he responded, "but my jailers never let me *do* anything. Every so often, I escape them. They are easily duped."

"Forgive me, Your Majesty, but is that wise as things stand here now?"

"I do not think it much matters," he replied with a shrug, discarding the core of the pear. Gripping the edge of the bench with both hands, he began swinging his feet beneath it. "I should be safe enough so long as both sides are fighting over me. This holy war is childish; grown men fighting over God. It will all be forgotten once they tire of the game, just as children tire of their toys. I trust none of them. Their play is too intense. If I am to be caught up in it, as I know I soon must be, and run the risk of dying for my pains, I shall have some fun first!"

"That you do not trust any of them is all the more reason why you ought to keep those who attend you close, I should think," Robert said with a humorless laugh.

"Ummm," the boy hummed, dismissing the thought with a hand gesture while scrutinizing him closely. "You now know that I am the king," he said, "but you have me at a disadvantage. I have no idea who you are, sir. Identify yourself."

"Forgive my want of conduct, Your Majesty," Robert said. Vaulting to his feet again, he offered another bow. "I am Robert Mack, of Paxton Keep, Laird of Berwickshire, Scotland, at your service, Your Majesty."

"Scotland? My, that is a distance. Your French is excellent. I would never have guessed. Ha! To think I've found a noble Scotsman blundering about my maze."

"It is an odd business I will allow," said Robert, taking his seat again in obedience to the king's gesture.

"Well, my lord," the king responded, "are all Scotsmen so lacking in manners that they remain helmed in a sovereign's presence? It is quite rude, you know."

"It is not meant to be, Your Majesty," Robert defended. "What lies beneath my helm is unpleasant to view. I wear it to spare myself embarrassment, and you the sight."

"I could command you to remove it."

"You could, Your Majesty, but I have never heard it said that you are a cruel sovereign."

"I shan't command it. I am simply . . . curious. That is my prerogative, of course, as both child and king. But I am more curious as to how you view our country, and with which side you are aligned."

Robert studied the boy's face. He seemed so very wise, and yet so adolescent all at once, and he tried to recall himself at age twelve, seeking some insight toward dealing with what could well be a dangerous situation. There was clearly no pretense. It was simply as the boy said; he was curious, nothing more. That he obviously did not fully understand the skullduggery afoot came as no surprise. He was far too steeped in the stew to savor the broth, nor was it something Robert could fathom wisely enough to enlighten the youth. He hadn't even begun to scratch the surface of the complexities of the conflict he'd become embroiled in himself.

"You do not want to commit yourself," the boy said to his hesitation.

Suddenly, Robert thought of Nostradamus, and tried to view his new acquaintance with his spirit—with his instinct, as the healer had so vividly stressed, wondering if this could be one of the occasions he had warned of. That experiment sired truth, and he answered the question honestly.

"No, Your Majesty," he said through a sigh, "I do not want to, but there is no disloyalty in it. I am unwittingly caught up in your madness here against my will."

"Explain."

Robert popped a cryptic laugh. "Hideous as my wretched head is, I should like to keep it yet awhile," he said, with candor.

"And you shall, I promise you," said the king. "I wish to hear tell of what has brought you here, and how you are . . . involved against your will. I like you. You speak openly— even now. Yes, I like you, indeed. Nobody does that with me, you know. That is why I didn't tell you right away that I am the king. I wanted some plain speech first. I am so weary of being fawned over and placated and, well, you know."

"I expect I do," Robert replied. "It must be . . . difficult."

"It is *boring*, my lord."

Robert laughed again. "Well, I cannot promise that you will find my tale any less tiresome," he said, "but I shall tell it, if you wish me to."

"Good!"

"I came to France for counsel with your Doctor Nostradamus over my . . . disfigurement. I had no other thought save that in coming. My uncle, a monk of Mount St. Michael Abbey, arranged that seigneur de Montaigne sponsor me during my stay in your country. Unfortunately, the cardinal was slighted that the honor was not delegated to himself, and he has conscripted me to fight the Huguenots . . ."

"*Out of spite!*" the king concluded for him.

"That could well be, yes," Robert responded warily. Now he understood the ways of walking the edge of a sword.

"He can be rather ... vengeful, the cardinal—far too vengeful for a holy man, I've often thought. I don't really like him, but it isn't permitted to dislike him openly. He is a Guise, and the cardinal atop it and Mama won't hear a whisper of disrespect toward him."

"What of the general?" Robert queried.

"Louis de Brach is afire to wipe the Huguenots from the face of the planet. He is a great warrior, and I like him well enough I suppose, but sometimes I must confess I do feel stifled enduring him. He is at odds with Admiral Coligny, and condemns some who stood beside my cradle. He would have me do likewise, and it often makes me ill at ease. I like the admiral. I think Mama does, too. She heeds him sometimes, but now that the duke is dead ..."

"Well, I cannot comment upon the admiral. I have not met the man. But from my brief encounter with the general, I do see what you mean about his fervor to champion the cause. They are both strong-willed souls, bigod, your cardinal and general, but so are you, Your Majesty. If I were called upon to give you counsel, I would say heed none of them completely, and trust your own instincts. For one so young, you have a remarkable insight. I envy it. Were I as perceptive, I would not be facing this dilemma here now."

"You will definitely fight, then?"

"I have no choice. I have given my word. The word of a Scot is his bond, Your Majesty, and now that I have met you, it will be easier."

"How?"

"No man wants to do battle, lest he be mad. We fight to defend our homes and family, our faith, our integrity, when we are driven to it. Common logic will tell you that a foreigner doing battle with a faceless foe who has done him no harm—with whom he has no personal grudge—would have to be caught in a somewhat less than savory situation. True, the cause we champion, you and I, is the same, yet it is very different. Surely you can see that? But now, having met you, having spoken so candidly with you, I can fight on your behalf. Even though the enemy remains faceless, he for whom I fight now has a face indeed, and thus the battle has taken on a personal nature."

"I wish I could feel the cause more acutely," the boy mused.

"You are thinking of those who stood beside your cradle," Robert pointed out. "Your Majesty, it is not the individual who threatens you, it is the movement that threatens us *all*. There is no shame in that you do not yet have the means to separate the two."

"I cannot hate them, the Huguenots."

"You shall be a well-loved sovereign."

"And you shall probably be killed," said the king.

Robert fell silent. Something in the sound of that wisdom from the boy's young lips wrenched his guts as though a fist had gripped them.

"Is that conjecture, or certainty, Your Majesty?" he ventured to ask.

"Let us just say," the boy replied on an audible breath, "that I, Charles, the king, command you to proceed from this bench here where we now sit with extreme caution. The ground hereabouts sits steady under no man's feet. Not even my own."

Seven

*R*obert *reluctantly accompanied the troops dispatched to the* Huguenot village the following night. General Louis de Brach came to collect him with an escort at dusk, and led him to the outskirts of the village, where the troops were gathered, well concealed within the forest. There they waited according to plan until the Huguenots slept, and all was still save a resident owl and the restless woodland creatures their intrusion had startled.

Overhead, no stars blinked down through the steadily gathering cloud fabric, thick and low in the night sky. A storm was approaching, and the risen wind had turned the crisp autumn air colder. Leaves filtered down, no longer able to cling to the trees' bony branches clacking together above. They smelled of dampness and decay, collecting in hushed whispers on the moss-clad forest floor.

Mounted, Robert waited at the head of the column he was to command, eyes close upon the general as he passed among the legion, the prohibitive helm with the visor in place affording him an advantage in that he could take stock of the situation, without the rest monitoring his scrutiny. This was not just a confrontation with the Calvinists. It was a fight for his survival. He was expendable—a problematic thorn in the cardinal's side because his presence among them was suspect, and unless he was mistaken, Louis de Brach had no intentions of letting him leave the field alive. When the general finally reached him, he was ready.

"It is time, my lord," de Brach growled. "The wind fights

with us. Not only will its wailing cover the sound of our approach, it will fan the flames and spread our handiwork. Assemble your men."

"What of the forest?" Robert queried.

"What of it?"

"If the flames should spread—"

"What matters the forest?" the general interrupted. "Let the damnable trees burn. With so much at stake here, you worry over *timber*—Huguenot timber, at that?"

"I worry over our retreat once the fray is done," Robert returned. "Can you not feel the wind? It blows in our direction."

"Yes, yes, and changes course with each breath it breathes in storms such as this bearing down upon us. Group your men, I say, and be quick about it. I think you are not quite resigned. That would be most unwise. You had best remember what is at stake here and have done over trifles. Time grows short. As I have said, the wind is with us, and I do not like repeating myself. The rain will not be so accommodating. Make ready!"

With no more said, he disappeared, and suddenly a sea of torches sprang to life in the ink-black night. Like disembodied souls, they bobbed, wraithlike, in the darkness—another and another until the landscape glowed blood-red with thatch-roofed dwellings engulfed in flames.

Flushed from their homes, the Huguenots fell helpless in the confusion just as he had predicted. The strident sounds of the terror-stricken and dying rose over the wail of the wind, many of them women and children, and he took a sudden chill despite the heat the holocaust generated. The wind was blowing toward the forest, just as he had warned.

Hypnotized by the flames, he stared into them, compelled, despite his occupation with the battle, while out of the midst of the rising columns of smoke and flame came the bone-chilling voice of Nostradamus. Loudly it echoed—almost too loudly to have been dredged of the stuff of dreams—waking or sleeping. Carried by the wind, it lingered: "All your life, the flames will stalk you, Robert of Paxton. Listen well and remember, for I speak this augur only once: The flames attend you. They will spring to life about you at each turning point your life takes 'til 'tis done, for the winds of change fan them like a bellows. Tempt them not, but heed them well—they will guard you, and they will guide you to the woman your heart desires, but they also herald Hell itself. You must learn to divine them, young Scot. You must learn to divine them quickly, and well or you will see all you hold dear lost to the flames."

Robert gave a battle cry as sparks flew from the edge of a Huguenot sword come down hard upon his own, snapping him out of his reverie. Dazed, he groaned as the man behind the weapon fell dead beneath his mount's prancing feet.

Glancing up, he searched the flaming pandemonium for Louis de Brach, having lost sight of him momentarily. Panicked by the blaze, the horse beneath him spun and reared, pawing the ground with its heavy forefeet. As the animal whirled in a mad frenzy, he caught sight of the hulking general setting his torch to a barn on the village fringes that skirted the forest to the north. A girl staggered through the wide-flung doors, slapping the rump of a crazed horse, then another, followed by several bellowing cows, and a flock of complaining chickens. The animals nearly unhorsed the general as they thundered past, but the girl seemed not to notice him in her path as she groped her way through the smoke, fiery straw, and thatch raining all around her. The haze parted just long enough for Robert to glimpse her frightened face. Violette! Her terrified shrieks joined the rest of the din as the general swooped down and seized her, dragging her alongside his mount until they were well out of sight behind the burning barn toward the forest's edge.

Fear rose with the flavor of bile in Robert's throat, and he dug his heels in, deeply driving his own mount toward their direction, only to be detained by a fresh onslaught of Huguenots, who had shed the dregs of sleep sufficiently enough to arm themselves and round up horses to join in the conflict. Most of the others were occupied behind him, and he quickly saw that those who were not engaged weren't overly eager to come to his aid. He took a deep wound in his left shoulder, and it was several minutes before he'd felled the man who had dealt the blow, and his comrades with him.

Cursing for the pain and the vertigo it caused, Robert set out again, and, rounding the corner of the barn, he saw the general's horse vacant. On the ground below, Louis de Brach was struggling atop Violette, grinding his powerful body against her as she struggled underneath him. Robert drove his horse straight toward them at a gallop, leaped off the animal's back, and wrenched the general off her.

Grappling with each other, they rolled down the hill away from the forest, which had also begun to blaze. Halfway down the steep grade, a sapling stopped their progress. They sprang to their feet, their drawn swords gleaming red in the glare of the flames springing up all around them. Despite the crippling wound, Robert had the advantages of height and strength over the general. Panting and cursing, Louis de Brach hacked wildly at the Scot, who was hard pressed to keep his footing on the steep incline, and their swords clashed, flinging sparks, as first one and then the other weapon sliced through the thick, smoke-filled air.

Behind them, the roar of the flames devouring the copse all but drowned out the distant sounds of battle, and the girl's panic-stricken sobs grew steadily more distant, as Robert dodged a thrust that caught his sword and spun it out of his hand.

Blood was flowing down his arm, sapping his strength, but the general was advancing, and Robert tore the *sgian dubh* from his boot, ducked as the general swung his sword, then surged up, and thrust the dirk. The general froze, then fell forward, the Scottish blade buried deep in his belly.

Through the swirling clouds of smoke, Robert caught sight of troops advancing. They were nearly upon him. With neither time nor thought wasted upon the fallen general, he spun facing the burning wood behind.

The silver helm grew unbearably hot so close to the inferno. Raising the visor, he called at the top of his voice: "Violette!" There was no answer, and, Louis de Brach forgotten, he recovered the sword the general had beaten from his hand, collected his mount, and swung himself clumsily upon the horse's lathered back. Then with his body bent low in the saddle, he drove the animal toward the forest using the sooty curtain as a blind.

"*Violette!*" he shouted, his eyes straining the smoke-filled air. "Speak out that I may find you! It is I, Robert Mack. I will help you, lass. Violette, in God's name, *answer me!*"

Still no answer came. His greatest fear was that he would not be able to bear the heat much longer. He was all but cooked beneath the helmet. Finally desperate, he tore it off, calling out again and again, the battle behind forgotten in his fever to find her. He'd nearly given in to hopelessness when his sharp eyes spied the shape of a distant silhouette groping amid the trees that had just begun to catch fire farther north. He reached her in seconds, scooped her up in his good arm, and drove the half-crazed horse beneath him in a southerly direction, away from the hungry flames eating the wood all around.

He set her down, tethered his mount, and went to her side. His breath caught at close sight of her. She was hysterical still, her long hair matted with dead leaves and straw, loose about her shoulders. Her skin was streaked and smudged with soot over her face and arms and full, round breasts, scarcely covered by the gaping shift.

Kneeling down beside her, Robert gingerly struggled out

of the chain mail armor the general had provided for the occasion. Despite it all, the sight of her had aroused him, and his hard sex strained against his codpiece. Her shift, torn at the shoulder, had fallen down around her waist, exposing the soft, lush breasts trembling beneath to the fire glow, their tawny nipples, tall and perfect buds protruding through the gossamer veil of honey-brown hair.

His left arm was all but useless, and it took more time than was bearable, all the way around, for him to work his way out of his doublet beneath and cover her with it. Even out of his view, the sight of her perfect body, the feel of that satiny, petal soft skin as his roughened fingers grazed it remained, gripping his loins in an iron fist. What would it be like to feel those breasts skin to skin? He stifled a moan imagining it.

"Violette, it is Robert Mack," he murmured, smoothing her hair back from her face with gentle hands. "I helped you by the bridge . . . drove off the rowdies. Do you know me, lass? Shhh, don't cry, you are safe now." But her shrieks only grew louder—into desperate, involuntary spasms, and he shook her. "Violette! Don't you know me? I righted your cart, and saved your coins before the gendarmes set upon me. Don't you remember? You tried to prevent them from taking me. You took my letter to seigneur de Montaigne. You saved my *life*. I've been trying to find you—to thank you."

The gauze of madness parted then, and she reached out, groping toward him, clutching fast to his blood-soaked shirt with all her strength. Clumsily, he embraced her. Her closeness was excruciating ecstasy, flooding his loins with fire, while he soothed her with a gentle voice until she finally lay still against him.

"Did he . . . spoil you, lass? Was I too late?" he urged.

"N-no," she moaned, "but if you had not come when you did . . . ! He . . . he was so strong, my lord. He hurt me."

Robert heaved a sigh of relief. "You are aright now," he said. "He shan't hurt you again. I have killed him. But why did you run from me? Surely you knew I wouldn't harm you?"

"I did not know it was you," she cried. "I am *blind*, my lord! Have you forgotten? I did not know what was happening. I was so frightened. I was asleep in the barn. The animals woke me in their fear when the fire started. I heard it . . . smelled it . . . felt the heat of it, and I set them free of their stalls. I was trying to flee myself, when the soldier grabbed me. When you came, I ran to get away from him. How was I to know that you were not his comrade? The soldiers were many . . . I heard them. They were taking the women down—fighting over them—*raping* them. I heard their screams! I ran to get away . . . I couldn't tell where I was going, I . . . I . . ."

"There, there, don't cry," he soothed. "You are safe now, but what in God's name were you doing in that barn? I have searched everywhere for you. You saved my life, child, and then you vanished. How have you come here? Is this your home, then? Are you one of these?"

"I have no home," she despaired. "The Huguenots, they took me in . . . gave me food and lodging in the barn in exchange for milking, and gathering of the eggs. I was grateful for it. I couldn't return to the city. The guards who seized you were dealt with severely. Several of the other vendors warned me that they sought me for vengeance as they promised they would if I spoke out against them. Those vendors helped me come here at night . . . in a cart filled with vegetables. I dared not show myself in the city."

"I thought it odd that no one would tell me where to find you."

"They were only trying to protect me. They trust no one here now."

The wind had shifted again, and smoke rose afresh in

Robert's nostrils. "We cannot stay here," he said. "The fire, it spreads rapidly. It will soon be upon us. We must go now, before it blocks our escape."

"You are wounded!" she cried, feeling the ooze from his gashed shoulder.

"It is nothing. Come," he coaxed. Staggering to his feet, he drew her up beside him, took back the doublet he'd covered her with, and helped her into it properly. "That's right, put it on," he said. "I will take you to seigneur de Montaigne. He will know what's to be done. He will give you shelter. You will be safe there. No one will harm you, I swear it."

"But . . . I do not understand," she said. "How did you come to the village? Why were you there?" Silence answered her, and she gasped. "*Mon Dieu!* You *were* his comrade. You were *with* them, the soldiers . . . you were one of them!"

"That is a lengthy tale, and there is no time for me to tell it here now," he said. Unable to bear the stricken look of her, he turned away, busying himself in collecting his helm and mail. "Come," he urged. "It is a very long way, and a storm is soon upon us."

"But . . . *why?*" she sobbed.

"Why, right now, is not important," he snapped. "Just thank God that I was among them, and be still. In my haste to come after you, I've left my Scottish blade behind in the belly of Louis de Brach. I cannot go back for it now, and there will be no question as to whom it belongs if he is found. These woods are very likely still alive with troops. We must be away quickly. If by some miracle we do elude the soldiers, we still must face the city. Quickly now, come!"

Despite the young Scot's fears, the soldiers soon vanished from the weald, their victory won, and their leader fallen. Robert's only regret was that the fire prevented him from going back for his *sgian dubh.* Fortune further smiled upon them when they reached Paris, for the city slept unaware as he walked his weary gelding across the deserted bridge in the teeming rain. It pelted down on a brutal slant out of the southbound wind. Sheltered from the brunt of it riding behind, the depleted girl clung listlessly to him, her head resting heavily upon the clenched muscles in his back. That soft, sweet body rubbing against him had aroused him so severely that his codpiece, which still contained his coins, was causing physical pain with the motion of the horse, and he had to raise it.

Freeing his engorged sex, he soothed it in his palm. At least, that was how it began, but his pelvis jerked forward, and the traitorous member leaped in his hand, hot and hard, palpitating in a steady rhythm. Behind, Violette stirred. She'd begun to doze and nearly slipped from the horse's back. As she seized him about the middle to steady herself, the soft, round orbs of her breasts pressed up against his broad back and his posture clenched. Even through their garments he could feel her heat, her supple roundness. Every curve of her body trembled against him, and he was undone. His breath caught in his throat. Waves of drenching fire exploded in his loins as the shuddering climax pumped him dry.

Release and blood loss had sapped his strength. His member, slow to return to a flaccid state, still throbbed a steady rhythm. And though he'd bound the wound tightly with a strip of homespun cloth Violette had bequeathed from the hem of her shift, he'd lost much blood beforehand. Vertigo caused his head to spin, and he fantasized laying upon the wool-stuffed mattresses between soft sheets. Rounding the bend in the road that led to the safe haven at last, he narrowed his eyes, scanning the needles of rain stabbing down for a glimpse of the familiar brick façade, only to rein in sharply and conceal his mount among the trees off the path at sight of the cardinal's standard born by a mounted escort.

They flanked a sedan chair, likewise emblazoned with the cardinal's device, and he didn't have to wonder who was seated inside. Robert started, fascinated. He had never seen the like of that conveyance in Scotland, or England either, for that matter, and he made a mental note to bring the concept of such technology home, if he ever did reach his beloved Scottish shores again. He was beginning to doubt he would.

It was scarcely two hours before dawn, and the cardinal's untimely presence at that hour could only mean one thing—Louis de Brach's body had been found with his Scottish *sgian dubh* sunken in his belly to the hilt.

He quickly dismounted, lifted Violette down beside him, and gave the gelding's rump a whack that sent the animal homeward along the road at a gallop, just as the admiral's men approached bearing torches and flinging turf churned up from the muddy track in their haste.

"What do you do?" she cried, bewildered, as the horse's hoofbeats grew distant.

"The cardinal and soldiers of Coligny are at the château. They are just now arriving. At least, I believe they are the admiral's men. They carry the Huguenot standard. They could only have come for me. I deserted the battle, when Louis de Brach set upon you. I killed him. We cannot stay here. I cannot bring this upon seigneur de Montaigne. 'Tis clear that both factions seek me now—the cardinal, because of Louis de Brach, and Coligny, because I took part in the slaughter of his flock at that village. Poor Michel. It is best that he think me dead—at least for the time being. It will protect him from accusation of complicity in my escape."

"*Dead?*" she breathed. "But . . . how? I do not understand."

"Forgive me, lass," said Robert. "You are so perceptive that I tend to forget that you are blind. When my riderless horse returns in full view of the cardinal and the rest, they will assume that I, too, have died in that battle. My blood is on the beast, and on his trappings. Come with me quickly, while they are occupied. I know of a place where we will both be safe until I rest my wounds awhile and form another plan. Hurry! We must reach it by dawn, or we will surely be seen."

"But—"

"Be still now, child, and pray that I remember how to find it."

Eight

The birds had begun to twitter awake, and the cock to crow as the fugitives reached the ruins. The rain had stopped falling, and an eerie, predawn mist hovered over the land in its place, all but hiding the wounded castle ruins from view. The attached smokehouse was the only viable option offering shelter and seclusion. They entered cautiously, for it, too, was strewn with rubble, and it would be awhile yet before first light illuminated the pitfalls.

Exhausted, Robert sank down on the moldy straw that carpeted the place, and groaned in response to the searing pain he had thus far put aside owing to the urgency of the journey. Now, having freed himself of the helm in Violette's blind presence, he indulged in the sheer pleasure of that groan, and lay still while her small, soft hands attended its cause.

"God, but you have a gentle touch," he told her, surrendering to it.

"You have lost much blood," she said. "This is no simple gash. A sword has cut deeply in. You are in grave need of a physician, my lord, and I know not where or how to fetch one."

"One is already fetched, little flower," said a shadowy shape emerging from the blackness.

Startled, Violette cried out, and Robert's narrowed eyes strained the first hint of dawn diluting the darkness astonished, as the flowing gown and angular headdress of Michel de Nostredame bled into focus.

"D-Doctor Nostradamus!" he murmured. "What are you doing here?"

"Awaiting you," the healer replied flatly.

"You are indeed a sorcerer. How could you know that I—that *we*—would come here, when I did not know myself, until the very last?"

Strolling closer, Nostradamus smiled. "It doesn't take a sorcerer to fathom what a cornered rat will do. But there is a certain facet of . . . perception afoot in all this. It was I who introduced you to this haven if you recall? And I told you we would meet again somewhat . . . abruptly, did I not? Some of that might well be deemed sorcery, but, for the most part, is pure logic; nothing more."

"Well, logic, accident, or black arts, I am glad, indeed, for the sight of you, sir."

"You have been wounded," the healer said, "and I see you have found our Violette."

"When I did not seek her, as you foretold," Robert realized.

"So I did. And you, child," said Nostradamus, scrutinizing Violette in his inimitable manner. "How did you come to be among the apostates? Surely, you have not converted?" he urged, his voice grown stern at the prospect. "That would be unwise."

"No, Doctor Nostradamus," she murmured demurely. "They gave me food and lodging in exchange for honest work among the beasts in their keeping."

"Ahhh," the healer said, clearly relieved, for it was well known that he would have no truck with Huguenots. "But you look a fright, girl. Are you in need of my unctions, also?"

"No, sir," she said. "I am in his lordship's debt over my good health, but he is gravely injured. Much blood has been lost, and the wound wants cleaning badly."

"Mmm," Nostradamus grunted. "Can you stand, young ram?"

"If I must," Robert replied.

The healer reached the brickwork that had once enclosed the ovens in two shuffling strides, and pressed heavily on a brick at the back of it. With that, a slab moved in the floor until a hole appeared at his feet.

"Come," he charged. "You cannot stay here. These old walls are far too pervious. Any façade that will let in the rays of dawn will also permit the eyes of Coligny's troops—not to mention the cardinal, who has the eyes of a ferret." He beckoned, and waited while Violette helped Robert up. "Come," he said, "we go below."

Robert stared bewildered at the gaping hole, and Nostradamus smiled. Producing a beeswax candle and tinderbox from the folds of his gown, he lit the candle.

"All old castles have their secret rooms," he said. "They were designed to protect women and children in times of siege. I found this one quite by accident some years ago. Old ruins fascinate me. There is a similar mechanism for opening it from below as well."

Holding the candle high, he led them below to a spacious chamber gouged into the very bowels of the foundation. A long straw pallet lay in the corner. Spared the dampness of the upper level, it was actually fresher than the one Robert had vacated above, and hadn't been visited by rats. It wasn't the soft mattress he had dreamed of, but he sank gratefully into it nonetheless.

"No one will sight the candle down here," the healer told him. "This sanctuary is most cleverly designed. Many of the dovetail joints in these walls have been altered to form vents that let in the air when needed, but in such a way that no telltale light will leak through. It was intended to shelter many indefinitely. There are other chambers also—a maze of them, but enough of pre-Crusade architecture. Let's have a look at that wound. Violette . . . ," he said, taking her hand, "let me lead you, child. I shall need you to assist me."

Saying no more, the aging physician drew a sack of herbs

and powders, and a skin of fresh water from the folds of his gown, which seemed to serve as his traveling apothecary. And, while Violette held the candle with his guiding, he proceeded to cleanse, purify, and cauterize Robert's wound, reviving him afterward with a medicinal cordial brewed of herbs.

"He will recover, no?" Violette begged.

"Most certainly, little flower," Nostradamus assured her, blatantly astonished at the question. "He will mend quickly with rest and tending."

"I will leave you a draught made from the poppy for pain that will allow him the sleep he needs, and another to bathe the wound for now. It needs a poultice of bread and cheese mold. I will bring some when I return. You must dress it morning and night after a thorough cleansing. Here are clean binding strips," he said, putting them in her hand.

"No . . . !" Robert moaned from his drug-induced consciousness, "she . . . cannot stay here. I was going to leave her in Montaigne's keeping. That is not possible now. The cardinal and Coligny's men are at the château seeking me. That's why we came here. They seek her also. The gendarmes, Jean-Claude and Henri, seek her. That is why she took refuge among the Huguenots. I am to blame for it. They would have liked to bury me in that filthy jail. But for her, I would be there still, or dead. For that, she will suffer if left unprotected."

"What is to be done with her, then?" asked Nostradamus.

"Have I no say?" Violette interrupted. "My lord, you need not trouble over me. I will make my own way, just as I have always done."

"How?" Robert challenged, "—blind, alone, and sought by the authorities? How, lass, the way you did with Louis de Brach? Things are different now. You can no longer 'do as you have always done.'"

"I am not your responsibility."

"I must leave France now, while they think me dead. But first I must know that you are safe and cared for. Doctor Nostradamus . . . can you shelter her?"

"No, young ram, I cannot, more's the pity. I had hoped to be on my way home to Salon by now, but the king has suffered a relapse. He is consumptive you know, in the early stages of the disease. The foolish child took an outing yesterday in the autumn air without my sanction or anyone's knowledge. It has set him back apace, I fear."

"God's teeth!" Robert gritted through rigid lips. Clenching his workable fist, he pounded the pallet. "It isn't serious?" he urged.

"It isn't fatal, if that's what you're asking," Nostradamus replied, "but it is serious enough to keep me here awhile longer—too long, I'm afraid, to be of service to our little flower here, and you are right, you must be away soon, young lord. The soldiers of Coligny shan't be duped for long. When your body is not found among the dead, they will certainly seek you among the living, and it is hardly going to be a simple task slipping through their fingers in that silver bonnet of yours."

"Suppose she were to stay here once I've gone? Could you . . . look after her, and perhaps see her south to some safe place, a convent, or an abbey, when you finally do depart from the city?"

The healer thought upon this, tugging at his beard. "I suppose that could be arranged," he said at last. "There are several fine convents in the south that I must pass by returning home. I am sure—"

"You speak as though I am not even here!" Violette cried, fiercely stamping her foot. "I am no piece of property to be disposed of! I will not be shut up in a nunnery!"

"Is there no one to care for you?" Robert pleaded. "No kindred whom perhaps you have overlooked, lass?"

"I never knew my parents," she murmured, shaking her

lowered head, "only that they loved me, and named me *Violette* because my mother so loved the violets that bloomed in the spring, when I was born. They both died shortly after, of a fever. My aunt Marie kept me until she died when I was eight. We frequented the vendors daily, and I became well acquainted with them. That is how I came to be one when she died. Jacques and Justine Delon had lost a child that autumn, and they took me in. The vendors are my friends. Any one of them would come to my aid now and suffer execution for it. More than friends—they are my *family*—poor folk who have no means to buy leniency. I cannot endanger them, and I do not want to be entombed in any nunnery!"

"What do you want, Violette?" Robert asked softly.

"I . . . I want to sell my flowers by the bridge," she sobbed bitterly, "and be free—as I have always been."

Robert sighed. "I am a blunderer at best, but *this*. This is the greatest blunder to my credit yet. Can you forgive me?"

"There is naught to forgive, my lord," she said, "but . . . please do not shut me up in the convent. I shall die if you do! I could not bear to be caged."

That admission struck a chord. Hadn't he said much the same to his uncle before this nightmare began? She was no more cut out for the religious life than he was. It was plain that the mere thought of it terrified her, and he had no words of consolation or persuasion. He would not force upon her what he would not himself endure. Not unless her very life depended upon it, and there were no other options. Her fierce spirit would never thrive there.

"Little flower," Nostradamus soothed in his most gentle voice, "you need not become a nun to take shelter in a nunnery. The good sisters will care for and feed you in exchange for performing chores, just as you did at the Huguenot village, until they find some other situation suitable for you. You will be protected there—given sanctuary. We are seeking a safe haven for you."

"But my flowers . . . ," she moaned.

"There, there, child, do not grieve so," Nostradamus comforted. "You cannot sell your flowers in Paris any longer. Besides, soon all the flowers will be gone until the spring. Do you trust me, Violette?"

She nodded.

"Ahhh, good!" said Nostradamus. "I will come again at dusk with food, and all you shall need. We will speak again of your dilemma then, once we have all had time to ponder it. You must never grieve over that which you have no power to control. Do not fly in the face of destiny. Whatever fabric it is that God weaves for your future already has its warp and weft. No tears that you can shed will shrink it, that tapestry."

"Doctor Nostradamas," Robert murmured haltingly, unable to hide his pain behind the stilted control of a voice grown husky, "you have done so much for me already . . . I hesitate to ask, but . . . is there any way that you could send word to my sponsor that I live? I would be eternally grateful, sir."

"That would not be . . . wise," Nostradamus warned.

"But, surely he will not betray me? He thinks me dead. Can I not spare him needless sorrow? He has been a good and generous friend to me in France."

"I did not say that I would not deliver your message, young ram," the healer said quietly, though his voice boomed like thunder, "—only that it is . . . unwise. But that, alas, is also part of the tapestry. Wisdom, or the lack of it, is no more than sand in God's mortar. I, it seems, am to be the pestle to grind the paste of your future. But who—or what—shall be the oil to bind the stuff? Or will it be venom that congeals it?"

"Oh, Christ, I beg you, please, no more idioms—no riddles—no cryptic verse. You waste your precious breath here now. In my present state, they are beyond my comprehending."

Nostradamus smiled. "Some things, I fear, are better left beyond our comprehending," he said. "This, my rash warlord, could well be one of them."

Nine

The bondservant, Francine, ushered the physician in at the château, and led him to the parlor study to wait for seigneur de Montaigne to join him. The sun had scarcely cleared the southern hills and its warmth had not yet reached the château. The air had grown cooler since the storm, promising an early frost. Such was the healer's view as he gazed through the leaded oriel window toward the courtyard beyond. When Montaigne entered through the open door behind him, though he had not heard him do so, Nostradamus spoke.

"Thank you for receiving me at such an early hour, Michel," he murmured, turning at last. "My business is urgent . . . and personal. Are we quite alone?"

Francine still waited close by, and the magistrate dismissed her with a hand gesture, and shut the door behind her. The healer listened for the scuffling sound of her footfalls receding along the passageway outside, but, strain though he did he heard no such sound.

"None but myself and the bondservants are in residence, Doctor, and they are all completely loyal to me." Montaigne assured him. He seemed pale and drawn, evidently for lack of sleep, judging from the dark shadows wreathing his bleary eyes.

Nostradamus nodded through a doubtful smile. "Yes, well, I will be brief," he intoned. "I have just come from the Laird of Berwickshire. He is wounded, but he lives. He was most distressed that you would presume him dead, despite the fact that he conceived the deception to spare you chastisement, and was anxious that I come with gentler news."

"*Praise God!*" Montaigne breathed. "But he is wounded, you say? How serious is it, Doctor Nostradamus?"

"A shoulder wound. He will recover."

"He has a natural talent for slight of hand I think," the magistrate observed. He breathed a heaving sigh of relief. "You have no inkling of my happiness at this news, sir, but he must be warned. I had half of Paris on my doorstep before dawn seeking him. Where is he? I will go to him at once."

The healer shook his head. "I believe it is best that you do not know his whereabouts," he responded. "He does not wish to involve you. If you do not know where he is, you cannot unwittingly lead the military to him. He is already warned, and he plans to leave France now, while it is still supposed that he died in that raid, before they tally the dead and find him not among them. It is best."

"But if he is wounded . . ."

"I will tend him, and the girl, Violette. She is with him now."

"The flower urchin?"

Nostradamus nodded.

"God's precious blood! But . . . *how?*"

"She had taken refuge among the Huguenots. When Louis de Brach and his troops raided the settlement, the Scot saved her from the other villagers' fate. He was bringing her here for sanctuary, when he saw the cardinal and Coligny's troops at your door. He will not hear of returning and entangling you in his misfortune. He sends you his eternal gratitude and unerring affection, and bids me speak his farewells."

"But the girl . . . surely she needs looking after now?"

"That is true. She can peddle her wares no more in Paris, Michel. The gendarmes seek her. They would repay her for their suffering over the Scot's imprisonment—especially now that he will be sought for treason."

"He is suspected of killing Louis de Brach."

"As well he did," said Nostradamus, "and left his Scottish dagger in him."

"*Mon Dieu!* So that is how they came to their conclusion. They did not share it with me. Only that he was under suspicion."

"He did so in defense of Violette's honor," the healer explained. "Now they are linked, and it is no longer safe for her here. I needn't tell you that men, women, even children are lost in the Bastille these days for far less than she has done, or cruelly used by men. Surely, you, a magistrate, know that far better than I."

"Well, *what*, then?"

Nostradamus hesitated. "I travel south to home soon," he said with raised voice, shuffling closer to the door as he spoke. Until then, he'd spoken in hushed tones, his keen ears alerted to any sound from the passageway beyond. Thus far, he had heard nothing, and now when he spoke, he did so to the door itself. "I shall see her safely to my château in Salon," he continued. "There, I will arrange for her care. She will be safe. Have no fear."

He turned back toward the magistrate, who was watching him with knit brows, clearly nonplussed by the attitude he'd taken beside the door. Nostradamus warned him from commenting on it with a quick wag of his head, and a crooked finger laid across his lips.

"Is there a message you would have me deliver to him?" he went on, his voice having gone up still another notch in volume. "I will be returning to him at sundown."

"Tell him Godspeed for me if you will," the magistrate said, still frowning, and clearly bewildered, though his voice did not betray it. "Tell him I will miss him greatly . . . and that my prayers go with him."

The healer nodded, grasping the door handle, and smiled to himself at the hasty patter of small feet receding along the passageway outside. "I will give him your message," he said. "But first, a bit of advice before I go . . . ?"

"Doctor?"

"Leave Paris at once. Go home, Michel. Your business here is . . . concluded."

"But—"

"Go *home*, Michel."

"Why?" the magistrate queried, gravel-voiced.

"It is not to question. There is much yet for you to do. Go home . . . and live to do it."

"Doctor Nostradamus, despite all that you say, I am still concerned for Robert. Might I see him . . . just a brief interview?"

The old healer smiled. "No," he said flatly. "Heed my words, and go *quickly* for, if you stay, all that he has suffered— and is about to suffer—will be for naught. Michel . . . *go home.*"

Robert slept for a time under the influence of the old physician's mysterious cordial, while Violette sat beside him, bathing his face. It was the soft touch of her hand on his brow feeling for fever, and the cool solution being stroked on his skin that woke him. He arrested the tiny hand ministering to him and pulled it away.

"Don't!" he snapped, wincing from the stabbing pain in his shoulder the sudden motion caused.

A muffled cry escaped her lips with the rough handling, and she shrank away from him, all but upsetting the basin beside her.

"Forgive me," he murmured, breathing a ragged sigh as he focused eyes still glazed with sleep upon the fright in her pale face. "It is just that . . . I do not like to be touched. Don't be afraid. I didn't mean to frighten you." After what he'd just saved her from the arms of Louis de Brach, he wasn't about to tell her that her touch aroused him. "Why aren't you asleep? We do not know what we face here next. You were supposed to rest as well."

"You cried out! I . . . I feared fever. My aunt . . . before she died, cried out just as you did, and a fever raged, and took her. We were so very poor. There was no medicine— naught save water to bathe her brow. It wasn't enough . . ."

"I am not going to die, child. I have sustained many greater wounds than this, and only once before did I succumb to fever." He reached and gave her hand a reassuring squeeze. "I shall mend admirably for having such a good and conscientious nurse to tend me."

"Where will you go once you have mended?"

"Home to Scotland," Robert told her. He popped a bitter laugh. "I never should have left there. I never should have come. Doctor Nostradamus cannot help me. And so, you see, all of this is for naught—a fool's errand, just as my uncle warned. I regret only that you have become embroiled in my folly."

"You came all this way in hopes that Doctor Nostradamus could heal you?"

"Yes, child."

"But . . . why?"

"*Why?*" he erupted. "My God, you *know* why. You heard the gendarmes when they removed my helm and saw my face."

"But . . . you are beautiful!"

"Lass, you *are* blind," he said.

"Oh, no," she contradicted. "My hands are my eyes, my lord, and they see quite well. I bathed your face a good many times while you slept. Your jaw is firm and squarely set, and your chin wears a fine, deep cleft. Your lips are strong, and your cheeks are like that of a marble statue I once touched in the great cathedral. Your nose is arrow-straight. It is the proud nose of a Celt, from what I have heard told—bent ever so slightly below the bridge. Your brow is broad, and flat, the eyes deeply set beneath the ledge of it. They are marvelous eyes. They are the most marvelous of all."

"Oh, child, you dream."

"No," she insisted. Grasping his hand, she raised it to his face. "Here . . . see for yourself." He tried to pull away, for he detested the feel of it, but she held his hand securely. "Trace the bones, my lord," she instructed. "Feel deeply . . . feel what lies beneath the scars. Pay them no mind. They only mar the skin on one side, and go no deeper. The other side was not touched by the flames. The bones themselves have not been harmed. Their structure is sound. Feel both sides now . . . see? You are beautiful! I can see you just as God made you."

Reluctantly, he did as she bade him, marveling at her enthusiasm, studying the gentle smile that had turned up the corners of her bowed lips.

"Beautiful," he ground out through clenched teeth, "only to you, child, in your blindness. If those magnificent eyes of yours were in this instant given sight, you would shrink and turn from me in horror and disgust just like all the others."

"Perhaps," she conceded, giving it honest thought, "but that is why at times such as this, I am almost . . . grateful that I am blind. The sighted all too often do not make use of their gift. They do not notice the thrush or the dove that hide right under their noses. They have no ear trained to detect them, you see. They do not know that moving water laughs and sings, or that the grasses dance and murmur. They view you and others like you by the standard of beauty, which their vain eye sets for them. My lord, *they* are the blind ones. Sometimes, I cannot help but pity them. Does that sound mad?"

"Mad?" he echoed. "No, child—no, indeed it does not. Doctor Nostradamus painted you well. He said you saw with your spirit far better than anyone with sight. He suggested that I cultivate the art."

"He is a very dear man. He often stops to buy flowers from my cart."

"He is a very wise man."

"Have you tried?" she asked him.

"Tried what?"

". . . To see with your spirit."

"I have labored at it," he admitted, "but I doubt I have the talent for it."

"But you tried," she rejoiced, smiling broadly. "You will succeed at it then. The trying is the hardest part. If you will do that, the rest will come. God lets no honest labor go without reward."

"Tell me," he mused, warmed by her joy, "in regard to my 'marvelous' eyes, can you tell me their color, my fine little sorceress?"

"Truth to tell, I do not understand color, my lord," she said, clouding. "I have tried and tried, but I do not know it. Oh, I know that the sky is blue, the apple red, the grass green, but for me to say to you, 'the sky is blue,' means nothing. I have not ever seen the sky. The grass is green, but I have never seen the grass to carry the picture of it in my mind. There is no one to explain it, and that is my greatest sorrow. My world is gray, sir. That, they tell me, is the color I see, and the only one I know . . ."

Moved by her speech, tears welled in his eyes then, and a lump constricted in his throat. How well he knew the emptiness of not being whole. How well he understood her despair. All at once, he longed to reach out and take her in his arms for the sole sake of giving comfort, but he did not— dared not. The little sorceress had bewitched him. When he spoke, he could not erase the tremor from his voice.

"Do you feel the vastness of the sky above, when you walk in the meadow? Do you sense the air . . . the openness?"

"Oh, yes, it is wonderful, and free. I cannot touch the boundaries of it. I think it has none."

"My eyes are like the sky in color."

"Ahhh," she breathed, "and mine?" she begged, wriggling excitedly. "Tell me of mine."

"Have you ever stroked a fawn or a doe in the forest?"

"Oh, yes!"

"Your eyes are a golden brown, like its coat."

"And my hair?"

"The same."

"And yours?"

He puzzled for a moment. "Almost the same . . . but . . . different. I'm sure you have felt the warmth of the sun as it rises?"

"Yes."

"It blazes brightly before dying . . . like fire," he said uneasily, not wanting the word to bring her unpleasant memories, as it did him. But he could think of no other comparison.

"Fire is warm . . . I cannot imagine its color."

"Have you never turned your face toward the sky at sunset?"

"I have," she said.

"The sun blazes before it dies. Does the gray you ordinarily see not change its hue a bit when you face the setting sun?"

"Yes . . . *yes*, it does!" she cried excitedly. "Oh, it *does* . . . !"

"Some of that warmth you see as the sun sets lights my hair."

"It must be beautiful," she murmured. She held her peace then for so long a time he thought their conversation was over before she finally straightened her posture and said, "Will you tell me truly . . . am I . . . fair?" The words scarcely out, she scowled, her quick hands flitting over her hair and clothing. "Oh, I do not mean now—not like this! I mean . . . well, you know what I mean."

"Oh, lass, has no one ever told you you are beautiful, then?" Astonished, he laughed.

She shook her head. "Never a lord."

Again, he laughed. There was poignancy in it. "You are exquisite," he told her. "I have never looked upon one so fair."

"It is so difficult to tell," she returned. "Oh, I can feel my features—my hair, my body, and they appear seemly, but I do not know what 'fair' is to a man, unless one tells me."

Robert stared, studying her excitement over the discoveries, convinced that ugliness could not exist in her presence—in the innocent aura of her spirit. How had he kindled such things as these to life in that gray void of a mind that stored no images? He did not know, but somehow it had happened. Somehow her view seemed clearer, and for a fleeting space of time she had actually convinced him that *he* was beautiful. His eyes had never before been compared to the sky, nor his hair to a deer, or the setting sun. Most wondrous of all, he'd made the comparisons himself. Contemplating that, and scarcely able to believe it, he'd forgotten his pain, and failed to hear the patter of hasty feet milling about overhead, until Violette's quick intake of breath jolted him back to a more familiar breed of awareness—that of a warrior.

Together, they held their breath, blind and sighted eyes trained upon the movable slab in the ceiling as it opened above the crudely hewn stone stairs. And when the grating sound it made ceased and a shaft of daylight wearing dust motes streamed down around them, Robert drew his sword and labored to his feet, shoving her out of the way behind him.

At sight of the ermine trim on Nostradamus's best robe of Lyons velvet, the Scot's posture collapsed, and he relaxed his grip on the sword, reassuring Violette. One look into the grim-faced healer's eyes, however, sent fingers of a cold chill crawling along his spine.

"Doctor Nostradamus!" he breathed. "Is something wrong? You were not to return until dusk."

"It is just past noon," he replied, shuffling toward them out of breath. He lowered a large sack he'd been toting with a grunt. "It is no longer safe for you here. I'm afraid there must be a change in the plan," he said. "You must go at once. I have delivered your message to Montaigne, and that, my young friend, is your undoing if you do not escape within the hour."

"But how?" Robert demanded. "I will not believe that he has betrayed me."

"No, young ram," the healer replied, "he has not. He sends naught but his prayers and fond affection. His bond-servant betrays you. At this very moment, she is carrying the tale to the cardinal, and Coligny. The greedy slattern will more than likely have her reward from both factions."

"Ahhh, yes . . . Francine," Robert growled, remembering. "She knows I am here at the ruins?"

"No. She does not know where you are, but only that you are alive, and wounded, and that I will seek you out at sunset. That is why I have come here now, to see you safe and away, and lead them on a merry chase while you put a goodly distance between yourself and the troops."

"No one followed you?"

"No, the wench eavesdropped while I was closeted with Montaigne. I saw to it that she heard what they would believe, and came here straightaway once I'd gathered your provisions. You are safe for now, but not for long. You must be away at once, lest it be too late." He frowned, taking the young Scot's measure. "Your wound concerns me. Are you strong enough?"

"Yes, I will have to be," Robert said. "But surely I will be recognized. How can I hope to hide like . . . like *this* in broad daylight?"

"Quite easily," said Nostradamus. "I must admit, I worried

over that awhile myself, but then it came to me. It's simple, really." Foraging through the sack, he produced a monk's robe with a deep cowl. "You will discard your helm for the time being, and wear this instead. The cowl will hide your face quite nicely, and should it fail we can thank God that few have seen you unmasked."

"This is insane! What of Violette?"

"She must go with you."

"*No!*" he thundered. "It is out of the question. She *cannot!*" The mere thought of the temptation—of the torture of her company on such a journey terrified him more than any fearsome enemy he might come up against on the field of battle.

"You *must* take her, young ram. They know she is alive and in your company. I have let it be known that I will see her south to Salon when I depart from the city. Instead, you will travel west, toward the coast. There is a convent on your way. It sits in a forest glade about sixty leagues this side of Nance. I have drawn you a map. You will leave her there in the sisters' keeping, and press on to the bay. Ships are plentiful, and you must be safely aboard one before word of you can spread to the coast. This must be. I cannot leave the city yet awhile, and she will not be safe here anywhere now. You have no choice, young ram, but to see her to sanctuary. I have a nun's habit for her here as well. No one will question a monk and good sister traveling together. It is a common enough sight. I have brought mounts, food, skins of water for the horses, and mead for yourselves, as well as medicine for your journey, and the moldy bread and cheese for your poultices. Do not be alarmed. It is quite maggoty, but that is for the good. Moisten it, slather it on, and bind the wound. Stay that look! Traveling thus is the only solution now. There is no other way."

"I will not go to the convent!" Violette shouted, turning both their heads.

"Be still," Robert snapped. "None of us have a choice

here now. We must do as he says." He turned back to Nostradamus. "What will you do once we have gone?"

"I will return to court and pay my daily visit to the king. I am expected. I must go every afternoon now until he is improved. That is why I cannot leave Paris. Then, I will go to my lodgings until 'tis time. At dusk, I will lead them to a place I know, well north of the Huguenot village. They will presume that you are hiding there. It is a shrewd move. They will assume that you hope to elude them hiding in the last place they would expect you—where you murdered. By time they discover their error, you will be well out of their reach, traveling in the opposite direction."

"What in God's name do I say to you?" Robert murmured. "How do I thank you?"

Nostradamus smiled his knowing smile. "There is no time for thanking," he said, "nor is there need. You'll likely curse me, before 'tis done. It is a long, hard press before you." Again he reached into the sack and produced a baked clay jar, crushing the young Scot's fingers around it. "Some sweets for your journey," he said. "Guard them well."

"*Sweets?*" Robert said, nonplussed.

"Oh, not ordinary confections by any means," the healer said. "These patties will safeguard you from plague. The recipe is my own, proven during the black death of 1546. Keep them close."

Robert removed the stopper and shrank back from the smell.

"Now, now, don't flinch," the healer chided. "They are quite tasty, made of roses picked at dawn, while the dew still bloomed upon their petals, together with a liqueur distilled from green cypress wood, cloves, sweet flag, lichen algae, essence of plum, and . . . other ingredients. When carried in the mouth, they will protect you."

Robert looked him long in the eyes and took a wracking chill at what he found there.

"Come," said the physician, breaking the spell. "We must make ready. I will help you, and see you on your way. It would be wise for you to pretend the disguise is authentic . . . even at the convent, so far as you are concerned. Now then, let me look at that wound before you go."

"Doctor Nostradamus," Robert said, struggling out of his shirt with the old man's help.

"No," the healer interrupted. "Ask me no more. There is enough food to chew on in what I have already told you. Digest that if you can on your journey, with keen eyes upon the flames. They have already turned you once. They will do so again, my blind young ram. See that they turn you rightly."

Ten

After careful deliberation, Robert decided to take only one mount. Were they to ride separately, the going would be dangerously slow, since Violette, in her blindness, would have to be led. That, coupled with the discovery that she had never before ridden a horse on her own, convinced him to sacrifice comfort for speed. It was the right decision, even though he couldn't help but remember what occurred the last time they rode double.

The wise old healer saw to it that they wasted no time setting out, and, finally, armed with the provisions and map he'd brought, they headed southward, keeping to the forest when they could. By dusk they had put a considerable distance between themselves and what was happening north of the Huguenot village. Robert was not concerned about Nostradamus. Whatever the situation, he was certain that the crafty old man's uncanny wisdom would be more than adequate to ensure his safety. What did worry him was Violette, and something cryptic he had seen in Nostradamus's eyes—something that had chilled him to the marrow. And he bitterly wished he'd never consented to cultivating the art of seeing with his spirit.

By nightfall, the Scot's wound had begun to throb like a pulse beat. They had made good progress, but it had not been an easy beginning. Frightened and reluctant, the girl clung to him with a relentless grip. The pressure of her pinching fingers grieved his shoulder painfully, and her whispered, soft sobs pricked incessantly at his nerves. She said little, but her silence was pregnant with dismay.

Robert endured as long as he could bear it. Then finally, as the moon rose high in the heavens, dodging wind-driven clouds, they came to a thicket. Walking the horse deeply into a tall stand of young trees at the edge of it, he helped Violette dismount and tethered the exhausted animal to a snarl of bracken. She sat quietly, leaning against a nearby stump while he tended the horse and offered nothing in the way of conversation. Above, the haloed moon was shining brightly down from a star-studded sky through a hole the risen wind had torn in the cloud fabric. It lit her pale, sad face framed by the draped headdress and sparkled in her sightless eyes, staring blankly in the direction of his footfalls disturbing the undergrowth.

Dropping the sack of provisions, Robert sank down close beside her, searching inside it for their food. Her fear was unmistakable then, and when he found a clerical stole and a pot of unction for the dying inside that the crafty old healer had put there, though the discovery made his skin crawl with gooseflesh, he made no mention of it. His hand closed next around the little crock of pastilles, and he slipped them into the pocket of his robe, making room inside to continue his search.

"The habit of a nun becomes you far better than my old battle-worn doublet," he told her, rummaging deeper in the sack. "You look quite regal in it."

She squirmed, tugging at the stiff, close-fitting headdress. "It itches," she complained. "Nuns have no hair to fit inside such things, and mine is much too long to be confined so tightly. I cannot bear restrictions . . . they remind me that I am no longer free."

"None of us are free unless we die, lass—especially in this godforsaken land. And God *has* forsaken it I think, though I cannot blame Him, since His children here shed each other's blood so wantonly in His holy name. All of us have some form of tethers—even that poor, tired beast there."

"I am certain God did not intend that all his creatures be . . . restrained," she said, scowling.

"Well, whether He did or didn't, you needn't suffer restraint here now. Remove the headdress, and do not pout so. It spoils your lovely face." Having found their food at last, he offered it. "Here . . . have some bread and cheese," he said. "You must be starving."

Closing her fingers around the offering, he watched while she raised it eagerly to her lips. Smiling, satisfied, he produced the skin of honey mead, leaned his weary head back against a straight-backed sapling, and downed a healthy swallow.

"Lack of food can make a body out of sorts," he said, tearing off a chunk of the bread for himself.

"I am not out of sorts," she defended.

Her tone, and the hasty downcast eyes, as prohibitive as his helm had ever been, contradicted her, and he set the bread and mead aside and leaned closer.

"Violette," he said velvet-voiced, "you mustn't be frightened. I know it must be terrifying alone here in a stranger's keeping with no familiar thing to give you comfort. I have tried to put myself in your place, and I cannot imagine it. But I promise you, there is naught to fear. I will let no harm befall you."

"I am not afraid of . . . that," she murmured.

"What, then? What frightens you?"

She shook her head, unwilling to answer.

He sighed. "Well, if you will not tell me what your fears are, how can I still them?"

"They cannot be stilled."

"You have suffered a great deal because of me. I cannot blame you for your resentment, but—"

Her head shot up, the blind eyes searching. "I do not resent you, my lord," she cried. "It is nothing like that."

"What is it, then, child?"

Again she shook her head and lowered her eyes.

He frowned. "I have been short with you I know. It is my way. I am a warrior, and I am not accustomed to young lassies. I . . . I apologize." Had he ever said that to a living soul before? Not that he could recall. He cleared his voice, grateful that she couldn't see the perspiration beading on his brow. "I have been under a great duress since I arrived here," he blundered on. "I did not ask for duty in that massacre. If I wanted to fight Protestants, I could have stayed at home to do it. It was forced upon me. Is that what troubles you, lass? Is that what has sewn seeds of mistrust?"

"You never told me why you were among those troops," she murmured, "why you helped them do that awful thing."

"My uncle snubbed the cardinal in naming seigneur de Montaigne my sponsor here rather than himself. My presence at that gruesome raid was solely to spare my uncle a chastisement. God knows, they'll probably have him imprisoned or killed here now for this, Montaigne as well. That *is* what's troubling you, lass, isn't it . . . that I was there . . . that I was among them?"

"He lives in Scotland, your uncle?"

"No, he is a monk at Mount St. Michael Abbey, off the Cornish coast of England."

"Oh, so that is why you press so for shutting me up in the convent!" she snapped.

"No, it is not," he said tersely. "I press for your incarceration to protect you—nothing more."

A lengthy pause ensued, and Robert took another rough swallow of the mead, wincing from the sharp pain that movement caused in his shoulder. It wanted tending, but he was too tired, and considering the way exhaustion charged his passions, he dared not risk her soft, gentle touch just then.

"Who is Francine?" she hurled at him out of the blue.

He stared, the mead skin suspended before his lips. Lowering it, he sighed. "A bondservant at the château," he said warily.

"Why did she betray you?"

"No doubt because I would not succumb to her seduction," he snapped. On the verge of anger at such a question, he had spoken sharply, that there be no mistaking his annoyance.

"Did you . . . lie with her?" she queried.

"*What?*" he cried with a start. "I have just told you 'no.' Look here, how have you knowledge of such things—you, a . . . a mere child?"

"I am a street vendor," she said haughtily, expanding her posture in a way that made his own clench. "I know of many shocking things—as many as you, perhaps even more. And I am no child, my lord. You may call me child as you will, but that by no means makes me one. I am in my nineteenth year. Many my age are already wed with families. That I am blind, sir, hardly makes me infantile, nor does it make me ignorant, only . . . restricted."

"Is that it, then?" he returned, "Have you a swain that all of this has parted you from? Is that the cause of your ill temper?"

"I have no 'ill temper'!" she shrilled, "and I have no swain, either."

"Well, all that remains is that you must be suffering from exhaustion. Tiring makes all children cross. Oh, but, do forgive me, I forget! You are no child, are you? I must try very hard in the future to remember that. But I am going to find it difficult if your disposition doesn't improve. So, I would suggest that you curl up there, my weary maid, and sleep. I will tend to my shoulder, and rest myself. We must set out before dawn if we are to reach the Loire tomorrow, and dawn comes quickly to the weary." No, indeed she was no child, but fixing her as such in his mind was the only way of getting through the ordeal of close proximity to her without being driven mad by the sight, smell, and feel of her.

"I will tend your wound, my lord," she offered, groping for the provisions sack.

"Ohhh, no, lass," he said, arresting the tiny hand with his own. "I will make the mold paste and tend it myself. Forgive me, but the way things stand with you here now, my own hand, awkward though it be, is bound to take my wound to task a good deal more kindly than yours."

But sleep did naught that he could see to sweeten Violette's disposition. She scarcely spoke two words while they broke their fast in the hazy predawn gloom, a phenomenon that, Robert surmised, had little to do with the climate. He wasn't given to premonitions, but neither could he deny that something eerie attended, and had done since he'd first met Doctor Nostradamus, and the look he'd last seen in those sharp gray eyes did nothing to ease his dread.

They took their midday meal at an abandoned gristmill well beyond Orleans, on the banks of the Loire, and pressed quickly on again. There was a dense weald at the river's edge, noted on the map Nostradamus had prepared, and Robert was anxious to reach it by nightfall, for that milestone would ensure that they would reach the convent by nightfall the following day.

Despite his apprehensions, all was going well. As the healer had predicted, no one paid them any mind in their habits, and they were free to drink in the breathtaking French countryside, so beautiful in autumn, despite the festering sky poised overhead that seemed to dog them. They passed by several farms as the cloud-banked sun sank low, giving way to the storm, and they reached the forest just as the cold, dreary rain began to fall. There, on a bed of plush green moss, well sheltered among the trees, they settled in to partake of a light evening meal. A brooding silence had come between them, and Robert made no attempt to spark conversation. Except to encourage that she sleep as soon as she'd eaten, he held his peace. And though he got the distinct impression that she longed to probe the strain between them by the way her beautiful mouth kept opening and snapping shut, he did not encourage her. He was neither fit nor patient enough for sparring.

He would have rather had her nod off first, but his eyes would not stay open, and he soon succumbed to sleep, but it wasn't long before the pressure of her body trembling against him snapped his dazed eyes open. He stiffened, and she scrambled backward.

"What is it, child?" he murmured.

"I . . . I thought you were sleeping," she demurred. "I meant no harm. I'm cold . . . and I'm . . . I'm . . ."

"What, child?"

"Afraid . . . !" she cried.

"Of what, Violette? I am not Nostradamus. I cannot read your mind. Why won't you tell me?"

"There is much that I fear," she said, low-voiced, her angst palpable.

He pulled her close with his good arm. "Tell me, then," he soothed. "There is nothing so grave that you cannot speak it to me. Are we not friends, you and I?"

She nodded against him.

"Well, then?"

"I fear the convent," she began.

"Violette, you will be safe there—cared for."

"The sisters will not welcome me once they discover that I do not wish to be one of them. I will be miserable. I will *die* shut up in such a place."

"I'm sure you won't be long in residence. They will find a suitable situation for you, child. I will plead your cause. I will stress it."

"What suitable situation can there be for me—blind—penniless—alone? No! You dream. They will keep me—make a slave of me! My blindness . . . it has always been my prison. It shackles my mind . . . and for a brief space of wonderful time, you unlocked those shackles and let me see through your eyes. Now, my body is to be imprisoned also, and you will not be there to help me see. I will not bear it. I cannot endure *both*."

"And I cannot put your mind at ease over that fear, lass, because—try as I might—you have painted a rigid picture in that sighted mind of yours that is false. I cannot erase it, but you will soon see that there is naught to fear, I promise you. Violette, I owe you my life. Do you honestly think I could be so cruel as to abandon you to such a fate as you imagine? My God, where is your perception? You always seemed to see more clearly than any man I've known. Where has your wisdom gone?"

"You would not . . . deliberately."

"I would not *at all*," he said, exasperated. "Rest assured that I will be well satisfied before I give you into *anyone's* hands. Now! No more about that. What else, lass? There is more. I can feel it."

She sighed deeply. "I do not know this place," she pointed out on the verge of tears. "In Paris I knew every cobblestone, every tree—every path and turn in it. Here I am lost, and I will stay lost, for there is no one to find me."

"Perhaps that is best for a while. You are wrong, child, there are many to find you if you aren't careful. It is best that you stay out of the public eye awhile."

Again she sighed.

"There is more?"

"The greatest fear," she said.

"And that is?"

"That we shall never meet again," she murmured, casting down sightless eyes.

He stared at her then, so desolate in his arms, and a curious breed of anger moved him suddenly.

"You do not know that," he said.

"Oh, yes, I do," she snapped. "You will have forgotten me before you ever reach the coast. You will be rid of me tomorrow, and glad of the lifted burden. I never meant to be a burden. I said the same to Doctor Nostradamus back at the ruins. I begged you both to trust in my ability to care for myself."

"That was madness! How could you hope to?"

"I always have in the past."

"I am not so sure that your account is accurate. You were in grave distress the day we met if you remember, and at that accursed Huguenot village."

"I remember. But do you suppose it was the first time I have suffered such? I will have you know, sir, that I have always managed to deal on my own with all manner of roaring boys and gendarmes and randy soldiers, such as your Louis de Brach, and I am a virgin still!" Pride stiffened her spine. "I call that not inept, considering."

"That is very commendable, but this is different here now." He gave her a gentle squeeze. "Violette, it is different, because I am to blame for all that has come upon you since we met. Like it or not, I am responsible for all that has befallen you in my blundering pursuit of the impossible. You wrongly accuse me. I am not anxious to be rid of you. I am anxious to see you out of danger before I do you greater harm, and then make an attempt to flee this place if I am able, with my head intact—hideous though it be."

"I like this not!" she cried. "I have no more control of my destiny. You would map it for me and then abandon me to it. No! I like this *not*!"

"Violette, we—none of us—have control of our destiny. God has chosen to cross our paths here to some purpose as yet unclear. He will make it known in time."

"I think I know His plan," she sobbed, tears rolling down the bright red cheeks that anger and embarrassment had painted, "but you would go against it."

He studied her then, staring long into her lovely face so

fraught with sorrows, and something primal stirred in his loins that stilled all voices in him save that of longing. The scent of rain-drenched gillyflowers drifted toward him from her hair and skin. It was intoxicating, blended with the pungent forest smells of bark and fern that assailed his senses. She was so very beautiful in the misty green darkness diluted by the storm.

The nagging wound forgotten, his hand reached out, caressed the rosy cheek wet with tears, and followed her slender neck to her shoulder, and the warm, round breast straining against her habit. Her sobs became something else, something deep and throaty, as he leaned fully against her, every sinew in the long, corded length of him stretched to its limit. All at once those renegade fingers fastened in the silken stream of hair that spilled over her shoulders, free of the constricting headdress. Hypnotized, he drew her close and seized her in a smothering embrace, his trembling hand seeking the sweet flesh of her breast until he'd freed it from the coarse homespun and cupped its lush fullness in his palm. The rosebud nipple hardened against his rough, calloused skin, sending shock waves of anticipation to every nerve in his body. She let out a soft whimper, and Robert froze. What kind of beast was he, that he would let this innocent give herself to him?

All at once she strained against him, and when her pleasure moans became a frightened cry, he let her go.

"You see?" he groaned. "Oh, Christ, this is madness! Not even *you* can bear it, my embrace."

"It is the anger I cannot bear," she cried, adjusting her garment. "I do not need to see, or even hear the anger in you. I can *feel* it."

"Can you not understand why?" he railed. "Can you not see that my selfish urges could well be the greatest danger of all? I am lonely, child—so lonely I would abuse you because of it, I am that selfish, and you would let me, you are that innocent! No, Violette, do not fear my rage, thank God for it. It keeps you safe. I am not angry with you, I am angry with myself for what I would succumb to . . . to slake what is no more than libidinous animal lust. That is not God's plan, lass, and but for the rage sprung from what little moral fiber still knits me together, I would be no less a savage than Louis de Brach—and spoil you for a fleeting moment of relief in that exquisite body, and destroy us both."

Suddenly, her posture clenched, and she gripped his arm. "Shhh, someone comes!" she whispered, fumbling with the cumbersome headdress she had discarded.

"I hear nothing," he snapped.

"You will, he is almost upon us," she said in an undertone.

Though he still did not hear what her heightened sense had obviously revealed to her, he was wise enough to trust it, and he gripped the sword at his side while, together, they held their breath, and waited until the sound came again, more clearly now—a hasty shuffling of feet, making no attempt to affect a cautious approach. Pitiful sobs accompanied the racket of displaced twigs and fallen leaves, and Robert quickly vaulted to his feet, adjusting the cowl to hide his face and tightening his grip on the sword. The sound grew louder still, and he worked the hilt in a white-knuckled fist, staring from the shadowy recesses of his cowl toward an aging peasant come suddenly to his knees and genuflecting before them.

Astonished, he was scarcely aware of Violette, who had won her battle with the headdress, groping toward the protection of his comforting arm. He drew her close and closer still as her body tensed and trembled against him.

"Good father, come, I beg you," the ragged man whined, his voice desperate. "My poor lady wife . . . she dies. I beseech you come and hear her last confession."

"Surely, my good man, you must have access to a parish

priest?" said Robert, holding the sword out of the peasant's view.

"No time!" he cried. "It is a half-day's distance. She will not last. Please, good father, come. Come *now*, I beg you, while she lingers."

"We are on a holy mission in most urgent haste," said Robert. "We tarry here but briefly to refresh ourselves and that poor beast there before we press on."

"You would *refuse* me?" the man breathed, slack-jawed. "—A holy man of God refuse the Sacrament of Extreme Unction to the dying? *Kyrie eleison?*" He was incredulous.

"Take ease, take ease," Robert soothed. "I have not refused you. I simply ask if there is no other that might fulfill your needs. It is imperative that our mission not be delayed . . . many lives depend upon us."

"I shan't detain you long," the man whined. "My dwelling is not far. You passed it by just now before you entered here. When I saw you, I knew that God had heard my prayers and sent you!" He took a pouch from the folds of his tunic. It dangled from a thong looped around his neck, and he jiggled the coins inside it. "It is a meager offering, I will allow," he said, "but, please, I beg you, do not turn me away."

"Take back your tribute, my son," Robert charged, "I want none of it. If you have no alternative, of course the good sister and I will come. A moment, while I fetch the unction."

"God bless you," the little man groaned, genuflecting again. He staggered to his feet. "This way . . . follow me," he charged, "and hurry, Father. Hurry, please!"

Following the little man, Robert hung back out of earshot and bent his cowled head low toward Violette. "Stay close beside me," he whispered. "It shan't take long, but we shall have to move on again immediately after. I am not at ease about this."

"What will you do?" she cried.

"*Shhh!* Be still," he cautioned her. "I will do what I must . . . administer the sacrament."

"But you *cannot*. You are not a priest!"

"I am a Catholic."

"But—"

"Child, we cannot betray our identity. I cannot put us to the hazard. The soldiers will search these parts eventually, when they realize what has happened. If we give no cause for suspicion, we might just see this odyssey through safely. I found this stole and unction in the provisions sack last night. Doctor Nostradamus did not put them there for naught. I swear to you, I do believe he did it a-purpose, knowing we would have need of them. He has uncanny foresight, and I think I see now what he meant when he said I would likely despise him before it was done."

"It is sacrilege!"

"It is *necessary*."

". . . But Extreme Unction! To tamper with a soul departing . . . !"

"Violette, that woman will depart this life in peace for having made her last confession. Believe me, I will pray for that. She will not know that I am not a priest. If there is any sin in what I do it will fall upon me, not her. She *dies*, child. We are living still, but not for long if you do not heed what I say and keep silent. Now, stay close beside me. He slows his pace. He mustn't overhear us. These are a cautious people, times being what they are, and if we are found out, he will tell the tale to any who will listen."

Violette said no more. There was no use. They had left the copse, and the little man urged them on to a small cottage beyond the meadow eastward.

"There, Father, is my home," the man panted. "I told you it wasn't far. Hurry, please . . . she is all alone."

"What ails her," said Robert, "what is her complaint?"

"A . . . a . . . fever," the man faltered. But there was no time to question him further. They were upon the threshold.

Violette stiffened as soon as the peasant threw the door open. The stench of disease rushed to meet them before they even entered. Her heightened sense of smell told her all too clearly that they had entered an unclean place. It tasted of death indeed, and she shrank back from it, burying her nose in the coarse homespun folds of Robert's sleeve. And as they drew nearer the deathbed she felt the muscles beneath that sleeve constrict and freeze as rigid as stone beneath her face.

Robert took up a candle from its stand and held it low, illuminating the stricken woman's face. Violette felt the heat of it, and she lurched as his breath caught, for the woman lay breathing her last through a death rattle. Cold chills gripped Violette's spine as she recalled the same sound coming from her aunt's throat just before she passed. She had been just a child, but the memory was so vivid it was as though it was happening all over again, and she tightened her grip upon his arm.

"This is plague here!" Robert breathed, supporting Violette as she cried out, quaking against him at the news. "She sweats. The fever rages! This canker on her neck, see how it oozes? I have seen it many times. Why did you not tell me, man?"

"Forgive me, Father," the peasant whined, "would you have come if I had?"

"It is too late for confession," Robert gritted. "She is in coma."

"No!" the man cried. "She is still conscious. See her eyes? They move! She is aware still. I beg you anoint her!"

Robert swallowed audibly, slipping the stole and pot of unction from the folds of his robe. Without further waste of words, he hurried through the prayers, anointed the woman, and hurried Violette out into the cool, rain-washed air.

The tearful little man followed after, spouting gratitude

with each jerky step, but Robert didn't respond. He let her go then, groping the pocket of his robe. Her hands, searching for him, felt the jar of lozenges that Nostradamus had given him. As he removed the stopper and thrust one toward the peasant, she shrank back from the smell.

"Carry this in your mouth; it is a remedy," Robert instructed the peasant, demonstrating by way of forcing one through her unsuspecting lips, and then his own. "Throw the door and windows wide, and wait. When your good lady wife has died, bury her at once, and burn each and every thing she has come in contact with from bedding to trencher—your clothing as well, and wash your whole body in clean water. May God have pity on you."

He turned then, and led her quickly away through the needles of rain stabbing down over the meadow to the forest, where the horse waited. Neither spoke until they had put some distance between themselves and the contaminated cottage. Clutching him close as they galloped through the darkness, Violette could still feel the tightness of anger in his well-muscled body, stiffened like marble against her through the coarse homespun robe, the heat of him so intense it was as though the blood had come to a boil in his veins. Between the horse's motion, and the foul-tasting lozenge, a queasy feeling settled in the pit of her stomach, and bile rose in her throat. Though she almost feared to break the pregnant silence, it was no use. She could no longer bear it.

"I cannot abide the remedy," she wailed. "I will retch! The taste . . . it is unbearable!"

"You will bear it," he spat.

"I will *retch*, I say!"

"You will *not!*" he commanded. "You would indeed have retched if you could have seen the sight of what I pray that damned remedy you revile so might spare you. Do not be a child. I cannot abide such as that here now."

"Can you at least slow our pace, then?" she pleaded. "I beg you! My stomach rejects this thing."

"Not until we have put this place behind us," he said. "Who is to say that what we have just left behind was an isolated case? More likely than not, the plague is widespread in these parts. I will be ill at ease until we reach the convent. I am sorry for your discomfort, lass, but you must trust my judgment. I will bear no more burden on my conscience over you."

She groaned again, but he didn't seem to notice, or feel her body constrict against him as she shivered and spat out the lozenge. She opened her mouth letting the rain in to wash it out, but not even that could rid her of the awful aftertaste the pastille had left behind.

It was well past midnight before they had finally purged the stench of plague with distance. Violette was exhausted, and wracked with chills in her wet habit, but she dared not complain. Something in the silence between them then— something in the stiff unbending posture that she clung to—told her all too well that he was still angry. Now, she sensed a facet of trepidation mingled with the rest that hadn't been there before. But she left that unexplored. Blind as she was, she saw quite clearly that this was no time for probing. Instead, she let him settle her beside the roots of an ancient oak tree, accepted the dry blanket he took from the sack, and slept.

Eleven

*R*obert *was weary of the journey and the worry and the* burden of thoughts he fought not to think, and feelings he struggled not to feel, his shoulder notwithstanding. The eager warmth of Violette's lush, supple body so close in his arms haunted him. The tender pressure of those pouting, heart-shaped lips trembling open beneath his own set his heart racing. A throbbing rush of icy fire gripped his loins when he recalled the touch of her petal-soft tongue, mating with his as he tasted her deeply. He relived the arousal that kiss had ignited, and it revisited him, more startling for the distance between them, and, to his horror, more acute.

He inched nearer the place where she lay. A wan, lackluster moon had broken through the clouds at last, and a shaft of its dappled light played softly upon her face through the trees. How gently it haloed her hair. How seductively it teased the rise and fall of her firm, uptilted breasts beneath the blanket. That they were hidden from view didn't matter. His mind's eye remembered, and he saw them just as vividly as he had at the Huguenot village, tinted a rosy golden hue by the flames. That reverie was so real that he could almost feel the heat of the holocaust. Or was that nothing more than the blood surging hot to his temples? He couldn't be sure. But whatever it was, it turned him away and kept him at his distance until dawn chased the visions away.

No, he would not succumb to such as that. He would not slake his bitter desperation in this innocent lass, who had invested her trust in his honor, even though he knew she would allow him. Was this love, then? He doubted it. Not under these bizarre circumstances. She was a woman, and he was sore for wanting one. He could put no other vestments on that specter. No, that was what it was, and he would not tamper with it. There were other vehicles for venting those passions. He had found them before. He would find them again. As repulsive and demoralizing as that prospect was, and despite that he had vowed against it, it suited him far better than the guilt-ridden alternative facing him now. A few more hours and she would tempt him no more. A brief, fleeting space of time, and he would bid farewell to this little sorceress, who had hopelessly muddled his thinking. Perhaps then he could concentrate upon getting safely back to Scotland—a thing that promised to be not so easily accomplished. He'd made no solid plan beyond seeing Violette safely to the nunnery, and with that goal as a prod, the vision of those soft, young breasts with their pink nipples whirling around in his brain notwithstanding, he initiated an early departure, and kept a relentless pace throughout the day.

He decided not to stop for an evening meal. That could be had at the convent, with a warm, dry bed to lie in while he plotted his escape. When daylight faded, he pressed his frazzled mount to continue, for according to the healer's map, it was only a little farther.

Fresh storm clouds had swallowed the moon momentarily, and the stars along with it. The night was as black as carbon ink around them. The only light for miles appeared as a rosy shimmer along the roadway in the valley below. A closer appraisal was denied him by trees dotting the landscape between. Assuming that whatever the cause of the phenomenon, it had to be close to the nunnery, he headed straight for it, promising Violette that she would soon be safe and warm and dry.

Driving the horse relentlessly, it did not take long to make his approach. The nearer he drew, the clearer the glow became, until he recognized it for what it was—a string of bonfires along the narrow road. The fire-hemmed track sidled toward a stone fortress, its tall open bell tower with its silent bell inside rising into the night—the convent, silhouetted against the vacant sky like a great black one-eyed giant lurking beyond a walled courtyard.

"*Fires!*" he groaned, recalling the healer's cryptic augur. "Good Christ, what could this be?"

Violette made no reply. She clung listlessly to him, so listlessly he feared she might fall off. Her head rested heavily against his back, and her tiny hands barely gripped his middle.

Walking the horse now, they passed between the fires flanking them on either side of the road, meanwhile soothing the animal shying away from the crackle and roar of snapping twigs, and rippling heat surging toward them. Straining his eyes, he caught sight of a robed figure shuffling toward them bearing a burden, which she fed to the anxious flames closest to the courtyard. A lively burst of sparks shot upward with the offering, and lit the woman's face, all but hidden beneath a prohibitive headdress and scarf of linen gauze that bound her nose and mouth. He adjusted his cowl, and as they came abreast of her, she waved them off with both hands held high.

"Go back! Away!" she shrilled. "Good brother, you cannot enter here. The pestilence! Go back, I say!"

"Good sister, I am a monk on sojourn from the south," he insisted, despite the warning. "I bring a child here for sanctuary. We cannot go back."

"The sister?"

"She is not a sister, but a blind child from the southern provinces, who has lost all in a fire that ravaged her village." It was half truth, and he would have to stretch it further, but he couldn't tell the whole truth. It was far too dangerous—even on holy ground—*especially* on holy ground. "The good sisters at the convent there provided the garments she wears," he went on convincingly. "She had naught but the flimsy shift she fled in. They had no room to keep her, and they sent me here. She must have care, and tending. I beseech you—"

"She cannot enter here!" The nun panicked. "You have not heard me . . . there is pestilence! To let her enter is sure and certain death. We have no remedy. We were forty strong on Tuesday last. Now, four and twenty remain, and half that number have fallen with the sickness."

"Are there no healers, then?"

The nun uttered a bitter laugh. "The plague has crippled the villages south of here. There are healers there, but not enough in number to meet our needs and theirs as well. The child cannot find sanctuary among us, lest you would bury her. I am sorry. You must turn back! We cannot help you here."

"Where then? Where do I go? I am a stranger to these parts."

"North, or east to Paris. There are no reports of pestilence in those quarters yet. I am sorry. God have mercy upon you. There is no mercy here."

"How many are you did you say?" he queried.

"We are four and twenty living."

"And half, you say, have fallen sick?"

She nodded.

"That leaves a dozen still untouched."

"But for how long?" the nun shrilled.

He took the jar of lozenges from the pocket sewn inside his robe, and counted them in the firelight.

"What have you there?" she begged him, braving a step closer.

He sighed. "A remedy," he said, "but it is not enough. If I keep one patty in reserve for the child, and one for myself, only seven will remain."

"I implore you, spare what you can—any token!"

"Have them, then," he said, thrusting the jar toward her outstretched hands. "Carry them in the mouth to forefend the disease. They are a remedy of Doctor Nostradamus."

"Praise God," she sobbed, crossing herself. "May He reward you for your kind compassion, good brother."

"Do not waste them on those who have fallen. I do not know that they will be effective once the plague has taken hold."

"I grieve that there is nothing I can give you in return, save perpetual prayers for your safety and reward."

"Pray them, then, and tell no man that we have passed this way. The child, in her innocence, gave aid to one sought by the troops of Coligny. She will be imprisoned . . . or worse if they find her, for naught save Christian charity."

"Coligny, the heretic?" She gasped, and crossed herself.

"The same. Can we depend upon your silence, sister?"

"I have not seen you, good brother, but God has. He will keep you safe. We will all pray for that." She turned then, pointing toward a dense weald behind. "The forest path will lead you northward toward the channel. There is a stream nearby, where you might refresh yourselves, and your poor beast. Should you decide to return as you have come, you will reach Paris in two days' time."

"Are there other convents in the north?" he urged.

She shook her head. "We are the last, but in Paris—"

"Thank you for your guiding, good sister," he interrupted. "Forgive me, but we must press on. We will find a haven somewhere. God keep you."

"And you, good brother. We will pray!" she shouted after them, for they had moved on.

They were well inside the forest before he slowed the horse's pace. Passing one of the two remaining lozenges to Violette, he sighed. "Have it now," he charged. "Let it dissolve slowly in your mouth."

"I cannot bear the taste," she cried, shuddering against him.

"I will force the damnable thing down your throat whole if you do not obey me!" he promised. Looking over his shoulder, he watched while she took it in her mouth, then turned back again, and did so several times more before he gave his full attention to the dark, narrow forest path ahead.

"You are not having yours," she pouted, shivering against him again.

"I will save it," he informed her, glancing over his shoulder again. "When it is needed, it will be had. It is all we have left. What ails you, are you cold?"

"The taste," she whined. "My stomach rejects it . . ."

"Nonsense," he scoffed, scowling at her contorted face and tearing eyes. "Stop complaining, and obey me! I am in no humor for childish rebellion. We must form another plan here now—and quickly. I need all of my wits about me to deal with that."

He turned back again, fixing his eyes on the path ahead, ignoring her sudden wracking cough and heaving body as it stiffened against him, dismissing it as obvious theatrics staged to win him over, though he cast her another scathing glance over his shoulder as it continued. How could she be such a child in one moment, and such a sensuous, passionate woman in the next? Having known none save strumpets in the stews at home, he had no understanding of the virtuous female psyche, though he had often fantasized about it. This female, however, had put his patience to the test. Despite it all, try though he did to deny it, he would miss her once they parted, and that nagging thought had contributed to his foul temper.

"What will we do?" she asked him warily, before he had a ready answer.

A muttered string of well-rehearsed oaths replied to that.

"Which way do we travel?"

"We cannot go south," he snapped. "You heard the sister,

the plague is rampant there, and we cannot return to Paris. That is certain death for us both. He *knew* this, damn him! Yes, he knew. What else does he know, I wonder?"

"Doctor Nostradamus?"

"Doctor Nostradamus," he echoed. "What is he, saint, or demon? I do not know, but I wish I'd never come seeking his counsel. I wish those blasted flames had eaten me whole in that damnable cradle. I wish . . . oh, Christ, I *wish*! You think that *you* are in prison? Hah!"

"But where will we go?" she persisted. "And do not blaspheme. We can ill afford to anger God here now."

"There is only one way we can go," he said "—north, to the channel. I will take you to the Mount. Uncle Aengus will know what to do. He will arrange sanctuary for you at the convent there."

"How long a journey is it?"

"How in God's name should I know that?" he responded. "I have never made it from this vantage. We shall have to rest awhile here in the forest before we set out in any case, else this poor beast fall down dead beneath us. Besides, I have not slept, and I can go no further."

"Your wound grieves you?"

"The devil take my wound!" he snarled, reining in beside the stream the nun had spoken of. "We will have to pass the night here." Lifting her down, he made her comfortable in a bed of leaves, tended the horse, and began rummaging through the provisions sack. "It is as good a spot as any, and there is water," he said. "Our skin is empty, and the horse is wanting." He studied her closely then, noting that her grimacing had miraculously ceased. "Have you finished your lozenge so soon?" he queried.

"Y-yes," she murmured.

"You haven't chewed it, have you?"

"No, I did not chew it, my lord."

"I have no doubt that we shall soon be disposed of," he

growled, setting a piece of bread, and a small wedge of cheese in her hands. "This is the last. If we are to depend upon Doctor Nostradamus's wisdom, this would indicate that soon now we reach the journey's end." Digging deeper in the sack, he found the map and spread it wide to the eerie fleeting bursts of moonlight filtering down through the trees, for the storm had passed over.

"God's precious blood!" he barked, tracing the old healer's skillful outline on the sheepskin. "I thought as much."

"What is it?" Violette murmured, the bread suspended halfway to her mouth.

"He has laid out our course through the channel, so it seems," he told her.

She gasped.

"I hadn't noticed before, but I see it here now. There are no markings at all to the south, yet the north is fully detailed. He knew we would be taking this direction. He meant for us to take this turn, God rot him!"

"How long before we reach the quay?"

"Not long, but any length is too long here now."

"What do you mean, my lord?"

"Nevermind," he snapped. The longer their journey together took, the greater the temptation she would become, and the more difficult it would be for him to part from her when the time came. But this he dared not let her know. This wasn't part of his plan. *She* wasn't part of his plan. But here she was in all her innocence, all soft and fresh and vulnerable . . . and willing—everything he could have hoped for—his for the taking, and yet he dared not if he were to satisfy his honor. "Finish that and go to sleep, child," he said. "On the morrow it will end, this nightmare, if I must die in the attempt."

Twelve

$\mathcal{I}$t was three days before Robert and his charge reached St. Michael's Mount. They replenished their food supply at the marketplace along the quay, but they consumed precious little of it. The channel crossing was a hazardous voyage fraught with howling winds that whipped up heaving white-capped swells of churning water, tossing the galley like a cork amid the froth and swill and spindrift at the mercy of the autumn sea. At times it seemed alive, a vengeful human entity full-bent upon swallowing them whole.

Violette clung so desperately to his homespun sleeve in her terror of the storm, that his arm beneath was sore and swollen from the outset. She scarcely touched the food, though she retched repeatedly, and he was thankful that he'd given her the lozenge long before they ever reached the coast or it would surely have been wasted. She told him that she had never traveled by sea before, and, though she didn't complain, her fear was obvious. Her trembling became quaking, and there was no color in her. He was no fonder of sea travel than she, but he was accustomed to it, and it was easier, being able to see the waves, to anticipate their direction, and to dodge the cruel spray and backwash from the sea. He couldn't begin to imagine what it must be like to suffer such a voyage blind, and he tried to soothe her with tenderness and compassion.

He managed to keep her fairly dry for the duration, but her trembling never ceased, and when they finally set foot on the rockbound shingle that girded the foot of the Mount, he held her even closer, for she reeled and staggered like a cup-shotten sailor. They had reached the summit before her feet seemed to remember that she walked again upon dry land.

No one paid them any mind on their way to the abbey. One more monk and nun were hardly conspicuous in a place where practically all the populous were religious, and Robert finally began to draw an easy breath. A strange monk showed them in and led them to the refectory, where he bade them wait, but it was not his uncle Aengus who joined them there, but the abbot himself. Puzzled, Robert rose and approached the elder cleric, whose cold, hooded eyes, the color of slate, shot him through with spine-tingling chills. Beyond that they were cold, unwelcoming, and unreadable.

"I am Robert Mack of Paxton, Laird of Berwickshire, nephew of Aengus Haddock of this abbey," he greeted.

"I know who you are, my lord," the abbot said stiffly.

"I seek audience with my uncle over a most urgent matter, good abbot . . . If I might see him but briefly?"

"He is no longer with us," the abbot intoned.

"He . . . he isn't . . . *isn't* . . . ?"

"Dead? I doubt it, but of course I cannot be certain."

"What riddle is this? Not here? Where is he, then?"

"He has been taken, my lord."

"Taken? Taken where?"

"To prison," the abbot said flatly.

"Prison? Who has taken him? Where? What prison?"

"Yesterday, the cardinal of Lorraine arrived with an entourage from Paris. They took him into custody, and departed again for that city less than an hour after they arrived."

"How did they come, by way of the Seine through the channel, or from Brittany, to the south?" Robert gritted through clenched teeth, his rigid arm impervious to Violette's pinching grip upon it.

"By way of the channel."

"You say they returned to Paris?"

The abbot nodded.

"That filthy, makeshift Bastille?" Robert breathed.

Again the abbot nodded.

"But why? What is the charge?"

"Treason against the Church," said the abbot. "He is chastised for *your* crime, young lord. You are not welcome here. I must ask that you leave the Mount at once. You are wanted for murder, and your uncle, our good brother, accused of heresy and sedition in light of your . . . misadventures in France. Did you expect that Mount St. Michael Abbey would embrace you with open arms?"

"I knew nothing of this until this moment, good abbot," Robert stammered. "I will return to Paris at once and see him released. He will not be punished for my crime, I promise you."

"It is far too late for noble heroics," the abbot said. "You should have thought beyond your actions beforehand. Nothing will sway the cardinal now. If you return, it will be to join your uncle, not to affect his release. In any event, you cannot remain here."

"I will leave at once, of course," said Robert, "but I beg you, let the child remain. She has done no wrong, and she is blind."

"I cannot do that. She is wanted also."

"On what charge?" Robert demanded, acutely aware of her hand tightening on his arm, not out of fright this time; she was clearly trying to restrain him.

"Heresy, and complicity in your escape," the abbot said with raised voice. "There is talk that sorcery is afoot, and that when she is caught, she will go before the Inquisitor. She *cannot* stay here. We cannot harbor her. It is treason to do so."

"You *must!*" Robert thundered.

"I beg your pardon?" the abbot intoned, incredulous. "Remember yourself, and where you are, my lord."

"I beseech you . . . she is blind," Robert persisted. "She has no one. Pestilence is widespread on the mainland. You seal her death warrant, sending her back there. She is but a child!"

"She is a Huguenot, and a heretic," the abbot corrected.

"Forgive me," Violette interrupted, turning both their heads, "but I am neither. I am Catholic, as yourself."

"Why, then, were you living amongst the heretics?" the abbot insisted.

"She tended their livestock for food and lodgings, nothing more," Robert put in.

"She can speak for herself, so it seems," said the abbot. "Hold your peace, and let her do so."

"He speaks truth," she murmured.

"And you would have me believe that you were not one of them?"

"It is true," she insisted.

"This man you cling to so tenaciously stands accused of the murder of General Louis de Brach, under the cardinal's command. What say you to that, child?"

"It is true, good abbot," Robert answered for her.

"Will you hold your tongue and let her speak?" the abbot thundered, "or must I separate you to have this sorted out?"

"General de Brach overpowered me while I was setting the cattle free of the burning barn where I slept, and made an attempt to . . . to take me down," she explained, her fingers pinching Robert's arm so acutely that he winced. Understanding their message, he kept silent. "If he had not intervened, the general would have . . . violated me. They fought, and the general was slain. Laird Mack was wounded also. The wound needs tending. I know it, though he will not admit it. Please, won't you help him?"

The abbot breathed a thoughtful sigh. "Is what she speaks the truth, my son?" he queried.

"All save that my wound is grievous. It is clean, and mending well enough. There is no need to trouble over it."

"Some of our own have sunken to the heretic's level so it seems," the abbot mused, "but that does not alter the charge against you, or the validity of it. You stand accused and guilty of the crime by your own admission. I will not judge you, but I cannot help you either, else we all be shut up in the Bastille. These are dangerous times. I am sorry, my lord, for you, and for the girl, and most of all, for Brother Aengus. A pity you sought to enmesh him and this abbey in your irresponsible misadventures. No. You must go at once from Mount St. Michael Abbey. There can be no help for you here."

"I seek none for myself, but please help the lass," Robert begged. "Or, at the very least, recommend a convent where she might find sanctuary."

"She cannot stay here, and I cannot recommend her. There can be no more complicity—no further accusation of sedition against this abbey. Do you know what it is that you ask? Your request is out of the question. Surely, you can see that?"

"I see a poor, blind, frightened child, whose only crime is that she happened to have the gross misfortune to be in the wrong place at the wrong time, and has managed to tangle herself into my misfortune in her helplessness. You would condemn her to death for that, a holy father—an *abbot of the Church*? I am loath to believe it."

"Believe this then—no holy Catholic sanctuary this close to France will have you—either of you, so long as treason and sorcery taint you, and it will be so long as Charles de Guise, Cardinal of Lorraine, draws breath. His influence is far-reaching. I am sorry. You must go. You have tarried too long here already. There are spies everywhere."

"I will take her to Scotland," Robert conceded, "but first I must go to Uncle Aengus. Please, will you keep her just until I return?"

"You will *never* return, my lord."

"I cannot take her back there, you know that. They will execute her!"

"I am thinking that sorcery really is afoot here," the abbot said. "I am thinking that this child bewitched Louis de Brach—and you—and now would try her sorcery upon *me* here in this holy place!"

"You cannot possibly believe that."

"Doctor Nostradamus's hand is in this, is it not? And has he not thrice been before the Inquisitor?"

"And twice *acquitted*," Robert hurled at him, his whole body delivering the word. "How do you dare accuse this child of witchcraft? *You* are the blind one. If nothing else, propriety dictates here. She cannot travel with me alone . . . unchaperoned, to God knows where for God knows how long. Can you give me no direction—no guidance at all?"

"Go home to Scotland, my lord," the abbot replied stonily. "There is nothing you can do here now save bring more death and destruction."

"I cannot abandon Uncle Aengus. How could you even think it?"

"There is nothing you can do for him. Take the girl and go home—go now, while you are still able. She will find sanctuary in Scotland. That is all the guidance I can give you."

"It sounds as though you want my uncle shut up in that dung heap. Is he your scapegoat, then? God forgive you. Love casteth out fear, but not at Mount St. Michael Abbey, eh? I may stand accused of sedition against the Church, but *you*! You stand guilty of sedition against Our Lord, and Jesus Christ! He never turned the blind away, or the innocent, or the guilty, for that matter, who came seeking sanctuary in His holy name. He never turned against His brethren in His hour of danger, either, but then, He didn't have to deal with Charles de Guise, did he? No. He only suffered under Pontius Pilate. I pray He pities you, Father. I, like yourself, am not Christian enough for that." He spun on his heels and handed Violette over the refectory threshold. "Come, lass," he murmured. "We will seek shelter elsewhere."

"One moment!" the abbot called after them, his thunder turning them toward him. "Be warned, I must report your coming; it was expected by the hierarchy. We are watched, and I am bound to give account. You would do well to heed my advice."

"You can make your report in hell," Robert snarled. "Your thirty pieces buys your passage. How quickly did you turn my uncle over? You wouldn't even grant him sanctuary in his own abbey! Why should we expect it? The holy Scriptures say that a man's pride shall bring him low. There is no lower level upon holy ground than that which ambition seeks. Sleep well, good abbot, and be of good cheer. He whom you serve is proud, indeed."

Neither of the fugitives spoke until they had boarded a barge anchored at the foot of the Mount. Although Violette was terrified at the prospect of another channel crossing, she dared not say so.

"You were wonderful," she marveled at last, giving his arm a squeeze. "I could never have stood up to an abbot so bravely."

"Sanctimonious old hypocrite," Robert growled. "There, bigod, is heresy! No Huguenot could hope to carry the banner as proudly. Good Christ! He offered Uncle Aengus up as a lamb to the slaughter to save his own reprehensible hide. *Blood sacrifice!* My God, is this what Christianity has come to?"

"You will help him, your uncle?" she murmured.

"Violette, I must. I have no choice. Have you so soon

forgotten that I myself suffered in that godforsaken pest-hole? He cannot die in that place. He will not—not while there is breath in my body."

"What will become of me now?" she queried, almost afraid of the answer. Just for a moment, when she thought he might actually take her with him to Scotland, her hopes had risen. Though she didn't fully understand the emotions that had overwhelmed her then, she did know that if they were to part, her heart would break. The kiss they'd shared, that warm, wonderful, urgent pressure of him leaning heavily against her, stirring passions and deep feelings that she didn't even know existed, had made her hunger for more. Was this love, then? Oh, yes . . . but not for him. He had made his position all too plain. He lusted . . . Only that. Her heart was breaking.

He sighed. "I must return to Paris, lass," he said. "We go there now. It is a lengthier voyage time-wise than it would have been had we not come to the Mount, and were making the journey overland on French soil, but safer, considering. I am sorry, Violette. I cannot leave you here."

"We go there . . . the whole distance by water?" she panicked.

"Yes, lass. All will be well. This vessel is quite large—much more sound and seaworthy than the last, and we shan't have to deal with the treacherous ocean currents down 'round Brittany. We go straight through the channel. I know it frightens you, but we have no choice."

"But . . . what will I do? Where will I go?"

"Since there is no sanctuary for you in the Church, I have no recourse save to involve seigneur de Montaigne. He will not turn you away, Violette. He is my friend, and yours. He has proven it, and he will not betray us.

"And what of your Francine?" she queried, pouting. Jealousy was new to her, making her say things she shouldn't—things that didn't seem to change anything, except to make matters worse, once she'd said them. Yet she couldn't help herself. It hurt too much to keep silent.

"She is not 'my' Francine; far from it. She is a strumpet— a bawd!"

"Does she whiten her face with alabaster powder, and paint her lips and cheeks with *focus*, and her eyes with kohl? I have heard of such practices by the strumpets, and court ladies as well. Oh, and, does she wear a caul of silk and pearls upon her head?" she added quickly. There was no mistaking the anger her words had stirred. His hot, moist breath was scorching, puffing down upon her like what she imagined might have just as easily come from a fire-breathing dragon, for he stood very close, and his hand had tightened ruthlessly around her arm.

"I'm sure I did not notice," he seethed.

"Well, will you, when you see her again? I cannot see for myself, after all, and I am . . . curious."

"I doubt I shall see her again," he snapped. "Montaigne would never stand for treason in his own household. He's doubtless sold her off by now, so you will just have to be curious. Enough now of Francine! She is the least of our worries. I am not liking that I must take you back to the city, but I have no choice. Let us pray that our disguises suffice us. If we can reach Montaigne's château unseen by nightfall, I will leave you in his keeping, and see to Uncle Aengus. Then I will return for you."

"They will capture you!" she cried. "You will be killed!"

"No. In this costume, I might just be able to get him out of that abomination. I must try."

"And . . . then?" she murmured, almost afraid of the answer.

"Return to Scotland," he replied.

"And . . . me . . . what of me?"

"If no miracle presents itself, I shall have no choice but to take you also, just as I told the abbot. The convents there are not so steeped in politics, since our own religious conflict. We have John Knox to contend with, 'tis true, but not all of Scotland has been converted, nor our convents and abbeys disbanded, though some say that is soon coming. At any rate, our beloved Queen Mary is come home and has held her own for a year, suing for peaceful coexistence. That is another bridge we must cross once we reach it. God alone knows what Scotland has come to since I left it. But you will fare well in my homeland, have no fear, and I will be close enough at hand there to make certain of it."

"I will do as you say," she murmured, her heart pounding in her ears at the prospect of a dream come true. She would make no fuss about convents now; that would come later if needs must . . . if she could only persuade him to take her with him . . .

"Violette, you must," he said, cutting into her reverie. "If you should come to harm here now after all my labor to prevent it, my conscience would not let me bear it."

The voyage was a kinder one than their first, as Robert had promised, but that did not spare Violette seasickness, or stark terror. By the time they reached the Paris fringes, she was weak from retching helplessly, and flushed, though she trembled with cold. And though he soothed her with gentle speech, promising all would be well once they reached the château, and he'd delivered her into sympathetic hands, she could not imagine it.

They came ashore at night, which, he told her, was what he had hoped. There would be less traffic on the roads and byways veining the city. They wasted no time collecting their mount from the steerage and made their way ashore traveling at a reasonable pace, so as not to arouse suspicion until they'd reached the château. But they found it in darkness, though the hour was not late. Robert adjusted his cowl to hide his face and spent several anxious minutes pounding at the door until the steward, Alain, answered.

"Good servant, we are a monk and sister from the south, come for audience with your master. May we enter? It has been a long, exhausting journey."

"Th-the master's gone," the man stammered.

"Gone? Gone where?"

"Why, to Bordeaux," said the servant, seeming surprised at the question.

"How long ago? When did he leave?" Robert asked the man.

"Sunup yesterday."

"Will he be returning?"

"Not likely 'til the spring," the steward told him. "I cannot have you in. I'm all that's left to tend the place, but for the scullions. He's taken the rest. My orders were to admit no one. Like as not, they'll give you shelter at the cathedral, or the abbey. You'll see the spires once you clear the wood. Just follow the road there east apace."

The door slammed shut in their faces then, and Robert led her back to their mount. He'd scarcely swung her up behind him on the animal's rippling back, when she stiffened against him, and tugged at the sleeve of his robe.

"Hold, my lord," she whispered. "Are we alone on this path, or does someone come?"

"There is no one else," he replied. "The road is quite vacant."

"I think not," she murmured. "Listen, do you not hear . . . something rustling the brush. I feel no wind, and yet the foliage, it chatters."

"I hear nothing, lass," Robert said on a sigh. "If there were spies afoot, they would have set upon and seized us by now."

"Still, I would be wary," she said. "My hearing is quite reliable, my lord, and I did hear . . . something."

"Do you hear it still?"

"No, not still . . . but I did. I'm certain."

"I will be watchful," he assured her.

"Where do we go?" she queried.

"Montaigne was my last hope," Robert said. "I need time to think, and there *is* no time."

"I am weary," she moaned, "and I am hot."

"I know," he murmured. "I know you are exhausted. The only other place I know of in these parts where we can go is the ruins. I will have to return you there. I will hide you where we hid before, until I can discover what has become of Uncle Aengus. We have come full circle—back to where we first began, and accomplished *nothing*. God's precious blood! This is madness!"

"Y-you would leave me there . . . *alone?*" The mere thought of it all but stopped her heart, which had begun to pound in her ears suddenly, beating a ragged rhythm.

"What other choice have I? I cannot march you into the Bastille alongside me. I am not liking this any more than you, believe me. The only other alternative that I can see is to involve your vendor friends. Would that suit you better, lass?"

"No, we cannot!" she cried. "They are innocent, and they struggle for their livelihood. Like as not, all save Jacques and Justine would turn me away here now. And even if another among them did consent to harbor me, they would have to renounce me should the soldiers come—they would have no choice, and even at that, they would more than likely die. I cannot bring that upon them—especially not Jacques and Justine, who took me in and raised me as their own."

"Then we go to the ruins," he said. "We have most of the provisions left. Somehow I will try to get word to Doctor Nostradamus. He frequents the ruins, you know. If he is still in Paris, he might even be there now. He will help us. Do you trust me, lass?"

"Y-yes," she sobbed, "I trust you, but I fear that they will *kill* you, and no one will ever find me in that awful tomb beneath the ruins. Do you not understand? All my years I have cared for myself. I have made my way. I have been independent. I know every curbstone—every cobblestone in Paris, my lord, and I was *happy*. I knew no fear. I want my freedom back, and I cannot have it. There, bigod, is the fear that grips me now . . . of things unknown . . . of places unfamiliar, where I cannot find my way on my own, much less make my own way in the world as I once did with my flower cart." She dared not tell him that above all that, her greatest fear, that which had shackled her most, was the dread of never seeing him again.

"This is my fault," Robert said. "And I will rectify it. That is why I wanted to see you in safe hands before I do this thing I'm planning . . . in case, well, let us not think about that now. You shan't be entombed at the ruins. I will show you the way to open the hatch from below if anything should . . . so you will not feel trapped. Before I deal with Uncle Aengus, I will first seek out Doctor Nostradamus. That is what must be. Now, hold fast! I will not be at ease until I have you safe below the castle ruins."

But her grip was weak, and she leaned heavily upon him as he drove the gelding through the darkness. The cold air stung her hot cheeks and she shuddered helplessly—wracking, involuntary spasms of chills that turned her clammy skin to gooseflesh beneath the habit. Her sour, queasy stomach threatened to retch again, and she could barely keep her eyes from sliding shut. It was as though they had been weighted down, but that weight seemed to be crushing her entire body as well. She began to pray in order to keep awake. Nothing seemed real anymore. Sweat oozing from her pores beaded on her brow and began running down her cheeks. And though she dreaded it, she prayed the ruins that she feared would materialize out of thin air, just so that she could rest.

They were still traveling at a moderate pace for fear of attracting attention, and it was some time before the steep incline that crawled up to the derelict castle presented itself in shrouded silhouette. Robert slowed the horse's pace to take the grade, and glanced back over his shoulder toward Violette, clinging listlessly to him.

"We are here, lass!" he said, turning his attention back to the horse. "I will have you safely inside, and then see to this poor beast."

But she didn't answer. Her grip at the waist of his robe failed, then her hands fell away altogether. She slid off the animal's back, and fell like a stone into a snarl of bramble and scrub that carpeted the knoll.

Robert vaulted from the saddle. "Violette! What is it, lass?" he murmured.

Unconscious, she made no reply.

They were halfway up the grade, and he tethered the horse in the bracken, and gathered her into his arms. The moon peeked through the clouds then and, as he turned, he thought he caught sight of a mounted rider standing at the edge of the wood they had just come from. He blinked, and the apparition was gone. Was he seeing specters now? Were his eyes playing tricks? He recalled Violette's warning at the château, and stared long and hard toward the tall stand of yews, where he'd seen . . . something. But there was nothing there now, and he dismissed it as exhaustion, slung the provisions sack over his shoulder, and continued his climb to the summit.

Once inside the smokehouse, he hurried Violette below to the hidden chamber, where he dared risk examining her by candlelight, and set her down on the pallet. His hands were no more use to him than two blunt clubs as he struggled with the flint, and it seemed an eternity before he managed to light the candle, still fastened to the floor with beeswax where they'd left it when they set out on their journey. Taking it up and holding it closer, his breath caught in a gasp, and his scalp drew back taut. She was burning with fever, her crimson face running with sweat and covered with puffy red blotches.

He tore off her headdress and opened the neck of her robe, spreading it wide. He groaned again at sight of the same red welts spread over her throat and shoulders, one of which had bloomed black, oozing puss.

He searched the pocket of his robe for the lozenge he'd held in reserve, praising God when he found it there after all they'd been through, and forced it between her parted lips.

"Oh, Christ! You have to help me here!" he pleaded, rocking her frantically in his arms. He lifted her closer and shook her, calling her name again and again, in a vain attempt to rouse her, and something rolled from the shallow pocket of her robe with the jostling, something round. He recognized it at once, the lozenge he had given her in the forest after they left the nunnery. It was scarcely altered.

"You foolish, foolish child!" he groaned. "What have you *done?*"

Thirteen

Time meant nothing to Robert then, shut up in the bowels of the castle ruins. Once he tethered and tended the horse in much the same place that he had Montaigne's bay on his first visit there, he sat wide-eyed beside Violette through the night, sponging her face with cool water from one of the skins he'd filled by the sparkling forest stream on their way to the coast. It was nearly gone now, since they had shared some with the gelding along the way. He knew that soon he would have to find a new source, and as the distant sound of bird music seeped through the dovetailed crevices, he left Violette and hurried outside with the water skins, anxious to have it accomplished while darkness still covered his movements.

He vaguely recalled having sighted the glint of a stream along the edge of the forest that bearded the foot of the knoll along the southern slope. Deciding that the spot would make a better place to hide the horse as well, since it was deeper into the weald, he quickly led the animal there, and tethered him beside the stream.

The water was sweet and icy-cool, running musically over watercress and pure white stones, sparkling in the predawn haze that would soon give way to a clear morning. He filled the skins, and ducked his head in the shallow flux in an attempt to rid himself of the weariness that had sapped his strength. The forest was thick and wild there, and content that it was unlikely anyone would stumble on the horse concealed in such a secluded place, he took up the water skins, and started back toward the ruins. As he lumbered up the hill, however, his new relief evaporated at sight of a shadow moving slowly through the drifting mist amid the crumbling castle walls—a horse and rider, black in silhouette against the slowly lightening sky.

Robert dropped down, flattening himself to the breast of the knoll, and watched, his breath suspended, while the rider swung himself down. It was still too dark to define the shape of the intruder, and he drew his sword and slithered closer, crawling on his belly through the tall grass spears, cold and wet with the autumn dew.

Close proximity did little to affect a clearer perspective, but now the horse's lusty snorting came clear, and he felt the tremor of the animal's heavy hoofs pawing the ground beneath him. Choosing his moment, the Scot surged to his full height without a sound and flattened himself against the angled smokehouse wall, the sword ready at his side. When the shadow moved alongside, he lunged and drove the man behind it to the ground, the sword blade at his throat.

"Hold there!" the man's winded voice cried, misshapen for the pressure of the sword flattening his Adam's apple.

Distorted though it was, there was something familiar in the sound, and Robert took a closer look at the man he'd pinned there.

"*Doctor Nostradamus?*" he breathed.

"Yes, my fine young ram," the healer choked. "Well met, or nearly, eh?"

"Good God, forgive me!" Robert groaned. "I had no idea it was you, Doctor. Have I hurt you, sir?"

"If you will haul that hulking carcass off me, I will try to rise and tell you," the healer said through a guttural chuckle.

Robert jumped to his feet and helped the healer up alongside him, holding his breath while the plump old man slapped the dirt from his Lyons velvet robe and snatched up his four-cornered hat, which had sailed a few yards off.

"I couldn't see you clearly," Robert told him. "You could have been a soldier—anyone in this deceiving predawn ink. I beg you, forgive me, sir. I am the prince of blunders."

"The king of them, if we would be accurate, but take ease, young lord. Nothing is broken as far as I can tell, save poise and bearing. It is good to see that you have come back safely. I have ventured here each morning at this hour for two days now in the hopes that I'd come upon you."

"You were expecting me?" Robert blurted. "Then that was you by the yews last night. Why didn't you make your presence known?"

The healer frowned. "If you saw someone by the forest, it was not me," he said.

"I thought I did," Robert mused, "but then, in the blink of an eye, the image vanished. It must have been my imagination. Violette thought she heard something at the château, and I have been overly cautious. That is probably what prompted it. But you were expecting me. How?"

"I knew you would return once you learned of your uncle's arrest," the healer explained. "With Montaigne gone south to the coast, this seemed your logical alternative. How fares the girl? The convent did not keep her, then?"

"She is with me still, and she has come down with plague, I think. I was praying that I could find you . . . praying that you hadn't left the city."

"Well, I am found. Take me to her. Has she had the remedy I gave you?"

"I thought she had," said Robert, leading him below, "but last night when I brought her here, the dose fell from her pocket scarcely touched."

"Hmmm, that is not good."

"We came upon plague twice along the journey. After the first encounter, I gave her one of the lozenges at once, but she complained that her stomach rejected the thing. Then at the convent, they would not admit us. The whole nunnery was down with the disease, save a handful. I reserved two patties for ourselves, and gave what remained to the sister we spoke with. I had Violette take one at once, of course, but I believe that was the one I found. Who is to say that the first was not discarded in the same manner?"

"But you did dose her last night?" the healer queried.

"Yes. She was in no condition to refuse it, but was it in time?"

"We shall see," Nostradamus replied, descending the stairs.

Below, Violette lay as Robert had left her, and the healer quickly scrutinized the scalding blotched skin and restless delirium.

"She comes to now and then, but makes no coherent sounds," Robert told him. "The fever rages. Can naught else be done? Can you not bleed her . . . or—"

"I do not hold with bloodletting," Nostradamus interrupted. "It is of no use with plague whatsoever, and only adds to the victim's discomfort. Phlebotomy is a ghoulish practice, to begin with, a ploy of the incompetent, and a barbaric hoax. I've seldom seen it prove effective in any respect, unless you consider draining the mad sufficiently enough to make them weak and docile 'effective.' I do not."

"What then? There has to be a nostrum . . . some herbal draught, perhaps?"

Nostradamus shook his head. "No medicinal cordial I have come upon yet has ever affected a cure for plague. That is why the death toll is so great in these cases."

Robert's heart leapt. "You aren't saying . . . ?" he murmured.

"No, not yet at least," the healer said. "It seems a mild case, so far as I can tell. It has not just come on her, either. Like as not, she came down with it upon your first encounter."

"How can you be so sure?"

"Do you see this, here?" the healer said, exposing the ugly, blackened canker on the side of her throat to his view.

"This is too far advanced for the disease to have been recent. The blackness is a good sign, believe it or not. It tells that her body is fighting back."

"She never complained," Robert murmured. "Only once did she confess that she was weary, and that was shortly before she fell. If only she'd taken that remedy . . ."

"Take ease, young ram. I have more lozenges, for you as well. This last that you gave her was your own, wasn't it?" He waved the question away with a hand gesture after his fashion. "Nevermind. We will use what I have, and wait." He laughed. "Don't look so wary. I have had astounding success with my confections in past epidemics. You might inquire of the good people of Ax, who have granted me a substantial life pension for the accomplishments of my curious pastilles there." He took one from the pouch he wore about his waist and extended it in his wrinkled palm. "You look at this here, and you see a withered mass of bark and leaf that resembles a turd and tastes not much better. I look at the self-same thing, and I see life. See with your spirit, Robert Mack, and it wouldn't hurt to pray. No remedy will work else God Himself prescribes it, and you *take* it."

"You are, indeed, a strange fellow," Robert said, thinking out loud.

"Many tell me so," the healer said, forcing the lozenge through Violette's blistered lips. He laughed again. "Many say that my cures and prophesying are accomplished by witchcraft and sorcery. Some even go so far as to suggest that those whose lives I do save are doomed to pay the penalty in everlasting hellfire."

"Is that true?"

"That you even ask tells me I waste my breath," the healer growled, arms akimbo.

"I am sorry," Robert murmured.

"You should be. And look at you! You are a fine specimen. I've seen healthier-looking cadavers in the surgery. How is that wound?"

"Well enough, I expect. I've had no time to trouble over it."

"Slip down that robe, and let me see," the healer charged. "And when was your last dose of my controversial remedy, eh?"

"I don't remember—two—three days ago."

"Hmmm, I thought as much. Well, we'll have you down here next. Have this," he ordered, thrusting a lozenge toward him. Robert took it without protest, and let him probe the wound. "Ummm," the healer grunted. "Despite your negligence, it mends well enough, so it seems."

"Nevermind me. What of her?"

The healer cocked his head and studied him. "She . . . matters to you, then?" he said at last.

"Well, of course she matters to me!"

"That is not exactly what I've asked."

Robert sputtered digesting that, but not for long. Behind, Violette stirred, and he vaulted to her side. She had begun to thrash about and moan, and he gathered her into his arms and sponged the sweat from her hot face with the cool water he'd brought from the stream.

"My lord," she cried, groping the air. "My lord, where are you?"

"Shhh, child," he soothed, brushing the tangled honey-brown hair back from her hot face. "I am right here beside you."

"My lord—*my lord*! Am I not allowed to call you by your given name as you do me? I knew it once, I think . . . I cannot remember," she moaned through a rattle that riddled him with cold chills. He had heard such before in the dying.

"You may call me Robert, lass, if it pleases you," he murmured, "—*anything*, lass, just do not die."

She didn't answer. The glazed, vacant eyes rolled back in

her head behind closed lids, and she drifted off again into senseless babbling.

"She is delirious," Nostradamus said, troubling his whiskers.

"No, she was coherent," Robert insisted.

The healer wagged his head. "Her subconscious speaks, young ram," he said. "No rational voice is in her now. She thrashes. She will break the canker open, and that will spread the poison. She will have to be tethered."

"You would restrain her?" Robert breathed, incredulous.

"You must sleep sometime," the healer pointed out.

"You mean to tie her down?"

Nostradamus nodded. "How else are we to prevent her doing herself harm? It is a common practice. She will come to no harm from tethers."

"But . . . she cannot bear restraints. She will be terrified."

"She will not even know," said the healer. "Those blotches there, on her face, her arms, and doubtless on the rest of her . . . if she were to scratch the surface they would leave ghastly scars behind. Scars may be in any case, but if we can prevent them . . ."

"You mean to say that she could be . . . disfigured?"

"It is a possibility."

"Oh, God, that foolish, foolish child!" he groaned.

"The prospect overwhelms you? Could that be because of your own disfiguration?" the healer said.

"She is so beautiful. I never thought about the possibility of . . . scars."

"Would you love her any the less?"

"*Love her?*"

The healer smiled. "That comes as a surprise to you, does it?" he chided.

"Are you mad?"

"No. Are you *blind?*" the healer parried.

"I have no right to love her, or anyone," Robert said flatly.

"And why is that?"

"*Now* who is blind?"

Nostradamus smiled. "She there in your arms will never have her sight. Let us pray that you gain yours while there is still time left for it to be of use to you."

"I am in no humor for your cryptic riddles, sir," Robert warned, easing Violette back against the pallet. "I have this nightmare with Uncle Aengus yet before me. I have no time to spare for solving riddles."

"Oh, so you would storm the Bastille single-handedly then, would you?"

"You mock me!"

"I marvel."

"I would attempt to liberate him, yes," said Robert. "Why bandy words. You've said as much."

"It is quite a task you undertake."

"But not impossible."

"Perhaps not."

"You mock me still!"

"Let us just say that I am awed by your zeal," Nostradamus replied, tongue-in-cheek. "It will not be easy, what you plan, or have you even formed a plan?"

"I've had no time with her like this," Robert admitted, raking his hair back roughly. "I am hoping I can get past the guards in this costume. If I can manage that, somehow I will liberate him."

"That is quite a strategy you have contrived, I dare say," Nostradamus said.

"There is only one person there inside those walls who has seen my face . . . Garboneaux, the jailer."

"Whom you will encounter at the outset, like it or not," the healer pointed out. "And he is jailer no longer, remember? He is reduced to sentry since Montaigne liberated you from that pest hold."

Robert rocked back on his haunches. "You obviously have suggestions," he said, waiting.

"Better than that," said the healer slyly. "I have the solution!"

"Share it then. I would be done with this inhospitable waste of God's good time—your beloved France."

"I appreciate your disenchantment with my land, but we French are not all inhospitable creatures. You have met three friends here, have you not? Montaigne, myself, and that exquisite child lying there that worships you."

"She wastes her worship," Robert snapped. "But for me, she would not *be* lying there."

"You cannot take the blame for all her woes, young son. Thinking such as that will solve naught here now."

"You said you have a solution. I would hear it."

"I cannot help you with Garboneaux. It is unfortunate that he has seen your face. It is not something that he would be likely to forget, and I doubt that habit will get you by him, since he has grown even more diligent now that he's trying to have his appointment as jailer reinstated. The rest, however, can be managed, but not alone."

"How, then?"

"I will help you."

"You? How?"

"There is to be a tour of that god-awful place two days hence," the healer explained. "The king wishes it. That is why I've sought you here so anxiously. It would be the best time to execute my plan. It will, of course, be dangerous. The cardinal is not scheduled to attend, nor the Queen Mother; she would not lower herself. I find that quite amusing, since she never leaves the king's side—even sleeps in his chamber. She governs as if *she* were king—appoints officers—grants pardons—keeps the seal, and has the last say in counsel, yet she will not set her pretty foot over the threshold of that pest hole. Admiral Coligny will be there, however, as will the Duke of Guise, and Ruggiero, the court astrologer—when she can't get hold of me, that is," he hastened to add. "The man has mediocre talent. He has not seen what I *know*—that pretty foot of hers is soon submerged in blood. I am scheduled to attend also. It is the admiral's intent to prove to our young sovereign that the Huguenots imprisoned there are not receiving equal treatment. I am to bear witness and offer impartial evaluations as a physician, so long as those evaluations are in the admiral's favor, that is. He raves injustice, and plays upon the king's sympathy to release some of those who could be useful to him while Condé is marshalling allies in the south. Naturally, security will be tight, especially since the Queen Mother will not be hovering, and Garboneaux will be on his best and most alert behavior."

"You hope to join me with their entourage?" Robert cried. "That is insane!"

"No, no, that could not be," Nostradamus returned. "I hope that in the mass confusion, while their heads are turned, two humble monks might well slip in unnoticed, or, at the very least, unscrutinized."

"*Two* monks?"

The healer nodded. "Your uncle is close in age to me, is he not?"

"Yes, but—"

"His build?"

"He is about your height, but he has no beard, and you are, well, you are a bit more . . ."

"Rounded?" Nostradamus concluded for him.

Robert nodded.

"Neither should present a real problem," the healer assured him. "Hopefully, the cowl will cover my beard once I've tucked it inside. We can cover our faces easily enough. The stink in that dung heap is suffocating. It would not seem odd that we would forefend it. And I am sure your uncle's cell will provide us with something we can pad him with."

"You cannot mean that you intend to masquerade as a monk also?"

Nostradamus nodded.

"But, why? Wouldn't it be easier to escort me in as you are? Surely no one would question me then—not in your esteemed company."

"It would be easier, of course, but how would we explain my taking one monk in, and bringing two monks out—one in Benedictine black?" He smiled toward Robert's brow pleated in a frown. "I will robe myself as you are robed," he went on. "Underneath, I will wear my usual attire. We will ply the guards with flagons of wine, which I will prepare with powders that will . . . shall we say . . . subdue them? Quite harmless stuff, but effective. When we enter your uncle's cell, I will give him my robe, and leave you. As I've said, I am expected. No one will view my presence in that dungeon as unusual. When you emerge with your uncle, I will be close by, and I will join you, pretending to recognize you both as old acquaintances. And then, as you suggested earlier, in my esteemed company, no one will hinder your departure."

"Your plan is brilliantly contrived," Robert admitted. "But why should you do such a thing—take such a risk, for someone you hardly know?"

The wise old seer smiled. "I've known you for eons, young ram; a pity that there are no more like you in France. Were that the case, she would not be so beleaguered with the burden of political madness. I have seen many men in this life—noble and peasant alike—but few have earned my admiration in the way that you have done."

"What could you possibly find in the likes of me to admire?" Robert wondered out loud.

"An inherent compassion, and a Christian heart, an innocence that does delight me, and a sense of honor that is hewn of the stuff of gods and kings. Your heart is pure, young Scot, though you've done murder—will do again—and nearly dishonored our Violette."

Robert's eyes flashed.

"Ahha!" Nostradamus erupted. "Only a sorcerer would know that, eh?" He laughed. It was a guttural chuckle that rumbled through his portly frame. "Take ease, take ease, there is no witchcraft here. I see the guilt of passion in those anxious eyes trained upon her. Your fortitude astounds me."

"It is *myth*!" Robert hurled at him.

Again the healer laughed. "You would not have me hoist you up too high upon the pedestal, lest you tumble down and disappoint me, eh? You shan't—disappoint me, that is. The mystery surrounding me is really quite a simple thing. I am a devout man, young son. God knows it; what mortal man chooses to call me matters not in view of that. I answer to Him only. He has given me the greatest gift—the ability to discern the spirits. With such comes the power to command those spirits, or, if you will, manipulate them. He has also given me sight—I think as a reward, I *know* as a necessity for the good of man—future man in particular, for some of what I see is not for now. I never abuse the gifts He has given me, nor do I ignore or waste them. If I would squander them upon you, the least that you can do is pay attention."

"More riddles?"

"Only if you choose to make it so."

"You speak now of Violette."

"You are learning."

Robert stared toward her, clouding. "She is just a child," he said, "a beautiful child, but a child nonetheless—an innocent—and I feel responsible for her and protective because of it."

"This is why you nearly ravished her?"

"I nearly ravished her because I am a man with needs that she does arouse. I lust, sir, nothing more."

"What stopped you?"

"My conscience!"

"I see . . . and was she willing?"

"Until I frightened her," Robert said dismally.

"Will you hear advice?"

"I will hear it."

"But will you *listen?*"

"Speak it!"

"You are so drowned in your own vain despair—so steeped in self-pity, that you can see naught beyond it. You have shed the helm from your face, but not from your mind. I tried to tell you once to learn to see with your spirit. It is a handsome spirit—as handsome as that half of your face there is ugly, and it will reward you handsomely if you would let it. But no, you will have none of it. And now, I tell you this—at some preordained moment, God gives each soul in whom He breathes the breath of life a special gift—an offering by way of opportunity. That soul has but to recognize what God offers and it is granted. The opportunity of which I speak comes only once, a test, if you will, of faith, of trust, and, yes, of courage. For sometimes that is what it takes to seize the gift and hold fast to it. Be of good courage, Robert Mack. It is not a prophesy, this, it is a warning. When God speaks to you, young son, you had best listen. The Scriptures will bear witness that the one thing He will not abide is wasted breath, and you can ill afford to tempt His wrath here now."

Nostradamus did not hover through those two endless days that brought Violette to the brink of crisis. He left Robert there alone with her to meditate upon his wisdom, explaining that it was important for him to go about his normal duties in the interim so as not to arouse suspicion. Subsequently, his comings and goings were cautions and brief, under cover of darkness.

Robert sat wide-eyed beside the delirious girl, sponging her face, which was on fire with fever, and forcing the lozenges through crusted lips that moaned and trembled, calling his name. Each time her ravings became violent, he tethered her in strong arms, for he would not allow the healer's restraints. Instead, he held her and rocked her and clamped massive fists around her slender wrists whenever she made attempts to gouge the blisters, until bracelets of bruised skin encircled them. Exhaustion was his enemy then. It weighed heavily upon him. His body cried for sleep. When he could no longer deny it, he drew her close and held her fast in such a grip that any movement she might make would surely wake him, in much the same way that he always slept clutching his sword in dangerous places. Only then would he shut his eyes. He'd slept for several hours, though it seemed only minutes, when the feeble sound of her voice so close in his ear woke him with a start.

"My lord," she murmured. "My *lord* . . . !" Reluctant to wake, he moaned, and she spoke again. "My lord . . . I thirst . . ."

Groggily, he vaulted upright, his hooded eyes staring out of focus, trying to decide if he'd dreamed the voice, or actually heard it. After a moment, his vision cleared, and he took her measure. She seemed less animated, her sightless stare less glazed, and her skin appeared to have fewer blotches. At the very least, he was certain some of what remained had lost its fire. A surge of relief washed over him, and something else—disappointment that she had called him 'my lord,' and not Robert, as she'd begged to in her delirium.

"Violette?" he cried, addressing what he prayed was a rational voice.

"I thirst . . . ," she moaned.

He snatched up the water skin and moistened her lips. They seemed cooler against the fingers that spread the droplets there. Supporting her in his arm, he let her drink from the skin, then felt her brow for fever. It had started to abate. Thanking God, he pulled her close, but he had scarcely gotten the supplication out, when anger flared again, and he shook her.

"You little fool!" he snapped. "I should up-end you here and now and thrash your bottom like the child you are. Why did you not take the remedy? Foolish child, we've nearly lost you."

"Thrash me . . . beat me . . . flay my body raw if it please you—anything, my lord, but . . . please, I beg you, do not leave me! Do not send me away. Please . . . I beseech you . . . do not shut me up in the convent."

"It was *deliberate*, this?" he breathed. The cold fingers of a chill crawled the length of his spine. "Answer me!"

"I . . . I knew no convent would have me with plague . . . not in this land . . . or yours."

"*God's beard!*" he gritted through clenched teeth. "Did it never occur to you that you might die?"

"I wish that I had," she sobbed. "That is what I truly wanted."

"Ahhh, child," he moaned, crushing her close.

"I am *not* a child," she reminded him with passion, "and I love you! Please do not abandon me."

Trembling with something he could not name, Robert searched her face. No. She was not delirious now. She was very much in earnest. Suddenly, his lips descended upon hers. Her weak arms were holding him fast in an embrace that drained his senses dry and brought him to full arousal, despite the impotence of her grip. He crushed her close, every cord and muscle in his battle-conditioned body on fire against her with the primal heat of passion. He gathered her closer still, drinking her in as though he would absorb her very being into his own.

"So! We are recovered!" said a voice from behind, and

Robert pulled back sharply spinning toward the sturdy, dark shape of Nostradamus. The man *was* a sorcerer. He hadn't even heard him enter or felt the rush of air funneling through the hatchway above that would have preceded him. In that heavenly, mind-altering embrace, the earth could have opened up and swallowed him. He would never have known.

"Th-the crisis is past," he stammered dumbly. Laying Violette back gently on the pallet, he raked his fingers through the hair waving across his moist brow.

"Or, has it just begun?" Nostradamus queried pointedly.

Robert ignored the innuendo, and moved aside to let the healer examine her.

"She mends," Nostradamus concurred, continuing his evaluation, "but she must have much rest if we would keep her. We are fortunate to have this place. We may need it for some time yet before she can move on, and being so isolated, we shan't spread plague through the city. The pallet should be burned, of course, but we cannot risk a bonfire. We shall have to remove it to the smokehouse and gather enough gleanings from nature to replace it. I have brought a fresh robe for her, however. That will have to suffice."

"She will recover—you are certain?"

"Her body will," said the healer, "quite unscathed, I expect, except for some minor scarring. See how the blotches fade? Most will disappear in time. But as to her spirit, that is quite another matter, and both are essential. The mind must will it, and I have no mystical remedy for that. That healing must come from within."

Robert swallowed dry around a constriction that had formed in his throat suddenly, but made no reply.

"And you?" the healer queried. "How are you faring, young ram? Mayhap, have you managed to contract the thing as reward for your . . . hovering?"

"No," Robert murmured.

"A miracle!" Nostradamus erupted.

"What now?" Robert asked him.

"She must have sleep," said the healer. Leading him out of the girl's range of hearing, he went on speaking in hushed tones. "I have a powder that, when mixed with wine, will make a cordial that will ensure she sleeps soundly, and that is best while we are away. It is time. We must be gone within the hour if we would execute my plan."

Robert cast a skeptical glance in Violette's direction. He had lost track of time, and now the prospect of leaving her alone so suddenly made him uneasy. He wanted to hold her again, to feel her arms around him, to hear her say those magical words once more just to be sure he hadn't imagined them.

"She will be quite safe," the healer assured him, producing a vial of powder and a cup of hammered silver from the pocket of his robe. "She will fall into a peaceful sleep that will let her body heal itself. She will not even miss us. And, God willing, we will return with your uncle before the nostrum has even begun to dissipate. We have no other choice. She cannot go with us. Would you rather that she lay here wakeful the whole while we are gone, fraught with worry? Think! In her blindness, still giddy from the fever, without reassurance she would go mad."

"Do you think your powdered sleep will spare me that?" Violette scorned, turning them both toward her. Robert had forgotten her enhanced hearing sense. "Not even the fever of plague could manage to keep me from the brink of madness," she confessed. "The dreams! I cannot bear them . . ."

"There will be no dreams in this sleep, little flower, I promise it," Nostradamus said, having mixed the cordial. "Take it, child," he charged, closing her reluctant fingers around the cup.

She hesitated, gripping the chalice. "You will be killed—

the pair of you, I know it," she sobbed, "and I shall wake alone here to . . . to . . . !"

Robert sprang to her then. Setting the cup aside, he took her in his arms. "You have that little faith in me, lass?" he scolded. "Have I not just wrestled death for you, and won the joust?"

"You will be killed!" she insisted.

"No, Violette, I will not," he promised. "I will not leave you in that way, or any other. I will return, I swear it, Uncle Aengus with me. I go to liberate the very priest whom I would have hear our vows."

A satisfied smile creased the healer's lips looking on, but Robert only gave it a passing glance. Gathering her into another embrace, he was aware of nothing but the warm and willing abandon of her, and the sweet, petal-soft lips that mated with his own. After a moment, those anxious lips parted, and Robert raised the cup on the floor beside them.

"Drink, Violette, and sleep," he murmured, his voice shaking with passion, and something he dared not endow with a name. "Have faith, if not in me, in God, that when you wake . . . if you are willing, it is your wedding day."

She took it then, and supporting her in his good arm, Robert helped her drain the cup to the dregs, cradling her gently in his arms until she'd fallen fast asleep.

Fourteen

*R*obed as monks, Robert and the healer wasted no time setting out, though the young laird had not laid all of his doubts to rest. The gnawing trepidation he wrestled with was clearly visible, and they hadn't gone far when Nostradamus addressed it.

"You cannot think about the girl now," he said. "Our success in this demands all of our wits be about us, and our full attention upon what lies before us. She will . . . fare well."

"You hesitate."

"I speak truth."

"Then I must believe it."

"You preach to her of faith. I advise you take your comfort from the same homily."

"It is . . . difficult," Robert admitted frankly. "She is so vulnerable . . . and so frightened."

"She is very brave," Nostradamus observed.

"How well I know it."

"You are resigned, then, no . . . misgivings?"

"I love her, if that is what you ask. But you knew that, didn't you?"

The healer nodded, cocking his head thoughtfully. "How is it that you would not admit it until now?" he queried.

"I am disfigured. She is blind. I had to be certain that it wasn't a selfish emotion bred of convenience. Surely, you can see how such a thing could happen. It seemed too . . . easy, too convenient."

"But she knows your face, young ram. She has seen it with her hands far better than any eyes could show it."

"I am aware of that. I wasn't putting her love to the test, it was *mine* I questioned."

"I see," said the healer. "And what happenstance was it that finally convinced you?"

Robert hesitated. "She was so very close to death," he said. "I had not . . . had her, Doctor Nostradamus, and when I feared that I might lose her . . . ! One cannot grieve so for the loss of something one has never had . . . unless he loves. I knew I could never leave her behind. I think I knew that from the start."

"Why have you never 'had her,' young ram? She seemed willing enough to me."

"I very nearly did," he confessed.

"What stopped you?"

"She already has one handicap," he replied. "She is proud of her virginity—proud that she has kept it in her blind innocence against all odds. If I were to take it from her—possibly leave her with child—and then fail in this madness . . . and die, what would become of her? I could not justify taking such a chance merely to satisfy my urges. I am no fool, sir. What we attempt is outright madness. The odds are hardly in our favor."

"Ahhhh," the healer warbled, nodding. "Commendable, young ram. But she is hardly your social equal. That matters not to you?"

"Not in the slightest," Robert said without hesitation, well aware that the crafty old healer was baiting him, searching his soul. "If she will have me, I am indeed beneath *her.* And, who is there to challenge me? My mother? She puts no such class distinctions in her prayers that I wed and give her grandchildren to coddle. It wouldn't matter if she did. It shan't be the first time Cupid has meddled with the class distinctions of noble Scots, herself included. That uncanny fellow's arrows go where they are sent. Mother would be the first to raise a loud huzzah to that, bigod! She has taken one beneath her station—despite the land and title awarded him—as consort, intending eventually to marry, and probably already has by now if I am any judge."

"You are learning," the healer returned.

"How long a time before Violette will be fit for travel?" Robert asked him. "Once we free Uncle Aengus, it will not be safe for us to tarry in these parts."

"That depends largely upon the girl herself, but I would venture an educated guess at a sennight if fortune smiles upon us—a fortnight . . . if not."

"We cannot stay here that long, can we," Robert said, answering his own question.

"Let's not speculate so early," the healer hedged. "We have enough to occupy us with the dilemma at hand without borrowing woes. Let the matter of our fair Violette lie awhile. Your uncle needs our total concentration here now."

"You are right, of course," Robert said. "I don't even know where to find him in that godforsaken labyrinth of death."

"Ahhh, but I *do*," said Nostradamus.

"You know?"

"You didn't think I'd leave that critical stone unturned, did you? I took the liberty of a pre-tour visit to just that purpose. Though I had to feign sympathy with the admiral's cause, and deal with much that was irrelevant, it wasn't such a difficult task. Garboneaux was quite accommodating. The dull-witted old maltworm was only too eager to point out the good monk's cell to me, not all that far from the cell which you had occupied, so he told me with not a little satisfaction. Considering that Montaigne had him so severely chastised for your entombment, he was only too anxious to gloat over your kin's incarceration."

"The whoreson!"

They had nearly reached the jail, and Nostradamus took his measure. "Look sharp now, and stay close beside me," he charged. "There is just one thing . . . your posture worries me."

"My *posture*, sir?" Robert said, puzzled.

"You are by far too stalwart a figure—too tall—too broad and muscular of shoulder for a monk, and too . . . noble. If you could hunch a bit—feign a limp . . . something. It needs humility, your bearing."

"I will try," Robert consented, "but I am charged for battle, and a warrior does not engage the enemy with humility."

"This one will."

Robert breathed a nasal sigh. "I will feel a good deal more at ease once you have left me and become yourself again," he admitted. "I do not want you to come to harm at my hands here. This is not your battle."

"But it is my victory. Be still now! And correct that posture. Our moment is upon us."

And indeed it was, for the infamous jail loomed before them, and Robert shuddered in spite of himself at the sight of it.

"The king's escort," Nostradamus whispered, pointing as they neared the mounted guards and runners stationed outside the royal sedan. "They have arrived. Pray that Garboneaux, in his new circumstance as head sentry, is occupied afield of the course we must travel, as jailer he would not be. Come."

Dismounting, they tethered their horses at a discrete distance from the royal entourage, though close enough to affect a hasty departure if needs must. That accomplished, they shuffled past the troops and guards and gendarmes waiting beside the portal, and entered in quite anonymously in their beaser-colored homespun. To their relief, it was the captain of the guard who met them and barred their way. Garboneaux was nowhere in sight.

"Hold there!" he barked, a hulking giant of a man standing in their path. "State your business here."

"Good captain," Nostradamus said, with disguised voice. "We are come to minister, and pray for the soul of our brother, Aengus—to plead and beg the Lord's forgiveness for his crime. We will not tarry long. Would you be so kind as to direct us?"

"The monk from St. Michael's Mount?" said the jailer.

Nostradamus nodded. "Forgive us our handkerchiefs, but . . . tell me, is the stench in here always so . . . arresting? How do you bear it?"

The captain laughed. "A body gets used to it," he said.

"Well, I fear that these bodies shall not," the healer groaned. "If you would but point out our direction, we will have our duty done, and be away, lest you, er . . . relish mopping up our bile?"

"Below," the captain growled with a shrug, jerking his helmed head in that general direction. "The guards at the bottom of the stairs will direct you. Let them clean up your vomit. Hah! The stink is worse below. Beware—and be *quick*. There's no time for your kind t'day. The admiral is abroad. Best not let him catch you. He's not too fond of papists."

Nostradamus affected a bow, and drew a small earthenware crock from the folds of his robe. "A token for your trouble," he said silkily, handing it over. "Fine wine from our vineyards in the south. To your good health, sir! It has been blessed."

The captain snatched the crock with a grunt, and with no more words wasted upon him, they hurried below.

"Come," Nostradamus whispered. "I know the way. The guards at the bottom of the stairs in his sector occupy a recessed alcove. There are five of them—a rowdy lot, but our offering should subdue them."

Robert followed his lead, a cautious hand straying to his waist for the comforting feel of the sword concealed beneath his robe. They passed no one in the cold, dank passageways, and heard no sound but the distant wails of the inmates, and now and then a spurt of raucous laughter echoing from the guards as they approached them below.

Reliving his all too recent entombment in that quadrant, Robert shuddered afresh. He longed to fling all the doors wide, that pitiful were the wretched cries of despair that had come to life so often in his memory. They were real again now, his uncle's among them, and with that to drive him, they reached the lower regions in record speed.

Nostradamus genuflected breathlessly before the guards come quickly to surround them. The eldest of the group swaggered close and stooped over, like a hovering vulture.

"And where do you think you're going?" he barked. "Who let you in here, eh? Well? Speak up, speak up, what do you want here?"

"Your good captain kindly granted us permission to minister to our brother, Aengus. A brief moment is all we ask."

"Indeed," the guard jeered. "Well, *I* am captain here below, and good Brother Aengus ain't receiving today. Be gone, holy ones. There is no soul in here worth saving, lest you fancy a go at ours."

The others joined in a burst of rowdy laughter, and Robert stiffened, but the crafty old healer showed no signs of intimidation.

"We have no doubt that you are all devout and wise," he flattered, "but, alas, our brother is not so blessed. We come to beg him mend his ways, and urge him—"

"Oh, he has been 'urged,'" the captain interrupted. "We urged him a'plenty, didn't we, now?" he said to his men, extracting yet another outburst of revelry.

Again, Robert's posture clenched, and Nostradamus went on quickly. "But, my good man, you do not let me finish," he said. "We commend you for your attempt, of course, but it is our duty, this pilgrimage." Producing a second crock of wine from his robe, he thrust it toward the guard. "Blessed wine, for you and your men," he said.

"Eh?" the captain snarled, constricting stony eyes. "What's this, then, a bribe?"

"No, no," said the healer, his voice sounding vexed, ". . . a token of our gratitude for your indulgence, nothing more."

"Ummm," the captain grunted, thinking on it, before he snatched it from the healer's hands and walked away.

The others came closer then, reaching toward it eagerly, and the captain held it high.

Nostradamus gave a dramatic gasp. "You would accept God's blessings from His messengers with no kindness rendered? *Kyrie eleison!*" he breathed, crossing himself.

The captain stopped in his tracks, slapping his comrade's hands away from the crock in his grip. "All right, all right, stop your puling! Five minutes—no more." Turning to the nearest man, he charged, "Jacques, you take them."

The reluctant appointee shuffled forward, hurrying them along the passageway, close eyes upon the wine crock being passed behind. When they reached the cell, and the man had flung the door wide, Nostradamus concealed his beard behind his handkerchief, and looked him squarely in the eyes with a burning stare that possessed the power to hypnotize, so thought Robert, or at the very least, the power to disarm.

"You had best get back before they drain that crock to the dregs," the crafty healer said levelly. "It would be a pity if you missed your share. I have no other to lend you. Do not trouble over the lock. What harm can we two helpless holy men do?"

"I'm supposed to lock it after you," the man protested.

"Yes, yes, I know," the healer said velvet-voiced, "but there is no need. Where could we go? There is no way out but back the way we came right past your station. By the time you lock us in the wine will be gone when you rejoin your friends, for the gluttons they are. Go and have your portion, and collect us in five minutes' time. Have no fear, my son. We do only God's work here."

The guard, grumbling in agreement, ran back the way they had come, and they plunged into the narrow, filthy cell and groped in the darkness for Aengus.

A feeble moan directed them at last, and while Nostradamus struggled out of his habit, Robert gathered his uncle in strong arms. What little light seeped through the small, barred aperture in the door showed the young laird clearly enough to see that Aengus had been severely beaten, and he crushed him close.

"Ahhh, Uncle Aengus, God forgive me," he sobbed.

"R-Robert?" his uncle moaned.

"*Shhh*, be still! We're going to get you out of here."

"Are you mad?" Aengus murmured. "I have prayed all this while that by now you would be safe and away. It is too late to help me here. Go quickly, before they find you out. Go, Robert! I will not suffer you to die on my account."

"Neither will I suffer you in such a place on mine," Robert gritted through clenched teeth. "Doctor Nostradamus and I have formed a plan. You will be out of here in minutes, if you will hold your peace and do as I command you."

"D-Doctor Nostradamus . . . *here?*"

"Yes, now let me help you into this," he charged, snatching the habit the healer thrust toward him, "and I shall introduce you."

"There is no time for amenities now," said the healer, taking cautious steps toward the door. "Go! Hurry, young ram. That guard will soon return."

Nostradamus disappeared then, but Robert scarcely noticed, struggling to help his uncle don the habit. The old monk could scarcely stand, and dressing him was clumsy in the darkness.

"No," Aengus moaned, arresting the frantic hands wrestling with the awkward homespun garment. "It is too late, Robert. There is no use. Save yourself. I . . . cannot. I am too weak."

"You are a Haddock," Robert seethed. "Call your strength from that. Nary a one of my mother's kin ever backed down from a fight, while breath was in his body. That blood flows in your veins, too. Now, come! I will support you, but you must help me. We have risked much in coming, and I will not leave this place without you." He hauled him to his full height. "Lean on me, and cover your face with the handkerchief," he said. "I will pretend that you have taken sick. The stench in here makes such a thing believable, bigod. Moan if you must, but do not speak aloud. Doctor Nostradamus is close by. He will help us to safety."

"You should be safe at home in Scotland. That dream made all of this worthwhile. We are dead men here now, you and I. I am not able, I tell you!"

"You *are*," Robert insisted. Stooping, he plumped up a mound of straw, and threw the fouled Bastille blanket over it. "Quickly! The guard comes," he warned. "We cannot let him enter in here now."

Supporting him in strong arms, Robert led him outside and closed the cell door behind them just as the guard approached. But, to Robert's horror, it was not Jacques whose quick step echoed so angrily along the passageway. It was Garboneaux, and Nostradamus was nowhere in sight.

"God's beard!" Robert muttered. "Be still, Uncle Aengus, and follow my lead. This jailer knows me well. There may be trouble here."

In the flickering torchlight set in motion by the jailer's hasty stride, Robert read the palpable anger in him, lowered his head in an attempt to escape without detection, and began speaking to his uncle, moaning now in earnest.

"Come along," he soothed. "I knew the strain would be too much for you, and it was all for naught. He will not repent, that one. We waste our pains, and our prayers upon him."

"All right, hold there! Who in the hell are you, and how did you get down here?" the sentry spat. Speak up! My guards all lie cup-shotten—besotted to the gills. Was it you, then, who brought that accursed wine? Answer me!"

"Your good captain permitted us," Robert said steadily, ignoring the issue of the wine. "We thought to persuade our brother of his folly for his soul's sake, but, of course, it was no use, and now my colleague is stricken. Forgive me, but I must get him to cleaner air."

"Must you now," said Garboneaux, looming over them. All at once he broke the pose. In the blink of an eye, he reached out and threw back the young laird's cowl. He gasped. "God's body! *You!*"

Robert shoved his uncle clear and drew his sword. "What? You did not expect me?" he responded. "You are more of a fool than I thought, Garboneaux."

Loosing a string of passionate curses, the sentry drew his own weapon and lunged, but Robert quickly sidestepped the thrust, and cold steel sparked in the shadowy passageway as their swords struck hard.

Robert cast a quick sidelong glance toward Aengus, slumped against the fouled wall slimed with mold. He was watching the exchange with anxious eyes, but there was no time to monitor him then. The monk's robe was a hindrance to his form. Awkward in it, his timing was off, and the sentry quickly got the better of him, rending the blade from his hand with a mighty, well-executed blow. It came to ground close to Aengus, and as Robert lunged to retrieve it, Garboneaux lunged also, with aim to run him through.

Sinking to the floor, the old cleric snatched up the sword and tossed it.

"Robert! Behind you!" he cried in time, for the young Scot caught the weapon and rolled over, impaling the sentry on the outstretched blade as he dove after him.

The combatants froze motionless. From somewhere on the peripheral fringes of that suspended moment, Robert heard Garboneaux's weapon strike stone as it dropped to the floor, and he watched while the sentry's burly hands gripped the blade embedded in his belly.

"Christ have mercy!" Aengus breathed, crossing himself.

Robert gave the sword in his hands one final thrust that pitched the sentry over sideways. With one mighty shove, he scrambled out from underneath the hulking giant, who lay dead on the filth-encrusted floor, and scrambled to his feet.

Taking back his sword, Robert quickly wiped it clean on Garboneaux's tunic, then sheathed the weapon out of sight again beneath his robe. Straightening up, he flexed his shoulder, for he'd taxed the wound in the foray, then dragging the sentry's bloodied corpse inside his uncle's cell, he shut the door upon it. Grabbing the extra sword, he gave it to his uncle, who was slumped against the wall, and turned him down the passageway.

"Conceal it," he charged. "We may have need of it before 'tis done, and we cannot leave it here. Lean on me. We will escape this pit of living death here yet."

Aengus made no reply, and when they reached the guards' station, they found them quite drunk and docile, and passed them by with hardly any notice.

"It will be some time before these find Garboneaux," Robert whispered. "Now all that remains is to elude the king, and Coligny."

"You are your father's son," Aengus murmured, "and to think that I envisioned you embracing *my* vocation."

In spite of himself, Robert laughed. "Do not bestow all the laurels upon me," he said. "The plan was hatched by Doctor Nostradamus. Be still now as we climb. I am hearing voices. Pray that the good doctor's is among them. I have no qualms over ending Coligny's days, but I have a liking for the boy king, and I do not want to spill his blood, though I will if needs must, to see you freed."

The voices came clearer, and as they rounded the angled wall that led to the upper level, they pulled up short before the admiral, the angular-featured, raisin-eyed astrologer Ruggiero, splendidly robed and trumpeting officiously, and the boy king himself. A string of guards had fanned out on the stairs behind, and Aengus moaned and sagged in Robert's arms, scarcely conscious as the formidable party approached.

"What's this?" Coligny erupted, pulling up short.

"Only two humble monks come to minister to the sick and dying," Robert said, bowing to the king, his voice driven up an octave, and muffled behind the handkerchief. "My brother here has taken sick from the stench below. I am in haste to see him into the fresh air before he vomits, my Lord Admiral."

"You know me?" Coligny blurted.

"All France knows the most esteemed Admiral," Robert flattered. "Would that the circumstances were less critical so that we might pay our respects properly. I beg you, please forgive us . . ."

While Coligny pondered that, Ruggiero craned his neck for a clearer view. The king ventured closer, studying Robert beneath the deep cowl that hid his face from the others in that dark place. But it could not hide it so completely from the boy at his vantage looking up. Their eyes locked, and in that terrible instant the Scot knew that, even though the young king hadn't seen his face without the helm that day in the maze, the boy had seen it now, and made the connection.

"I think I know this man," said the king. "I do not recall his name, but, yes, we met at court, this . . . monk and I. We strolled in the palace garden."

Robert swallowed hard. There was nothing in the boy king's voice to assure safety, though he plumbed for it, and Coligny's scrutiny riddled him as well now, clearly evaluating yet another rival vying for the boy king's support.

Robert took the gamble. "Yes, Your Majesty," he said, steadily, offering another bow. "We are acquainted."

The king continued to stare. There was no mistaking the shiver in that stare. Was he boy or monarch today? And which one would spare him? Young Charles studied him thoroughly. It was the longest moment Robert had ever suffered, and then he realized *the boy knew*. The king glanced beyond toward the lower regions thoughtfully. It was just a fleeting glance, though the Scot read it well the instant the boy's eyes fastened upon Aengus.

"Well?" barked the admiral. He shifted his weight and posed, the picture of impatience, arms folded across his chest. "Are these monks acceptable, Your Majesty?" he urged. "We do not relish papist vomit upon our footwear."

"Oh, quite," said the king. Taking out his own handkerchief, he passed it beneath his angular nose. "I doubt that I can bear that stench below, either," he choked.

"But, Your Majesty!"

"Enough, Coligny!" the king decreed. "I have seen all I need to see here. You've made your point. You have valid cause for indignation. I needn't lose my last meal to satisfy you. Mama shan't be pleased if I do. She was not given over to my coming so soon after my chill. And you are quite right. She shan't thank you for it if I am toted home, with my new hose and doublet painted with bile. Come! Let us help these two away. That poor soul there is barely conscious."

The admiral nodded briskly at that, and several guards came forward.

"Thank you, but no. I can manage this," Robert insisted. "It would be best that you do not come in too close contact. I am sure it's nothing, but with so much plague about, I think it wise to err on the side of caution and not jeopardize yourselves . . . or our good king. I have been stricken and recovered. There is no danger in my laying hold of him. If you would but let us pass, I would seek a physician before we return to our abbey."

Ruggiero backpedaled so quickly he nearly lost his footing. "Your Majesty, my Lord Admiral, I beg you come away!" he wheezed, shielding his nose and mouth with a gaudily beringed hand. "This does not bode well here."

The soldiers fanned out wide then, scattering, but as the Scot eased his uncle by them, the king's voice rose above their anxious murmuring.

"We spoke that day of loyalty and wisdom, as I recall?" he said to Robert as they came abreast of him.

"Yes, Your Majesty, we did."

"And I was touched that you imparted both to me."

"I am glad, Your Majesty."

"Do you recall our parting words that day, good monk?"

"I think I do, Your Majesty."

"Ahhh, good. I gave you food for thought on that occasion. We had so fine a . . . theological discussion it would have disappointed me if you had forgotten. I do so hate to waste my breath. Perhaps one day we might find time to talk again."

"I would like that, Your Majesty."

"Good!" said the king. "Safe . . . *home*, then?"

"Yes, Your Majesty," Robert murmured, reading his message well, "my eternal praise and gratitude, as always."

"Ahhh, look!" the king rejoiced, turning toward the stairs that led to the upper regions. "Here is Doctor Nostradamus now," he cried, beckoning. "Good doctor, come! I fear we have a patient for you."

Winded, the old physician lumbered down the stairs to meet them. "Brother Raphael, Brother Andre? Is that you, there? Why, bless my soul, it is! What do you here?"

"A mission of mercy," said Robert. "Brother . . . Andre here has been overcome, I fear, and I myself am on the verge. The stench, sir, it overwhelms us. I'm sure that is all it is."

"You know these also, Doctor?" the admiral said from behind knit brows.

"Oh, yes, they are old friends, my Lord Admiral. If it please you, stand aside. I shall get them out from underfoot and attend to them." He took firm hold of Aengus. "Come, Andre," he said, "let us hope there is no contagion. Fresh air is my first prescription. Then we shall see, eh? Let me help you." Leading them, the sly old seer turned. "If I am excused, of course," he said to Coligny. "I have gathered enough evidence to support you in your cause, sir—more than enough."

"Yes, yes, we are done here," Coligny growled, waving him off with a hand gesture, "but first I seek Garboneaux. I would have a word with him before we go. He courts another demotion. There's not a sober guard above this level. Excuse me. I go below."

Robert stiffened, and the healer responded. "Oh, he is not below," he said smoothly. "I passed him above just now on my way down, traveling westward in a dreadful snit. Why, he all but threw me down, the clod." Then over his shoulder to the king, he said, "You had best be away, Your Majesty. That is a foul, unhealthy stench coming from the lower regions. Why, *I* won't even chance it. There is much sickness in it, and you are just now recovering. You are courting relapse, and your good mother will never forgive any one of us should you come down here over something so plebeian as reprimanding a common sentry."

The boy king nodded in agreement, and sealed the decision to leave with a hand gesture. The admiral growled something incoherent, moved aside to let Nostradamus pass, and turned back again in obedience to the king's command. Charles and his entire entourage followed, and Nostradamus quickened his step, leading Robert and Aengus well out of earshot.

"Is he dead?" the healer whispered, leaning close to Robert's ear.

The Scot nodded in reply.

"Christ have mercy!"

"So will Uncle Aengus be if we do not tend him quickly. He has been brutalized unmercifully."

"Take ease, take ease, young ram, all goes well."

"*Too* well," Robert gritted. "The king knows. He recognized me."

"You are certain?"

"Oh, yes," Robert muttered.

"And he . . . did not betray you?"

"No, not yet. But how long is my reprieve?"

"It only need be long enough to get you out of here alive. That, it seems, is done. Thank God for it, and *hurry*! I do believe you're right. It goes too well, indeed. I like it not."

Fifteen

$\mathcal{D}$espite the healer's apprehensions, no one hindered their departure from the jail. It was managed so flawlessly, in fact, that all three marveled. They dared not return to the ruins by the same route they had traveled coming. Instead, Nostradamus led them eastward, toward his lodgings, though they did not enter there. Losing themselves amid the crowded streets, they slipped away unnoticed toward the Huguenot village, and doubled back southward through the dense, black forest. It was a lengthier journey to the ruins from that distance, and made even longer because Robert's horse bore a double weight. Nightfall was upon them before they reached the southern wood that crept up to the foot of the knoll where Nostradamus made a a quick evaluation of Aengus's condition and imparted a draught for pain after promising Robert that the scourging was not fatal.

With that news to ease him, all Robert thought about was Violette, alone in the secret chamber below the smokehouse. Surely she would be awake by now, and frightened. Once they reached the foot of the knoll and tethered their mounts in the copse, he left his uncle for the doctor to manage, and hurried on ahead, bounding over the rut-scarred incline. The others were still struggling with the steep grade, when he opened the slab and hurried below, calling her name. But he leaped down only to stand frozen in horror. In the glow of the candle that had almost burned down, the room yawned empty before him. Violette was gone.

Screaming her name at the top of his voice, Robert scanned the room, praying that she would materialize before him, but naught save echoes answered, though his shouts brought the healer, who settled Aengus on the smokehouse floor above and hurried down the coarsely hewn chamber stairs, his velvet robe spread wide.

"She is gone!" Robert cried. "How? How could she be? Where? *She is blind!*"

"Take ease, take ease," Nostradamus snapped, out of breath from his steep descent. "Raving will serve naught." He glanced around the room, his silver eyes sparkling in the candlelight. "She is not long gone I'm thinking," he observed, "and there seems to be no sign of a struggle."

"No," Robert agreed, "but she could not have moved that stone herself. She would have barely had the strength for such a feat in good health, let alone drained weak from plague."

"She was probably still unconscious when they took her," the healer opined. His sharp gaze scrutinized the room. Something shiny caught his eye near the pallet in the straw, and he stooped and snatched it up, studying it beside the candle flame.

"What have you got there?" Robert said, coming closer. "What is it?"

"A silver crucifix," said Nostradamus, exhibiting it. "This is not one that I issued you with your disguise."

"No," Robert responded. "What does it mean?"

"A calling card," the healer answered, "left here deliberately, no doubt. You are invited to retrieve her. They wanted you to find this. That's why they left the candle burning."

"The cardinal?"

Nostradamus nodded. "I would expect so," he said. "You must have been seen coming here with the girl. No doubt we were seen leaving today as well."

"She told me she heard something outside Montaigne's château. I should have trusted her hearing. Then here . . . I told you I thought I saw someone by the edge of the wood below." He awarded his forehead a scathing blow with the heel of his open palm. "Of course! They were the cardinal's spies. That is why they didn't take us into custody."

"The rest is fairly obvious."

"Not to me," Robert blurted. "Where has he got her? The Bastille?"

Nostradamus shook his head. "No," he said. "I thought it odd that he did not put in an appearance there today, even though he was not scheduled to do so. That sanctimonious old fox would scarcely let so juicy an opportunity escape him . . . unless it served his purpose somehow. He has a talent for intercepting the king whenever Coligny is involved. There is a jealous animosity between those two."

"Where, then? Where has he taken her?"

"To Notre Dame, I have no doubt, and you are expected."

"I will not disappoint him," Robert snarled. Stripping off the monk's robe, he darted toward the stairs.

"Hold there!" the healer thundered, stopping him midstep. "That is not the way. You cannot march on Notre Dame. You will be caught, and sent to the Bastille before you even reach the threshold. Have you forgotten what we have just left behind? By now, it is a safe assumption that Garboneaux's body has been found. It is also a safe assumption that the gendarmes will be here directly. We must get away from here—and quickly—to the forest. I will tend your uncle, and we will form a strategy for this misadventure. It needs careful planning."

"But Violette! She will be terrified. She is not yet recovered. They will kill her!"

"No," Nostradamus refuted. "She will come to no harm. He will not even breathe a word to the authorities that he has her—not yet. The cardinal wants *you*, young ram. It is you who have bested and offended him. She is his insurance that you will come. He waits, expecting you to do exactly what you are set to do here—fall right into his trap. You must not. You *cannot*, else you will both be lost."

"We are already," Robert groaned.

"No, this can be managed, but I can no longer help you now, save to give counsel. After our little farce today, my usefulness is ended here. I am old. I have foreseen my death, and it is not far off. I would spend what few scant years remain in my family's company at home in Salon. God has much yet for me to do before I join him. He would not have given me the sight if I were not to pass on what I have seen to others. There is a grave lesson in it. It is best now that we part, for your own sake as well as mine."

"Then I am alone here," Robert realized.

"No," said Nostradamus. "You are not alone, Robert of Paxton. One who I have counseled has not heeded my advice . . . not totally at any rate, and that, if you have paid close attention to my counsel now, might just save you."

They reached the copse below not a minute too soon. They had scarcely taken cover amid the trees, when the summit above was lit as bright as midday from the storm of torchbearing troops that flooded the castle ruins. Like so many ants, they scurried helter-skelter, leaving no crevice unscrutinized, igniting that which would burn as if, not having found their quarry, they would punish the refuse itself for spite.

The parched straw that carpeted the secret chamber was dry tinder, and great shafts of flame shot up through the smokehouse. Writhing columns of blood-red flames climbed up the castle's wounded walls. Tall clouds of sparkembroidered smoke belched from the castle's bowels and drifted low over the forest, where the three crouched watching. But the troops were long gone then. They had disappeared into the darkness behind the holocaust.

"Which way will the flames turn you this time?" Nostradamus mused.

Robert's eyes flashed toward him. "They didn't even seek us here," he marveled. "Why?"

"They would not search a weald so vast as this in darkness. They are but a handful, not nearly enough in number to comb the forest by night. There are too many places for you to elude them, and they are a lazy, self-serving lot. No doubt the cardinal has told them where to find you. Unwittingly, they have underscored his message, and at the same time made it impossible for you to return here. That is all this is about."

"They will return," Robert said. This was definitely not the type of warfare waged in Scotland. He did not understand this devious French battle mentality. Things were much simpler at home, where battle was joined in the open, and fought to the death hand-to-hand in plain sight.

"Anything is possible," Nostradamus replied, "and we must, of course, be prepared for all possibilities. I have tended your uncle. He sleeps now, and will for some time."

"How serious is it?"

"He will recover. The beatings were severe, and he is not a young man, but with rest and care—"

"How can I provide rest and care for him here now?" Robert interrupted.

"You cannot," the healer said succinctly.

"He must leave France!" the laird ranted.

"I know, young ram, but first he must be fit to leave France."

"You have a plan," Robert said, answering his own question.

The old healer nodded. "I will see him safely to Montaigne's château, and—"

"That is no use," Robert cut in. "His servant turned us away. He will not admit him. Even if he did, he wouldn't be safe there. Who is to say that the steward wasn't the one who betrayed us?"

"You are too impetuous," the healer scolded. "You do not let me finish. Not here in Paris. In Bordeaux."

"Bordeaux?"

Again the healer nodded. "I told you I will go south to home now. On my way, I shall deliver your uncle to the magistrate myself."

"I am not familiar with your land, 'tis true," said Robert, "but I have seen maps and Bordeaux is quite a distance from Salon, I think."

"I know," the healer replied. "Aside from plotting this new escapade of yours, it is the last service I can render you."

"I am in your debt for life, sir—"

"—which will not be a lengthy span of time if you do not step cautiously here now, and heed me," Nostradamus added.

"I will do as you say," Robert conceded.

"Good. These ruins are no longer safe. The forest must shelter you now, until this is accomplished."

"That is the least of my worries. How do I liberate Violette?"

The crafty old seer smiled and cocked his head. "You must first find her," he said. "I must return now to the city. I will go to the king, for I need his sanction to depart. I will discern how closely he is aligned in your . . . situation. I must render my findings at the Bastille in any case. If I can learn her whereabouts, it will be all the easier. If I cannot . . . well, we will deal with that if it comes to pass."

"You cannot go to the king! They will arrest you for complicity."

"No, no, I am quite beyond reproach, young ram. I can easily profess that you duped me as you did the rest."

"No one will believe that, especially if our comings and goings have been monitored."

Again, the old healer smiled. "You do not understand," he said. "I am needed here—France needs me. The Queen

Mother knows it, and champions me because of it. I have her favor. Given that, they know it will be expedient for them to believe me, should I say black is white, and white is purple. Besides, the king himself recognized you. If he holds *his* position, how dare they question me?"

"No man is indispensable here now," Robert said. "The king said that to me once, also."

"Do you trust me, Robert of Paxton?"

"Yes, I trust you, but I do not trust them—any of them."

"That, of course, is wise. But you can trust this—no harm will come to me unless God wills it. I shall glean what news I can of the girl, and conclude my business. Remain here in the forest. When the sun sets on the morrow, I will return with my carriage. It is not my preferred mode of travel, that awkward, rickety old wooden box on wheels. Such conveyances will not always be so inhospitable. Alas, I shall not live to see that come to pass. I much prefer my mule for travel. My servant will have to tie him on behind. Then I will counsel you toward your course, and see your uncle safely to Montaigne."

"And . . . if you do not return?"

"But I must, mustn't I?" the seer replied. "And I shall, else all this has been for naught." He laughed, and said, "Don't look so wretched. Your course is far from run. Sleep, and tend to Aengus. Only one thing in all this muddle is certain— you will need all the strength you can muster for what now lies before you."

It was well past the noon hour the next day before the healer had his audience with the king. It was a rather warm day, with cloudless skies, and softly sighing breezes, more like spring than autumn. Eager for the meeting, and knowing that a private interview was called for, the healer suggested a stroll in the palace garden. The king walked with him in the open among the sculptured yews. Well out of range of jealous ears, the young monarch spoke frankly, his voice mature for one so young. Nostradamus had always admired this in the boy, and credited it to the fact that he spent much of his time in the company of intellectual adults, rather than children his own age. For all that the boy had the makings of a proper hypochondriac, and was easily led. He also had the makings of a monarch in him. But the healer had seen that outcome as well, and walking with the still innocent boy then, he saw again the bloodbath to come, and shuddered in spite of himself, for he knew that he would not be there to prevent it.

"I am glad to have this chance to speak with you privately before you leave the city," the king said. "Tell me . . . our bold Scot, is he safe?"

Nostradamus studied him. It would not do to be hasty. "Would that please you, Your Majesty?" he probed at last.

"I like that fellow," the boy confided. "I did from our first encounter."

"I have heard it said that he greatly admires you as well," said Nostradamus.

"And where would you have heard something such as that?" he queried.

"From a reliable source, Your Majesty."

"He is well, then?"

Nostradamus nodded.

"Come, come, Doctor! Surely you are aware that I recognized him yesterday?" the boy snapped. "If I was going to see him clapped in irons that would have been the time to do it. I know that he liberated that uncle of his, and I know that he killed the fool Garboneaux in the process. I should imagine that I have proven my loyalty well enough in abetting his escape. I even tried to warn him to leave France now as best I could under the circumstances."

Nostradamus smiled. "Surely the admiral knows that?" he queried.

"Nothing of the kind," said the king, "though he can think whatever he likes, of course, and doubtless does, but should I say that monk was Jesus Christ Himself, *I am the king*! How dare he—how dare *anyone*—question me?"

"I am . . . grateful, Your Majesty."

"And I am worried," the king admitted. "All factions seek the Scot. I have done everything I can do. Is he safe and away? Has he returned to Scotland? They cannot touch him there."

"There is a slight . . . problem, Your Majesty. I am in hopes that you might be able to alleviate it."

"If I can. Tell it me."

"I do have your allegiance?" the healer hedged.

The boy king stopped in his tracks and stared, incredulous. "Has your hearing become impaired, then? If you did not, he never would have left the Bastille alive yesterday."

Nostradamus nodded. "Forgive me, I had to be certain," he said humbly. "There is a young blind girl, a flower vendor, whom he seeks to wed and take to Scotland with him. He was attempting to escape the country with her, when he had news of Brother Aengus's arrest. That turned him 'round, and he set out with the girl to liberate him. She came down with a mild case of plague en route. Mild, because I prepared them for it with my lozenges, which she foolishly discarded. I doctored her, and she has passed the crisis, but while our Scot left her unattended yesterday to free the monk, someone stole her from their hiding place."

"And you would know who took her, and her whereabouts," the king surmised.

"If you have knowledge, and would share it, I would be eternally grateful, Your Majesty."

"She is detained at Notre Dame Cathedral," said the king. "The cardinal and the Guises's loyals took her there. I wondered what the urgency was all about—and the secrecy over a mere street urchin. Now it becomes clear. The cardinal would claim the Scot's head as a personal trophy. The fellow's made a fool of him. And that is simply not allowed. He obviously means to see our friend pay the penalty."

"I assumed such was the case. I needed to be certain."

"Surely, he cannot mean to lay siege to Notre Dame?" the king asked.

"Hardly 'lay siege,' but, yes, he does mean to retrieve her. He will not leave France without the girl."

"But he *must.* He is one man alone. He has no hope against the cardinal and his allies—against the Guise machine, for it is that well-oiled, and at the ready."

"And . . . if he does as you urge, what will happen to the girl then?"

"She will be arrested, of course, for complicity," the king pronounced. "And they will shut her up in that prison and forget her, or put her to death."

"What if the powers that be . . . the gendarmes take her from the cathedral now?"

"They cannot," said the king. "So long as she is under the protection of Notre Dame, she has sanctuary. No legal means can touch her. When she no longer serves the cardinal's purpose, he will, of course, remand her to the authorities. It is only a matter of time."

"I see. He must move quickly, then."

The boy king gave a start. "You're serious!" he cried. "He actually means to stage another daring rescue!"

"He means to see that no guiltless man suffers for the crimes of which he is accused."

"He will be killed."

"Possibly."

"He is mad!"

"He is a Scot."

"That's said it, bigod!" the king shouted. "Are they all mad, our Scottish cousins?"

"They are all, for the most part, honorable, something

that is often accompanied by a jot of madness. The times dictate it, Your Majesty."

The boy king breathed a ragged sigh. "I will, of course, keep your confidence, but I cannot help you in this. Sanctuary of the Church cannot be violated. Not even by the king himself without extreme circumstances. There are no such circumstances here, and you well know the extent of my actual power. My mother—"

"Yes, yes, I know," Nostradamus interrupted. "I did by no means expect you to abet me. I sought only information that might lead us to the girl."

"Hah!" the king cried. "I wonder if our esteemed cardinal would have been so quick to lay hands upon her, were he aware that she emerged so recently from the pestilence. Half the clergy in Paris will be down with the pox here now, no doubt. There is almost justice in it that, at least, as Coligny will view it. But, of course, you seek explicit information. To my knowledge, she is held below the nave, in the lower regions. Guards are posted at all the portals. No doubt many are disguised. Specifics will not help you. It is impossible— suicide."

"Perhaps," said the healer, "but hasn't all of France gone suicidal here of late?"

"But *this*," the king breathed.

"Forgive me," Nostradamus interrupted. "The hour grows late. I regret that I can tarry here no longer. I thank you for your compassion and honesty. Both qualities are rare jewels that offset any sovereign. Wear them always, Your Majesty. I doubt that France is worthy of you, or that she will even show her true appreciation. You are a remarkable boy. You will be a . . . remembered king. If you would do as I have told him, forget all outward influence, and learn to see with your spirit, history will reward you. May God attend you, Your Majesty."

"And you likewise," the king returned. "Tell the Scot . . ."

"Yes, Your Majesty?" Nostradamus prompted, through the boy's hesitation.

"Tell him that I pray we meet again one day, when times are saner."

"I will convey your message," the healer promised, bowing, "but I fear such times will never be. Insanity is king of all the earth, 'til God Himself descends again, and walks upon it."

True to his word, Nostradamus's carriage penetrated the wood just after the sun disappeared. It did indeed resemble a box on wheels, lumbering wooden wheels, at that, somewhat out of round for warping and disuse. It boasted open holes for doors, and was being pulled by two heavy horses, driven by the healer's mute servant. The man saw Aengus settled safely inside the seat facing forward, which had been prepared with a padding of *dagswain*, and blankets of fustian wool for his comfort. There he would remain out of sight, where the crude wooden seat itself could be lowered over him and sat upon if needs must, should they be stopped. The servant showed Aengus how to bring the seat down and secure it from below if necessary. Carriages were not unknown, but few save royalty and the very rich possessed them. Consequently, they were a curiosity, attracting the notice of peasant and gendarme alike, and oftentimes a following. The hollow seats had served Nostradamus in the past as a means of transporting forbidden books and documents and recipes for his medicines, slipping them past the watchful eyes of the Inquisitor's men undetected. Now, they held a far more precious cargo. The healer guided Robert toward the gurgling stream to walk awhile before departing.

"The king will keep your confidence," he told him. "He wishes you well, and prays you meet again under less . . . severe circumstances."

"God save him," Robert murmured.

"As I suspected, Charles de Guise has conveyed Violette to Notre Dame. It is a trap. Guards man the portals, and she is safe there until you are in custody. Then, she, too, will suffer under all factions' wrath. She is expendable. She has no ties."

"Where have they got her in that place?"

"She is confined to the lower regions."

"If I go by night . . . ?"

The healer shook his head. "Have you seen Notre Dame?" he queried.

"No, but—"

"It crouches on Île de la Cité, an island in the very heart of the Seine. It is immense, young ram. It can easily hold thirteen thousand persons. It is well staffed. You cannot hope to approach it unseen. It is quite impossible. And the cardinal knows it."

"What do I do, then?" Robert urged.

"There is one way that you can enter, in full view of the cardinal himself if needs must be, without detection."

"And that is?"

"Dead."

"*Dead?*"

"It is arranged," Nostradamus replied. "The plan will get you in, but getting you out again is quite another matter. That cannot be plotted. There are too many incalculable aspects. You will be on your own resources in that, I'm afraid."

"Just get me in. I will attend to the rest. Go on, Doctor Nostradamus, let me hear this."

"At midnight, make your way to the vendors' quarter. Just south of the bridge, a narrow lane forks southward. Number twelve is the house you seek. It bears a broken gargoyle over the portal. Knock once and the door will open to you."

"You went to the vendors?" Robert asked, his voice edged with objection.

"There was no other choice."

"I know the street of which you speak. But she did not want to involve those people. Besides, none there would help me. I spoke with every tenant when I first sought her."

"She no longer has a choice if we are to save her, and they are willing."

"That may well be, but what can a handful of hawkers do? It is madness, this!"

The old healer smiled. "They can take their poor dead brother to the nave for prayers before his burial," he said. "He was a wealthy shopkeeper, as hawkers go. A cloth merchant with his own fine stall, God rest him, and they are prepared with a substantial contribution to the churchmens' coffers for their inconvenience at the untimely pilgrimage. The coffin will not be disturbed once tales spread that the poor devil was crushed to death—quite hideously mangled beneath the hoofs of a frenzied horse."

"They would convey me in a . . . a coffin?"

A smug nod answered him.

"You paid the tribute, didn't you?" Robert surmised.

"A good investment."

The Scot heaved a mammoth sigh, and raked his hair back roughly. "I hope you're right," he said.

"What? You do not like the plan? I thought it quite brilliant."

"It isn't that," the young laird returned. "How do I get out of the abominable thing in full view of the priests—feign resurrection?"

"At some predetermined point, which you will arrange with the vendors, their grief will overcome them. They will converge upon the coffin and shroud your escape from it with their bodies en masse."

"What then?"

Nostradamus shrugged. "You are on your own. They will request time to recover for a bit in one of the two chapels set between the flying buttresses before they depart the cathedral. The donation is sufficient enough that there should be no resistance. They will wait a reasonable time— you know it cannot be lengthy. If in that time you can manage to find the girl and convey her to the coffin, they will carry her out in it as they have carried you in. You, of course, will be left on your own. Ideally, you might follow along with the crowd, but that is hardly likely—not with that face. Besides, I would suggest that you wear the habit. It will help you in the lower regions, but it will be noticed if you attempt to leave with the rest. This, as I've said, is the ideal. More than likely, you will be left there facing escape with Violette on your own. The maze of Notre Dame Cathedral's bowels is no mere closet, young ram."

"I suppose this is the only hope I have?" Robert replied, praying he was mistaken.

"Of gaining entrance to Notre Dame while all Paris seeks you? Yes."

"So be it, then! What happens next?"

"If you are separated, you will return to the same house under cover of darkness. Violette will not be there. The vendors will have spirited her away to some safe place, and you will be given directions to join her. The coffin will be buried, as though it actually did have a body in it, which it probably will by the time it reaches the graveyard, since I have just come from there, and several of their number breathe their last. If you are forced to escape together, the plan must be of your own design."

"And . . . Uncle Aengus?"

"Put him from your mind. I will see that Montaigne secures him safe passage to Scotland once he is fit. He cannot return to the Mount."

"I do not like involving the vendors. The risk is great."

"It is far greater if you try and enter the cathedral on your own with no hope of any means to cover or conceal you."

"Have you no riddles, no metaphors, no cryptic verse to

mark this mad venture, then?" Robert probed, in need of a positive thought.

Nostradamus laughed outright. "Even such as that, which you do so renounce, would be welcome in the shadow of such folly as this, eh?"

Robert hung his head. "Before, it was none save myself I needed to worry over," he said. "I was a warrior doing battle. Warriors need no omens, and they are better left without . . . sight. A warrior needs only a steady hand, and a rational mind—quick to calculate. Now, there is Violette. Love dilutes reason, sir. A warrior should have no truck with it. And then there are the vendors."

"But you are the warrior still."

"True," Robert agreed, "as I always will be."

"Then, draw your strength from that. Forget all else, take up your sword, and go carve out your destiny."

There was a long, silent moment then—so solemn that not even the woodland creatures' voices violated it.

"We will not meet again," Robert said.

"No, Robert of Paxton, Laird of Berwickshire, we will not," Nostradamus confirmed. "Our paths divide here in this wood. I have done all that I can to groom your spirit for this moment. I told you once that I would not be there when an even greater sight was vital to your life. That hour is upon you."

"You also told me once that you were not my last hope. If that is so and we are parting, won't you tell me who is?"

The healer cast him a disdainful smile. "Not 'who,' *what*," he scorned. "Violette is not the only blind one, but no matter. *Love* is your last hope, Robert of Paxton. It is the physician that you seek. You already have it in your Violette. Now see if you can keep it. Step cautiously, young ram. Your horns are locked with greater antlers—greater than you have the power to subdue. Charge with your spirit—your inner eye. It is the only legacy that I can leave you." He turned to go then, but gave a lurch and waddled back, producing a pouch from the pocket of his gown. "I nearly forgot," he said, handing it over. "A parting gift."

Puzzled, Robert hefted the sack in his hand to judge its contents, and thrust his chin in query.

"Sulfur ash," the healer explained. "I would treat it carefully."

"Sulfur ash? The sorcerer's ploy?"

A wry smile crimped the healer's jowls, and he breathed a nasal sigh. "Have you not long since exhausted your supply of natural ploys?" he chided. "Is your Violette not worth a . . . supernatural weapon?"

"You test me!"

"I mock your righteous indignation, and your blindness. It is no wonder that you and Montaigne get on so famously. You are both hewn of the same immovable rock." He threw up his hands. "I will speak plain. Lord knows that it will matter. A pinch or two of that cast down at the proper time and place might save your life, my fine-feathered skeptic. Not all weapons bear a cutting edge."

Sixteen

Robert did not ride boldly through the streets of Paris at midnight. Familiar with the vendors' quarter from his earlier search for Violette, he tethered his mount in a remembered grove nearby, and made his cautious way on foot.

All went as Doctor Nostradamus predicted, and he was admitted at number twelve, the house with the broken gargoyle that the healer had described, by a short, plump woman, who introduced herself only as Madeline. Well past middle age, she was possessed of a sparse crop of yellow-gray hair, and small eyes all but lost in the flab of her round face. This was not the house of Jacques and Justine Delon, where the girl had lodged. They, too, were in their later years, and in order that no suspicion should fall upon them if the plan should fail, Nostradamus had seen to it that they were spirited away from the quarter beforehand.

A cold, dreary rain had begun to fall, and Madeline offered the bedraggled laird a piece of fresh baked bread, a trencher of pottage, and a tankard of sack before the blazing kitchen hearth. He was famished, and he took the trencher with anxious hands, threw back the cowl, and began to wolf down the stew greedily.

At sight of his face, the woman gasped, making the sign of the cross over her tremendous bosom, and for the first time since he had set his helmet aside in exchange for the cowl, Robert remembered his disfigurement, marveling that something had actually made him forget the despair that had brought him to France in the first place and begun this madness. He couldn't even pinpoint when it had ceased to be the foremost thought in his mind, only that Nostradamus was right—Violette was at the root of it. It was a rude awakening, but Robert tried to concentrate on the day to come, and once he'd met briefly with several others who were privy to the clever healer's plot, he succumbed to sleep beside that wonderful crackling hearth.

The full scope of the ruse was not apparent until the dismal dawn broke over the vendors' quarter the next morning. The handful of wary, inept peasants he had envisioned was in fact a sturdy force nearly one hundred strong. Wearing humble mourning garments, they made a striking show indeed, down to a very authentic embalmer robed in the proper, somber countenance befitting the occasion. The coffin had been his contribution to the event, and as Robert let them shut him up inside it, he prayed that it was not an omen.

A cold autumn rain beat down on the procession that crawled slowly over the cobblestone streets of Paris. The rain drummed upon the coffin lid, so close above the Scot's face in the darkness beneath. It resounded like thunder in the ears that strained to hear any sounds of danger. There were none, though that did not ease the tension that had drawn every sinew so taut he feared they would snap for the strain.

Not until they reached the Pont Neuf, a narrow bridge that spanned the Seine to the Île de la Cité and gave access to the towering cathedral, did they meet with opposition. There, a detachment of gendarmes patrolled the approach and called the procession to a halt.

Robert held his breath at the sound of heavy boots striking slick cobblestones, but over the din of the rain and the sobs and the shouted commands, the embalmer's voice became clear.

"Would you disturb the dead?" he cried, for one of the soldiers had laid hold the coffin. Robert stiffened inside.

"Have you no respect, sir? You would risk a curse upon your house to view that mangled corpse in there?"

"Curse, eh?" the guard scoffed, drawing the coffin closer. "Get out of the way, undertaker."

"If you are possessed of a strong stomach, sir, lift off the lid," the embalmer said. Robert gripped his sword. "Our poor departed brother inside was trampled—crushed to death under the hooves of a crazed horse in the street!"

The gendarme, paying him no mind, still struggled with the lid, but Robert had secured the clever latch inside that had been placed there for just such an emergency.

"Here, let me help you if you must," said the embalmer, "though I should warn you that he who lies inside took the faltering step that led to his demise while suffering from a fever of rather . . . doubtful origins."

"*Plague?*" the gendarme cried, leaping back from the cart.

"Who can say?" the embalmer replied. "There wasn't enough left of the poor soul to be certain, God pity him," he said, his own hands on the lid now. "But if you must have your duty done . . ."

"No! Hold there! Leave it. Be on your way—the lot of you!" he barked, instructing his men to give the procession a wide berth.

"As you wish, sir," said the embalmer, straightening the coffin in the cart. Robert heaved a sigh of relief inside, as the sounds of horse's hooves and sharp commands grew distant, and the congregation lumbered on.

He had begun to sweat profusely, and though there was a crevice here and there designed to let air in, he could scarcely breathe. His heart was racing, and by the time they'd crossed the little bridge and reached the cathedral, he was certain the thundering beat of it could be heard above the clatter of the rain. Another delay halted the procession, but it wasn't as dramatic. Having been allowed to cross to the Île de la Cité, the sentries posted at the cathedral assumed that the gendarmes on the other side of Pont Neuf had done their duty. After hearing the same deterring tale, they made no attempt to disturb the coffin, and the mourners were admitted without suspicion. They were not, however, allowed to congregate in the nave as planned. They were herded instead into the west side chapel, where several priests attended, and they bore the coffin along the buttressed wall and set it down at a discreet distance while the spokesman approached the clerics. This placed Robert advantageously close to an arch that partially obscured the coffin, and led to a narrow passageway beyond. It was at that moment, when the embalmer had captured the priests' attention with the generous contribution, that a sharp rap on the coffin lid signaled Robert to make ready, as the vendors began their realistic charade.

Uttering a grief-stricken wail, the woman, Madeline, feigned a swoon and fell prostrate upon the coffin. The others rallied around then, and the melancholy hum of their grief echoed through the empty chapel. The wall of their animated bodies became a shield that hid Robert's escape from the casket, and let him slither away along the marble floor and disappear into the darkened passageway that led toward access to the lower regions.

Fortune had smiled upon the hour of the escape, in that it came before the priests began the service. This would allow a little extra margin to Robert's chances of finding Violette below, and getting her back to the vendors in time to be carried out as he was carried in.

But he still had to act quickly, and at sight of the maze of darkened turns and alcoves, his heart sank. He had never seen anything like it. Looking up, he was awed by the height of the intricate arches and domes and buttresses. How vast could the place be? But he moved boldly through the passageways, feeling confident in his monk's attire, throwing open doors to storage chambers and cubicles along the way. None were inhabited, and he dared not call out for fear of attracting the wrong sort of response. His heart had begun to pound again, and cold sweat ran down his pleated brow despite the drafty chill that clung to the damp, musty corridor. Aside from the putrid stench of mold that called to mind the Bastille, Notre Dame smelled of sickly sweet, stale incense and tallow, threatening to make him retch.

Precious minutes were slipping away. Robert couldn't spare them, and he couldn't stop them. What he needed was a signpost to guide him. Nostradamus was right. This was no mere closet. It was, in fact, so vast and intricate a labyrinth that he wondered that he would be able to find his way back to the chapel again.

Suddenly there was a sound, amplified by the acoustics, and he drew his sword and flattened himself in the shadows, listening. It came clearer—the hollow clop and shuffle of footfalls echoing along the passageway, and he held his breath awaiting the author of the noise. At last, the figure of a man bled through the darkness. He was garbed in the robes of a priest, and Robert lunged and hooked his arm around the man's throat as he passed, pulling him close, the pressure of hard, corded muscle on the priest's larynx stifling his cry.

"The blind girl," he spat, close in the sputtering priest's ear. "Take me to her."

Whining and gasping, the priest struggled, but the tip of Robert's sword indenting his side soon quieted him.

"One careless step—one outcry, and I will skewer you through," the young laird promised. "Do we understand one another?"

The frantic priest's bobbing head replied to that, and he nodded in the direction from which he had come.

Robert relaxed his grip just enough so that his captive could walk, wondering how he could have missed the chamber where they had her, but he didn't release the priest, nor did he remove the sword while he moved alongside down a narrow passageway off to the left, so obscured in shadow he'd passed it by earlier.

"You cannot escape, you know," the priest choked, retracing his steps.

Robert jerked him closer in lieu of conversation, though the gesture spoke louder than any words he might have voiced.

"God have mercy upon you!" the holy man shrilled.

Robert tightened his grip, and jabbed deeper with the sword. "Sanctimonious toad," he spat. "You had best beg God's mercy for yourself, if so much as one hair of that lass's head has been harmed."

They descended toward the wine cellar. When they reached the great arched door that confined it, the terrified priest waved a trembling hand. Snatching the key chatelaine dangling from the chain that girded the man, Robert unlocked the cellar and propelled him inside. A quick glance was all it took to be certain that the priest had not deceived him. Violette lay bound among the casks. Delivering a swift blow to the priest's head, he let the man drop and ran to her.

Hysterical, she made no coherent sounds while he unfastened the ropes that bound her hands.

"Violette, it is I," he soothed, lifting her to her feet beside him. "I am going to get you out of here. You must be still now, and do exactly as I say."

She searched his scarred face, her tiny fingers flitting over every contour, and she groaned, pulling him into her arms.

"Oh, my lord, it *is* you!" she sobbed. "Your uncle . . . is he safe?"

"Yes, but nevermind all that now. We must hurry, lass."

"You should not have come. It is what they intended. They will kill you!"

A small flare set in its bracket on the wall had nearly

burned out. In the waning light he could see that her face was bruised, and that her wrists were raw from the bite of coarse, abrasive ropes. He drew her closer in his arms, finding her trembling mouth with his own.

She clung to him desperately, and he moaned, crushing her closer still, at the mercy of her passion. Nothing else existed then. His senses had exploded. The scent of her surrounded him and, for the moment, left him dazed. That soon passed, however, chased by a rush of adrenaline that called him back to the present. He held her at arm's distance.

"There is no time to explain. You must trust and obey me now, or all of this is for naught." Releasing her, he stalked to the unconscious priest, snatched a wine-stained serviette from a pile of soiled linen on the corner shelf, and jammed it into the cleric's mouth.

"Where have you gone?" she panicked, groping the air in mad circles. "What do you do?"

"Shhh!" he said, collecting the ropes. "I bind your jailer as you were bound," he said. "Should he come 'round now, he will alert the others."

"They will kill you, I say . . . these 'holy men'—I know it," she moaned.

Having tied the senseless priest securely, he reached her again in two great strides, and seized her close in comforting arms, torn between longing and the desperation of the moment.

"Not if you do as I say," he murmured, finding her lips again. They were hot and dry, and he laid a hand against her face, searching the glazed, sightless eyes that so desperately sought him in their blindness.

"You are still burning with fever," he said. "Come, the vendors wait. They will see you safely away, but we must hurry."

Leading her, he darted from the cellar and began his

winding way upward toward the chapel as best he remembered.

"The vendors?" she cried. "No!"

"Shhh, be still!" he snapped. "They wait in the chapel above. If we are not too late, they will see you safely out of this tomb." For that is what it seemed to him in its dank, inhospitable emptiness.

"But what of you?" she sobbed. "How will you escape?"

"Nevermind about that now," he said. "I will. That is all you need know, and I will join you just as quickly as I can. It is all arranged."

"I do not even know what it is, this place," she said, low-voiced. "Where are we—where?"

"Notre Dame Cathedral," he told her.

Groaning, she sagged against him. "*Mon Dieu!*" she murmured. "You will never escape from here. It is impossible."

"It was impossible that I gain entrance," he said. "I have done that, haven't I? I will escape as well."

She was limp in his arm, as though all the life in her had been siphoned off suddenly, and when they reached the chapel arch, he had to leave her leaning against the wall, while he crept close enough to observe the situation. The vendors had begun to make their reluctant departure, for they dared wait no longer if they would avoid suspicion. The priests were nowhere in sight then, and without a second thought, the young laird grabbed Violette and thrust her toward the anxious gathering.

"No!" she cried. "No, I won't leave you!"

He shook her. "You will be still," he gritted out. "You will make no sound, or all these will die with you. They are a hundred strong!" He lowered his lips to her own again in a scorching kiss. Then, gathering her up in his arms, he laid her in the coffin. "Not one sound," he warned, and darted back into the shadows as they lowered the coffin lid and bore her away.

The embalmer hung back. "Come away with us, please," he begged. "You cannot escape alone from this place. It is madness—suicide!"

"No," said Robert. "I cannot come with you. The guards will surely have been warned of my disfigurement, and without this habit and cowl . . . my face . . . it is impossible. If I attempt it, you will all die—Violette and myself as well. Take her to safety. I will wait long enough for you to return to the vendors' quarter if I can. Then I will attempt escape. If I succeed, I will join you. Look after her!" he charged them, and moved back into the murky shadows of the passageway. For, had he lingered there another moment as he was, still atremble from Violette's passionate embrace, he would have let the man persuade him.

The worst still lay before him, and he focused upon that as he flattened himself against the cold stone wall in the darkness, wracking his brain for a viable plan of escape from the fortified cathedral. This could not be managed from any of the portals. They were too well guarded. Escape by any means in broad daylight was indeed suicidal, but he dared not wait until nightfall. Someone was certain to miss the priest he'd tethered in the wine cellar long before then, and the vendors' successful escape would gain them nothing once that occurred. They were no fools. They would certainly connect the coincidences.

The ideal would be to affect a hasty escape, collect Violette, and be away from the city before the priest was missed. But footfalls quickly put an end to hopes of that, and he watched with sinking heart as two robed figures passed by his shadowy alcove.

Without a sound, he drew his sword and set out in the opposite direction, back into the west chapel. Moving with caution, he approached the vaulted apse in the clerestory, where a narrow stained glass window had caught his attention earlier. That recess seemed as good a place as any to hide for the moment. Any second now, the priests would come running with their liberated brother from the wine cellar. The niche was nicely shadowed, and the window was noteworthy as a possible means of escape. He'd nearly reached it when the cardinal's voice arrested him, booming through the echo-infested chapel with all the subtlety of a thunder roll.

"Stand where you are, heretic!" he commanded.

Robert spun, his sword extended toward the formidable figure of Charles de Guise, emerging from the chapel arch opposite. But he had no chance to reply, for just then the priests from below came running, their outcries—riding the echoes—resounding in advance of their appearance.

"Fetch the guards!" the cardinal shouted, and they skittered off toward the nave with robes spread wide.

Robert's hand plunged into his boot, and his steady fingers closed around the pouch of sulfur ash he'd hidden there in case of capture.

"I knew the girl would flush you out, young zealot," the cardinal triumphed, strolling confidently closer.

"And, did you know, when you abducted her so cleverly, that her fever was plague, Your Eminence?" Robert queried. The cardinal stopped in his tracks, a tremor in his cold eyes, and the laird burst into laughter.

"You lie!" the cardinal spat, his whole body delivering the words.

"Do I?" Robert said, triumphant. "She burns with it still. You were safe until you brought her into the city. It spreads like wildfire. When your cohorts come down with it you will know how well I lie."

Footfalls from the passageway beyond sent Robert's blood surging through his veins. His sharp eyes caught the glint of a nearby crosier standing tall in its bracket. He edged closer to it.

"You cannot escape," the cardinal bellowed, as a troop of

soldiers poured into the chapel. "It is over, my fine Scottish traitor. It is finished!"

"Forgive me," Robert contradicted, "but I do not think so." Tearing open the pouch, he threw down the sulfur ash. A mild explosion fraught with bilious green clouds of spark-clad fog momentarily blotted the cardinal from view. Taking good advantage, Robert snatched up the crosier. Lowering it broadside to the window at his back, he plunged it through in a shower of brightly colored glass that spilled out over the manicured grounds below, then leapt through the twisted lead after it.

The window was a jot higher up than he'd calculated. Though he landed for the most part on his feet, his breath caught at the shock. His knees gave way beneath his weight, and it was a moment before he caught his balance and scrambled toward the not too distant bank of the Seine.

Arrows rained down all around him. When he turned to gauge their trajectory he was overwhelmed by the architecture, the gargoyles high atop the bell tower, the jamb figures, the capitals and column figures that seemed to wind along the buttressed Royal Portal of the west façade. In awe of what he had escaped from, he hesitated. It was only a brief hitch in the long-legged stride carrying him swiftly out of range, but it was enough. One of the missiles struck his good shoulder and drove him into the water. He was a strong swimmer, and the current was mild, but negotiating the Seine in a weighty woolen monk's robe with an arrow in his shoulder quickly sapped his strength. More arrows pierced the water, and he held his breath, ducked beneath, and swam along the shore of the isle without breaking the surface until he'd nearly put himself in the shadow of Pont Neuf before he gulped air again.

The arrows had ceased flying. De Guise and his men had surely seen him struck. Could they think him dead? That had been the plan. Praying that it had worked, he ducked beneath the water again and followed the bridge to a grove that hemmed the unkempt shore of the mainland. Slithering out of the water, he dove in among the yews, unseen to assess and tend his wound.

Seventeen

Michel seigneur de Montaigne had nearly reached Limoges when a crossroads presented itself, and he reined in to deliberate his direction. But there was no real choice. That was as far south as his conscience would allow him to travel, and he wheeled the horse around, spurring the gray gelding back the way he'd come, sorry now, that he'd sent the rest of his entourage—provisions cart and all—on ahead. He must return to Paris. Why he'd ever let Doctor Nostradamus persuade him to leave, he couldn't imagine.

The good doctor was probably right in his cryptic warning, he had no doubt of that, but being a man of principle, Michel could not justify sacrificing another man's life for his own safety. In his view, that is what it would amount to were he to turn his back on the Scottish laird, whom he'd agreed to sponsor, at the first whiff of danger—even if that danger came at the merciless hands of the Guises. He liked and admired Robert of Paxton, his heart went out to him in his hopeless quest, and even though he knew that in no way could he be held responsible for the coil the laird found himself tangled in, that it all had begun in his kitchen garden kept him from being absolved. If the headstrong Scot was still alive, he saw it as his duty to help him.

It was several days before he reached the city, though he drove the horse beneath him relentlessly. Stopping first at the château, he learned of the strange monk who had come with Violette, seeking him. He lingered there only long enough to collect a hooded mantle, which he put on over his gown for anonymity, and give Alain and the other servants stern instructions to pretend they'd never seen him. He set out at dusk for Nostradamus's lodgings in the city. To his dismay, he found the healer's rooms there were shut up tight—abandoned. When he inquired of the other residents in the lane, they told him the good doctor had closed down his city residence and returned to Salon indefinitely.

It was too late now to trouble the vendors, and he didn't want to return to the château unless he had to. Perhaps he'd find the duke and the girl at the ruins. Now that he knew they were traveling together, it seemed a logical choice. It was worth a try, and he rode there under cover of darkness, for there was no moon, only to find the gutted remains of the wounded castle, still stinking of burnt timbers and debris in the cool night air.

How had so much occurred in his short absence from the city? In mere days, Nostradamus had gone south, the ruins had been burned out, and the Scot had disappeared with Violette without a trace. Now where was he to go? He dared not return to the château—that would be the first place the cardinal's men would seek him. He wasn't prepared to sleep in the open, either. After much deliberation, he decided to return to the city and take a room at the Inn of St. Michael. It was a bold move, for he was certainly well known in Paris, but he was not a patron of the inn. Praying that he could hide there in plain sight until dawn, he made his way back to the city, wishing he'd never left it.

Robert bided his time deep in the grove until dark. His pain was excruciating. He'd broken the arrow off, but it was driven too deeply into his right shoulder to pull it out, and he couldn't push it through without help. His robe was fouled with blood, though much had washed away in the Seine. Still, it would be noticeable. Somehow, he had to reach the vendors' quarter, find out where they had taken Violette, and retrieve his traveling sack with the spare robe and his helmet. He waited as long as he dared, and then, hugging the façades along the lane, he crept through the shadows and knocked once at number twelve. But it wasn't Madeline who threw the door open to him. It was Gaspard de Coligny, Admiral of France.

"Come in, my lord," he said. "We have been expecting you."

Three Huguenot soldiers emerged from the shadows, seized him, and handed him over the threshold into the kitchen, where Madeline sat sobbing with her head in her hands. Winded, and weak from blood loss, the laird staggered as they hauled him close to the admiral, who threw back his cowl and took a step back from him, scrutinizing his face in the firelight.

"These good people have done no wrong," Robert defended. "They meant only to help me right a terrible injustice."

The admiral smiled coldly. "Take ease," he said. "These 'good people' are in no danger from me. I am not Charles de Guise. My business is with you, Robert of Paxton. You were so busy minding the cardinal's movements you were oblivious of ours. I find that unimpressive for a warrior—even a Scottish warrior."

"Battles are not quite so deviously fought in Scotland," Robert muttered, for the wound was throbbing. His head was reeling, but he dared not lose consciousness until he'd learned what had become of Violette.

"Evidently," the admiral pronounced, tongue-in-cheek. "You have been wounded, and from the look of it, you've lost much blood. That needs tending. We shall see to it, and then we shall talk, you and I. You have much to answer for. But not here."

"What have you done with Violette?" Robert asked, almost afraid of the answer. He couldn't see past the triumph in the admiral's cold eyes, and he repeated his question over and over, as they dragged him back out into the shadows of the dark lane, bound him, and loaded him in a cart that had been hidden in the mews.

"In due time, my lord," the admiral assured him. "Don't fly in the face of fortune. You have very . . . influential friends. But for that, I would have cut you down long since. However, let me warn you: you are quite alone with me here now, and there is only so much condescension I am prepared to suffer on the whim of a mere twelve-year-old puppet—king or no. Now, if you had his mother's favor, it might be quite a different matter altogether. But you do not. I doubt she even knows that you exist. So, hold your peace! And thank your Catholic idols that you've found me in an amiable humor. Such moods come rarely to me of late. If you would have it continue, I advise while we travel that you prepare a brilliant defense. Much depends upon it."

But Robert scarcely heard this. The admiral nodded to the driver and slapped the rump of the mule harnessed to the cart. It was a rickety conveyance, padded with moldy alfalfa, and between the nauseating, sickeningly sweet smell and the sudden jolt of motion, he spiraled into unconsciousness.

The nightmares were the worst of it—dark, lurking visions of buttresses and passageways—all dead ends. Of seeking, and not finding, but not finding *what*? There were creatures— dragons, no, *gargoyles*, hideous creatures staring down from great spired heights—mocking him. Then there was the pain in his shoulder. One had healed, but the other now burned as though someone had set it afire. How would he wield his sword? But he had no sword. It lay somewhere in the muddy silt at the bottom of the Seine. It was all trickling back. Someone groaned. It was several minutes before he realized the sound had come from his own parched throat. He gave a lurch, but a strong hand prevented him from rising.

"So! You have come 'round," the gruff voice behind it said. "Good! We shall have our talk, then, Robert of Paxton."

Slowly, the Scot's bleary eyes came open to the massive figure of Gaspard de Coligny, standing arms akimbo now above the pallet where he lay half naked, shed of his robe, shirt, and doublet; only his breeches remained. The arrow had been removed from his shoulder, and clean linen bandages swathed it. From the stench of burnt flesh flaring his nostrils, he knew the wound had been cauterized.

He was in a small cubicle, sparsely furnished and steeped in shadow. An oaken table, a Glastonbury chair, and a large coffer were the only pieces. Two armed sentries occupied the coffer and sat looking on while the admiral took his seat in the X-shaped Glastonbury chair facing the pallet for the interrogation.

"We have met before I think," the admiral mused, "when you were staging the dashing rescue of your papist uncle from the Bastille. I must commend you. Well done!"

"I did not set out to kill the jailer," Robert defended. "He recognized me. I had no choice."

The admiral smiled his cold smile. "That is no concern of mine," he said. "Garboneaux was an odious toad, who mistreated my imprisoned brethren in that pest hole—gave them not the sort of treatment he gave the Catholics entombed there. That was the reason for my little inspection. I'd hoped to persuade the king to rectify the situation."

"Well, if he has treated your brethren worse than he did me—a Catholic—during my incarceration in that place, he has received his just deserts," Robert gritted through a humorless chuckle.

"Ummmm," the admiral hummed, drumming his fingers on his knee. "Do you know where you are, my lord?" he queried.

"No," Robert murmured, shaking his head as best he could. There was no bolster or pillow beneath it, and the movement shot him through with needles of punishing pain.

"You are at the village you helped ravage," said the admiral, drawing his fingers into white-knuckled fists. "But I am a fair man. I would hear your account of that unfortunate foray."

Robert sighed. Something in the inscrutable eyes holding him relentlessly made him doubt the wisdom of telling the truth. He hardly believed it himself any longer.

"I came to Paris on a peaceful mission," he began, against his better judgment.

"In search of Doctor Nostradamus, yes, yes, I've heard the tale. And, looking at you now, I see the folly of it. What I wish to know is how you came to be among the raiding party with Louis de Brach, and the cardinal's men?"

A peasant woman entered bearing a water crock, her eyes seeking the admiral's permission to offer it. Through the open doorway, Robert saw that it was daylight. Coligny nodded, and the laird gulped the crock dry. Afterward, the woman bowed and left them.

"My uncle . . . the monk I liberated, served the Church in France . . . under the Cardinal of Lorraine . . . when all this madness started," Robert began again, out of breath for having raised himself on his elbow to drink.

"What has that got to do—"

"Please," Robert interrupted. "If I am to tell it, you must hear it all. I know some of your background, my Lord Admiral, and it is most impressive, but I also know that you have only these three years past publicly confessed your conversion to Protestantism. I appeal to the Catholic soul you once possessed to listen with an open mind."

"Very well, then, tell it," the admiral begrudged.

"Uncle Aengus opposed the cardinal's methods of dealing with the Huguenots—the very methods you abhor. For his pains, Charles de Guise had him banished to the abbey on St. Michael's Mount. My uncle is a humble monk, who spends his life in prayer, and means ill to no one. When I approached him seeking a sponsor for my journey here, instead of Cardinal de Guise, he referred me to seigneur de Montaigne. The cardinal was slighted, and as appeasement for the insult, I was forced to attend the raid on this village. I did so against my will and under protest. I had then, and have now, no designs upon involving myself in *any* insurrection—religious, political, or otherwise. I did so to spare my uncle and Montaigne a chastisement, and Uncle Aengus was punished anyway."

"Ummm," the admiral growled. "You were conscripted?"

"I was *taken hostage!*" Robert bellowed. "That is what it amounted to. The cardinal's armed men came for me. I had no choice. I feared for my uncle, and my friend. Surely you are no stranger to the ruthless brutality of the cardinal's chastisements?"

The admiral ground out a guttural chuckle. There was no humor in it. "The 'Cardinal,' Charles de Guise, ordered all Huguenots to leave Paris or be burned at the stake; many were," he said. "He ordered all those who lived in his own town, where he is archbishop, mind, to be killed, and their pitiful bodies floated down the river as a lesson to any who would defy him. On the first of March, in this year of Our Lord, fifteen sixty-two, the cardinal's brother Francis, le Duc de Guise, set fire to an obscure tavern on the outskirts of Vassy, where a harmless Huguenot prayer meeting was taking place, and ordered his troops to attack. Twenty-three unsuspecting Huguenots were put to the sword, and one hundred and thirty more were wounded. Yes, my lord, I know well the ruthless capabilities of the cardinal's chastisements."

"Well then, you know I speak the truth of him," Robert said. "Who is the leader of your movement here now? Perhaps if I could speak with him . . . I might be able to persuade him of my unfortunate situation. I like it not!"

"Le Duc de Condé leads us now that the conflict has become a full-blown war, but I am in command here while he is traveling south to counsel at the border with our ally, Henry of Navarre, and you are indeed fortunate that you must answer to me. Le Duc de Condé is far less . . . understanding."

"I was present at the raid, yes, I cannot deny it," Robert admitted, "but I did precious little to harm your people; I was too busy trying to thwart assassination. Neither the cardinal, nor his general expected me to leave the field alive."

"Who killed Louis de Brach?" the admiral demanded.

"I did," Robert responded without hesitation. There was no reason to lie.

"Explain."

"The young blind girl that you have taken sought refuge here amongst your people after she defended me, and openly accused the gendarmes who arrested me for naught. It was no longer safe for her to sell her flowers in the city, and these people here gave her shelter in exchange for chores. At the height of the battle, Louis de Brach had taken her down to rape her. I intervened, we fought, and I planted my *sgian dubh*—my Scottish dagger—in his belly. I then left the fray and went in search of Violette. She had wandered off in her fright, and blundered headlong into the burning forest."

"Ummmm," the admiral grunted, considering it. "It is the tale I have been told. I needed to have it from you. Where stand you now? With which side are you aligned?"

"I have no alignment, my Lord Admiral. I never have had. Why is that so difficult to make any of you see? I came on a fool's errand—a vain quest to try and make myself presentable enough to find a wife and get heirs upon her. I have no siblings. An heir is necessary, lest the noble Mack line die out with me, and none but whores will come near enough to my face to let my cock prove me."

"And the girl? Where does she stand in this?"

Robert breathed a nasal sigh. "I love her," he replied. "She is the only thing that I have gained from this mad quest, and I will not leave France without her. She is safe in this country no longer, because of me. She was taken from our hiding place while I was freeing Uncle Aengus, and held against her will at Notre Dame by the cardinal in order to bring me. I killed his general. He means to see I pay for that. Well and good, I will allow, but he may not harm Violette. I got her out, and meant to join her and leave France, and then you . . . prevented me."

"Where is your uncle now?" the admiral interrupted.

How much should he tell this man? How much should he confide? He had been truthful thus far, but those unreadable eyes dilated in the dying candlelight in that dark, windowless room, and were not trustworthy.

"Gone back to Scotland," Robert replied, praying it was the truth. He would not involve Nostradamus—never that. After all the wise, old healer had done for his foolish cause he would not leave him at the mercy of any of them. "Violette?" he pleaded. "What have you done with Violette?"

"She is safe," the admiral grunted.

"But she must be frightened—terrified beyond reason. I beg you let me see her."

"Not just yet," the admiral pronounced. "She will be freed, but you have yet to prove yourself, my lord."

"You cannot set her free alone here now!" Robert erupted. "The cardinal's men . . . they will kill her. She is blind! She has nowhere to go. Let me take her away—home to Scotland."

"I cannot allow that," the admiral said. "As I've said, and I do not like repeating myself, you must prove yourself."

"*How?* I have told you the truth—to the very letter. What more must I do to prove myself?"

"You must do for me what you did for Charles de Guise. You must even the score."

"But I have evened the score," Robert protested. "Have I not killed Louis de Brach? Are you no better than the cardinal that you would force me to fight against my will?" It was a rash remark that caused the admiral to stiffen, but the laird was not sorry he'd made it.

"If you will not, your alignment is proven, and you will die, my lord," Coligny said flatly. "It is that simple."

Robert stared. How could this be? Was it jealous rivalry, not religious freedom that drove this war? And which side was God on, he wondered? Or had He turned His back upon both factions? That seemed the most logical answer, since neither side had prospered much from what he could see, but then, he was no theologian.

"What would you have me do, exactly?" he queried, knowing full well that the crafty admiral, bested by the cardinal at his hands—albeit unavoidably—expected him to fight.

"That wound will not take long to mend enough for you to travel," Coligny opined, "—a sennight at the outside, and you should be able to sit a horse. Then you will come with us to Normandy, where we shall do unto the Catholics there as the Guises have done unto us here . . . and elsewhere. But *we* will be merciful. We will not burn them at the stake, or send their mangled, headless bodies floating downriver. No. And we will not tax you overmuch expecting you to join in the thick of battle risen so soon from your sickbed. We will hang them in the public squares and *you*, our duly appointed hangman, will loop the noose 'round their worthless necks, my lord; that is what I would have you do."

"And Violette? What will become of her?"

"I told you. I will set her free."

"But you cannot, my Lord Admiral! You sign her death warrant. I will do what you ask, but in the end, I must take Violette safely home to Scotland. Either that, or kill me now. You mean to do that anyway, once I slake your jealous passion for vengeance on me. I am no fool."

"And I am no Charles de Guise!" the admiral shot back. Anger flared his nostrils now. Robert knew he had gone too far. It didn't matter. He had reached the end of his tether.

Blue eyes jousted with gray, or were they blue as well, or brown? He couldn't say. They were dilated black and seething with palpable passion. Both were immovable.

"There has to be someone to care for the girl," the admiral finally growled.

"There was. Seigneur de Montaigne," Robert replied, "but I am sure you must know that he has left the city, and gone to his home on the coast, where he will harvest his vineyards and winter. He shan't return to Paris 'til the spring, and there is no one else that will protect her from the cardinal, and the troops of his brother, the duke. She will not see the vendors who have sheltered her subjected to the Guises's retribution."

A commotion outside turned the admiral's head then, and he threw the door open to his sentries, who had laid hold of a robed figure on the threshold.

"Let me in, Coligny," the man cried, struggling to free himself from the soldiers' grip. "I know you have him here, and the king knows I have come. Have these gudgeons unhand me—*at once!*"

"Montaigne?" the admiral erupted, casting a suspicious scowl over his shoulder toward Robert.

The young laird sagged back against the pallet. Had he not just told the admiral that Montaigne had left the city? How much would he believe now, with the man standing— large as life—upon his doorstep?

"Let him go," the admiral growled, and Montaigne crossed the threshold, strutting like a cock with ruffled feathers, tugging his mantle straight and slapping at the dust on it relentlessly.

"Michel!" Robert cried. "What are you doing here?" Did

it sound as false to Coligny as it did to him? He prayed not, but he feared so.

"Yes, Montaigne," the admiral parroted, "what are you doing here? Your protégé has just told me a fantasy that you had left the city."

"As well I did, and was halfway home before my conscience drove me back again to finish my obligation to the laird here. Is this your handiwork, then?" he demanded, wagging a stiff finger toward Robert's bandaged wound.

"No, it's not," the admiral grunted. " 'Tis the cardinal's doing, that, none of mine."

"How did you find me, Michel?" Robert queried.

"I sought you everywhere, and then, the vendors—"

"You weren't seen?" Robert begged him, interrupting.

"No, no. Give me some credit," the magistrate replied, "ergo, the disguise," he added, holding his mantle wide. "I never wear the damnable thing. It makes me look much fatter than I am, but it fitted the occasion today."

"My Lord Admiral, may we speak privately?" Robert requested. "Could the guards not wait outside while seigneur and I converse? Have pity. Where can I go?"

"Surely you jest," the admiral chortled. "There shall be no more 'speaking privately' here now."

"Very well, then," Robert snapped. "Since you insist." He switched his glance to the magistrate. "He has Violette, and means to set her free. She cannot be set free here now with no one to protect her. The cardinal's men will kill her!" Before he realized what had happened, the whole twisted coil unraveled then and there. He didn't stop speaking until he had told the magistrate all that had occurred since their last meeting. Halfway through, Montaigne lost his color, and the admiral vacated the Glastonbury chair and let him sink into it, backing away at the mention of plague. Finally, Robert in conclusion said, ". . . and he has her here somewhere, and means to set her free—on her own! She has passed the crisis, thanks to Doctor Nostradamus's lozenges, but she has fever still, I felt it myself. I fear relapse if she is misused."

"Look here, you told me naught of *plague!*" the admiral thundered, backing farther away. The two sentries had vaulted from the coffer, edging toward the door, their eyes pleading with their superior to be dismissed from the cubicle.

"You needn't fear contagion from me," Robert assured him. "If I have not come down with it by now, the doctor's pastilles have made me immune, for I have been in the thick of it several times. Pestilence is rampant in the south."

"You mean to hold him to this jealous madness?" Montaigne demanded of the admiral.

Coligny gave a crisp nod. "I do," he retorted unequivocally. "You have no jurisdiction over me, Montaigne."

"No, I do not, but God does, and I leave you to Him." Dismissing Coligny, he turned to Robert. "I will take the girl, and keep her 'til you come," he said. "And you *will come*," he intoned, hard eyes upon the admiral, "or the king will know why. Have I made myself plain, Coligny?"

"As I have just told him—I am no Charles de Guise," the admiral reiterated.

"Yes, well, we shall see," Montaigne snapped. "Now, bring the girl, and leave us. We shall let these two lovers meet and say their farewells in peace."

Eighteen

*W*e haven't much time," Montaigne said in hushed tones. "You have your tale of plague to thank for that. They will want her quickly away now." They were alone, the others having fled, and his speech was replete with animated hand gestures.

"Where will you take her?" Robert asked him, struggling to a sitting position.

"To my home on the coast," said the magistrate. Reaching into the folds of his mantle, he produced a crudely drawn map. "Memorize this, I cannot give it you," he said. "Should things turn sour, 'tis best that they do not know your exact destination, or your means of reaching it. We do not know which way the wind blows here now; it changes so capriciously, it is best to trust no one."

"God's bones!" Robert seethed, remembering. "Uncle Aengus! Doctor Nostradamus has smuggled him out of Paris, and, even now, takes him to your home in Bordeaux! If you are not there to admit him—"

"Take ease, take ease," Montaigne soothed. "My steward will admit them."

"Hah! Like Alain admitted Violette, and I? The door was literally slammed shut in our faces."

"Gaspard, my steward on the coast, is well acquainted with the good doctor. All will be well. How do they go?"

"By carriage."

"How long ago?"

"Two days—three . . . I have lost track of time."

"I will give you some time with the girl, and then set out with her at once."

"On horseback? No! She cannot ride. In her blindness—"

"Shhhh, Robert," Montaigne soothed. "Panic serves you not. I, too, have a carriage, remember? It is not how I planned to travel. I purposely left it behind when I began my first journey to the coast in order to save time, but that cannot be helped here now, and it is fortunate that I did leave it, as it turns out. You must put the girl, and all this from your mind now, and concentrate upon what lies before you. It will be difficult, fighting with one shoulder just mending and the other freshly wounded."

"According to the admiral, we go to Normandy, and I am to be his hangman."

"*Mon Dieu!*" the magistrate murmured. "And there is no way 'round it, I know him well, the admiral. He is rock-ribbed—unbending."

"What manner of man is he . . . underneath all that bluster?" Robert queried, anxious to know what he was up against—just how much power he was dealing with in this man, who seemed no better than the cardinal in his ruthlessness. "Was he appointed by the king, or the Queen Mother?"

"He is no mere appointee," the magistrate returned. "He has earned his laurels. He came early on to Court, with designs upon rising in the ranks, and made a name for himself in the Italian Wars, at Ceresole, back in forty-four, when he was barely twenty-five—younger than us. That got him promoted to Colonel General of Infantry, and ten years ago, he became Admiral of France. He sways from side to side—first Catholic and now Huguenot, undoubtedly he sees some personal future in the rising tide of Protestantism, and then there is his hatred of the Guises. Whichever, his zeal is personal before religious or political. No matter which of his demons drives him, once he makes his mind up he is immutable. Just remember this—there is no shame in retreat if needs must. This is not your war, Robert. Your fight is on a different shore. It is rumored that Northumberland—even now—is driving at your borders again, while Knox forces the thin edge of the wedge deeper, rending Scotland apart from within. You must live to return and defend your own, and take your Violette with you."

"And you have managed somehow to escape this madness here," Robert marveled. "I wish I knew your secret."

"My Jewish faith, that to which I do subscribe, and would even if I did *not* in order to be of service to France here now has spared me from this 'madness,' yes."

"You are a great man," Robert said, sighing.

"History will tell if I am great," Montaigne said wryly. "For now, I am content with being clever."

Together, they poured over Montaigne's map until Robert had committed it to memory. The magistrate pointed out the shortest route to Bordeaux from Normandy, highlighting the main arteries as well as the less-traveled byways, should there be need to avoid pursuit. Great attention was given to detail, every river, lake, and stream—every prominent village gone over again and again. And when the young laird had fixed it in his mind, the magistrate took the sheepskin back and tucked it away again inside his gown none too soon. He had scarcely concealed it, when the door burst open, and one of the sentries prodded Violette over the threshold with the hilt of his sword. His disdain for the chore was clearly visible on his pinched face—the mouth screwed tight, nostrils compressed, head turned to the side as though he held his breath, before he slammed the door shut at her back.

"Admiral says, be quick—and then away!" the soldier barked from the other side.

Robert vaulted to his feet, and staggered toward the whimpering girl, carving wide circles in the air in her blindness as she advanced. Montaigne quickly cupped her elbow, murmuring soothing words as he handed her to him. The laird staggered, and the magistrate led them to the pallet, where Robert fell down embracing her, scarcely aware that Montaigne had left them.

First she groped his face, her tiny fingers feeling for the very thing that all else shrank from, and, wonder of wonders, delighting in her find. Traveling down his neck to his shoulder, they grazed the linen bandages, and her smile dissolved as the dainty fingers searched its perimeter, discovering dampness where the oozing blood had not yet dried.

"You are injured!" she cried. "This is not the same wound. It is the other shoulder. Did these that keep me do this?"

"No, lass, they have done me no harm," Robert murmured. "Those that took you from the ruins did this whilst I was escaping. I had lost much blood by time it was tended, but it is not serious—not nearly as serious as the first."

She settled down then, her posture relaxed somewhat as she lay beside him on the pallet where he'd fallen. Her closeness was excruciating ecstasy, every nerve ending in his lean, corded body awakened to the sensation of arousal invading his loins—every feathery light touch of her hands— her lips on his hair, on his face. In her innocent eagerness to express her sheer joy in his presence, wherever she touched him, she ignited a searing, swelling, all-consuming ache in the blood coursing through his veins—pounding relentlessly in his fogged brain. He was besotted with her, and, his pain forgotten, he drew her to him, fondling the softness of her breasts beneath the coarse homespun of her robe.

He took her lips, and her moan echoed in his throat as their tongues entwined. He wrenched her closer, fully aroused, and her gentle hand explored him. It was unimaginably sweet agony, the feather-light touch of those fingers inching beneath his codpiece. His heart leapt, and he groaned, wrenching her closer still.

"I want you to . . . have me," she murmured against his

ear. Her breath was warm, and moist, and his manhood responded to its sweetness, throbbing against her hand.

Oh, how he wanted her—wanted to bury his longing in that exquisite body. But he could not have her, and he could not tell her why. He dared not admit to fear that he might not return from this new press—from this dreaded campaign in Normandy, under the yoke of Gaspard de Coligny. Then, what would she do?

She was ripe for it. He could allow his swollen member to relieve itself in her, answer the demands of the hot blood thrumming through his body, but that would make him no better than a randy goat. Spoil that sweet flesh for naught . . . *and leave her?* Never. Every instinct in him warned he would be facing the flames of Hell itself if he were to die in battle after such as that, and justly so.

"No," he panted, capturing the hand that had nearly exposed his member and made deliberation a moot point. "We cannot," he said with a ragged sigh, lifting a hand to his lips. "There is no time, Violette."

"You do not want me," she despaired. "I knew it—I have always known it."

"Are you mad?" he groaned, driving her hand down to his member again. "You can feel how I want you. But you are an innocent. Innocence must be taken gently . . . slowly, not like this."

"I wish I never told you I was a virgin," she pouted, pulling her hand away from his hardness. "Mayhap I'm not. Mayhap I *lied.*"

"Oh, lass," Robert chuckled. "You are too precious to be taken thus. I will bed you properly and well, you have my oath, but when we are wed . . . when there is time . . . when I am strong enough to do it properly. I have waited a very long time for you, *mon amour.*"

He kissed her then, to make an end to her petulance and her questions—mostly her questions, fearing what might come from that sweet mouth next. The worst was still before him. He had to prepare her for her journey with Montaigne. She would not want to leave him, and that happenstance was imminent.

"Violette," he began softly, though his body tensed, "you trust me, do you not?"

She nodded acquiescence against his chest.

"You trust seigneur de Montaigne as well, is that not so?"

Again she nodded against him.

"That is good, lass, because you must go away with him to his château in the south, to wait for me to join you and take you home with me to Scotland."

She bolted upright. "*Leave you?*" she cried. "I have just found you!"

"You must," he said sternly. "Doctor Nostradamus has already taken my uncle there. If he has recovered enough to travel, he may have already returned to Scotland. If not, he will remain with you there until I join you, marry us, and we will—all three—go home together. Either way you will wait there, where you will be safe under seigneur's protection until I come for you."

"Why can you not come with us?" she asked, the picture of dejection.

"Because I am not yet strong enough and you cannot stay here until I am. The cardinal's men seek you, Violette. You are safe here no longer, and Admiral Coligny has need of me yet awhile." It was half truth, but he could not tell her more for fear of frightening her. "It will not be a long while, I vow."

"You will fight," she wailed, "and you will be killed. I will never see you again!"

Her cries brought Montaigne, who had been waiting outside. Motioning them toward silence, he came nearer, and Robert saw something in his eyes that demanded caution.

"We must leave," the magistrate whispered. "Dusk has

fallen. Coligny gave me no more time than that. We are fortunate that he has allowed her to remain this long. I begged for it so that we might collect my carriage under cover of darkness. It isn't likely that the château is being watched, since everyone thinks that I have long since left the city. The vendors' quarter is certain to be under surveillance, and, more than likely, this village. We cannot be too careful."

Violette began to protest, and the magistrate quickly took hold of her and clapped his hand over her mouth, while Robert struggled to his feet again.

"Child, you will stop that caterwauling at once!" Montaigne demanded. "I am trying to save your life—and his. I will take my hand away, but you must be still. Do I have your word?" She nodded, and he let the hand drop. "Good. That is a start. I will tell you what will be, so that you both know my plan. We go now to my château. There, I will gather provisions, collect my carriage, conceal you inside, and put as much distance between us and the city as possible before first light. I know less traveled routes south. We will make our way slowly, so as not to cause suspicion. You must do exactly as I say, Violette, and trust my discretion, and we will reach my vineyards safely, where we will wait for Laird Mack to join us."

Robert took her in his arms. "Do as he says, lass," he murmured, then kissed her long and hard and thrust her toward the magistrate. "Take her," he commanded, turning away from the devastating sight of those vacant, sightless eyes. He raked his damp hair back with a steady hand, and when he turned again, though he hadn't heard the door of the one-room dwelling close behind them, they were gone.

Violette was no fool. She would not settle for this without a fight. Fearful that if she left Robert in the hands of the Huguenots she would never see him again, she could not sit idly by and let Montaigne spirit her away. Robert's pleas that she obey Montaigne fell upon deaf ears. There was no question that she would be safe in the magistrate's hands—as safe as could be expected with the winds of change blowing every which way. But what good was safety if she were to be denied the man she loved, and had loved since they met at the foot of the little bridge by the Seine, when the boys tipped over her flower cart.

How could he think himself ugly? Laird Robert Mack was the most beautiful creature she had ever known. Sometimes the blind had more vision than the sighted, she decided. The fact remained that fate had brought them together, and she would not let her blundering separate them now. If he had left her and gone back to Scotland as he'd wanted, he wouldn't be lying captive at the hands of the ruthless Admiral Gaspard de Coligny, whom she feared would use him and then murder him. The nightmare of that possibility had been festering since Montaigne spirited her away, for she knew the ways of such political men firsthand. Had not they sent her into the exile that began this nightmare?

She held her peace until they reached the little bridge over the Seine, the last lap of the journey to reach Montaigne's château. The minute she heard the water music, the gentle gurgling the river made rushing under the bridge, she fisted her hands in the back of the magistrate's cloak.

"Take me back!" she cried. "Please, seigneur, you *must*. These are ruthless, vicious men. They will not let Robert go. They will make use of him and then *kill* him. Don't you see? They cannot let him live. They do not need him for this mad raid they are planning. They take him only to toy with him—to make of him a puppet, with the hope of release afterward. It will come, that release, but at the point of a sword. How can you abandon him thus? Please, I beg you, take me back!"

Montaigne's broad back became as hard as steel beneath her pinching fingers. "And what good do you suppose you can do?" he gritted out through clenched teeth. "They will kill you, too."

"That would be better than *this!*" she cried. "Never to know what has become of him. . . . Never to have tried to forefend it. Much of this is my fault, seigneur. We are betrothed. I want to be with him. Perhaps if I am . . ."

"What? You think your presence would sway them? Hah! It would only make an end of him sooner. They are obsessed with battle madness. They want the blood of Catholics to flow in reparation for the Huguenot souls who died at Vassy. They see naught beyond blind vengeance. They can no longer see that retribution serves them not, that they have become the very thing they abhor. And as if that is not enough, little flower, they think you still carry *plague!* If you had your sight, you would know the terror in the eyes of those who shooed us away, their noses and mouths covered for fear of breathing the very air you breathe. The only reason we got clear of that camp is that you are in my company. They dare not meddle with me. But *you!* You are expendable. Go back there now and they will run you through and toss your body on the bonfire they leave behind when they march on Normandy. Robert is not blind, Violette. You would want him to see that? Is this how well you love him, child?"

"He needs an ally now. I know being blind is a hindrance, but surely any ally is better than none."

"What makes you think he needs one? He is a force to be reckoned with, believe me—a warrior well seasoned, with a sense of honor and decency seldom seen in these troubled times—or any times, come to that."

"You do not need to sell his honor to me, seigneur," Violette sallied. "He is honorable to a fault, or I am simply not satisfactory. I can think of no other reason why he will not have me."

"Did it never occur to you that without you underfoot in

your . . . affliction, he might be free to concentrate upon just the sort of strategy necessary to best Coligny? You need to leave him, Violette, and let him be about the business he knows well without distraction. While he worries over you, he is vulnerable to *them*."

"I love him so . . ." she sobbed. "What if he never comes to Bordeaux? How will we ever know what has become of him?"

"You love him, and I have come to look upon him as a brother, lass," Montaigne said. "Trust me to know what is best in this. If things go as he plans, he will come to Bordeaux straightaway, and if you are not there, what then? Trust us to know what is best in this, little flower."

Violette did not hold the same view. His method would not see her safely into Robert's strong, warm arms. If she were to take action, it had to be now, and here, where she knew every inch of the city—where she had friends in the vendors' quarter who could see her back to the Huguenot village as they had once before.

She gave Montaigne's argument next to no credence. It didn't matter that her alternative was rash, or that it offered little or no hope of success. She had to do *something*. She could not bear to think that she had just spent the last moments she would ever spend in the arms of the man she loved. He had braved the halls of Notre Dame Cathedral to liberate her. Could she do less than try to help him now?

They had reached the foot of the little bridge, and without a second thought, Violette slid off the horse's back, turned to the east, and ran along the lane to the vendors' quarter she knew so well.

"*Violette!*" the magistrate cried.

But she paid him no mind, not even when she heard the horse's frenzied cries as it reared, pawing the cobblestones, frightened by her hasty leap off its back and Montaigne's shrill oaths and commands. On she ran until her foot struck a paving stone and she fell sprawled on her belly with the wind knocked from her lungs.

Strong hands hauled her erect and shook her none too gently. "Enough, now!" Montaigne admonished her. "These streets are crawling with gendarmes. Do you want to be shut up in the Bastille?"

"The vendors will take me back if you will not," she argued.

"They will not!" Montaigne said. "Now come! Let Robert Mack do what needs must without the obvious distraction of you. Then maybe . . . just maybe, with his wits about him, he might manage to reach Bordeaux alive."

Nineteen

For the most part, Robert was placed under guard and forgotten. He saw little of Coligny during the week that followed. Anxious to leave for Normandy, however, the admiral sent his healer regularly, a hawk-faced little man known to Robert only as Guerisseur who spoke in some harsh-sounding dialect he couldn't place. The healer fed him foul-tasting febrifuge tinctures, and plastered his wound with thick poultices of fermented balsam and vinegar to "cure" the wound—cure as in 'preserve,' more than heal as the young laird understood it. By the third day, Robert's shoulder more closely resembled coarsely tanned leather than human skin, but it was beginning to heal. That notwithstanding, he hated to see the odious little man coming, and noted with not a little amusement that he wore around his neck, on a twisted silk cord, a garishly large orange-red jacinth stone—the legendary amulet for warding off plague. It dangled down in plain view against his black physician's robe, like a shield, which he obviously believed it to be, for he fondled it often.

Robert thought of Nostradamus's lozenges, a cure he'd trust against an amulet any day. No, there was no comparison between the two physicians' skill. Guerisseur may call himself a 'healer,' but that did not make him one. The man's manner was brusque, his long, bony fingers were merciless, his breath smelled of badly digested onions and garlic, and his credentials were suspect. Coligny was anxious to march on Normandy, and this odious charlatan was assigned to expedite the matter. It was that simple.

Robert longed for the steady, skilled hands of Doctor

Nostradamus instead, and for the mold poultices that seemed to work like magic and were kinder to the skin— maggots and all—than the itching, burning fermentation of balsam and vinegar. He longed for the gentle, feather-light touch of Violette's soft fingers—ached for her sweet breath, and the scent that drifted from her skin and hair.

Waking and sleeping, he was haunted by the soft, supple pressure of her lithe body rubbing up against his broad back as they rode through the rain returning from the very village where he now lay at the mercy of the Huguenots. Again and again, he relived the insatiable hunger that had ignited a climax like no other. What would it be like to immerse himself in that willing flesh, to love her as a woman needed to be loved, to know the warm silky feel of her come alive for him—for *him*, just as he was? She had taken possession of him—heart and soul. With his mind thus clouded, he was ill equipped to enter into the admiral's conflict, or any other, come to that, until he'd had her, until those dreams became reality.

He wondered how Violette's journey with the magistrate was progressing, and spent every spare minute going over the contours of the map Montaigne had showed him in his mind, lest it fade from his memory. He was anxious to have the Normandy raid behind him—to slake the admiral's bloodthirsty craving for revenge sufficiently enough to buy his freedom, and somehow manage it with a minimum of innocent blood being shed. Just how he planned to manage that feat was a mystery to him then, but manage it, he would. He was resigned. He was also straining at the tether, and just when he thought he could bear no more of the awful waiting, the admiral paid him a visit.

Robert hadn't touched his food. Instead he paced the length of the small one-room dwelling as he exercised his arm, and when the door came open in the admiral's grizzled hand, the Scot stopped mid-stride.

"I am glad to see you so . . . improved, my lord," Coligny said, taking his measure. "It is good, because enough time has been wasted. We march at dawn, and I shouldn't want to have to lash you to your saddle. Our target is Rouen."

"I am not familiar with your country," Robert growled. "I have no idea where this 'Rouen' is."

"It lies about eighty-five miles northwest of here, on the right bank of the Seine River."

"That far north," Robert mused, thinking—so close to the channel . . . and home—so far from Bordeaux, and those dear to him depending upon him. It did not bode well.

"It is an inland seaport that serves Paris, and a great Catholic cultural center. There are many churches to despoil, and a great cathedral that also bears the name of Notre Dame. The Archbishop's Palace adjoins it. Behind that lies Saint Maclou, a garishly flamboyant church, then several streets to the north is Saint Ouen, originally a Benedictine abbey church, and the very one where Jeanne d'Arc was sentenced to death. There isn't much inside it, but ahhhhh, those windows! *Mon Dieu!* If we can only reach them. There is no question. We will take the city."

Robert did not have to be told about Saint Ouen. He had been raised hearing tales of the legendary Jeanne d'Arc told by his uncle, who was never remiss in pointing out that the famous church's roots were Benedictine. Could he have a hand in sacking such a place and face Aengus ever again? He couldn't imagine it, nor did he want to.

"Here," said the admiral excitedly, unfurling a map drawn on sheepskin on an oaken table beneath the fading rush dip. "This is a map of the city. You can see here how these churches are like links in a chain that we shall disassemble. Then, here," he added, pointing to a crude X drawn not far from the cathedral, "is the giant clock—Gros Horloge, set in a gateway. We will break its hands, and stop its ticking to mark our visit. And there, adjacent, is the belfry tower where we will station a lookout. It affords a panoramic view of the city."

"I will be that lookout?" Robert said, hopeful.

The admiral's rapture faded and he scowled at him, his eyes narrowed and cold. "*You?* A lookout? I think not. Were you a 'lookout' for the Guises? You were in the thick of things, as I have it—close enough to the battle to take out its leader, were you not? You are disappointed. You do not wish to fight in this war, do you, my lord?"

"I do not wish to fight in any war but that which wages on my own soil, my Lord Admiral," Robert hurled at him.

"But you *did* fight for Charles de Guise."

"Under protest, as his hostage, as I have told you."

"And so you shall fight for me . . . as mine."

"Then let us have done. My own lands are under siege at home, and I am needed there. Do we go by water?"

"What? And have them burn our barges in the Seine and leave us like wharf rats with our backs to river? There are twelve miles of docks along that port. They run along the Seine as far as Bouille. We will go by land, and take them unaware in their sleep."

"I told you I know naught of this France of yours," Robert snarled. "We do not have such problems north of Hadrian's Wall. We fight hand-to-hand in the open—'tis honest warfare—aye, honest and honorable. We do not skulk about in the dark, roust inept holy men from their beds, and hang them in the public square like plucked chickens."

"Wait," the admiral mouthed complacently. "You will. There is John Knox on your shore, and you will soon be one of us, my lord. Your Queen Mary tries to glue the land together by permitting each man to worship according to his own conscience, but there is only one true religion, and now that Henry's red-haired hellion has replaced Bloody Mary on the throne of England, you will soon see the feathers fly. She is her father's daughter—as jealous as King Henry ever was. There are English here now fighting in France, and we have learned much news from them. Wait, my lord, and learn your art well here, for you will soon enough be hanging Scottish holy men in your own land."

"And what am I to fight with?" Robert snapped sarcastically. "Am I to enter into battle bare-handed?"

"Are you resigned to your fate?" the admiral queried.

"Hardly. I have, however, given my word, as you have given yours to release me after . . . Rouen."

The admiral nodded. "After Rouen," he parroted. "Once you have given me the same 'courtesy' you gave to Charles de Guise."

"I killed none in that fray save his own general, and one who took me by surprise, to my knowledge. Any wounds that I inflicted otherwise were purely to defend myself."

"Which is why I shall have you kill only holy men." Coligny said. "I like the irony . . . seeing you kill your own kind after staging such a brilliant rescue of your papist uncle. It excites me." He tore a sword from its scabbard at his side and laid it on the table. Robert stiffened, but he did not flinch as his *sgian dubh* joined it. "A token of my trust in your . . . Scottish loyalty," he intoned, "and I do not fear to give it to you. We know where Montaigne has taken your betrothed, Laird Mack, and we go south to rendezvous with Condé after the victory. We must pass right by Bordeaux along the way. It would serve you well to keep that in mind if you ever want to see any of your . . . friends again. Now then, we form ranks an hour before dawn. I would suggest you get some sleep. It is to be a long journey, and you will want to be at your most powerful. This is one battle you can ill afford to lose."

They reached Rouen in three days' time, but not as a unit. Detachments set out separately. They would join forces once again in the forest outside the city for their final orders before converging upon the seaport in a semicircular, surrounding formation at midnight on the third day. Coligny kept Robert in his company during the march, and though he rode armed at the admiral's side, he remained under guard.

Divested of his monk's robe and dressed as a soldier with a coarsely woven cloth traveling mask in place instead of his helm, the laird made no attempt to run. He had no qualms about defending himself in battle. He was a warrior after all. He had, however, become resigned that he would have no truck with hanging holy men. Regardless. He would bide his time—watch, and wait. Give the admiral no reason to doubt him. If only he could talk Coligny into letting him go on ahead and scout the area, then mayhap— just mayhap he might be able to warn the clerics somehow and disappear in the thick of battle. He said he would go with the Huguenot troops to Rouen and fight. He never said for which side. It was a far-fetched plan, but a plan nonetheless—one he could live with, and it sustained him until they reached the forest outside the Rouen city limits in a chilly autumn drizzle just before midnight.

Coligny had begun to order his men, when Robert interrupted him. "Let me go in ahead," he suggested boldly, causing the admiral to give a start and face him.

"*You?*" the admiral blurted. "So you can run? Are you mad, my lord, or do you think that I am? You stay in my sight. Besides, you said yourself you are unfamiliar with this land. What will it benefit me letting you blunder into strange territory, eh?"

"Scouting is what I do best," Robert lied. "At home all the neighboring clans call upon me to venture into unfamiliar quarters—to scout, and mark the best course. I have a knack. If you want me to prove myself useful, you will have to loosen the tether and allow me."

Coligny narrowed cold steel eyes. "You really do think I am the fool," he snarled.

"I needn't go alone," Robert said. "Send another with me—no more, though. Too many strangers would look suspicious should townsfolk still be milling about." He shrugged through the admiral's thoughtful hesitation. "But, of course, if you'd rather not take advantage of my special skills . . ."

"Etienne!" the admiral barked in a hoarse whisper toward a soldier watering his horse nearby. He gave a silent command that brought the man. "Go with him," he charged. "Do not leave his side. You will scout the area."

"Are you familiar with the perimeter of this city?" Robert asked Etienne.

"No," the man grunted, clearly unhappy with the order. He was young, built well enough for his height, with broad shoulders, and a sparse, short-cropped beard.

"Hah! And you criticize me," Robert chided, casting hard eyes toward Coligny. "It shouldn't be too difficult a task even without your impressive map, my Lord Admiral. I can see the cathedral spires from here. First we pass it by, and then the adjoining Archbishop's Palace. We then move on past Saint-Maclou," he continued, pointing the way on the sheepskin map Coligny had unfurled, "and finally, Saint-Ouen. We look for activity, and assess the guards at all three. Are there taverns?" he asked the admiral.

"Several," Coligny returned, "and a few stews, but they pose no threat to our raid. Those in the taverns will be cupshotten, and the ruttish patrons of the stews will be . . . occupied. We'll take the taverns just as they did ours at Vassy."

"Give us enough time to make the rounds," Robert said, hardly able to believe his good fortune in convincing the admiral of his prowess so easily. Scarcely breathing, he went on to the most critical part. "Do not wait for us to return, lest we be followed," he said, his tone forceful and self-assured, for all that his heart was pounding so loud he was certain they could hear its thunder. "Such a seaport will not be left without sentries. If the guards are too many and you need warning, we will know at the outset and return at once, otherwise we will join with you at the clock once we have disabled it."

"No," the admiral interrupted. "I will send another to disable the clock and climb the belfry. It will be accomplished when you reach it, with an arquebus mounted at the top. So, should you be entertaining any thoughts of escape, I would advise that you rethink them. That tower offers a *bel vieu* of the city."

"Etienne here will see that I do not escape," Robert assured him. "Is that not why you have chosen him?"

"You mock me?"

"I remind you."

"You are a clever devil, my lord. Let us see if your reputation is well earned, eh? You had best pray that it is, Robert of Paxton. Now, go. This drizzle will soon become a tempest. Let us have this done beforehand. I am not fond of fighting in the rain."

Midnight was fast approaching, and Robert set out with Etienne along the dark, winding streets. The taverns and stews they passed were the only establishments still serving patrons. The tavern doors were open, spilling light in their path from tallow candles inside, set in candle beams made of iron suspended from the ceiling. The stench of strong onions and spilt wine rushed at them, making Robert grimace. Raucous laughter filtered out with it, suggesting that it would be awhile yet before the tavern keeper employed the pulley and extinguished the candles, a less than subtle signal to the cup-shotten patrons that it was time for them to leave.

The stews were more discretely lit. Lightskirts languished inside and out, calling to them as they passed. Apple-squires could be seen flitting to and fro inside as they served the customers. They seemed like shadow puppets, backlit by softer shafts of defused light blinking from the doorways and windows, where candlesticks of latten and brass on ornate tripods beckoned to prospective patrons among the passersby. Etienne eyed these houses of ill repute longingly. Considering what Robert was planning, he was almost sorry he couldn't let him indulge, since he was about to meet his maker. He couldn't warn the clergy until he'd disposed of Etienne, and while he regretted the necessity of that, he was resigned. Better that one Huguenot be sacrificed than a city full of unsuspecting clerics, as he saw it, and he led him steadily away from the hub of activity, hopefully toward the riverbank. There was no way to know for certain, being unfamiliar with Rouen, but if he were to dispose of the Huguenot's body. . . .

"Where do we go?" Etienne questioned. "This is not the way to the cathedral."

Indeed it was not. The cathedral, with its majestic three-portal façade, decorated with lacey stonework and statues in gaudy profusion stood in the center of the city, not far from the clock that Robert knew by now would have been disabled. The spires of Notre Dame were clearly visible, and he was straying farther and farther away from the clergy he was committed to warn.

There was no more time. Glancing about the street, he spied an alleyway with a darkened mews behind. It was enclosed, with no outlet; not what he'd hoped for, since the body would certainly be found there, but it would have to do. The alley was deserted, and he propelled the Huguenot along it over the damp cobblestones.

"Quickly," he whispered. "Someone comes!"

"I don't see—"

Robert's hand clamped over Etienne's lips silenced him, and his *sgian dubh*, driven deep into the struggling Huguenot's throat, made an end to the protest. Dragging the body into the shadows, Robert cleaned the dagger on the dead man's doublet, thrust it back into his boot, and ran back toward the heart of the city.

He wasted no time bothering with the cathedral, since there would be no clergy there at that hour, but went instead to the adjoining Archbishop's Palace, intending to wake the priests, and then do the same at the Church of Saint-Maclou behind. He would surely find unsuspecting clergy at both. What he did find, however, were guards, and they seized him before he'd scaled the Archbishop's Palace steps.

"Please! I come to warn you!" he cried, struggling with two gendarmes in the square. "The Huguenots! They come to sack and plunder here this night. You must alert the priests!"

"Eh?" one grunted. "And how would you know that, citizen?"

"Because I was with them—against my will," Robert said. "They mean to take the city and hang every priest, monk, and cleric they can lay hands on in retaliation for Vassy. You waste precious time. You must warn them, I say!"

As they danced there restraining him, the silent one removed Robert's mask, let him go, and staggered backward, crossing himself. "*Mon Dieu!* He has *plague!*" he shrilled.

The other, meanwhile, had taken Robert's sword, and the Scot prayed that neither would find the *sgian dubh* hidden in his boot. He was almost relieved when the skittish guard took hold of him again. His struggling hadn't afforded them the opportunity to search his person further. He wasn't going to make it easy for either of them, and he fought them valiantly, continuing his loud protest in a desperate attempt if nothing else, to see the clergy spared.

"I have no plague," he trumpeted, "—no contagion. Deal with me how you will, but I implore you, sound the alarm! The clergy must be warned. The admiral's troops have come to slaughter them!"

The words were barely out, when strident shouts and the screams of hysterical women funneled down the lane in their direction from the outskirts of the city, filling the square with the truth of his words. A faint crimson glow bled into the black night sky from the taverns and stews he'd passed by earlier. It had begun—the slaughter. The acrid smell of smoke flared his nostrils. More fires sprang to life in a surrounding formation ringing the city. Cold chills gripped him as he recalled Nostradamus's prophecy.

"*Now* do you believe me, you nodcocks?" Robert thundered. "Sound the alarm!"

The hilt of the sword they'd taken from him crashed against the back of his head. His knees buckled with the blow, but it took a second to render him unconscious as they dragged him off toward an anonymous destination, which, in his spiral into unconsciousness, he heard them call 'the keep.'

Robert opened his eyes to the sight of a robed cleric dangling overhead. It was the sound of the rope around the unfortunate priest's neck creaking that nudged him toward consciousness. He lay at the base of a makeshift gallows in the center of the street. The cathedral doors were flung wide, and piles of debris—broken statues, relics, and church trappings—littered the square. It was too late. The Huguenots had taken the city.

His head ached where the gendarme had struck him with the hilt of the sword, and his vision was blurred. The last thing he remembered was talk of a keep. This was no keep. Huguenots were milling everywhere, their raucous shouts and clanging swords banging around in his brain until his head throbbed unmercifully. Nonetheless, he tried to vault upright, and fell back again. His hands were bound with rope. A length tied to a spiked iron collar around his neck tethered him to the gallows as well, and he shook his head like a dog shedding water in a desperate attempt to clear the cobwebs from it and command his vision, praying that the gruesome sight above him was a figment of his dazed imagination. A familiar laugh close by told him otherwise.

"So, Laird Mack, this is your 'knack,' your 'special skill' is it?" said Coligny stooping over him, fists braced upon his hips. "Your 'skill,' I think, is murder."

"H-how did I come here?" Robert stammered, knowing full well that the troops must have overtaken the gendarmes; they were everywhere. He shook his head again. Why wouldn't his head clear? He needed his wits about him now. "Why am I tied?" he demanded.

"Hold your tongue! You waste your breath," Coligny snarled. "We have found Etienne. What? Did you think you could escape from me so easily—from me, Gaspard de Chatillon, Comte de Coligny? You are more of a fool than I thought, Robert of Paxton."

Robert's breath hissed from his lungs. It was useless to make a pretense. He knew when circumstance dictated that he must give in, but that by no means meant he was ready to give up. Unless he missed his guess, his *sgian dubh* was still wedged in his boot. Its bulk chafed against his ankle through the hose as he lay there with his full weight upon it. Did these Frenchmen not know where a Scot carried his dagger? Evidently not, since theirs were worn on their belts in plain view. Besides, they probably didn't give it a thought, since the gendarmes would surely have disarmed him. He swallowed dry, and licked parched lips. The deadly black knife was so close. . . .

"What do you mean to do with me?" he said steadily.

"What? You aren't even going to try and deny it? I'm disappointed. You like to make a fool of your betters, don't you, my lord? You made a fool of the cardinal"—he shrugged, and waved his hand in a gesture of dismissal—"and I have no objection to that, but you shan't make one of me."

"What you do here is wrong," Robert insisted. "These holy men have done you no harm. To sack and burn their trappings is one thing, but *this*," he gritted his teeth, nodding toward the swaying cleric dangling overhead. "This is sacrilege, and—"

The toe of the admiral's boot in his face cut him short. "This is necessary," Coligny contradicted. "These are idolaters—heretics. Catholics showed no mercy to unarmed civilians at Vassy—the troops of Charles de Guise cut them down like wheat spears. This is only the beginning. We will bury them."

Robert spat out blood. "God have mercy on your souls."

Another boot replied, this time to the young Scot's ribs. "Enough!" Coligny growled. "You will not go free. You will die like the rest here in this street—on this very gallows, but not yet, my lord. First, you will hang the others—you and Jacques." He nodded toward a mounted soldier a few yards off that Robert hadn't even noticed, who quickly backed his horse up toward the gallows in response to the silent command. The dead cleric plummeted to the ground alongside him. "I hope you were paying attention," Coligny went on. "You will man the noose, and Jacques will . . . well, you are no simpleton. You, of course, will be last, once you have seen to all these." He swept his arm wide toward a huddled group of well-guarded priests and monks behind him, their ashen faces tinted red in the glow of the bonfire the troops had made of their church trappings. The stink of burnt tapestries, perfumed with stale incense, of beeswax and tallow and ancient wood, flared Robert's nostrils and threatened to make him retch.

"And how do you expect me to do that like this?" Robert snapped, exhibiting his bound wrists.

"You will manage," said the admiral, a triumphant smile fixed in place. "You are quite the enterprising fellow."

"The king will not thank you for this, Coligny."

The admiral laughed. "The king will be content in the knowledge that you died for our cause nobly in battle—it may even prosper from it—the cause, that is. It might just be the prod to nudge him over to our side . . . considering his fondness for you, and considering that he is so filled with idealistic fantasies, and is so easily led. Be assured I will tell His Majesty how bravely you died . . . for the cause."

Just then a disturbance on the far side of the bonfire turned the admiral's head. Some of the troops were herding the whores from the stews into the square, and the soldiers were joining them, their lewd, jeering laughter testimony to their intent. Coligny scowled toward the mob they had become. His cold eyes narrowed in the heat of the flames that had crawled closer to the gallows, belching plumes of thick black smoke and spitting tufts of fiery ash into the misty drizzle.

The admiral drew his sword and beckoned to Jacques to follow him. Then turning on his heels, he plunged into the melee, leaving Robert without a backward glance, and only a scant few soldiers guarding the clergy that had been prodded nearer the gallows because of the fire.

Robert wasted no time wriggling into position to retrieve the *sgian dubh* from his boot, but the soldiers guarding the clerics were closer now, and he had to work quickly, keeping a close eye on the disturbance. The admiral would not leave him unattended long—even tethered. He would soon return, or send Jacques back to stand guard. He was working desperately against time. It had served him in the past, and he prayed with all his strength that it would serve him now.

Inch by inch, he slipped the blade along inside the boot until he was able to grip the handle and coax it closer to his fingers. Glancing toward the soldiers keeping the holy men contained, he noticed that some of the monks were watching him, and were silently alerting the others. He made eye contact with them. Freedom was within his reach, but there was nothing he could do to help them. Reading their expressions, it was clear that they knew it.

In one covert motion, Robert withdrew the *sgian dubh*. Working in the shadow of the portly body that had fallen alongside him, he began sawing at the ropes, with a close eye upon the soldiers. Thus far, they had been craning their necks toward the fracas that was taking place beyond the bonfire, clearly anxious to join in the licentious revelry with the rest. Now they were growing restless and impatient, and he'd almost severed his bonds, when he noticed one closest to the gallows begin to turn.

Heart pounding, Robert stopped mid-stroke, his breath suspended—scarcely believing his eyes—as the captive clergymen began to wail and thrash about, raising their arms toward heaven in a chanting, moaning supplication in unison that captured the guards' attention.

For a split second Robert stared slack-jawed, until he caught the pleading eye of one of the elder priests, and then he sawed like a madman while the soldiers were occupied until the rope finally fell away. After severing the length attached to the iron collar, he crawled off into the smoke-filled darkness.

Robert didn't want to think about the fate of the holy men he was leaving behind. He prayed that some had broken free and stolen away as he had done, but he didn't think it likely. They were being too closely watched. That he would be hunted was a foregone conclusion. He was a fugitive sought by all factions now. Alone in the rain-swept darkness, in an unfamiliar place, he was at a grave disadvantage. He no longer had his helm or the cloth traveling mask for anonymity, and the spiked iron collar was still fastened around his neck. If he were seen, he would be remembered, and surely betrayed to that fearsome, intimidating army of marauding Huguenots.

It was a certainty that Coligny would follow after him. Now that he had taken Rouen, the admiral would establish a garrison, leave some of the troops behind in the city, and head south with the rest to join Condé, sacking God knew how many other cities in his path along the way. Bordeaux could well be one of them. Montaigne was in danger, not to mention Aengus and Violette. The admiral knew they were at Montaigne's château. He would certainly go there now. It was a point of honor. There was no time to waste, and he wracked his addled brain to recall the map the magistrate had made him memorize before they parted.

The strident sounds of the melee grew louder, the priests' raised voices having joined the noise. Flattened up against the buttressed wall of the cathedral, Robert assessed the perimeter. Which way to go? The city was crawling with Huguenots. It was impossible to elude them on foot. He glanced behind toward the direction of the square, thankful that he could not see what was happening to the priests that had abetted his escape. They were close enough to the gallows to have overheard his conversation with Coligny, and to realize that he was no Huguenot. They had saved him, and his heart ached that he could not return the favor in kind. But then, of course, they knew that when they staged the disturbance that set him free. That their sacrifice shouldn't have been in vain, he covered his ears to shut out their cries, and stumbled off in the darkness in search of a horse he could steal that would see him south. First, however, he had to find his way out of the city.

Twenty

Only one thing was certain. Robert needed to put as much physical distance between himself and the Huguenots as possible. Dangerous as flight in the open was, he had to risk it. He could not linger. No longer afforded the protection of the cathedral's tall, shadowy façade, he inched his way through the deserted streets of Rouen. Flattening himself against other, less majestic buildings in his path, he moved toward the southern outskirts of the city, away from the pandemonium building in the village square behind, audible clear to the wheat fields he'd plunged headlong into.

The drizzle had become a downpour, bending the wheat spears low around him, and his prayers of thanks that the harvest was late that year were short-lived, as the shelter the tall crop growth had promised was stripped away. Lightning speared down, flooding the fields with an eerie blue-white glare that illuminated a barn not too far distant. It stood alone; no farmhouse nearby that he could see, though he knew there had to be one somewhere in close proximity considering the lay of land so richly planted. Praying now that such was so, and that a horse would be kept there, he ran full-bent toward the weathered structure, and reached it just as an ear-splitting crack of thunder extracted a nervous equine response from the shadows within that told him fortune had once more smiled upon him.

It was a swayback mare, not nearly as grand as Montaigne's bay, and certainly not bred for speed, unmistakably a plow horse. It would have to do—at least until he could steal another. Bit and bridle hung on a rusty nail on the wall, and he quickly snatched it and fixed it in place. There was no saddle, and doubting that the animal had rarely—if ever—seen one, Robert swung himself up bareback, and kneed the sluggish nag out into the rain.

Over and over again, he called to mind the map Montaigne had made him memorize. It was two hundred miles as the crow flies from Rouen to Bordeaux; it would be closer to three hundred following the magistrate's convoluted intricacy of detours and byways, which would take him first to Brittany, back through the forests of Tours, then along the Loire River in a zigzag course that threaded along the outskirts of Richelieu and Poitiers, and finally into yet another deep, dense forest that bypassed La Rochelle, and would shelter him as he followed the coast due south to Bordeaux. But which direction would Coligny and his men take? Certainly one more direct—one that would see them to Bordeaux in record speed, with bloodlust to drive the fast horses underneath them.

There was no question that Montaigne's route would have to be altered, and with palpable dread that Coligny might reach Bordeaux first, and Violette's beautiful frightened-doe image dangling before him like a carrot before a hungry horse, he spent all his energies on shortening the distance between them. Regardless, the journey would take many days.

Bypassing Brittany altogether, the young laird spurred his mount in a straight southwesterly line toward Alençon, avoiding the city proper, and staying well within the forest, always keeping a river or stream in sight, since water would have to be gotten for man and horse alike en route. Food was another matter entirely. Gleaning what edibles he could from the land sufficed for a time, but he knew that soon he would have to venture into the open and find more satisfying fare, if he were to keep up his strength coming back so soon from two serious wounds that had weakened him considerably. Except that he was traveling south, he had no knowledge of the lay of the land, and no idea where he was going. He needed reliable guidance Quickly.

Then he saw it—a church spire rising from the twilight through the trees. As if lightning-struck, he knew what he must do, and he broke through the thicket and urged the swayback mare straight toward it. It was a small church nestled in a little glade. He surmised that it served more than one of the surrounding pastoral communities, judging from the clusters of modest dwellings looming in the near and far distance, and not another spire in sight.

Lazy plumes of smoke rose from chimneys of the sleepy little village closest to the wood he traveled through. He'd passed many like it along the way. All around, the hills were white with sheep, their bleating carried on the evening breeze. A beautiful sight, if he were at liberty to enjoy it. As it was, he wasted no time addressing the door panels of the priest's residence—no more than a cubicle—attached to the back of the church alongside a dilapidated smokehouse.

A narrow aperture in the door came open partway.

"Who comes?" said a thin voice from inside.

"Good priest, there is no time for proper introductions. I come to warn you." Robert said. "Huguenots led by Coligny ride south to rendezvous with their ally, Henry of Navarre. They come from Rouen, where they slaughtered many of your brethren, and sacked the cathedrals in retaliation for Vassy. The city there is reduced to rubble."

"*Mon Dieu!*" said the priest. "But what would they want here? We are a humble parish—no cathedral."

"That matters not to men driven by lust for the blood of Catholics, good father."

"How do you know this?"

"I was there—I saw—I overheard them say that they would sack and burn churches all the way to the border on their way south. They will surely pass this way. It is the shortest route, I think. I travel south myself and I must reach Bordeaux before they do else my uncle, a humble monk from St. Michael's Mount, and an innocent blind lass, be taken unaware and slain, and I am unsure of the way."

There was a shuffling noise from within, then the rasp of the bolt being thrown and the priest opened the creaking door and faced him, making the sign of the cross as they stood face-to-face.

"It is not plague," said Robert, having become accustomed to making that defense since he first set foot on French soil. "A fire marked me in my cradle."

The priest gasped. He was well past his prime, of an age, Robert suspected, few lived to see in such times. He was short, and rotund in stature, with articulate hands. Working them ceaselessly, he pointed toward the nag.

"Is *that* how you mean to travel south ahead of Coligny's Huguenots?" he said.

"She was the best I could steal," said Robert.

"You haven't stolen much," said the priest, "she's hardly worth imposing penance over. If you've ridden her from Rouen, I marvel that she hasn't dropped down dead. You are no judge of horses, my son."

"I am no judge of anything in this accursed land," Robert said, "but I know the men of whom I speak firsthand. The threat is real. I beg you, hide your trappings amongst your congregation—bury them if needs must, or you will lose them."

"Come," said the priest, standing aside for Robert to enter. "You speak the language as if you were born to it, but you are no Frenchman. From whence do you come?"

"I hail from the Scottish borderlands north of Hadrian's Wall," said Robert.

"A *Scot*," the priest marveled.

"I am Robert Mack, of Paxton, Laird of Berwickshire,"

the young Scot replied. "I have come to France on a fool's errand, and unwittingly put those I love in danger. I am trying to make amends."

The priest led him into the kitchen, where he prepared a sack of bread, cheese, apples, and a skin of wine. By the time he finished the chore and handed it over, Robert had unburdened himself.

". . . They helped me escape, and I could do nothing to save them," he concluded, moved by the telling of it, "but I can warn other clergy of what is to come. It is why I cannot linger. I may have stayed too long already. I mean to stop at every church and chapel I find on my way south to warn of the storm that is coming. What I need is good directions that I might keep ahead of these men in order to do it. The map seigneur de Montaigne made me memorize was designed to confuse them. It was elaborately contrived, but it would take too long to reach my destination as things are now. I am in need of a more direct route."

"I shall draw you a map, young son," said the priest, "that will see you south through the forests. You will pass many churches, where you may do penance for the souls lost in Rouen—" he crossed himself—"by way of warning the living of the fate of the martyred dead that rests so heavily upon your conscience. Behind the smokehouse, you will find a horse. Leave the mare, and take him instead. He is a swifter mount—the gift of one in my parish, but what need have I of a swift mount, eh? The mare will suit me better . . . until I find her owner, of course," he hastened to add. He sighed. "These are indeed troubled times."

"I shan't forget your kindness," Robert said. "Few here have shown me hospitality. I shall keep you in my prayers, Father . . . ?"

"Pierre," said the priest, "and I shall keep you in mine, my son. Now let us get you on you way, eh? I will fetch tools to remove that collar, and then we make the map."

It was fully dark by the time Robert helped the priest distribute the church vessels amongst the villagers for safekeeping. Persuading the obstinate cleric to abandon his church and find a safe place among them was another matter entirely, which he relegated to his congregation to sort out. He dared stay no longer.

By midnight, wrapped in a hooded cloak offered by one of the locals, he'd made good progress on the swifter gelding the priest had given him. He was exhausted, but he dared not slow his pace. Not yet, not until he'd put a little more distance between himself and the bloodthirsty mob he knew was nipping at his heels.

He rode through the night, and stopped before dawn to warn the clergy at two more churches along the route Father Pierre had mapped out for him. He plodded on until midday before he and the horse could go on no longer without rest. Finding no shelter, he walked the animal into the wood that hemmed the road he traveled to a little brook, where he tethered him to graze. Then, choosing a spot where he could watch the road unseen—where passersby would wake him—he succumbed to sleep at last.

The sun had nearly set when the thunder of horses' hooves jolted him awake. He strained bleary eyes toward the road, and his scalp drew taut with gooseflesh when they focused. It wasn't the Huguenot banner these riders carried. It was the standard of Charles de Guise. His heart leapt. The cardinal's men traveling south at breakneck speed could only mean one thing. Assuming that Montaigne was still his sponsor, they, too, were set to lay siege to the magistrate's vineyards. He was caught between two factions, and he had to reach Bordeaux before either of them.

Cursing under his breath that Dr. Nostradamus hadn't

shared this augur, Robert bolted back through the trees to where he'd tethered the gelding, with intent to reach him before he answered the call of the other horses streaking by. He found the animal milling in place, his ears pricked up and cupped toward the strident sounds coming from the dusty road. Robert snatched the horse's reins, and soothed him with gentle hands until the thunder became a distant rumble. After mounting, he plunged deeper into the forest and made straight for the coast.

He'd come nearly halfway. There could be no more stopping to rest. With both the Huguenots and the cardinal's men seeking him, he dared not show himself, or risk being caught between them. There was nothing for it but to stay ahead of the one, while attempting to bypass the other, if he was to reach Montaigne before they did. That meant approaching Bordeaux by *sea*. It was his only hope, and he kept within the forest and followed the tributaries to the quay at La Rochelle, praying for a sturdy barge and fair winds to help him do it.

Twenty-one

*V*iolette reached Montaigne's rambling château at Bordeaux without incident, except, of course, for the time she tried to leave the coach in another attempt to return to Robert with or without the magistrate. Montaigne made her as comfortable as was possible on such a long, slow journey, but no manner of reassurance would still her fear that she would never see Robert again.

It was nearly time to harvest the grapes when they arrived. A fortnight and the harvest would be in full swing. The château was understaffed as it always was in the magistrate's absence, and Montaigne left Violette in Brother Aengus's keeping several days after they arrived, and went in search of pickers in the neighboring villages.

The day was fair, and mild enough to spend time on the terrace, which was where Montaigne settled them. There wouldn't be too many more mornings such as this, however. The days were drawing in. It wouldn't be long before the air turned crisp, and such outings would be abandoned until the spring. Today, birds twittered sweetly in the nearby branches, and the sun was warm on Violette's face. The air was sweet with the heady scent of grapes ripening on the vine, and though Violette inhaled deeply, she let her breath out on a long, labored sigh.

"I like this not," she said. "Robert should have come by now. It has been many days—too many, I'm thinking."

"It is a long way from Rouen to Bordeaux," said Aengus. "Who is to say how long the journey to Rouen took from the Huguenot village. There are storms this time of year."

"I shall never see him again," she despaired. "I *did* see him, you know . . . with my hands . . . with the eye in my mind that isn't blind." Somehow it was important that the monk know that.

"Poor child, how difficult it must be to have patience when you have no sight," said Aengus. "I will not pretend that there is no danger. You would not believe me if I did, but I have known my nephew longer than you do. He has an iron will, and is tenacious, that one. If you could have seen his daring feats liberating me from that filthy jail—"

"And rescuing me from Notre Dame," she interrupted. "But how long can favor smile upon him in his recklessness?"

"As long as needs must to see you both safely out of France, please God," Aengus responded.

Violette said no more. She prayed, and sat beside the sickly monk while the sun rose steadily, until it beat down upon her head at midday, then slid lower and cooled as the golden gray she saw behind her sightless eyes turned darker and the warmth went with it on the brink of twilight. Aengus was just about to see her inside, when the sound of hoofbeats tearing up the lane turned them both around. Aengus gasped.

"What is it?" Violette cried.

"Someone comes," the monk said, ". . . Montaigne, I think, coming on at a pace. He is not alone. There is another with him."

Robert and Montaigne reined in their mounts at the château portal in a cloud of dust they'd raised from the parched roadway. Climbing down, he reached Violette in two strides, and gathered her close in his arms.

"Collect your things, both of you," he said. "We must be away at once. I've brought the wrath of France down upon our heads."

"What now?" asked Aengus, coming nearer.

"There's no time to tell it," Robert responded. "Thank God that I blundered into Michel trying to find my way here, or I never would have come in time. Bordeaux is no small city, and the cardinal's men are at the gates. Fetch your belongings. We will ride to the quay and catch the evening tide."

Still mounted, Montaigne glanced behind, his narrowed eyes straining the twilight down the lane, where another, greater cloud of dust was rising in the distance.

"They are not at the gates, they have passed through them," he cried. "Quickly! There is no more time." Cupping his hands around his mouth, he threw the château portal open, and called out: "*Gaspard . . . Peter . . . come!*"

Seconds later, the steward and two house servants poured through the door, gaping at the gathering.

"Gaspard, bring oil, and torches—all we have, and tinder. Hurry!" he charged.

"What are you doing?" said Robert, still soothing Violette.

"I will see you safe and away," said the magistrate.

"How?" Robert asked. "We will ride right into them."

"Not so," said Montaigne, pointing. "There is another way, beyond the vineyards through the forest. It is a longer route, I'll own, but the path, though narrow, is well defined. Enter between those two tall pines. Farther in, there is a brook. Keep it within your hearing. It will lead you to the quay, and your escape through the inlet."

"We will be seen. They are upon us!"

The servants ran out then, burdened with the oil and torches the magistrate had ordered, and he climbed down from his horse and crushed Robert's hand around the reins.

"Take him," he said, meanwhile helping the steward and the others light the pitch-soaked firebrands. "Two mounts will have to suffice. There is no time to fetch another."

"But you can't mean to—"

"There is no other way." Montaigne cut in. He turned to

the servants. "Spread the oil, and fire the vineyards. Don't just stand there gaping like simpletons!" He gestured toward the lane. "That is *death* beating a path to our door! Set the vines afire, and take care not to catch fire yourselves. There's been no rain for weeks; they'll go up in seconds, and so will you if you're not careful. Here . . . give me one of those torches. I join you presently."

"You cannot fire your vineyards," Robert cried. "My conscience will not stand the loss."

"And mine will not stand your death upon my doorstep after all I've done to prevent it. The grapes will grow again. Will you—any of you—if they cut you down—or I, if they find us in collaboration here?"

The servants had begun to set fire to the vineyards. Thick black smoke rose into the twilight, spreading the scent of dry tinder and cooking grapes. Flames shot up—walls of them—as first one row and then another shot fiery tongues spitting sparks high into the darkening sky.

"But what of you?" Robert persisted, despite his uncle's hand tugging on his arm, and Violette's urging that they do as the magistrate said. "This is madness! How can I leave you to face my folly here alone?"

"How can you not? If you stay, you bring us all low. Go now, while the fire makes a blind to shield your escape. When they arrive, they will not find you—or any trace of you: All in residence will disavow your presence here. What they will find is myself, and my house servants, desperately trying to put out the fire—so few to battle such a blaze, since I am just come home and we are short-staffed until the harvest. I will fare well, believe me. Go—*now*, while you still can. I feel the vibration of their mounts beneath my feet! I can smell their horseflesh over the stench of the blaze. Go, Robert. We are well met. Now, hail and farewell! 'Tis time we part."

"These are not all that come," said Robert. "The

Huguenots follow also, seeking Violette . . . and me. I could not do what they bade me. I could not kill the priests, though many died because of me. Coligny and his men were a day behind me when I took to the sea. It is too much for you alone!"

"You underestimate me," said Montaigne. "Before I'm done, I'll have them working side by side—Catholic and Huguenot alike—to put out this holocaust. Now *go!* I have not seen you—any of you. Your uncle and our Violette left for Scotland days ago. I will occupy them while you make your escape. Good-bye, my friend . . ."

His last words trailed off on the wind, for he had left them, and was running toward the south vineyard, which hadn't yet caught fire, as he spoke it. Without a minute to spare, Robert mounted Montaigne's horse and swung Violette up behind him, while Aengus climbed up on the mild-mannered gelding. Then, as Montaigne designed, using the flaming vineyards as blinds, they drove the animals beneath them toward the forest at full gallop.

Once inside the ancient weald, Robert cast a glance back toward the pandemonium they'd left behind. The cardinal's men were swarming over Montaigne's estate. Backlit by the wall of flames that had lit the night to day, he saw that they were many in number. From the way they were milling about, it was clear that what they found was not what they expected. The roar of the fire was deafening— even at their distance. Robert's eyes smarted from the smoke, or were those tears he blinked back staring toward Montaigne's sacrifice?

"Robert, we cannot linger here," said Aengus, ranging his mount alongside. "None venture near, but that is not to say that one among them might just find this path, and us. These are a clever lot. We need to be away while the fire has their full attention."

"I doubt they'd try to track us in the dark, even if they did know we were somewhere hereabout," said Robert, turning his mount. "They aren't that clever, Uncle Aengus. I wanted to be sure Montaigne fares well amongst them."

"He fares well enough, or they would be upon us."

"But the loss . . ."

"God will reward him for his sacrifice, if not in this life, in the next. Now, come. There is nothing you can do here now save lay the plan Montaigne's contrived to waste and us with it. The lass is exhausted. She's had scant sleep since she arrived, and according to Montaigne, precious little on the journey here. We must rest soon, and we cannot do that until we leave this place well behind."

There was no disputing that. One last look behind, and Robert led the way deep into the weald, following the narrow path that sidled like a lazy snake through the trees. How good it was to feel the pressure of Violette's slender arms around his middle, her tiny hands fisted in his donated cloak. It was well past midnight when her grip relaxed, and her head leaned heavily upon his back. She'd begun to doze. Another minute and she would fall to the ground. He was certain of it.

The babbling of running water caught his attention. It was coming from deeper within the wood, and he turned his mount toward the sound, motioning Aengus to follow. Was this the brook Montaigne had spoken of? Assuming it was, he followed the musical sound until he saw it, glistening in the fractured moonlight filtering through the boughs above. The thirsty horses led him to it, and he signaled Aengus to help Violette down, and dismounted himself.

How good the cold, clear water tasted. He cupped some in his hands and urged Violette to drink, then settled her on the mossy forest floor to sleep. It was the first time she'd let go of him since he seized her on Montaigne's terrace. Aengus drank as well, and slumped breathless against a tall, gnarled pine trunk, his breath coming short.

"Are you all right, Uncle Aengus?" Robert asked him. The old cleric's face was ghostly white in the semidarkness.

Aengus waved him off with a hand gesture, and shut his eyes.

"You aren't, are you?" Robert said. "All this has come too soon after your ordeal in that prison. We will soon be ... home." But Scotland wasn't Aengus's home any longer. With so much happening, Robert had never broached the subject with him. "Will you miss the Mount, Uncle?" he probed.

"That is irrelevant," said Aengus. "A priest of the Church goes where he's sent ... or where he's banished, as I was to the Mount, without question, son. One gets accustomed to it. Once Scotland was my home ... so long ago, it seems like another lifetime. I will not know it now, I fear. So much has ... changed."

"And the Mount?" said Robert.

Aengus shrugged. "I grew accustomed to it ... to my brothers there."

"Your brothers betrayed you—turned you over to the enemy," Robert reminded him.

"They had little choice, Robert," Aengus returned. "These are troubled times, and you now know firsthand how far-reaching the cardinal's hand can be. I cannot fault them."

"It nearly reached us this night—and would have done but for Montaigne," he said. "There is a truly noble fellow. They could well have overtaken you and Doctor Nostradamus coming here. Did nothing untoward happen?"

"To be in that man's presence is an 'untoward' happening," said Aengus. "I will admit, he was not at all what I expected, given his rather dubious reputation. I was impressed in the depth of the man, and in his aptitude for kindness. He is quite devout, and would, I think, defend his faith to the death if needs must."

"Did he have a message for me?"

"Not for you ... directly. His words were meant for me, Robert."

"Will you share them?"

Aengus hesitated, and Robert's heart leapt at the look of him then.

"I've tried and tried, but I cannot fathom his meaning," he replied at last. "He spoke of the flames that marked you . . . that will turn you toward your destiny again and again this life, and of a time when flames would rain down from the sky. He said, when such a thing occurred, it would turn us both, you and I. I told him that I did not understand his speech, but he said that I would when the time came. I thought he might have meant the fire at Montaigne's vineyards, but no flames rained down upon us from above on that occasion." He grunted. "Here I am, the unbeliever, putting stock in that odd fellow's cryptic augur. I must be getting old, indeed."

"If he said flames will rain down from heaven itself, I would believe it," Robert said, "and you can trust that one day you will understand their meaning—at least that is how it has always been with me."

Silence settled over them for an awkward space of time, before the old cleric spoke again. When he broke it, his voice was low, and strained.

"Do you still mean to marry the lass, Robert?" he said.

"Yes, Uncle . . ."

"Then we'd best have it done."

"*Now?*"

"When dawn breaks," said Aengus, "before we press on."

"I thought to wait until we reached Scottish soil, and do it properly."

"If you would marry, and have me say the blessing, we will do it here, beside this brook, at first light, Robert," the old cleric said, and said no more.

Twenty-two

Dawn broke soft with rain. It was his wedding day, but the danger was far from over. He had no idea how long a journey it was to reach the quay, and then there was the long voyage home, facing autumn currents that spawned violent storms the length of the coast they must travel. He would not mention that to Violette just yet. She had been so brave in their travels for one without sight who had never left the Paris city limits before they met. But now *he* was at a disadvantage. He owed her honesty, and how could he reassure her, when he'd never experienced himself what they now faced?

The Huguenots would have reached Bordeaux by now. Would they be more tenacious than the cardinal's men and follow them into the forest? It would not do to linger and find out that both factions were bearing down upon them.

He still had some of the bread and cheese given him at the last church he'd stopped at along the way. He woke Violette and Aengus, and gave them portions. Once they'd eaten, while Violette refreshed herself beside the brook, Robert took Aengus aside.

"We are not yet out of this," he said, low-voiced. "You must promise me that you will see Violette safely to Scotland if anything should . . . prevent me. She can no longer remain here in France. All factions seek her. Her death warrant would be sealed were she to remain here now."

"Have you told her yet what is to be?"

"That we shall wed here? No. I will do that now."

"Then you had best be at it. The sun will soon rise, and we should be on our way."

"You have not promised, Uncle."

"If God wills that I reach Scottish shores, she will be beside me, I vow," Aengus responded.

Something cryptic in the tone of the old monk's voice made Robert's blood run cold. Aengus Haddock was tired. Praying that was all that prompted such a speech, Robert gripped his arm and went in search of Violette. He found her on her knees picking wildflowers at the edge of the brook, and though he didn't speak, she answered his step.

"I followed their scent," she said, exhibiting her find. "How strong it is, carried on the dawn breeze. See? Clover and pink, snowdrop and gillyflower . . . and these I've just plucked are harebell, wet with the morning dew."

Squatting on his haunches, Robert cupped her hands in his. "I see with both eyes very well," he said, enchanted, "yet I cannot name a one."

"Smell," she said, raising them up. His hands went with them, gripping hers tighter.

"They are your wedding posies," he said, brushing her forehead with his lips. It was soft and white and cool as marble, without blemish after the plague. "Uncle Aengus means to marry us before we press on, Violette. That is . . . if you are still willing."

"He does not think we will escape," she said dully. Her hands fell away, though she kept the flowers. "It is a token he offers us."

"I do not think it that at all," said Robert, giving it honest thought. He hesitated. Pondering it through the night, he had struggled to see with his spirit, as Nostradamus had counseled, and come to a conclusion, one that he was almost afraid to speak aloud. "He is unwell, Violette," he said. "He is not a young man. The maltreatment he suffered in that jail has brought him low. He wants to give the blessing, and I think he fears that if we wait . . ."

"I will make ready," she said.

"It is just to please him," Robert said, studying her downcast expression. "Once we reach my keep, we shall have a proper ceremony, the sort that all young lasses dream of, in a fine cathedral, with merriment and feasting after."

"This is all I need," she said, "—no merriment, no feasting. We have this beautiful place, where flowers scent the air, and running water trills and sings, and a holy man to say the words over us. God sees it, and we know it. What else matters?"

"Be quick then, making ready," Robert urged, embracing her. "We leave the minute the blessing is spoken."

They said their vows beside the brook, where the trees thinned farther west, and the bank was carpeted with the striking gold and russet wildflowers of autumn. Violette wound the blossoms she'd picked earlier into a wreath for her hair. The sight of her took Robert's breath away. He had never seen any living creature as beautiful.

After the blessing was spoken, they made their way back to the forest path, and followed it westward. The rain slackened to a misty drizzle by noon. As Montaigne told him, the brook became a stream, and by what he assumed to be mid-afternoon, for there was no sun to go by, and the docks were visible through the thinning trees. Keeping well hidden among the pines, they waited, monitoring the activity along the wharf for some sign that heralded danger.

"We cannot ride out together—blind lass, monk, and me as I am," Robert said, assessing the situation. "Such a lot would surely be remembered. Who knows but that word of us has already reached this quarter?"

"We will need tribute to book passage," Aengus said. "I don't suppose—"

"I still have most of my coins," Robert interrupted, "—enough to buy us passage on one of those rickety galleys."

"Give it me," said Aengus, holding out his hand. "I am the least likely to raise suspicion, a humble monk on sojourn."

"Shouldn't we wait until dark?"

"To leave, yes, but not to arrange it. Would a fugitive venture forth in broad daylight on such a mission? I think not. Neither of you is suited to the task. We waste time. Give it here."

Robert did as his uncle bade him, watching with breath suspended as Aengus left the forest behind and set out toward the docks. His hand worked the hilt of the *sgian dubh* wedged in his boot. The Scottish blade was a fearsome weapon, but he would have felt more secure with a sword at his side.

"We go by water?" said Violette.

He lurched at the sound of her voice so close in his ear. Intent upon the activity along the docks, he didn't hear her creep alongside. He hadn't broached the subject of the voyage before, meaning to leave that news until last, considering her disdain for sea travel. Steeling himself for the worst, he gripped her hand.

"Yes," he said. "There is no other way to reach my homeland from here but by sea. Uncle Aengus arranges our passage. Please God, we sail on the evening tide."

"Is it a . . . long journey?" she said, her voice thin and faltering.

"I'll not lie to you, lass, it will take many days—even with fair winds, but you will be safe, I swear it, and once we reach the borderlands, none here will ever harm you. We go to Paxton Keep, my home, a fine, strong castle protected by my legions. My mother lives there . . . and her consort. You will be welcomed as nobility—cared for and loved—never to struggle for your livelihood again. You are my wife now, Violette. There, we will begin our life together."

"Are there flowers in Scotland?"

"Oh yes, lass, heather carpets the hills and there are more wildflowers than I can name . . . if I knew their names. The land is rife with them."

"I am not fond of sea travel," she said, "but I would brave a thousand seas as long as you are with me. My greatest fear this whole while was that one day you would . . . leave me."

"Never, lass, until death part us," Robert assured her. "We are one, Violette. Soon now, I will show you what that means."

"I know what it means," she returned. "I told you once that just because—"

"I know," he cut in, "you are a worldly lass despite your blindness, and your innocence, yes, but there are some things that must be experienced, pleasures that can not be known elsewise, because they must be tasted for true understanding. You will see."

He took her in his arms, and she melted against him. Finding her lips, he took them. They were like petals, soft and yielding, opening to him, blooming beneath his own. Their touch alone aroused him. It would be so easy to give in to his desire, but he needed his wits about him now, and he shifted his lips to her forehead instead.

"You must do just exactly as I say once we leave this wood," he said, cupping her face in his hands, "—without question, Violette. We are not safe until we ride the waves you fear so."

He said no more. Relieved that he'd gotten off with less difficulty than he'd expected, he turned his gaze back on the docks, and it wasn't long before he spied Aengus returning. The old cleric looked more haggard now than he had when he set out. Sliding off the horse's back, he had to steady himself, and more than once Robert saw him stagger as he made his approach.

"We sail at dusk," he said, sinking down on a tree stump.

"The tribute?"

"It was enough, with some left over," said Aengus, handing him a few gold coins. "Tuck them away. You may need them before 'tis done."

"What did you tell them?"

"That passage for three was wanted to the Scottish borderlands on the first vessel departing. She sails with the tide. Do not let them know you have more gold. These are naught but freebooters—not to be trusted."

"And the ship?"

"The *Toledo*. A seaworthy galley, small, but strongly built, and there is room for our mounts. They were only too glad of them for ballast. The captain's name is Blount."

"*English?*"

Aengus nodded. "Take ease, nephew, he's an outcast—a pirate. He pledges allegiance to no country. Coin is his king. There are many like him on the high seas. He seems more trustworthy than most that I've encountered, but do not relax your guard. Keep your face covered beneath the hood, and lass," he said to Violette, "tie up your hair, and do the same. Call no attention to yourself. See to it, Robert. The sight of her would tempt the dead!"

The laird had no quarrel with that assessment. Despite the urgent press of his circumstances, it was all he could do to honor the commitment he'd made himself to wait until he'd seen her to safety before consummating their marriage.

As soon as darkness fell, they set out for the docks. The young Scot kept a close eye on the surrounding land as they progressed. It wasn't a long distance to the wharf from their vantage in the forest, but it offered too many places where ambushers could hide without being seen for his liking. Nothing met his eyes. That in itself warranted caution. His instincts had always served him well in the past, and they were vying for his attention now. The hairs on the back of his neck were standing on end. Cold sweat beaded on his brow, and his hands were clammy-cold. These were not good signs.

When they reached the gangplank, Aengus hung back. "Take her aboard," he said, "I'll follow after."

"You feel it, too, don't you, Uncle?"

"I feel . . . something. Hurry! Do as I've said."

Robert dismounted, and led Violette on board. Gentle ripples lapped the bulkhead as the galley shifted with their weight, spreading the odor of tar and salt-besotted timbers that creaked under the strain. Still Aengus didn't follow. With a close eye on him, Robert settled Violette aft, and consigned their mount to steerage.

"Hurry, Uncle!" he called. The seamen were throwing the ropes off. "No, wait," he said to the three scurrying over the deck making ready to sail, "my uncle comes . . ."

He'd scarcely spoken, when the thunder of hoofbeats bled into the quiet, and a hail of flaming arrows rained down upon them. Aengus had just begun to lead his mount toward the gangplank, when one of the arrows struck his leg, and he wheeled the animal around.

"*Uncle!*" Robert thundered. Violette's terrified scream ripped through the racket, and he was caught between the horrifying scene along the dock, and the flaming arrows that had fallen all around her.

"*Go, Robert!*" his uncle called. "My course is run. This is what he meant, your healer. See to your bride, and *go with God . . . !*"

It was the cardinal's men.

Helpless to prevent it, the young Scot watched his uncle ride straight toward the line of oncoming soldiers, then veer off, leading them away from the dock. Fanned by the wind that had risen with the turn of the tide and his motion, the flaming arrow imbedded in the old cleric's leg had set fire to his habit. Robert looked away, grateful for the darkness that would spare him the sight of Aengus Haddock's last moments.

The deck was alive with crewmen trying to extinguish the fire the arrows had started along the gunwales. Robert ran to Violette, led her out of harm's way, and lent his hand to the chore.

More arrows rained down, but the risen wind had carried the galley out of their reach, and the flaming missiles sank hissing into the inlet. Bucket after bucket was hauled up over the side and dumped on the starboard gunwales. More was brought up and sloshed over the aft deck that had started to burn before the fire was finally extinguished.

Violette had calmed by the time he reached her, which amazed him considering her blindness, and he took her in his arms and led her below.

"It is over," he said. "You are very brave."

"Once I could no longer feel the heat of the flames, I knew there was no danger . . . that you would not let me come to harm."

"I wish *I'd* known it," Robert gritted through clenched teeth.

"Your uncle . . . ?"

"Dead."

She gasped.

"He sacrificed himself for us—made straight for the cardinal's men. They must have seen him booking our passage earlier. We rode right into their trap."

"Are we . . . safe now?" she murmured.

"We have to be," said Robert. "I have to believe it, because if we aren't, Uncle Aengus has died for naught."

Twenty-three

*W*hen they set out, Violette had no idea of the length of their journey. Had she been aware when they left Bordeaux that they must navigate through the Channel and follow the coast of England north in order to reach her husband's keep in Scotland, she mightn't have pretended to be so brave.

Once the voyage was underway, Robert told her that it would doubtless take longer than anticipated, given the fickle currents. When wicked autumn tempests weren't blowing ships off course, staid calms would slow their speed to a standstill. But these reprieves from dirty weather that always seemed to happen during the day, while terrible squalls plagued the nights, grew few and far between, and ceased altogether when they neared the Scottish border. There, wicked maelstroms fraught with white-capped swells and following seas became the order of the day and night until they had nearly reached their destination.

Then, too, there were stops along the way to unload and take on cargo and supplies, further delaying the journey's progress. In her blindness, one endless day of pitching, rolling terror bled into the next, though Violette would not show her fear to Robert. Except for the terrible retching that she couldn't hide, she steeled herself for whatever her new circumstance held in store. He had stilled her greatest fear, quelled her most dreaded despair. He hadn't abandoned her. That was all that mattered. Given that, he would soon see he was dealing with quite a different Violette.

One thing troubled her as the days wore on. Though they

were wed, Robert had not claimed his husbandly rights. They shared a tiny cubicle below deck not far removed from steerage, but despite the closeness, he kept her at a distance. Something was not as it should be. He was grieving for his uncle, it was true, and for the sacrifice seigneur de Montaigne had made giving up his vineyards to aid their escape, but there was something else between them now, something she didn't understand, and it frightened her.

Finally, the wind held its breath, and on the first calm night since they'd set out, she let Robert lead her on deck for a breath of air that didn't smell of horseflesh and dung. She inhaled deeply as she clung to him. Even though the seas were calm, she had never gotten used to the pitch and roll of a ship riding the waves, nor would she.

"Are there seas in Scotland . . . like this . . . Will we have to travel on them?" she said, gripping his arm as a rolling swell challenged her footing.

"No, lass," he said, "not like this. There are brooks and streams and lakes, yes, but once we reach Scottish shores our voyaging is ended. Then we travel by land the rest of the distance to Paxton Keep, and but for the moat about it that we cross by bridge, you'll come upon no body of water for leagues."

"That . . . is good," she responded.

"Ahhh, lass," he said, "It isn't long now before we stand on dry land again. You are so clear of mind I sometimes forget that you cannot see. If you could, and I gave you a spyglass to look through, you could see the English coastline we follow. Once we reach Scotland, we travel west, over land . . . no more than a day's ride. A high wall separates us from the English, but raiders often cross over, and we must be prepared. We follow the River Tweed, but there is a bridge to cross it, and then we shall pass through rolling hills, forests, and land much like your French countryside before we reach the keep."

"Will you want me then?" she said, low-voiced. The muscles in his arm tensed under her fingers. She held her breath. When he hesitated, she reached to touch his face with the fingers that were her eyes, but he cupped her hands in his and held them away.

"Will I *want you?*" he said. "Violette, you know I want you. I would take you right now, if . . ."

"If what?"

"Why can you not trust me just a little longer?" he said, pulling her close in his arms.

"Something has . . . changed in you. I know you grieve, but it is something . . . more. I sense things, Robert . . . I *feel* what others see. I feel a difference in you . . . in your touch. We lie together below, and yet you will not love me. I'm thinking that you have wed me out of obligation and that once we reach your homeland—"

He shook her none too gently. "You want the truth?" he said. "It will frighten you to hear it, and I need you to be brave."

"I do not understand . . ."

"The danger is not over," he said, his voice soft, and forced. The sound of it turned her blood cold. "I would have had you long ago, if I didn't fear that something might . . . happen to me, and then you would be . . . alone, blind and helpless—possibly with child, and now in a strange land. While Uncle Aengus was with us, we were stronger. Now, we have no allies 'til we reach Paxton Keep, and there is danger from the English raiders coming from Northumbria, to pillage, and . . . rape. I am one against God knows how many, should we be set upon. I will not leave you vulnerable. I did not want to speak of this, because I did not want to frighten you. How you have survived this ordeal as it is is quite beyond my comprehension."

"But we are *wed* now," she reminded him.

"That matters not to English raiders, Violette."

"And if you were . . . struck down—what then?"

Again he hesitated. "Just pray it doesn't happen," he said.

Robert couldn't bring himself to tell her that he'd take her life before he let her fall into the hands of marauding raiders. It was too terrible to think about, let alone speak. They said no more about consummating their marriage, though what was left unspoken festered between them. He hadn't convinced her that it wasn't solely out of obligation that he'd brought her with him. They were almost home. Soon he would prove how much she was wanted, but for now, he needed to marshal all his energies, and concentrate on reaching Paxton Keep in order to do it.

He wished Dr. Nostradamus had shed more light on his current predicament. Did the healer's silence mean that all was well, or was omission his means of sparing him foreknowledge of some calamity yet to befall them? He would not dwell upon it. His mind must be clear. His body must be rested. If all went well, he would be safely reunited with his kin in less than a day.

He led his bride ashore on the banks of the Tweed River at first light. He lifted her up on the horse's back, mounted himself, and rode west, at last on familiar ground. The day dawned clear after a soft lowland mist that burned off after the sun rose. It was fanned by a gentle breeze blowing down from the Highlands that grew stronger by noon.

"What is that wonderful smell?" Violette breathed, inhaling deeply. "Flowers, I think, but I do not know it."

Robert smiled. "The last of the autumn heather," he said. "Even when these wither and turn black, the fragrance lingers. The hills are covered with it here."

"What does it look like?"

"Small stalks—some white, some different shades of purple. I know that you do not know color, but white, I think, is what you must see when the sun strikes you full in the face and dilutes the gray. I cannot think of a way to show you purple, else it be likened to the evening shadows."

"Oh," she said. "It must be beautiful. Is there heather by your keep?"

"Not close enough to visit on your own," he told her. "The keep sits upon higher, rockier ground. There is a courtyard, but I doubt it has been planted, what with so much press over raiders, and no wildflowers grow beyond the moat. There are many different species in Scotland. I promise you will come to know them all—even the ones I cannot name. I will see to it."

Again she inhaled. "In times such as this, I do so wish that I could *see*," she said with passion.

Robert hesitated. He didn't want to stop until he reached his stronghold. He looked about. There was nothing moving but the heather, and the tall grass swaying in the breeze for as far as he could see in any direction. Reining in his mount, he set her down among the flowers. Violette squealed in delight, frolicking in the heather. She knelt in it, and picked handfuls, which she tucked into the pocket she wore on a cord over her apron. She tucked some into her cap, her sleeves—anywhere she could fit the delicate, spriglike blooms.

Robert climbed down from the horse and strode toward her. "These are not the last in all Scotland," he said through a chuckle. "They will come again in the spring. You needn't ravage the countryside."

"I think I shall like your Scotland," she said.

Reaching toward him, she made wide circles in the air. He breached the gap and took her hands. How beautiful she looked with the sun shining on her face. The sight alone aroused him. How could she question that he wanted her? How, when he'd nearly succumbed to her charms at every pass since their odyssey began. As if his fingers had a will of their own, they began sliding up her arms. She smelled of the heather, and of the sun.

Leaning into him, Violette pulled him close—too close. His posture clenched, and he held her at arm's distance.

"*No!*" he said. "No, Violette, I should not have. It shan't be long now. We are almost home, where there are others to care for you if I . . . cannot."

She looked up at him with those vacant, unseeing eyes, so filled with hurt. All he could think of was that he had put it there. "Violette . . . ," he murmured.

"I am right," she cried, breaking away. "You do not want me now, here in your homeland, where you can have your pick of sighted women. I've felt it since we left seigneur Montaigne's. I am not satisfactory."

He jerked her around, for she'd started to bolt. "Once we reach the keep, you will see how foolish this notion of yours is," he said. "You are here with me, aren't you? Did I leave you behind, as you feared I would? I love you, Violette, but my conscience—"

"Conscience, conscience—always your *conscience!*" she cried. "Before—yes, though I did not agree, I could see the reasoning behind your 'conscience,' but no longer. There is no more need to keep your distance, else it be that you regret our joining, Robert. We are *wed!*"

The young Scot stared down at the despair in her sightless eyes, her words an echo in the scented air. Was this the time to tell her what her fate would be if they were set upon by raiders from the south? Was the stark reality that he may have brought her to his homeland only to end her existence at the mercy of his deadly *sgian dubh* to spare her from marauding invaders enough to make her understand the dictates of his conscience—that he see her safely to his kindred, who would keep her, and care for her, should he die in the battle he feared was imminent? If only she were sighted, there might be a chance of her fending for herself in a strange land—even a land under siege. But *blind*! It was an aspect of the situation that he'd never taken into account . . . until now.

Robert Mack was a seasoned warrior. His intuition in such circumstances had never failed him in the past. Even if he hadn't had word that the English raiders were on the march again attacking the borderlands, he would have known it. The innocent lay of the land before him, with nothing in motion save the last of the autumn heather rippling in the breeze, did not ease his mind. His hackles were raised, and there was a cold metallic taste at the back of his palate, like blood—like death. Those signs were inherent. They were in the ancestral memories of warriors long dead, carried in the bloodline from generation to generation, and they never occurred unless he was in the presence of danger.

No. He would not frighten her. It would be best that she be taken by surprise if he was forced to do the thing he feared most. If that moment came, his thrust must be quick, and clean. It would be kinder if she were unaware. Could he do it? *A warrior ought have no truck with love*, he thought bitterly, wrestling with that.

"If we ride hard, we will reach the keep by nightfall," he said. "There, you will be safe. We are not safe here—*you* are not safe, blind, and alone, if something were to happen to me, Violette. This is my land, and I know it. I know when it is safe, and when it is not. You must trust me. Now, enough! I shall put you back on the horse, and we will ride for Paxton Keep. I never should have let you do this. We waste precious time."

"With no soft word . . . no comforting embrace . . . no lover's kiss?" she cried. "You speak the right words, but you have changed toward me. I know it . . . I can *feel* it. No! I cannot bear it, this." Breaking away, she ran through the heather, her arms outstretched before her, her sobs riding the wind.

Robert ran after her, calling her name at the top of his voice. Behind, the horse he'd left grazing shied and complained at the sound of his footsteps and the sudden appearance of a flock of airborne thrushes their feet had raised from the tall grass.

Robert stopped in his tracks, his attention oscillating between the frightened horse ready to bolt, and Violette running headlong toward the brow of a lowland vale. It wasn't a dangerous drop, but blind. . . .

"Violette! *Stop!*" he called at the top of his voice. "The land falls away . . . you'll go over the edge!"

If she even heard over her sobs, she made no response, and cold chills gripped him, recalling the sight of her running in her blindness straight toward the burning forest beside the Huguenot village. If he hadn't reached her when he did on that occasion, she would have blundered into the burning wood.

Caught between two urgencies, he hesitated, deciding. She wasn't that far distant. He could reach her with ease on horseback, and he ran back the way he'd come. Without a horse to speed them to the keep, it would be days before they reached it over the rough terrain on foot.

It was too late. Frightened by the birds, the untethered horse galloped off before Robert could reach him, scattering irate thrushes dropping half-eaten berries in all directions. The sky was gray with them. It wasn't until then that Robert spied the patch of bramble bushes where they had been feeding, obscured by the tall grass, where the heather thinned to the south. They had unwittingly disbursed them, and he loosed a troop of curses after them, and after the animal that had carried off their provisions as well.

The horse had galloped out of sight, but Robert wasn't given long to lament the loss. A blood-chilling scream turned him around, and he scanned the crest of the hill with frantic eyes.

"*Violette!*" he thundered, scanning the perimeter for some sign of her, but there was none. She was gone.

Twenty-four

The Scot raced over the uneven ground, his heart hammering against his ribs, to the place he'd last glimpsed Violette. Traveling the brow of the hill, he scanned the valley below. The descent was steeper and rockier than he'd thought, snarled with bracken and thistles and all manner of ground-creeping vines. It was a moment before a splotch of indigo caught his eye. It seemed like a lifetime.

"*Violette!*" he cried, slipping and sliding down the grade until he reached her, lying in a bed of thistles. Lifting her into his arms, he carried her lower, and set her down on softer ground beneath a rock that formed a natural shelter, addressing her sobs.

"Are you hurt?" he urged, feeling for broken bones, and picking the thistles from her hair.

"N-no . . . just winded," she moaned.

"Your nonsense has cost us the horse—and our provisions into the bargain. Have you any idea how long it will take us to reach Paxton Keep afoot? What would have taken hours on horseback will now take days."

"I . . . I'm sorry," she murmured.

"Where did you think you were going?"

"Away from a man who doesn't love me," she shot back, ". . . where it matters not."

Robert stared. How beautiful she was with the sun beaming down on her face, on her moist doelike eyes looking right into it. A sighted lass would have shielded her eyes from the glare. How fragrant she was surrounded by the heather. What still remained of the blooms that she had gleaned before and tucked into her bodice and pockets had been bruised in her fall, making their fragrance more acute. It assailed his senses, and a throbbing sensation began in his sex. Her words haunted him. "*We are wed* . . ." The worst of it was, she was right.

It was no use. Nobility and conscience be damned! The sight and scent of her, the malleable pressure of her soft flesh pressed up against his hard body had aroused him, and he seized her in a smothering embrace, and laid her back in the heather.

"This is not how I wanted it to be," he said as she clung to him. "I wanted to have you in a proper bed, made with quilts and bolsters and pillows of down."

"What finer bed could there be than these wonderful flowers," she murmured, reaching for his lips.

Robert's heart raced. He had fantasized about this moment since fate thrust them together, but she was a virgin. With no experience save bedding whores, he had no knowledge of the protocol of deflowering maidens. It would be awkward at best, but nothing would deter him now. It had gone too far for that.

Her hands groped his face, his body. Nothing mattered then but her feather-light touch, seeking to pleasure him, and the excruciating ecstasy that touch ignited. He had never felt the like. All at once Nostradamus's words assailed his ears as if he stood beside them: ". . . Not whom, *what*. Love is your last hope, young ram . . ."

So this was love, this all-consuming, conscience-killing agony—this sorcery that made him forget the reason for his mad journey. He couldn't remember when he'd last thought about his face. Time and place, purpose and resolve, meant nothing then. Lost in the magic of her embrace, and no longer able to deny the demands of his body, he ripped off his codpiece, and exposed his sex to her hand. When her hand stroked it tenderly, it responded against her fingers, and he groaned.

"Does this seem like the member of a man who finds you . . . unsatisfactory?" he panted against her ear. "I think not." He bared her breasts to his lips. They were full and round, just as he remembered from the Huguenot village, when his eyes had first feasted upon them. She shuddered with pleasure as his tongue caressed the nipples, first one, and then the other, tugging them erect until the rosy peaks hardened against his lips, and the surrounding puckered flesh was flushed with the bloom of arousal.

"There may be pain." he said. "You are a virgin, and I have never taken one. I am not skilled enough to do it painlessly. It will not always be so, but this first time—"

Her fingers pressed against his mouth quieted whatever blundering words he might have spoken next, and when her lips replaced them, he gathered her to him greedily, sliding his hand over her belly and thighs. Inching the skirt of her frock up, he reached beneath. How soft her skin was, how supple and warm to the touch. The silky hair between her thighs was moist with the essence of her first awakening. He probed deeper to the engorged bud of her sex and the swollen folds beneath.

Arching her body against his hand, Violette spread her legs, and he struggled between them, acutely aware of the tender flesh he was about to penetrate. Her breath caught when his member touched it, caught again as he moved against her—slow, shallow strokes at first, taking her deeper with each thrust until she clasped him tighter, clinging to him—crying out as he entered her.

How sweet, how yielding she was. How perfectly they fitted together, just as he knew they would. Clinging to his back, she swayed to the rhythm of his thrusts as his hands roamed over her body in an unstoppable frenzy to know every inch of her and make it his own.

Blistering waves of pulsating heat raced through his loins. He felt as if he would shatter in her arms as her hands explored him just as his explored her, seeking skin beneath the layers of cloth that girded him.

On the brink of release, he slowed his pace in a vain attempt to prolong her pleasure, but she forestalled that by wrapping her legs around his waist, and took him deeper still—too deep to stave off the climax. He moaned as her sex gripped him in palpitating contractions, and cried out as the warm rush of his seed filled her. Though he froze in her arms, she moved against him still, until her own breath caught, then left her lungs in the shape of a deep, throaty groan, siphoned off on the wind that stirred the heather all around them.

Robert dropped his head down on her shoulder. His hot brow was running with sweat, and his heart hammered against his ribs—echoing through his body until the last shuddering eruption drained his strength.

She was his. There would be no more talk of being unsatisfactory. Robert heaved a ragged sigh. *What have I done?* said his conscience, come alive again. *Have I planted the seed of my heir in this exquisite body?* He couldn't shake the feelings of unease. He wasn't given the chance. Robert had scarcely withdrawn himself and gathered her into his arms, when a vibration in the earth beneath them clenched every fiber in his body. He stopped fondling her and listened, urging her to be still with a gentle hand clamped over the sweet mouth murmuring soft words in his ear.

"What is it?" she whispered.

"Horses—many horses," he said. "They come this way. No—do not move. You cannot be seen beneath this ledge. If they are ours, we are safe home, if not . . ."

"Where are you going?" she cried as he fastened his codpiece in place and crawled toward the sound of the horses' hooves.

"*Stay*, I said," he charged. "I need to see if these soldiers are mine."

"D-don't leave me," she murmured, clutching the sleeve of his tunic.

"I will never leave you, Violette," he whispered, "but if these are my legions, and we let them pass us by . . ."

With no more said, he raised his head above the grass spears just high enough to observe the lay of the land. Disobedient to a fault, Violette raised hers also, and he shoved it down in the tall grass with a quick hand.

"Lie still, I say," he gritted. "What use for you to rise? You cannot see."

"I do not need to see," she returned, "—only to hear." She inclined her head toward the noise, grown louder now. "They are many," she said, "not so many as a legion . . . not so few as a scouting party. More than a hundred strong, I think—*warhorses*, dressed for battle. Some are armored, others clad in leather. I hear the clinking of the one, and the thud of the other. Their masters drive them cruelly. Don't you hear their complaints?"

Dumbstruck, Robert stared. Indeed, it was a column of great horses, more than a hundred strong—closer to two hundred—some sporting silvery armor that shone in the sun, others wearing pierced, fringed leather, studded with nail heads. Robert's heart sank. The striped banner the standard bearer carried was red and gold. *Northumberland's men!*

"Are they your soldiers?" she said.

"What? You can't tell?" he flashed wryly. Her perception never ceased to amaze him.

"You mock me now," she pouted.

"No, my love," he murmured. "I am in awe. I forget how your other senses are enhanced. You had them to a fault, just now, and no, they are not my men, they are the raiders I feared we'd come upon . . . from Northumbria. We must be very careful now, Violette. Unless I miscalculate, they head for Paxton Keep. The only other fortress hereabouts is Hume Castle, and they are too few in number to take it. Unless more follow, they will strike hard, pillage, and withdraw to the border to report their conquest before regrouping. I have seen it many times. These leave a swath of blood behind. If my mother's consort is the man I think him to be, he will make short work of them, but I have not been home in some time to prove him. In any case, he must be warned, and we must warn him. How, I do not know, but we must try. There is a forest on the far side of the vale. Once I am certain that these are gone, we make for it. There is a village some leagues west that we will reach by nightfall if we hurry. There, with the help of God, we will find horses."

Violette cleaned herself with grass, and he helped her order her clothing, and hide her flowing hair beneath her cap and hood. That done, they waited what seemed an eternity to Robert before he dared lead her into the valley. The sun was sliding low in the midafternoon sky by the time they reached the wood. Safely inside, yet close enough to the thicket to see all comers, they picked their way west through the ancient pines toward the village that Robert hoped the raiders had passed by.

It was cool and fragrant inside the forest. Fallen needles crunched under their feet, spreading their heady pine scent. Violette breathed it in deeply.

"I have caused our misfortune," she said, low-voiced. "If I hadn't made such a scene and wandered off—"

"If you hadn't 'run' off, when you did," he amended, "we would have been out in the open, in full view, and they would have overtaken us, Violette. Do not reproach yourself. Just do not entertain the thought of doing anything similar again, now that we know what we are facing here. These men are dangerous, and I am useless against them— one against two hundred. They would slaughter us both."

She said no more, and by dusk, the trees began to thin where the land dipped low again. To the south, a ribbon of water snaked its way through the valley, catching glints of the sun in the west.

"Soon we lose our cover," he told her, "but the village I spoke of isn't far. We will reach it by dark, and if we can find a mount, we'll be at the keep by dawn. You must follow my lead, and do exactly as I say now, Violette; our lives could well depend upon it. These raiders carry swords and axes. I have only my *sgian dubh*." She made no reply, though her hand tightened on his arm as he led her along.

The moon rose at dusk, veiled with a misty halo. The day would dawn soft with rain, but that was still far off. Just after dark, a new odor bled into the rest. Violette smelled it first.

"Are there fires in the village?" she said, craning her neck toward the west.

"I cannot even see the village yet," he returned.

"You will," she said. "Breathe in. These are not hearth fires that I smell . . . it is like the Huguenot village—*the forest*," she shrilled. "Does it burn?"

"Shhhh! Be still," he cautioned. "We do not know whose ears are near enough to hear us. We have nearly left the forest. There is no danger, Violette, unless it be that soon we lose the trees' protection." He took a deeper breath, and strained through the trees with narrowed eyes toward the clearing.

"Something burns, I tell you!" she insisted. "I smell it . . ."

All at once, so did he. Close scrutiny toward the land ahead proved that her warning was sound. It wasn't the forest. It was the village, well on the way of being reduced to cinder, slag, and ash.

Robert uttered a string of oaths under his breath, and pulled up short just inside the thinning trees that marked the end of their protection.

"What is it?" she murmured.

"The village," he said emptily. "They have sacked it."

"What will we do?"

"There is nothing we can do," he said. "We will wait for the moon to rise higher and show us if they have moved on, or if some still linger."

"The horses?"

"It isn't likely that we'll find any fit to ride here now. They will have taken what there was. If I didn't have you with me, I would go on ahead and scout." He popped a cryptic laugh, remembering his last attempt at that, at Rouen. That all seemed so long ago to him now, like another lifetime.

"You won't leave me?" she cried.

"Never, Violette. Whatever happens to us now, happens to us both."

He said no more. The moon soon rose higher in the ink-black vault above, and stars winked down through the clouds that had begun to drift overland from the east off the sea. Seeing no movement, they crept closer to the village—close enough for Robert to see the smoldering remains of thatched-roof dwellings tinting the night sky an unearthly shade of red.

Bodies of the dead were strewn about the streets, and the Scot was glad that Violette was blind.

"There is death here," she murmured. "I am smelling blood."

"These people have been taken unaware. They never had a chance."

The echo of dogs barking in the distance sent cold chills down Robert's spine. They had seen the carnage, and were running mad with fright. He prayed they wouldn't meet them. But those words were scarcely murmured when they met with something else—something far more dangerous. They'd nearly left the village behind, when two lingering warriors strode from one of the dwellings that hadn't been burned. The sound of female moans leaking through the open doorway told all too well what had detained them. Cold sweat ran over Robert's raised hackles and he shoved Violette behind him.

"Stand still!" he charged, ripping the *sgian dubh* from his boot. "The land hereabout is open and fairly level. If I tell you, you must run! I will find you."

But there was nowhere to run. They stood face-to-face with two armed Northumbrian warriors, whose shouts brought two others from behind.

They were surrounded.

Twenty-five

*R*obert's *footwork earned him a sword when his* sgian dubh found its mark in the belly of one soldier, while the boot he'd drawn it from temporarily stayed the advance of another. Now he had two weapons, and he quickly sheathed the *sgian dubh* again and hefted the Northumbrian's sword. Violette screamed, and he spun toward the sound. The other two latecomers had grabbed her, and he lunged at the men, his sword at the ready, but the winded warrior, on his feet now, was attacking him from behind.

Sparks flew from edged cold steel in the darkness. All around, new fires were flaring up. Loose thatch trailing flames broke free and rained down in the dusty street as the combatants hacked at each other in the moonlight.

Violette's screams ran the young Scot through like javelins, as he battled the Northumbrian, matching thrust for thrust. In quick glimpses, he caught sight of her struggling with the men who had seized her, just as she had struggled with the gendarmes beside the bridge in Paris, when they first met, though these were far from drunk. She pummeled them with her fists, and drubbed their shins with the toes of her slippers. She used her teeth when all else failed, and it took the two of them to hold her.

Impaling the soldier he'd engaged upon his sword at last, Robert withdrew the blade and shoved the warrior down. Then spinning on his heels, he dove for the two who had hold of Violette. But while he struggled with one, the other let her go, and thrust his sword. It sliced through Robert's leather jerkin and pierced his side.

Robert hesitated. Pain starred his vision. The blow caused a shift in his rhythm momentarily. This was no mere surface wound. It was serious. He was losing blood. This he could not let either of the raiders see, and he raised both blades with a savage cry on his lips and met the warrior who had run him through head-on.

Violette's screams assailed his ears as though they were coming from an echo chamber in competition with the pulse thudding in his brain. The other Northumbrian had hold of her again, and he struck her a blow to the face that knocked her to the ground. Sudden blood loss was sapping the young Scot's strength. This was his worst fear—that he would die and leave her at the mercy of such as these that had hold of her now. Grinding clenched teeth, he lunged, driving the Northumbrian down, then rolled as the man righted himself and thrust his sword with all his strength. It was much the same maneuver that he'd employed against Garboneaux at the prison. It struck true, and the raider fell upon him, dead.

Robert rolled the fallen raider off his body. He had suffered many battle wounds, but this was different. It wasn't the pain, it was the weakness that struck terror in his heart—terror at the prospect that he would not be able to spare Violette a cruel fate at the raider's hands. The warrior who had hold of her didn't seem to view him as a threat, writhing in the dust as he crawled toward them. That gave him an advantage. Violette was semiconscious from the blow. She could no longer defend herself. Robert, in that instant, knew it wasn't likely that he would survive hand-to-hand combat with this seasoned warrior, but he still possessed enough strength to cheat him of his prize. He needed precious little to plunge his blade into Violette's tender flesh. Only courage. It would be quick and clean . . . and he would soon follow.

Intent upon attempting to tear Violette's shift away, the

soldier didn't see Robert drag himself to his knees. Robert dropped the sword. He hadn't strength enough to wield it. Instead, he raised the *sgian dubh* that fit his hand as though he'd been born with it, and hesitated.

More fires had flared up, shooting long, lean tongues of flame into the night sky. Why was the ground shaking? He was losing consciousness. That must be it. It wasn't the ground. It was his *knees* that were shaking as he inched his way closer.

One of the fires that spread from roof to roof was engulfing the cottage the first two warriors had quit when he and Violette first entered the village. All at once the figure of a woman reeled through the flaming doorframe. Her shift hung in tatters from her shoulders, her naked body beneath smeared with soot and slime and blood. Staggering over the lane studded with bits of burning thatch barefoot, she bore down upon them whimpering, a burning wattle raised above her head.

Robert's eyes oscillated between his bride and the woman approaching, the *sgian dubh* raised in both his hands, and he was poised to strike the blow that would free Violette and break his heart. Struggling with Violette's skirts, the Northumbrian had left her throat exposed. Robert was about to seize the opportunity to come from behind and drive the blade home, when the flaming wattle in the advancing woman's hands came crashing down upon the raider's head and shoulders, setting the man's hair and tunic afire.

"He rapes no more!" the woman shrilled, shuffling away, her wails siphoned off on the wind. As she disappeared in a belching cloud of smoke, Robert lunged, but not at Violette. With all his strength, he sank the *sgian dubh* into the Northumbrian raider's back, as he twisted in a vain attempt to escape the flames that had set fire to his torso. Shoving the man aside, he turned to Violette. Groping the ground, she had grabbed the flaming wattle the woman had dropped, and commenced beating the raider with it. Dodging her random swings, Robert took it from her, and gathered her into his arms.

"Enough," he said, holding her close. "He is done . . ."

She groped his face. *"You live!"* she cried. "I thought they'd killed you . . ."

Robert didn't answer. Holding her close, he buried his face in her hair, and she clung to him, sliding her hands the length of his body. When they touched the blood oozing from his side, he flinched.

"You are hurt!" she cried. " 'Tis deep, this . . ."

"It is . . . nothing," he lied, prying his black dagger loose from the dead raider's back.

"Listen!" she cried. "More horses come . . . many more than before."

He felt the vibration again, and recognized it for what it was—not his weakened knees as he'd supposed, but horses indeed, and he gripped the *sgian dubh* in a white knuckled fist, and poised it over his bride's slender throat.

"These do not come from the same direction," she said, ignorant of the blade that was about to take her life. "Listen! They come from before us, not behind, like the others."

Robert strained his ears for the sound her extraordinary hearing had already made plain to her. The ground beneath them now shook with the thunder of many heavy horses approaching—*from the west*. Were these the rest of the raiding party returning . . . or . . . ?

All at once, they were surrounded. Soldiers mounted on warhorses flooded the lane, but *whose* soldiers? He had no better advantage than she did, trying to penetrate the thick clouds of smoke with dazed eyes all but blind from blood loss.

"Seize them!" their leader thundered, dismounting, while two others, already on the ground, laid hands on Robert and disarmed him.

The leader strode closer, and pulled up short.

Robert was afraid to trust his eyes.

"God's toenails!" the towering, red-haired warrior brayed. Reaching down, he gripped the Scot's forearm in a burly fist. "Robert Mack!" he said. "Well met! We'd given you up for dead."

It was Hamish Greenlaw, his mother's consort, and keeper of his legions.

"And who is this pretty flower you've plucked?" said Greenlaw.

"My lady wife," Robert returned. "She is blind, Hamish . . . Uncle Aengus gave the blessing . . . before he died."

"Ahhh, sad news to bring your mother," Greenlaw said, his expression clouding. His eyes narrowed when he caught sight of Robert's injury.

Greenlaw squatted down and examined the wound, then vaulted to his feet and spun toward his men.

"Bind his wound, and make a litter," he commanded. "This is your liege wounded here." He turned back to Robert. "You have need of Baldric's skills," he said. "I send you and your lady wife to him with my escort. I cannot escort you myself. We seek the rest of these that you have slain here. The whoresons tried to raze Paxton Keep not two hours ago. I saw this fire, and thought mayhap they had sacked this village instead. If we hadn't come this way . . ."

If he said more, Robert didn't hear. Groaning, he spiraled into the dizzying mist of unconsciousness.

It was a sennight before Baldric was ready to declare Robert officially among the living. Several days later, he opened his eyes to the sight of two doting women fussing about the elevated bed, where he lay heaped with quilts in his sleeping chamber.

"You will stay at home now awhile, I think," said his mother. Her eyes were moist with unshed tears. "This fine daughter you have brought me has shared shocking tales of your adventures. That you have come home at all is a miracle."

"Can you not wait until I'm on my feet to admonish me, Mother?" said Robert, as Violette went into his arms.

"He cannot leave again 'til he has shown me every flower in Scotland," his radiant bride said. "He promised."

"Then he will be at home for some time," Lady Gwen replied.

"I am outnumbered," Robert said, embracing his bride. "I have no need to go abroad again. All that I want or need, or ever will is here."

"I won't deceive you, my son," his mother said. "There are grave dangers here at home that were only rumors when you left. John Knox will not rest 'til all in Scotland become slaves to the Protestant religion. What we face here now is not dissimilar from what you faced in France, Robert. These are troubled times. Heads will roll—nobility among them. No one stands upon firm ground here anymore, else he knows which way to swing, and when."

"I've had my fill of politics—religious or otherwise," Robert said, brushing Violette's brow with his lips. "I've seen firsthand what lust for power amongst religious factions does to men in the name of God." He brushed her brow again. She smelled of heather, reminding him. He admired the fine shift and tunic of embroidered silk his mother had provided. It was a shade of blue that rivaled the sky, and her long honey-brown hair was dressed with pearls. "I promised my lady wife a bed made with quilts and bolsters and pillows of down," he said. "The politics of that are all that moves me now." He stroked her face, as she reclined beside him atop the coverlet and nestled in the crook of his arm. "How do you find it, Violette, this bed of mine?"

"It is soft, and fine," she said, "but not so fine as the bed of heather in the valley—no bed will ever be."

How soft and warm she was in his arms. She would never know how close he'd come to sending her into the afterlife and following himself. It was a secret he would carry to his grave, and he made a solemn vow that he would never face such a test again.

"...*Love is your last hope*...," said Nostradamus's resonant voice, echoing across his memory. Did the crafty old healer foresee this last—his trial by fire? How many more would there be? He had no way of knowing, but he did know that the flames had turned him yet again, just as Nostradamus said they would, this time toward a future bright with promise no matter what lay ahead. For he would no longer face what dangers may come alone, he would meet whatever else the fickle winds of fortune had in store for him with his Violette by his side. His precious Violette, who called him "beautiful," and loved him just as he was.

☐ **YES!**

Sign me up for the Historical Romance Book Club and send my FREE BOOKS! If I choose to stay in the club, I will pay only $8.50* each month, a savings of $6.48!

NAME: _____

ADDRESS: _____

TELEPHONE: _____

EMAIL: _____

☐ I want to pay by credit card.

☐ VISA   ☐ MasterCard   ☐ DISCOVER

ACCOUNT #: _____

EXPIRATION DATE: _____

SIGNATURE: _____

Mail this page along with $2.00 shipping and handling to:

Historical Romance Book Club
PO Box 6640
Wayne, PA 19087

Or fax (must include credit card information) to:
610-995-9274

You can also sign up online at **www.dorchesterpub.com**.

*Plus $2.00 for shipping. Offer open to residents of the U.S. and Canada only. Canadian residents please call 1-800-481-9191 for pricing information.

If under 18, a parent or guardian must sign. Terms, prices and conditions subject to change. Subscription subject to acceptance. Dorchester Publishing reserves the right to reject any order or cancel any subscription.